THE COST
OF LIVING

THE COST OF LIVING

OF LIVING

DAISY DEMAY

atmosphere press

To the slayer of monstrosities lurking in the dark. Defender of the unaware from creatures that slither and crawl alike. A hunter of the unseen things that go bump in the night. A savior I did not know I needed but one that made sure I knew how many times you had to save me. You were constantly warning me to be careful. Your ability to tell a story at a young age always made me smile. You would have grown into a great writer. I love you with all my heart and miss you terribly.

– Brysom 2010-2013

PART ONE

SARA

Chapter 1

I truly believed I had prepared myself for the inevitable. Unfortunately, I underestimated how I would react when confronted with chaos and deadly destruction. The wind roared in my ears while the ground vibrated from the bolts of lightning crackling down. I covered my ears with my back pressed against the cold stone foundation. The rigidity of the storm deafened all the senses. As the house shook around me, my ears felt on the verge of imploding. The noise danced around my brain, reverberating in my skull—excruciating. The fear was like none I had experienced before; I was scared for my life. To occupy my mind, I tried to focus on a happier time.

Automatically, I pictured a time during a different storm. It didn't seem like so many years ago since I would sit outside and watch the dark clouds cascade throughout the sky, bringing along a storm, yet thinking about it now made me realize how much I had changed since those early days of love and marriage. The memory flooded me, containing all the images of a moment long gone, yet still fresh in my mind. We were barely twenty, living in our first home, and believed love could conquer anything the world threw at us.

"Sara, what are you doing?" Kyle asked as he walked up behind me.

His breath was on the back of my neck for a second before

his hands slid around my waist, pulling me into him.

I couldn't help but sigh; nothing felt better than his strong arms protecting me from everything.

I inhaled the fragrance, taking it into my lungs as deeply as possible. "Kyle, do you smell that? That's what rain smells like before it starts to come down."

"We need to get inside," he urged.

"It's so beautiful out here. Why would you want to be cooped up inside the house? Look at those clouds—they are so dark they look purple. The breeze barely has a chill, and it smells like the incoming rain, and if you look, you can see the lighting dancing through the clouds. It's magnificent!" I finished.

Kyle pressed his face into my shoulder and gently kissed my neck below my ear. "Yes, it is spectacular out here, but amongst all the beauty you have found is the sound of the sirens going off to let us know this is dangerous. We have to get to the basement."

"You worry too much. With as many warnings as we have experienced, I would expect you to understand the need to watch the changes in the sky," I said, my attention never leaving the show in front of us.

Kyle moved my hair away from my neck and placed featherlight kisses along my neck as he spoke. "I have an idea of what we could do together in the shelter of the basement."

I tilted my head slightly to allow him better access to my neck, closed my eyes, and softly replied, "Like?"

"If you follow me to the basement, we could light some candles and turn on the radio." His mouth continued its assault on my neck. A moment before his lips gently caressed my skin, the feeling of his warm breath caused my body to erupt with goosebumps. A shiver ran down my spine as the whisper-soft kisses developed into more vigorous and deliberate motions. Unconsciously, I pushed myself further into his embrace.

"And then?" I asked, whispering softly.

He pulled my shirt away from my neck, giving him more access to the junction where my neck and shoulder met. My legs turned to Jell-O as I melted into a pool of ecstasy, only still standing because his arms held firm. I could feel his smile against my skin when he noticed how quickly I became putty in his embrace.

"I would lead you to the table and set you down on the edge so I could kiss you like I know you want me to."

The minute he grazed his teeth across my flesh, I raked my hands in his hair and dragged my nails along his scalp.

"Then?" I asked as I exhaled.

"Then we're going to sit down and play a game of chess," he chuckled.

I couldn't possibly have heard him correctly. I opened my eyes and turned around to look at him. The large grin on his face told me I heard correctly. Then I shot him an evil glare before storming past him into the house as the rain finally let loose.

The memory was one of a truly happier time. When we got to the basement, what we did had little to do with playing chess and more to do with melding together. How quickly the time had passed us by. We'd been married for three years when we bought this house, and that was the first of many storms we shared in our home.

Pulling my thoughts from the euphoria, I was alerted to the rapid tapping noise above me. I was beginning to think the crescendo of sounds would never stop. Yet, it was done as quickly as the massive storms exploded into the sky. Then, finally, I was left with silence.

Taking a deep breath, I opened my eyes to the pitch-black void surrounding me. In the deadening air, nothing seemed to be alive. No birds, crickets, or car alarms. In that instant, the neighborhood was at a standstill. The world had gone silent.

I felt like a coward, hiding in the far corner of my basement, covered with the mattress to protect myself from whatever the massive tornadoes decided to drop on me. Meanwhile, my kids were suffering through this at school and not here with me.

I told Kyle I didn't want them to go to school today. I had a bad feeling this morning. He told me I was paranoid; his kids were going to school. I don't know how long I sat there replaying his words.

Once I was sure the worst of it had passed, I pushed the mattress off. I was surprised to see the basement reasonably intact. Rays of light were shining down the stairs. This was a heinous sight because it meant my house was destroyed. I scrambled to my feet and cautiously moved to the opening of the stairs. I walked up the first three steps and could see my house was not destroyed: it was gone. Nothing was left but a neighborhood full of debris, the pieces of once beautiful homes unfolded and ripped apart.

As I surveyed my surroundings, I quickly discovered I wasn't trying to understand what was left. Instead, I was searching for a way out. The road was covered with wood, bricks, downed power lines, and a few small, misplaced cars. A sliver of my garage was still standing, and my vehicle was nowhere in sight. My rational side deduced that I should *"Stay and wait for help,"* while the mother inside screamed, "Check on your children!"

I pulled my cell phone out and tried to call the school, but got nothing—not even a dial tone. I had three numbers programmed in my phone, the school, the police, and my husband. He always said those were the only people I needed to try and reach. My mind focused on my husband briefly, but I quickly discarded it. He was strong and intelligent; he'd be fine. However, I wasn't as confident about the kids or the structure of their school.

With my mind racing through unpleasant scenarios, what-ifs, and all possibilities, I returned to the basement. I had to get to my kids no matter what. I grabbed my old Schwinn bike that I'd stored out of the way and quickly picked up the backpack containing disaster supplies, cautiously making sure the straps felt secure on my shoulders. Smiling, I wiped the years of dust off the frame. Kyle wanted me to get rid of it, but it was a gift, and I tend to have sentimental attachments to any item someone has put thought into getting me. I had tucked it away in the back corner of the basement, out of the way, near where the Christmas decorations sat. Since the basement was untouched by the storms, the bike was in proper working order. Satisfied, I made my way up the stairs.

The school wasn't too far away. Eight minutes, give or take, by car. I had to get to my kids—I needed to see with my eyes that they were safe. Since I kept pushing off getting into better shape, this would be challenging. I needed to focus on the kids; I knew I could get there. Whenever I tried to walk, Kyle would make it a point to work overtime or go out with his friends. If I mentioned joining a club, he would inform me that it took money and we had nothing left to spend on frivolous things. Instead, he told me to stop eating, and then I could simultaneously lose weight and save money.

I tried to keep my hopes high as I started to peddle and maneuver around the bits and pieces of our scattered civilization. You always remember how to ride a bike, even if it has been more than three years since you went for a ride. I used to have a little buggy hooked to the back and would take the kids for rides until they got too big. I wanted to get them their own and teach them, but again, like always, money was an issue.

The sky was horrifyingly dark; beyond the deepest purple—just a shade away from black—there were a few stray rays of sunlight escaping. You wouldn't have believed it was early afternoon, as the sun was being held captive behind the wall of dark clouds. The rain was still falling but much calmer than moments before, the wind now barely noticeable.

It was challenging to stay focused on what I was doing amongst all the destruction. I would have never believed this disaster was my neighborhood had I not seen it with my own eyes. Weaving in and out of the trees, turned-over cars, and broken power poles proved more complex than I expected.

The neighborhood wasn't vast, with a few houses along the opposite side of the street and even fewer on my side. We lived outside of town, far enough away from the hordes of people but within driving distance of everything. The backyards were sprinkled with the lives of my neighbors. I could see appliances dotting the landscape, along with beds, couches, and shattered pictures.

As I approached a significant crossroad, something on the corner caught my eye. My mind was playing tricks on me. I shook my head and looked again. *I thought it had to be a little doll*, noticing its dirty pink dress. I was almost on top of it when I heard, "Mama! Mama, where are you!"

Pure terror was plastered on her small face. She couldn't have been more than four years old. There she stood, shaking, crying, and screaming for her mother. Her cries pulled on my maternal heartstrings, but I couldn't stop to help her. My focus was on my children—I had to ensure they were okay. I had to put my kids above anyone else. I gave one final glance before continuing, only to see her gone. What the hell is happening to me? Why am I hallucinating? I jumped off the bike and ran into the overgrowth to check. There she was, lying face up in the grass, glass eyes staring into the sky—a doll. She looked so real; I touched her face to make sure.

How had they made her so lifelike? She had to be a specialized order. I leaned in closer, and it spoke in a perfect little girl's voice: "Mama! Mama, where are you!"

I don't have time for this. So, I left it as it was and returned to the original task of finding my children.

The highway was the quickest route to school. Hopefully, it would be the clearest. I turned west and focused on not hyperventilating by picturing my kids' faces and the encouraging words they would say, *"You got this, Mom, don't give up, find us."*

I gave a small chuckle; who would have thought this curvy

middle-aged woman would be huffing and puffing her way to school on a bike? I hadn't done that since high school. My thighs burned more than my lungs. My throat felt like I was breathing in razors, but I pushed on.

I shut my mind to keep it from questioning what I saw. The devastation around me was far worse than I could have imagined. Was there an inch of town spared from the tornadoes' rage? Cars were piled on top of one another, and someone was sitting beside the wreckage every few feet or pacing aimlessly.

I could only presume they were in shock, looking but not seeing and walking without a clear destination. Some were half-dressed as if interrupted while doing mundane things. Many had blood dripping from different places on their body. One gentleman held his mangled arm close to his chest, rocking back and forth. I didn't recognize any of them. I wasn't going to help them, so without thinking, I pushed forward.

The overwhelming bleakness hit me like a two-ton boulder when I got within eyesight of the school or what was left of it. The mesmerizing glow of lights illuminated the sky surrounding the parking lot. The beauteous flashes of red, white, and blue were captivating. A few fire trucks, but no police cars, no ambulances. Where were the police?

Scanning the remnants of the school took away what little breath was left in my chest. The east, west, and south corridors had completely collapsed. The north and center of the school appeared to have minor damage. I continued to pedal, trying to go faster, but the burning in my thighs slowed me. I was covered in a layer of perspiration, and my body was protesting every move. Finally, I reached the outer edge of the parking lot and froze.

I let the bike fall to the side; my focus was locked on the east corridor. This was where my children's classes were. Collapsed bricks, exposed wires, and shattered glass occupied the space where their classrooms were. It looked like the tornado played hopscotch along the building and surrounding neighborhood.

It demolished some but then would leave something standing in almost perfect condition. The field behind the school had bits of bricks, books, computers, and gym equipment, but nothing too noticeable. The house next to the school had multiple cars stacked one on top of the other, and I could see fragments of people, a hand sticking from one, a leg from another.

"Ma'am, can you hear me?" a man yelled.

I shook my head out of my trance to see a handsome young firefighter standing in front of me, looking worn and frustrated.

"Ma'am, are you okay?" he asked again.

"Yes, I'm okay, but my kids are in there," I stuttered and pointed.

"Are you hurt?" he asked.

What an odd question to ask someone who clearly didn't come out of the wreckage. I hadn't thought about what I must have looked like, covered in sweat and mud, drenched from the rain.

"No! I'm fine, but I have to find my kids."

"We are searching for survivors, and they're being moved into the tents. You could help us more by going into the tents and lending a hand. Go on, go and see if you can help them." He pointed to a half-dozen tents set up in the parking lot.

"Uhm, okay," I agreed readily.

He gently pushed me toward the tents with his hand on my shoulder. How could I have forgotten about the tents? This was the week of Thanksgiving, and the school always had a big dinner celebration. Luckily some of the tents were still standing.

Thanksgiving reminded me that my family was gone. I lost my brother the summer before I turned twelve. I lost my dad the year I got married and my mom two years after. I had to admit I was glad she wasn't around to see the person her daughter turned out to be. Regardless, none of them ever got to meet my kids.

Still in shock, I followed the path to the tents without argument. When I got to the nearest one, I could hear children crying; they were in agony and afraid. I took a deep breath and walked in. People were moving around everywhere, and kids were lying on blankets on the ground. Some were grouped together, and others were by themselves.

The school was lucky to be positioned near the only firehouse in the town, and those guys had to have made the school their top priority. I was thankful they did. The firehouse shared space with EMTs; we didn't have an enormous hospital, and the closest large one was almost thirty miles away.

"I was told to come help," I tried to tell a man who rushed by me without a glance. "Excuse me, I was told to help," I said to another person hustling by. Unfortunately, no one noticed I was there, and despite my tries, I couldn't get their attention.

I walked closer to two men who were talking in hushed tones. I could only hear fragments of the conversation.

The tall one was saying, "—going to kill everyone if it is left on...still not safe."

The heavy man replied, "We got the all-clear, and turning it off was never my job."

"It is now. Go turn off the power grid," the lanky man scolded.

The chubby man huffed and stormed out of the tent.

"I want my mommy!" a lonely boy cried from the blanket nearest me.

I bent down beside him and brushed his hair out of his eyes.

"Will you find my mommy?" he begged.

It took me a moment to realize who I was looking at.

"Brady, sweetie, your mom will be here as soon as possible. She has to ensure all her students are safe, and then I'm sure she will come running in here to be with you!" I lied.

Brady was in first grade, and his mom was a fifth-grade teacher. I'd met a lot of the staff since my kids started school.

Her class was in the west corridor. I didn't know whether she was okay, and I had no way of knowing if she had survived. I held my breath to calm the agonizing sting of despair threatening to catch my voice.

"Will you stay with me, please, Tina's mom?" he whispered.

I squeezed his hand. "I'm not going anywhere."

His tiny hand fit into mine completely. It was freezing. Even with the dropping temperatures outside, the tent was warming up from all the propane heaters. The sound of the generators filled the inside of the tent with a slow, low hum. They must have been from the fire station; the school didn't have anything like that.

"Brady, I'm going to grab you another blanket," I stated before I walked to the dwindling pile and snatched one. I sat back down next to him and put the blanket over him.

"I see my mommy," he softly spoke as he tried to sit up.

"Don't try to sit up; lay down, and she will come over to you. Where is she?" I questioned while tucking him back under the blankets.

"Look, over there. You were right. She did come to get me." He gestured to the opposite side of the tent.

I looked where he was pointing, but didn't see anything. I glanced back at him and once more followed his finger. Still, I saw nothing; there wasn't an opening on that side of the enclosure.

"Brady?" I barely got the question out before he started speaking again.

"Mom says thank you, Sara, and she wants you to know she will take good care of Tina till you get there with us. She wanted me to tell you she won't go until she finds Tommy. Tina knows where he is. So, when she finds him, she will watch after him too." He smiled the warmest smile I had ever seen.

"Uhm," is all I could muster. What he was saying didn't register with me at that moment. His words touched me on a level I wasn't ready to admit to. I blindly sought out what he was looking at, but still saw nothing. I told myself he must have severe head trauma; it was the only possible explanation.

"Mommy, wait for me. I'm coming," Brady breathed.

Still dumbfounded by his words, I stared at the wall he kept pointing to.

"Brady, honey, I don't..."

Before I could understand what he was seeing, his weak grip on my hand let go. "Brady, Brady?" I began to panic. "No, no. Help, someone help him—hurry!" I screamed.

A woman ran over with a stethoscope, shoving me out of her way. She bent down and listened to his chest. She searched for a pulse on his wrist and again on his neck, then shook her head.

"Don't just look at me shaking your head, do something!" I crowed at her.

"He needed surgery. He'd been crushed, and there was nothing more we could do for him. All we could do was keep him comfortable and hope his mom came before he passed," she calmly replied before leaving.

I grabbed her wrist, stopped her, and yelled in her face, "What do you mean there's nothing more you can do for him? Like hell there is! This is a child. Try CPR—where are the ambulances?"

"I am truly sorry, but at the moment, we have to concentrate on the living," she stated coldly before prying her wrist from my grasp and moving on.

"He would be living if you would help him. He would be living if you gave a damn!" I screamed.

I'd never felt this much rage boiling inside of me. I couldn't stand to be there anymore. Rushing out of the tent, I decided to try another one. Undoubtedly, the other tents weren't going to be like that. There had to be at least one person who truly wanted to help these children and not push them aside. I held on to the anger; it felt easier to deal with it all while blinded by rage. I walked toward another tent in the line.

Everyone outside of the tents was busy with the main task of removing rubble and looking for survivors. Injured people were walking around the parking lot in a daze, looking but not really seeing. I recognized some office staff and a few parent volunteers like myself. However, there were fewer firefighters and volunteers than I initially thought I saw. Three people dressed in EMT uniforms but no doctors, still no police. I took a few deep breaths to cool my blood before going inside.

"You don't want to go in there!" a man's deep voice echoed behind me.

Ignoring him, I took three more steps towards the flap leading into the closed tent. This place was the only one that didn't have as much commotion.

"Listen, you really don't want to go in there!" he said again while putting his hand on my shoulder, letting me know precisely how close he was to me.

"You know what, jerk, I just held the hand of a little boy who...while he...I have to find my kids." I swallowed the knot in my throat, refusing to let a single tear fall. *I'll cry for Brady later when I have my kids safely in my arms.*

I rolled my shoulder and tried to take another step into the large tent.

"There are no survivors in there. This is the place for the dead," he solemnly replied, his voice raw with emotion he was so desperately trying to hide.

"I understand, but I need to know." I pushed his hand off and walked in.

I stood right inside the entrance and looked at four neat rows of blankets. Every head was enveloped with cloth, but their little feet were sticking out of the bottom of the covers. I heard the flap behind me open and then close, but I didn't care to see who had joined me. The hum of a large generator swelled as it powered the lights, and two stand-up, shop-style lanterns gave a narrow view of the massive tent, but it was enough to see something. The only way I would know if my kids were here was to look for their shoes.

I crouched down on the damp asphalt between the rows on the far left and examined the shoes. With every pair, my heart dropped a bit more. Pink, blue, red, purple, and green ones—so many little feet that couldn't have been more than five to ten years old. Every pair of tiny shoes belonged to a child, a child who had a mother who loved them and a father who adored them.

Not even halfway through, I couldn't breathe. The lump growing in my throat was now closing off my ventilation. The tears I fought to not let fall were rushing down my face. I wanted to vomit; so many innocents were lost. I needed to detach my feelings from the chaos around me and focus on the task.

I could still hear the person behind me, remaining close but never saying anything.

Wiping the blur from my eyes again, I continued down the line. Finally, I came up to the feet I had been glancing at for a while: the ones with the sparkly pink sneakers. I tried to pull air into my lungs as I pushed the blanket up a little to reveal the neon orange socks, and my heart seized in my chest. I forced myself to hold in the sob threatening to break free.

I stared at how she had put her socks on that morning, knee-high length but shoved down to her ankles. Her laces only had one loop on both shoes, tiny circles from her walking on her laces.

Every part of me knew I was gazing at my daughter's body before I saw her face. I couldn't help but think that if I didn't look, there would still be a chance she was alive in the school.

"I told her I loved her this morning just like I do every morning, but thinking back, did she think it was just routine, or did she truly know how much she meant to me? She had so much life in her. What am I going to do without her?" I asked the figure who was standing behind me.

I could hear them shift their body weight, but they abstained from speaking. Honestly, I didn't want them to.

I draped the blanket back over her socks and thought twice about retying her shoes, but couldn't. That was a part of her. She had always tied to one side; therefore, she constantly walked on it.

Taking a deep breath, I stood up and repositioned myself by her head. I grabbed the cover and lowered it to see my baby girl. Her chestnut hair was lying flat against her cheek, her glasses broken but still on her face.

It felt as if my heart was genuinely breaking inside my chest. I lost my breath and let the pain radiate from my heart, encasing my chest. Wiping my eyes once again, I took my backpack off. Without saying a word, I rummaged through the supplies. I found a little comb and gently caressed her hair back into place. There were small smudges of dirt on her cheek and a trickle of blood running across her forehead. I couldn't leave her like this. Mechanically, I dove back into the bag for the wet wipes to wash away the dirt and continued to remove the blood from her head. I couldn't think about what I was doing because I would fall apart if I put any thought into it. I worked with precision and logic; the emotions would overtake me soon enough. Once cleaned, a small scratch was revealed, and I grabbed a bandage from the bag and placed it over her wound. Finally, I removed her broken frames and replaced them with the spare pair I had in the bag.

There she was. My firstborn was in front of me, looking like she was sleeping. I wanted her to open her eyes, glance at me, and say, "Mom, why are you staring at me?" so I could say, "Because you're beautiful, and I love to look at you!" However, that wasn't going to happen; she would never catch me watching her sleep again.

I sat next to her, memorizing every feature of her face, ensuring I would never forget an inch of her. Not one ounce of her would fade from my memory, not her spattering of freckles or the small scar she got when her little brother threw a toy at her; I wouldn't allow it.

I ran my hand down the side of her face and slid it around her neck to lift her. I needed to hold her. She was cold, but she was my little girl, and I wanted to wrap my arms around her. When I tried to pull her onto my lap, it felt like she was caught on something.

I tossed the blanket away from her arm, and what I saw was worse than I could have imagined. In Tina's hand laid a smaller one, intertwined with her own. I believed I couldn't hurt any more than I was, but I was wrong.

"She never let him go. Not even for a second," the male softly spoke compassionately.

"Tina has always been kindhearted, always willing to help. This morning we talked about love, and I told them I loved them. Tina looked at Thomas and said, 'I love you, Tommy!' to which he said, 'Yuck,' and I had to sternly say, 'Thomas.' He sighed and said, 'Love you too, Tina,' and I said, 'Thank you.' I can only imagine the terror in his eyes as the tornadoes hit, but I know my Tina told him they would be okay because they were together and I would save them."

The words sputtered out before I lowered the blanket next to Tina.

I shook my head and silently thanked the firefighters for not pulling them apart and placing them together as they found them.

There was dirt in his light, auburn hair, and blood running from both ears. As I did for his sister, I pulled out the wipes and a duplicate of Thomas' favorite action figure. Funny to think I kept an extra toy in my disaster bag, but I knew if he couldn't find it amongst the destruction, it would break his heart. I combed the dirt granules from his hair, washed his face, and did my best to clean the blood from his ears. I stuffed the action hero into his front pocket, exactly where it would be if he was home.

I ran my hand across his forehead, then bent down and kissed his cheek. I removed my lips from his cold little cheek, leaned over, and kissed his sister on the forehead.

I wanted to hold them both. Thomas was the lighter of the two. I raised him up and slid behind him so he rested against my chest. I kissed his head and leaned in to grab his sister.

I started to pull her up onto the side of my leg, and the man who had been watching this whole time said, "Let me help you."

He reached down to pull their hands apart.

"Don't you dare," I hissed with more venom than I thought I could spit.

He quickly moved his hands and maneuvered himself up by me. He grabbed Tina by her waist and helped lift her onto me, so her head rested on my shoulder. Then, tilting her face toward me, I kissed her forehead again.

I sat in the cold, wet, dimly lit tent and held the two most precious things in the world to me. Within my arms were the extension of their father and me, lying quietly pressed against me.

I closed my eyes and could still hear their laughter. Even with all the commotion outside, all I heard was, "I love you, Mommy."

With the tears gushing down my face and my heart dying inside my chest, I didn't care about anything. Suddenly the outside got quiet, so quiet the shadow of the man running out of the tent was all I caught when I opened my eyes.

A loud sob tore from my throat, and I cried hysterically for a few minutes. Then, pulling in a few deep breaths, I managed to contain myself again. What was going on outside no longer concerned me, but I couldn't help watching the man shadowing my movements return. The tent entrance flew open, and he ran in with purpose.

"Get up; we've got to go now!" he yelled.

"No!" I shrieked.

"You don't understand. There are more tornadoes out there. I can see them perfectly—we need to take cover!" he screamed, urging me to move.

The sound hit the tent like a thousand train horns going off at once.

"We have to go, now!" he exclaimed, clearly agitated from the lack of concern over my own wellbeing.

"No, dammit. God already took away the two reasons I lived this hell we call life. If he wants to send another tornado to take my babies' bodies, then dammit, he can take me too! I'm not leaving them, not again. I will die before I leave!" I bellowed.

"Don't be stupid, Sara. Get up," he demanded, glancing back and forth between my face and the tent around us.

"I don't know you, so don't presume to know me. I didn't ask you to follow me in here. I didn't ask for your help, and I'm not asking you to stay. These two little people are my life; I have no reason to live without them, so get the hell out and save yourself!" I squawked.

"I won't leave you here to die," he responded.

The sound was getting louder, and the wind was picking up.

"If God wants me, he can have me!" I screamed.

"You are a stupid person," he groaned.

"You obviously don't have kids, so don't tell me I'm stupid."

"Shit, Sara!" he exclaimed before running back out.

"I'm not going to leave you, not again," I whispered to my kids before setting Tina down and wrapping my arms and legs over them both.

After lacing my arms around them, I bent my head down and closed my eyes. *If God wants me, he can have me. Life isn't worth living without my babies.*

"God, I don't call on you enough. I've always believed you were there watching, helping, and guiding. I should have thanked you more for what you gave me, but was I so bad that you had to take it away? Was I so evil that you felt you needed to punish me?" I lifted my head and screamed towards the sky,

"Take me too! Let me come with them because I don't want to try to live without them."

My ears ached from the screeching sounds surrounding me. I wanted to cover them, but I would have to let go of the kids, which wouldn't happen. I refused.

As I sat there waiting for my world to end, a strong voice rang through my head. *"I have not forsaken you. I have saved the children. One day, you will understand. One day, you will thank me."*

I opened my eyes to see who was talking, but there wasn't anyone around. The wind died down as quickly as it appeared. The tent flew open again, and the same man came rushing back in.

"Give me a break," I mumbled under my breath.

"Listen, you don't think you know me, but you do. I am Sam Alperstein. We went to high school together, and my daughter goes to school with your kids," he quickly sputtered at me.

"Sam Alperstein? You've got to be kidding me." My voice dripped with sarcasm.

"Look, I'll explain, but it's not safe here. You need to go home." I could see the weight of everything weighing on him; he slumped his shoulders, ran his fingers through his hair, and released an exasperated sigh.

"Home...Well, there's a funny thing about my home. The first string of tornadoes today leveled it." I laughed in a cold, despondent voice.

"Do you have a basement? Is it still covered?" he asked quickly.

"Yes, actually, the basement is fine," I smirked.

"Good, then we can go there."

"We? What exactly do you mean when you say we?" I exclaimed, the pain of years past trying to push its way to the forefront of my brain.

"I assume you're not going to leave the kids. I know you don't have a car, but I do," he interjected.

"Why would you help me? We haven't spoken to one another in over fifteen years," I hatefully spat at him.

"Because, if you haven't noticed, the world is turning to shit, and we're going to need people we can trust. I trust you even if you don't trust me," he answered softly.

"Maybe I don't trust you."

"Do you want my help or not?"

"Yes, what do I need to do?" What choice did I have? I wanted my kids out of this place, and he was offering. I trusted the old Sam with my life. If he decided to be a crazy axe murderer and kill me, there was no one left to miss me. Kyle had me isolated. He monitored my phone calls and never let me go anywhere. He had a tracker in my car and required detailed information about where I was and why. The only people I spoke to were one neighbor and the staff at the school. None of them were what you would call friends. Neither of my parents had siblings, and Kyle disowned his family years ago. I wasn't good. I didn't help people. I lived in my sheltered bubble and hid from life. I told myself it was to keep Kyle happy, but I'm not sure anymore. If my choice to follow him led to my death, it would have been deserved.

"I've got the car pulled up to the tent. As much as you don't want to, you're going to have to separate their hands. I can carry Tina out if you can carry Thomas. The police and fire departments will tell you to leave them here, and they'll make arrangements to take them to a funeral home. Let's face reality; how long do you think it will take for them to rebuild and then help you? If this was my little girl, I would want to bury her at home. If you agree, we need to hurry," he whispered.

There was no thought needed. I grabbed the kids' hands, kissing Tina's first and then Thomas' before unlacing them. Sam bent down and picked Tina up. I pulled Thomas' lifeless body up into my arms and headed to the entrance.

Outside the tent sat a silver Ford Excursion. It was enormous. The rear door was open, and the seats were flat. I maneuvered my way into it and laid Thomas down. I looked to see

Sam holding Tina, then helped him place her next to Thomas.

Sam closed the doors, climbed in on the driver's side, and started the SUV. I took a few extra deep breaths before bringing myself into the vehicle with him. I looked over where I had left my bike, and it was gone; the last thing from my mom was lost, just like me.

He proceeded to drive forward in silence. The last set of tornadoes had taken down what was remaining of the school and devastated the volunteer efforts. The only tent left standing was the one holding the dead. It was as if God knew he had already claimed those and had no need to decimate them. The soccer field that held little before was covered in vehicles, and the fire trucks were flipped over down the block. People were face down in the mud, unmoving, lifeless. I wanted to puke; this shouldn't be happening. I looked back at my kids, and my heart, already shredded, screamed; I had to tell their father they had died. As we drove in silence, the words echoed in my head: *"One day, you will thank me."*

"Are you and Kyle still living in the same place?" Sam broke the silence.

"Yep, we've been there for thirteen years," I softly answered. "Oh, Sam, how will I tell Kyle about the kids?" I asked, not wanting an answer. "How did you get your vehicle here? The roads are covered." I added, trying to make small talk and not think about Kyle.

"The interstate was clear, and it wasn't too difficult to get through the rest." Even though he answered honestly, it made me feel stupid, like somehow, I should have known.

The past ten years had been rocky between Kyle and me. To say our marriage was struggling was an understatement. Between the hours he worked and the things I did with the kids, there was little time for us. Slowly things morphed and changed into what it was today. Kyle was always mad about something, so I tried to do what he asked of me. I made the bed the way he liked and cooked only things I knew he would eat, yet it wasn't enough. Kyle had something terrible to say about everything I tried to do. Finally, when my actions didn't adequately fuel his rage, he started to remark about how I had let myself go.

We drove on in tense silence. I had questions, but they didn't matter. Kyle told me I talked too much; I needed to stop and learn to listen.

"I can't drive down your road. There is too much stuff all over it. Hold on, it's going to get bumpy," Sam said before turning into the yard at the beginning of the street.

He dodged and weaved around the debris. There was less in the grass and more in the road. The neighborhood had acquired some overturned farming equipment and dead livestock. The one dog in my area was sitting next to a body that had to be his owner. I didn't know them, but I'd seen him walking his dog. Not one of my neighbors was anywhere in sight. Surprisingly, there weren't any emergency vehicles either. We drove through the grass and stopped towards the west side of my house. He parked the car, then got out and opened the door closest to me.

"Show me your basement. They will be fine in here for a few moments," Sam plainly stated while looking down at my kids.

It took me a few minutes to get my bearings and figure out the outline of the house. The last set of tornadoes had stolen the rest of my garage and thrown junk into the stairwell to the basement.

"Over here!" I yelled at Sam. "Help me move this stuff. This is the entrance to the basement," I finished.

I began grabbing pieces of boards and debris out of the stairwell. It took us a few minutes to clear it out. I was afraid we would find a dead body in this mess, but it was mostly drywall, shards of glass, and a few shreds of materials. The steps were slick, and a pool of water formed at the base of the stairs. We walked down together, and Sam glanced around.

"It stayed fairly dry here; that's really good. This should keep you safe," he said confidently.

"Safe?" I scoffed. I didn't care about being safe; I wanted to die.

"What's wrong with being safe?" he snapped, his eyes blazing fiercely.

"Safe? What do I need to be safe from, Sam? Do I need to be terrified of zombies?" I laughed.

"Joke all you want, but when this all finally sinks into your thick head, you're going to see there are far worse things to be scared of than zombies," he warned. "We need to find a way to secure that opening to your basement. Right now, it's just a huge hole in the ground. So, anyone and anything could fall down right into our laps. On top of that are the crazy weather patterns. I mean, do you want any uninvited guests wandering in here at night?" he added quickly, moving back up the stairs. "See what you can find to close most of this up!" he barked at me without glancing back at me.

What did he expect me to find, a door to throw overtop the large hole? I walked around aimlessly, kicking a few things here and there, but I wouldn't say I was looking. Purely by accident, I found a hammer. I bent down to pick it up and saw a broken frame beside it. I flipped it over to see the faces of my family picture. The one we had taken last summer. I pulled the back off, pulling it from the broken frame, then folded it up and shoved it into my pocket.

"Great, you found a hammer. Come help me move this section of the wall. If we can find some nails, we can cover most of the opening with this," Sam advised, a hint of excitement in his voice as he waved me over.

Why does he not realize my life has fallen apart in less than six hours? How can he expect me to be on task?

I went over to him and tried my hardest to help move the section of the wall. In all honesty, he did most of it. It was a decent amount of the exterior wall, and with the added weight of plywood and siding, it was complicated to move. If we were having this much trouble getting it into place, I wondered if anyone else would attempt to move it.

"Did you find any nails?" Sam asked, while maneuvering the wall into the correct position.

"When was I supposed to find them? You just said something two seconds ago...Oh, never mind. The garage was over there, so maybe I'll find some there," I mumbled before walking off.

"We need to hurry. I can't see it staying quiet for much longer, and we need to get this secured," he warned.

Blah, blah, blah, whatever. I really couldn't have cared less. I could have dropped dead where I stood and wouldn't have minded in the slightest.

The one wall that was upright hours earlier had collapsed onto itself. I tried to lift it and see if anything was usable underneath, but it wouldn't budge.

Frustration set in, and the curses flew. "Dammit all to hell. Shit, Sam!"

I dropped to my knees and stared into the abyss surrounding us. *Is this how my life is meant to be from now on?*

"Sara, it's going to be okay," Sam urged, trying to reassure me. "I'll lift, you look," he finished before raising the wall above his head.

I quickly crawled under the wall and found Kyle's tray with all the nails in it. There were other things inside the assorted caverns. I crawled out from the mess and gave a slight yell. "I'm out!"

Sam dropped the wall; it hit the ground with a loud thud. The force of the aftershock blew across my ankles, and I realized how heavy that wall really was. It was stupid of me to think I could lift it.

Sitting there watching Sam secure the makeshift cover made me think about Kyle. I didn't know where he was or if he was okay, and though I still loved him, I wasn't worried. He had told me too many times over the years I wasn't his keeper, so I had become accustomed to not worrying over when he would be home. Maybe a tiny piece of me was hoping he wouldn't come home or that I wouldn't be alive to see him if he did.

Sam worked quickly and with what seemed to be little effort. He made his way around the first wall piece and double-checked to ensure it was secure.

"Okay, I think if we get that door over in your neighbor's yard, I should be able to secure it over the rest of this opening. If this works the way I think it will, we should be able to make it lockable. It should hold for a few days at least," Sam stated while pointing to the door buried in my neighbor's yard.

"Oh, right. Me, the gopher; I'll go for it," I sarcastically hissed.

"I am trying to help you!" Sam yelled at me.

"I know," I said, waving at the door as I walked aggressively toward it.

I maneuvered past the foundation's edge and started across the field between us. It wasn't that far to the neighbor's house, but my foot seemed to sink into the wet grass a few centimeters with each step. The rich collection of mud made each stride harder than the last.

The door was half-exposed, so I had to dig it out. I still wasn't in the mood, but I pushed on. I started yanking and throwing the small pieces of debris away from the pile, not paying any attention to where it was going. Piece by piece, I moved the junk clear of the door. It was a slow process, but I finally got it exposed. Placing one hand on either side of the solid wood, I pulled as hard as possible.

Nothing; it didn't budge.

I repositioned myself to get a better base and yanked again. Still no movement. *What is holding this thing in place?* My frustration had boiled over, and I was pulling and tugging like a mad woman, cursing and screaming the entire time.

"It won't budge!" I yelled back at Sam, who was already

walking my way.

"Help me," a faint voice whispered.

Great, now I'm hearing things. This day couldn't get any worse.

"Sara, please help me," the voice whispered again.

"Mrs. Johnston, is that you?" I tried to peer through the wreckage that was once her home.

"Sara, I'm so glad to see you," she groaned.

"Do you see me? Mrs. Johnston, where are you?" I questioned while trying to maneuver to where her voice was coming from.

"Down here, my dear," she moaned.

Out of the corner of my eye, I caught subtle movement. I turned my head quickly to see her hand waving between two fallen walls.

"Sam, help me!" I screamed, running over and trying to push one of the walls off.

Her house was a traditional ranch, but the debris pile was more extensive than just her home. It was hard to imagine what could have her pinned inside her residence. Sam got to me just when I decided to brace my back against it and push with my legs to knock it over. He looked concerned, but I had to help Mrs. Johnston.

He ran over and braced himself, preparing to help. Together we pushed the wall out of the way, revealing what was hidden under it, causing the massive pile. My face must have screamed absolute shock when I saw her. She waved me down to her. She was pinned under a small foreign car that had been thrown into her house. Bending down beside her head, I grabbed her hand. She was the only neighbor to greet us when we moved in. Her husband had died a few years before, and she doted over my kids as much as Kyle would allow.

"Sam, call for help. Please, call somebody for help," I said as calmly as possible, though I was sure the phones were still down.

Kyle worked for a phone company. Whenever the central

tower in town went out, we were without a signal until it was repaired, and looking at the wreckage that was the world at the moment, it didn't surprise me that he had no indication.

Mrs. Johnston smiled at me and softly said, "There is no one to help me anymore."

"No, don't think that way; we'll get an ambulance here to help you. You're going to be fine," I reassured, fighting the crack in my voice.

"Damned phone company," Sam cursed. He took in a deep breath and sighed before continuing. "The lines are down. I can't get a signal."

"Sara, you and I need a coming-to-Jesus moment. I know you are not stupid, yet you continue to stay with that hateful man. I watched as he yelled at you and saw how he bullied you and the kids. All those nights, you thought you were alone crying on the back deck; I saw that too. I should have called child services on him years ago, but that asshole threatened to burn my damn house down. I have stood by and watched instead of acting, and it's almost too late. You don't need him; you can do it all without him. He needs a swift kick in the ass or a quick bullet to the back of the head. I will die knowing I didn't intervene sooner and should have. Walk away from him, take those babies, and be someone else. None of you deserve the abuse he puts you through," she firmly stated.

"You're wrong; I protected the kids, sheltered them from the bad stuff." I defended with more venom than needed.

"I'm here to tell you that you didn't shelter them from it; they lived it every day with you." She sighed.

"No, I...tried..." I hiccupped.

"Stop being stupid and single-minded. I'm not your grandma, but you need some hard facts and truth. Everything you felt, they felt too. You choose to keep not only yourself in that life, but you choose for them too. Shame on you. Change it now..." She stopped in the middle of her sentence, her life bleeding out.

Dumbfounded, I stood up, walked back to the door that started my journey over here, and kicked that thing six times as hard as possible.

Sam came up behind me. He took the hammer and broke the frame around it at the top and sides. I chuckled to myself; leave it to me to grab the door still attached to something. Sam picked it up quickly, and we proceeded back to my house.

I sauntered, looking at the ground, trying to find a reason for the destruction.

Sam worked feverishly. The rain went from a continuous struggle of light sprinkles to a heavy downpour.

"This should work for tonight. I'll see if I can find more supplies and try to stabilize this tomorrow. Come over here and help me cover part of this up. We need to bury it, so it doesn't look as obvious," he shouted as he threw odds and ends on the new doorway.

Quietly, I did as he asked and threw whatever I could find around the doorway.

This is all that's left of my house...Not much to brag about. My car was missing, and my furniture—everything that had made this structure a home—was gone, including half of its inhabitants.

"Open the door," Sam urged.

He came upon me with Tina in his arms, and I moved quickly to open it. I turned to look at the vehicle where Thomas lay.

"I will get him. Just come down here and show me where you want me to place her," Sam interjected.

I followed him into the dark basement, fumbling to find a flashlight for a bit of light. I finally found one, but only after walking into a pole. After turning it on, I guided Sam to the mattress I had used earlier to shelter my face from the destruction of the storm. He softly placed Tina on it and hurried out to get Thomas. I took a moment to grab a few more flashlights from the stockpile I had and placed them around.

"How did you get so much light down here?" Sam asked, while descending the stairs with Thomas.

"Uhm, if you take the flashlight and stand it up on its end, it lights up a larger area. My little girl taught that to me," I plainly answered.

Sam placed Thomas next to Tina as they had been in his SUV. The amount of tenderness he showed pulled at my heart.

"Do you have somewhere to stay? I mean, you're welcome to crash here if you need somewhere with a roof," I mumbled.

I almost regretted it the moment the words left my lips. After all, I hadn't been in contact with him for many years, and who knew what kind of person he was. I owed him an out-standing debt of thanks for all his help. Yet, that didn't mean I wanted him here while I slept. Who was I kidding? I wasn't going to be sleeping.

"Thank you, but I must make my way to my house and see if I can salvage anything. Then I have to find Samantha. She wasn't at school. Her mom called her in sick. I spoke with the secretary before I saw you standing in the tent. I knew what was there because I was also looking for my daughter amongst the dead." Sam sighed.

"I understand, and if I can help, let me know. It's the least I can do," I added, running on auto-pilot.

"Stay safe," he said before heading back up the stairs.

I watched him until he was out of sight. Then, I stood over my children, lying on the bed covered in their own blankets. Then I knelt at the foot of the mattress and spoke to them as if they were still with me.

"I know you're safe. I love you both very much, and the thought of life without you is ripping me apart. The key is to survive. I'm not sure how I will do this without the two of you. I'm sorry I wasn't there; I should have been. Tina, I'm sure you took care of your little brother. I could always count on you to help keep him safe no matter what. Thomas, I know you were scared, and I have no doubt you were calling my name. I hope your sister was able to calm your fears and walk with you into Heaven. I am curious to know if your dad is with you. If he is, then one day, I will join you. If he hasn't made it there yet, one day, we will both be with you. I miss your smiles and your laughter. You two are my sunshine and my world. I love you so much."

After finishing, I placed my hands over my face and let the agony run through me.

Finally, I could let the pain escape and mourn the loss of my kids. I lay down at their feet and screamed into the mattress. I wanted this whole thing to be a bad dream and wished I could wake up with everything back to normal. My chest was tight; I could barely breathe, yet every inhale followed a fierce scream on the exhale. I would lose my voice, but I had to numb the pain.

How had my life turned out like this? All I ever wanted was to be a good wife and mother. I failed daily at being a good wife, but I knew I was a great mother in my heart, and now that was gone. I gulped air through my ever-tightening throat and tried to get my sobs under control. My chest physically hurt. It felt like my heart was shredding in my chest; the pain was real and intense. I cried until I couldn't cry anymore.

Chapter 2

No matter how hard I tried, I couldn't force myself to fall asleep. My eyes burned from crying, and my throat was overly sensitive from screaming. Once I couldn't wait any longer, I got up and grabbed another blanket. The storms started back up again, and the temperature dropped.

It was only a matter of time before one of the tornadoes threw something hard enough to crash through the floor and land on me. How much more could the world take? With the blanket around me, I went back to the foot of the bed. I kept the flashlights on in case Kyle showed up, but I held little hope of ever seeing him again. I stared into the darkest corner of the basement and let my mind drift.

A few months ago, to the day, I purchased the cover that was now draped over me.

"Why are you buying yet another blanket?" Kyle barked.

"I told you my reasoning," I whispered.

"We will not have a harsh enough winter to need extra blankets, Sara. You're being idiotic!" he yelled.

"Kyle, please keep your voice down," I urged him.

"No, I will not, dammit. I work for the money you're using to buy this nonsense!" he screamed at me.

"This is not appropriate behavior from an adult," I said quietly, trying not to draw much attention.

"When winter is over, and I am right, you are going to place an ad in the paper publicly stating how wrong you were. I want everyone to know how much of a complete moron my wife is. Then people will understand what I have to put up with," he hissed before storming away from me.

I finished shopping and found Kyle waiting in the car for me. I unloaded the cart and took my place in the passenger seat.

"You embarrassed me in there, you know that? You are absurd and delusional and...and you wonder why I'm constantly correcting you. This behavior is why I am correcting you. If you keep this up, Sara, I will have you committed," Kyle forcefully spat at me.

"Kyle, haven't you ever just had a feeling you couldn't explain?"

"Sara, everything is explainable. Stop this bullshit now before we go get the kids. I can't believe I took the day off to listen to this crap spilling out of your mouth again." He stated this as if it was a normal thing to say.

"You took the day off to play golf, but it got rained out," I interjected.

"Shut up. Did that sound like I was asking you a question? You would think after all these years you would know your place," he hissed.

"I'm not your property," I scolded.

"Yes, you are! You don't work or make any kind of money. That means I pay the bill to feed you, clothe you, and get you medical attention. I pay for everything needed for your survival; that damn well means I own you."

I shook my head vigorously. I needed to get myself out of that conversation. Now was the time to remember when Kyle and I were in love, not when our marriage had become strained.

When we first married all those years ago, we were happy. He loved me and never had a bad word to say about me. We spent hours at night holding one another and kissing until the sun rose. He loved me with every breath he took and couldn't imagine life without me.

I tried hard to remember those days, but my mind would not allow it. It kept going back to that bad day.

"You cannot own another person; that's slavery," I spat.

"Shut the hell up, you stupid bitch. I swear I don't want to hear another word come out of your useless mouth. You are an absolute waste of space, and I cannot figure out why I didn't divorce your ass years ago. I would say it was for your cooking, but that would be a lie. You're a horrible housekeeper, and I doubt you have the intellect to raise my kids. You coast through life daily, hoping someone else will come and take care of your mess. Sara, I'm tired of cleaning up after you," he coldly stated.

Once again, my hold fell. This wasn't the first time Kyle informed me about how horrible I was. I tried not to let his every word cut through me, but I was to the point that I believed each he said to me.

Thinking to myself about how horrible I was made me let out a sigh.

"Poor Sara, are we feeling bad about ourselves? I will tell you these things so you can fix them. You're worse than the kids. Why do I constantly have to repeat myself over and over again to you? If you just listened, we wouldn't have to have the same conversation again and again," he stated.

"Perhaps I should leave," I tried to say confidently, but it came out like the words of a scared child.

"Leave, haha. Where would you go? There isn't a man alive who would want to deal with you. No one will ever love you as much as I do. Any man that got a look at you would run away, and then if he was crazy enough to see what it was like to have sex with you—haha, you would scare him away from women for life. So, your leaving is the funniest thing you have ever said to me. Thanks for the laugh. I quite enjoyed that." He chuckled.

After laughing uncontrollably, he wiped away a tiny tear and said, "Stop talking. We have to get the kids. Put a smile on your face and pretend you love them."

I took a deep breath and put on my smile. Not to pretend to love the kids, but because the children were the best thing to come out of our marriage. My little ones meant more to me than my happiness, and if the ultimate sacrifice was to stay married to their father, I would.

We arrived at the school, and I stared out the window, waiting to see them. When I saw their smiling faces running out the double doors, all my sadness melted away. They were my reason for living.

I placed my hand on my head and tried to force the memory of their smiles to stay brightly active in my brain. Yet, when it faded, I looked beside me to see my reasons for living lying motionless next to me.

The rain was rushing outside again. It had not let up for hours. My legs quickly became numb, so I stood up and walked to the farthest flashlight to turn it off. I went to the others, making all but one small section dark. I was the only one there, so it seemed pointless to waste batteries.

The world had gone silent. I told Kyle this was bound to happen, and he said I was paranoid. I couldn't wait for him to walk down those stairs, so I could finally say, "I told you so."

It would be a pointless win, but at least I would know I wasn't a loser, and there were times when I had been right. I hated what I had allowed him to turn me into, but I must have believed it on some level, or else I wouldn't have let it get to me.

Things were going to change between us, and we had to work together to get through this with our sanity intact. Whenever he came home, I would do better and be the best wife I could be. I wouldn't make him angry anymore, and I would do everything correctly the first time, so he wouldn't have to correct me.

I continued to survey the basement and what I had saved up before everything happened. I knew water could be a possible problem, so I had 10 cases of small bottles and a half-dozen 5-gallon bottles. There was one entire shelf dedicated to batteries and three designated to candles. Thomas wasn't a fan of the dark, so I wanted to ensure I could always have a light on for him.

Shelves on top of racks of canned goods, veggies, meat— anything that could be canned, I got. I had even made sure I had Tina's allergy medicine on hand. For the last three months, I had given her a pill every other night to ensure I had some to tide us over until the world got back on track.

I was sure I had anticipated everything, except I never thought about dealing with this alone.

Thus far, the weather had been unseasonably warm, but that was also changing quickly. Although I was still wrapped in a large blanket, the cold chilled me. My breath hovered in front of my face, and I began to shiver. With my mind clouded in grief, I let the cold seep deeper.

I didn't drink often, but I was no stranger to the warmth good liquor could provide. I grabbed the first bottle of alcohol I could find; it was an extraordinary black rum, eighty-proof. I cracked the lid and took a large gulp. It burned through my mouth and down the back of my throat. I shuddered slightly and tipped the bottle a second and third time. The burn caused my eyes to well, and an uncontrollable cough ensued.

I yanked another comforter from the pile, watching one of the hidden erotic novels fall to the floor. I couldn't care less if Kyle found them now. He thought they were dumb and put unrealistic notions in my head. I longed to experience what it felt like to be desired and wanted by more than one man. The thought led to sexual flutters exploding, causing a sharp sting of desire to rush through me. I picked the book up and placed it on the shelf. Turned and returned to the children. Lining the two blankets, I pulled them up and over my head.

I hid inside the plush world I created and continued to drink from the bottle. Every swallow tasted better than the last, and before I realized it, my body was on fire, sweat breaking out above my lip and brow.

I'd always hated alcohol. On the few occasions I drank, I was mean, and I didn't want my kids to see me that way. With no one around, I began to banter with myself. "It's his fault. Yep, if he had only listened to my warnings, we would've all been here, but nooooooo, I'm stupid. Ha-ha, stupid Sara, yet I survived. How stupid am I now? Jerk, no one needs a jerk."

I wiped my mouth with my shirt and then dropped the half-empty bottle. I flung and fought the blanket to free myself from its prison, then stumbled to the stairs, almost falling twice.

Making my way up them hand over hand, foot over foot, I went out the homemade door and stood at the top of the steps. The rain was now filled with sharp shards of ice, more ice than water. It felt like a razor slicing at my bare face whenever one hit me.

I stumbled to stay upright. Finally, I got my footing and screamed, "I hate you, dammit. I hate you! You killed my children, you bastard. I hate you; I hate you, I hate me!"

I fell to my knees and cried through the tears, "I killed my kids. God, take me. I beg you—don't leave me here."

I couldn't keep balanced on my knees and allowed my body to fall sideways. The brunt of the hit landed on my shoulder, but my head still hit the floor. I could feel my heart beating in my temples; bright lights shot behind my eyes, causing my vision to waver. Everything was encased in a thin layer of ice. Yet, through my blurred vision, the ice wasn't too thick.

I didn't make any attempt to get up. I had no reason to. Instead, I pulled my knees into my chest and brought my head down to them, curling into a ball with my arms shielding my face.

While I lay there, the sharp sting of the ice slowly stopped;

my body was too cold to feel when it landed on my skin. I was
ready to go to sleep and never wake up. Why was it taking my
body so long to give up? I peered past my knees and could see
the light coming toward me. Not caring about the consequences, I tried to scream, "Just kill me, please kill me!" yet my voice
was long gone, and all that came out was a breathy whisper.

I blinked my eyes once and then again as the light seemed
to get closer. I had no curiosity about what this might be, and
by the third time, I blinked; I couldn't reopen my eyes. I was
in blackness when the light was gone, gladly racing toward
the end.

The dark void enveloped me and held tightly to my skin. I
couldn't see my features even though my hand was raised in
front of my face. Subtle words echoed around me: *"Hold on,
and fight."*

The voice was faint, and I didn't recognize it. I could no
longer feel my extremities, and standing in the darkness, I
shook from the cold. The bitterness of its rage hit me hard,
and I could feel my heartbeat fading. Despite everything I had
witnessed, it was a shock to dream of nothingness—to see the
end blank, empty coldness and dead.

"Hold on," again it rang through the darkness. This time
louder and with much more force than before.

I felt something burning hot touch my skin. It wrapped itself around me tightly, and I heard a subtle "hssss" come from
it. It squeezed me close, and every inch of my body it touched
felt like hot coals scoring my flesh. Its constricting grip moved
around my back and intertwined with my body, coiling me in
a snake-like grasp. I could feel it pressing hard into my flesh,
covering my chest and around my back. It was gripping my
waist and midway down my legs, its hot breath scorching the
side of my face and head. I wanted to scream in agony, but I
couldn't. I was lodged tightly in my fear and pain.

Again, I heard "hssss," and the creature shifted against me;
I could feel its fire searing my flesh. There was a brief moment

when its hold was released, and I thought it had given up. Then, a few seconds later, it was again wrapping around me, but its flesh burned hotter against mine this time.

I closed my eyes to accept my fate and tried to allow my body to drop to the ground. I released all muscle functions and went into a state of playing dead, but the creature wrapped around me so tightly—it wouldn't let me fall. I tried to let go of life, to allow the devil and his snake to take me toward the fate I deserved. The more I tried to give up, the harder my body fought to stay.

Suddenly I heard a forceful shout: "Open your eyes!"

I did as commanded. I opened my eyes to look at a solid male face staring at me. With my dream trail still lingering, I realized he was the hotness coiling around me. It took me a few minutes to focus on the handsome face of Sam staring at me. I looked into his eyes and could feel his overwhelming concern. He was close to me. Why was he so close? His exposed flesh was burning me.

With a quick jolt, my body began to convulse involuntarily. The movements were rigid and full of hate. My body was fighting me.

"Sam..." I tried to shout, but it came out as a soft cry.

"Oh Sara, hold on, you're going into shock," he stated.

His voice was softer in tone, laced with worry.

It was a timbre I hadn't gotten from my husband in a long time. The way he spoke to me lingered in my mind before the reality of the words sank in. Shock, why was I going into shock?

The tension in my muscles slowly began to relax, and the convulsions slowed to shakes.

"You need some electrolytes. Do you have anything in your vast arrangement of supplies?" he whispered; his mouth close to my ear.

The feel of his warm breath against my skin stirred emotions no man other than my husband should have been able to kindle. I found it challenging to think and harder to answer his simple question. I opened my mouth and managed a few words through the scratchy dryness of my throat. "Gatorade, bottom, back."

Sam hurried away to the shelves. At that moment, I observed two things I hadn't before. One being Sam had nothing on, and the second being without his fiery flesh next to mine, I was freezing. I was too caught up in my body's reaction to honestly think about Sam's nakedness.

When Sam returned, I stretched my arm out to grab the bottle from him and screamed when I saw my hand.

It couldn't have been my hand. It was a crimson color, and the large pus-filled nodules made it challenging to differentiate between the fingers. The fear over my hand subsided slowly as I observed a reflection farther behind where Sam stood. I barely noticed Sam slip on his boxers. I lowered my arm and fingers back down to my side and watched as the candlelight danced across the mother-of-pearl surface, a new addition to the basement. It was spectacular; it looked like something you would find in an exotic palace.

Sam curled back next to me and proceeded to take his place wrapped around me. When his arm touched the small of my back, I noticed I, too, wasn't wearing anything. Yet, at that moment, I only cared about where the delicate, small coffin came from.

"The other one behind it is a pearlescent pink," Sam whispered, reading my thoughts through my expression.

"How?" was all I managed to say breathlessly.

Sam continued to put light pressure on my back, urging me to rise up and take a few drinks. I followed his lead and worked on sitting up. I parted my lips slightly as he held the Gatorade to my mouth. I was desperate for the liquid and growled when he pulled it away after a few small drinks.

"You need bandages and antibiotics. Once I get your body temperature back to normal, I can get you some. If Kyle comes home, he can take my place beside you, and I could go sooner," Sam insisted while positioning us back under the covers.

"He wouldn't lay with me to save me. He would tell me to get over it. We haven't held one another for a very long time, and he makes sure I know how disgusted he is by my body. Don't count on him relieving you if your goal is to save me," I plainly stated. I couldn't work up the energy to be offended by how I knew Kyle would treat me.

Sam had no outward response to what I said, but I felt his body tense slightly, and he simply pulled me against him tighter. I had the vague feeling that he kissed my hair but was too weak to contemplate. It felt good to have somebody hold me again. I didn't mind that it seemed like he was burning me with every touch.

"What happened to me?" I squeaked through the soreness grasping at the base of my throat.

"I found you outside about six hours ago. When I got back here, I thought you were dead. I didn't see you at first, but when I found you, you were barely breathing and already showing signs of hypothermia. You were covered in a layer of ice, all of your exposed skin has frostbite, and luckily the worse of it was localized to your hand. You had yourself tucked into a fetal position. I picked you up and brought you back inside, stripped us down, and began warming you up." He moved slightly, trying to pull our bodies closer together. "You are all I have. We need each other to cope with what is happening, and I didn't want to lose you again," he softly finished.

"I don't understand why you would care so much?"

"Because, Sara, someone has to."

His answer was direct, and I could feel the passion behind it. Perhaps he had found his daughter, and she, too, had perished. But nevertheless, I couldn't bring myself to ask him this simple question.

"If Kyle is so horrible to you, why do you stay with him? Why would you stay in that situation if he is as mean and hateful as you say?"

"I never said he was mean and hateful," I argued.

"You didn't have to say those words for me to hear what you were leaving out."

I knew what he was getting at and couldn't deny the truth. I meant what I said about Kyle leaving me to die, and Sam heard the words I didn't include—that he was a heartless bastard.

"It wasn't always that way. There was a time when he truly loved me and would have done anything to make me happy."

"What happened? When did things change?"

I closed my eyes so Sam wouldn't see the pain my words would cause me. I could try and fool myself into thinking it didn't upset me anymore, but he would know the truth in my eyes, in my unshed tears.

"I honestly don't know. It was little things at first, an unkind word, a disgusted look at something I would say. I tried to change. Whenever he commented about me doing something horrible, I tried to adjust. I would change the way he wanted, but even that would be wrong. Eventually, it got to the point where I felt no matter what I did, I wasn't good enough for him.

"Regardless of what I wanted or how hard I tried to keep him happy, nothing I did pleased him. It could have been me. Maybe I changed him. He was wonderful when we got married. Attentive, loving, and concerned about me all the time. I crave that; I miss who Kyle was. I have fallen into a life of going through the motions. I do what I know he wants because it's easier to keep him content than worry about my happiness. One day he will see everything I do for him. He loves me the only way he knows how, and that has to be good enough for me."

"Why did you marry him?" Sam forcefully spat, causing me to hesitate.

"He was the most beautiful thing that had ever happened

to me. He seemed to love me for me. He accepted me even with all of my quirky and unusual ways of doing things. He never laughed at my notions or acted like I didn't know what I was doing, even when I didn't. Instead, he made me feel like his life revolved around being with me, which made me feel important.

"When we were in high school, I thought I had the world figured out, and he stood beside me, never once questioning my thought process. I was young and ignorant of the world around me, but he never treated me like what I said wasn't important to him. He held me when I cried, he laughed with me, and if I was scared, he tried to be a great protector. When he asked me to marry him, there was no thought needed. He was my match, my soul mate. He was the one I wanted to spend the rest of my life with. He was the man I wanted to call my husband and the father of my children. I was so sure about who he was, what he stood for, and what our lives would be like. I never thought we would end up like this. We were supposed to change and grow together, not apart.

"Slowly, things changed. First, it was the clothes I could wear, then it was what I could watch on TV. He constantly said he was protecting me, which sometimes meant he had to save me from myself. Day by day, he got more insistent. First, he canceled the satellite, citing that I spent too much of my day watching it. His next issue was that I was surfing the internet too much, so he password-protected it, and I wasn't allowed to use it. He checked my emails and sat with me when I wanted to look something up online. He threw out anything he didn't like me to wear and blocked my cell phone from contacting anyone but him or the authorities. He controlled every piece of my life, and I let him with no complaints because I was his wife.

"Once I was isolated from everyone, I knew he started saying things that made me question my own self-worth. He never called me anything horrible, but every compliment was backhanded. One time we were supposed to go out, and I was getting ready when I asked if he approved my choice. He looked me in the face and said, 'That's good; at least it doesn't make you look as fat.' I actually thought it was a compliment. I let him consume me, and I didn't fight it. Who does that?" I finished as Sam gently wiped the tears from my face.

I did miss the old Kyle. He was my life, and now lying here in the arms of another man, I couldn't have cared less if he came walking down the stairs. I didn't want him to die, but I was not worried about where he was or if he was okay. The revelation should have been disappointing, but it was long overdue. I loved him with all my heart, but I was sick and tired of him. Exhausted by the way he made me feel. No matter what he said now, I wasn't sure he would be able to change that.

"I understand where you're coming from. I thought Ellen and I would be married forever. Some things are meant to last, but she and I weren't. We never talked or argued; we never discussed anything. Our marriage was missing a key element, communication. I came home from work one day to find her saying enough was enough, and she was leaving. The worst part was that she never gave me a chance to change. She just packed her and Samantha's things and left. The following week I got served with divorce papers citing un-reconcilable differences. I never stood a chance."

I didn't know what to say. Nothing I could say would make a difference to how he felt. I appreciated his opening up to me about his problems. He helped me understand that I wasn't alone. The tone of his voice showed he was upset over the incident. But, if I had to guess, he still loved Ellen very much.

"Your love for her is beautiful." It was more of a whispered thought.

I didn't realize he had heard me until he replied, "I'm not sure I ever really loved her. She reminded me of someone I had loved for years but couldn't be with. I was subconsciously trying to extend my love for the other woman by marrying Ellen. I think I thought if I loved Ellen that I would stop loving the other woman. I loved Ellen in my own way, but I'm not in love with her."

His confession tore at my heart. To hear him speak honestly about something so hard to accept in yourself made me think the one he loved was an imbecile for not taking everything he had to offer. Only now was I starting to see how brainwashed I was by Kyle. Not everyone was like him, but I didn't know how to be anything other than what he had shaped me into. I was jaded and on guard, stuck in a mindset of *"they must want something from me because no one is nice without wanting something in return."* I didn't know how to be, feel, or react around other people. Who was I without Kyle? Who did I want to be?

My body finally stopped shaking, and the feel of Sam's soft, luscious skin next to mine felt nice. The fiery sensation he had initially brought to me was subsiding, and I was beginning to warm up. I tried not to think about the pain or that my hands were throbbing as if they had their own heartbeat. I wanted to enjoy the moment, the quietness that was all around us. It had been a devastating day, and having someone hold me tightly felt wonderful. When was the last time Kyle and I had been intimate, the last time we made love? Had he ever held me like this? When did he stop wanting me? When did I stop caring? The end of the world had brought up things I had locked up, not wanting to face them for fear of rejection.

"I think the neighbor had some prescriptions in her medicine cabinet. Since I've stopped shaking and convulsing, can you go check? If you could find something to help ease the pain in my hands, I would appreciate it. There used to be a drugstore up off Route Nine. If it is still there, maybe they could help us," I tried to say confidently.

"I'm not sure I should leave you yet. I don't want you to have a relapse or worse. You have to stay in this spot until I get back. Can you promise me you will not get up or try to move around?" Sam roughly stated.

"I promise I will only move from this spot once you return. I hurt too badly to want to move, so I don't foresee it being a problem."

Sam took in a deep breath and let it out. He pulled his arm around my back and gently placed his hand against my cheek. He looked deeply into my eyes as he said, "I will return to you. I know you remember who I am. You have to because we are all we have."

He leaned in and pressed his lips gently to my forehead, then maneuvered out of the blanket, ensuring I was completely covered before he even thought to get dressed. I should've turned and given him some privacy, but I didn't. Not because he didn't deserve my respect but because it hurt to move. As he pulled on his jeans, I watched his muscles flex and move gracefully. His back was toward me, and I marveled at how the human body looked so beautiful doing the simplest things.

I sighed. What I had managed to do to myself was unfathomable. I couldn't get dying right.

Sam pulled his shirt down and slid his boots on. He put on a flannel, then a sweatshirt, and continued bundling himself in coat layers. When I was outside, it didn't seem to be freezing. It was cold, but not as much as he was insinuating. So, what was with all of the extra insulation? I had been drunk, which could have affected my temperature perception.

I watched him walk up the stairs and go outside. I wondered whether or not Kyle would make it home. No matter how hard I tried to tell myself I didn't care if Kyle survived, a part of me was worried for him. I didn't owe him my devotion and love, but it was hard to reprogram the years. I'd been programmed to follow him. So how would I act if he didn't return? Sam didn't worry me; he had already proven he could survive.

It had been less than two days since everything had gone

to hell. I had no idea what the world outside my little neighborhood held for us. Maybe I was over-exaggerating and there could still be a chance that only our city was hit by the storms. No rule of nature stated everybody had to be hit by the same stuff or at the same time.

I was deluding myself; I knew the world was gone. Before we got hit by the storms, there were news reports from around the world telling of unnatural storms writhing throughout. Rescue workers and volunteers had spent the previous months trying to help clean up the aftermath. To sit here and try to convince me that the world was not hurting was a childish game. It wasn't time for games or comforting lies; it was time for cold hard facts. No sirens, no planes flying over, and I hadn't heard the lifeline helicopter once. If there was a chance of rescue, I should have seen signs of the government, military, or any form of law.

Laying on my side helped me focus on the beautiful little coffin. I knew that Thomas was in white and Tina was in pink. Sam brought me something magnificent to bury my children in. Although, if it was as cold as Sam made me believe, I don't know how we would get them in the ground.

Thinking about any one thing for too long was difficult. Too much was running through my head to stay focused.

My mind shifted, and I wondered if any other body part was as disgusting as my hand. The two parts of my body that were not shielded with clothing were my hands and my face. Did this mean my face looked like my hand? I already knew what my right hand looked like, so I slowly pulled my left hand up and out from under the blanket. I was surprised it hadn't suffered the same fate as my right. It was a deep crimson red but didn't have the same pus-filled nodules. I could move my fingers. It hurt like hell, but I could do it. I glanced down at my body to see it was covered in a light red color. It looked like I had been to the beach and had forgotten to wear sunblock. The pain that came with the burn was worse than any sunburn I had ever experienced.

I looked around the basement and saw that Sam had lit candles. He also had found the oil lamps I had buried on a shelf. The number of candles seemed excessive, given the fact it was just us down here. Then I realized he was also using them for heat.

Everything around me was still silent. By now, you would think I would be able to hear something. Any kind of noise would've been a welcome sound. A dog barking, birds chirping, car alarms going off uncontrollably, a siren or two showing there was life still moving out there. But when I closed my eyes, I heard nothing.

I could tell my body was warming up to the proper temperature because the pain was becoming unbearable. I tried to concentrate on the simplest things, such as my name, but I couldn't hold the thought for long.

Sam insisted I remembered him from high school. I didn't want him to know that I did recognize him. Every memory of him was burned into my mind. I had spent years of my life trying to erase what high school was for me, and here he was telling me I needed to re-live it.

There was nothing about that time in my life that I was required to remember. Sam had not been a memory of mine for many years. It was a choice he forced on me at the time, and I was not going to re-live it.

I waited for what seemed like an eternity listening carefully for the sound of Sam's boots on the wood above me. Finally, I heard him hit the floor and run to the only way into the basement. I looked over at him, and when the door opened, I could see the snow falling all around. It was a blizzard outside. All I saw was white and nothing else. He came down the stairs in a huff and quickly began to undress, ensuring that his coat was hanging to allow it to dry. Beside his boots sat a suitcase that he had brought in with him.

I half expected him to strip down and crawl back in bed with me, but he didn't. Instead, he grabbed the suitcase and came and sat beside me.

"Do you think you can handle wearing some clothes?" he joked.

"If you can give me something for the pain, I will wear whatever you like!"

"You will feel cold, but I need to have you come out from under the covers. We have to get you wrapped up. If you give me your hand first, I will start there," he urged.

"Did you find something for the pain?" I quickly asked, focused on finding relief from the excruciating ache.

"Yes, I did. I found you some naproxen." He smiled.

"Tell me you're joking. Naproxen is nice, but tell me she had something stronger, perhaps something with codeine," I insisted.

"Yes, she also had Darvocet and hydrocodone. Have you taken either of these?" he questioned as he pulled the pills from the suitcase.

"Yes, both, but I want the hydrocodone."

"Okay, let's get it into your system," he chuckled.

I rose onto my elbow, and Sam helped me sit up. I took my left hand and stretched it out for the pills. Sam grabbed the Gatorade and took the lid off. He placed a tablet in my hand, and I threw it into my mouth without a second thought. I grabbed the bottle from his outstretched hand and washed down the pill. I returned the bottle to Sam and extended my right hand to him.

"This is going to hurt, and I'm sorry for that, but I have to keep it from getting infected," Sam explained.

He took my offered appendage in his hand and squeezed a large glop of antibacterial ointment on my hand. Carefully, he spread it all over. I felt every muscle in my body tense, and I wanted to yank my hand from him. But instead, I pulled in a large gulp of air through my teeth. Sam recognized the sound and looked up at me.

"I'm sorry; I know it hurts. I'm trying to be gentle. I'm

almost done," he reassured.

I closed my eyes and held my breath. It was the only thing that seemed to help with the pain. Once he started wrapping my hand, the ache subsided slightly, and it was easier to take the pressure he was placing on my hand.

"Thank you!" I smiled.

"It's getting colder by the hour. Our best bet at surviving the night is to stay close. Our body heat will keep us warm. It will give us a better chance of lasting till the sun comes up, and I can figure out a better solution."

"Yeah, I understand. We have to be close to survive; I agree with you. After all, you saved my life. So, the least I can do is help to keep us alive. Can I wear something, perhaps my bra and panties?" I chuckled.

"Technically skin to skin is the best way to stay warm, but if it makes you uncomfortable. I can get you your clothes."

"Maybe I can just wear my undergarments and your T-shirt?" I stuttered.

"I think that's acceptable."

If I wasn't already crimson, I would have blushed bright red over asking permission to wear clothes while sharing a bed with a man who wasn't my husband.

Sam finished wrapping my hand and took his shirt off. He walked over to a pile of clothes and pulled my bra and panties from it. He gave a slight smile as he came back to me. He sat next to me on the edge of the bed and pulled the covers down.

"Hey," I muttered while trying to put them back over myself.

He quietly chuckled before speaking. "You can't get dressed buried under the covers."

"I could if I could use both of my hands."

I gave him the evilest glare I could muster. I huffed and maneuvered my way to the edge of the mattress and pushed myself to stand up. I stumbled a little and found Sam's fingers on my waist to help me steady myself.

I placed my good hand on his shoulder and tried not to think about what he was helping me do. I settled my balance and set one foot in my panties and then the other. I held my breath as his hands gently grazed the outside of my thighs while he pulled my panties in place. I felt his muscles tense, and his breath started to quicken.

He rose up without making a sound and guided me to turn around. He stood behind me, reached in front of me, and helped me place my hands into my bra. I held perfectly still as he guided the straps up my arms and pulled the closure in the back together.

Who would have ever thought putting clothes back on could be so exhilarating? I felt him bend down and grab his shirt. He placed it in my arm and moved quickly to put space between us.

I understood his need for distance; I required it too. I struggled at first to get the shirt over my head with one hand. Once Sam saw me grappling with it, he quickly returned to help. I moved back under the covers and watched him strip down to his boxers. I could see he was as affected by the sensuality in the little act of getting dressed as I was. He hurried to get under the large pile of covers with me.

My pain was finally coming to a stop, and I felt my eyes getting heavy.

"Your best bet at staying close to me is to spoon me. I get warm when I sleep, and I can't stand hot breath on my face," I mumbled before rolling over to my side.

With how my body was deceiving my mind, I didn't think I could handle looking at him at this moment, anyway.

"I have no problem with that," Sam agreed.

He positioned himself behind me and allowed his free arm to drape across the front of me, his body mimicking my every curve. He was close enough for me to feel his heart beating in his chest.

The effects of the hydrocodone were starting to affect my

thinking. I lost all ability to process what I wanted to say before it came out and to control my body. My head felt as if it was floating, and for once in my adult life, my thoughts and actions were unguarded. I wanted to feel Sam's body pressed against mine. I tried to tell him how much I hated life even before all the mayhem. My limbs felt heavier; moving took more energy than it usually would.

I scooted closer to him, snuggling my butt into his hips to feel him tighter against me.

"Does your heart always beat so fast, or is it because you're lying next to a half-naked woman?" I giggled.

I knew my question embarrassed him because he immediately tried to pull away.

"No, don't move. I wasn't saying it was a bad thing. I like the feel of your heart beating against my back; it's very soothing," I plainly stated.

I moved my hair off my shoulder and turned to look at him.

"Are you coming back over here? Sam," I sighed. "After all those nights in high school, I figured your shyness towards me was gone," I squeaked as my thoughts and voice faded.

He moved back into his previous spot and rested his head just over my ear.

"You do remember me?" he whispered.

"You're a hard person to forget," I slurred while settling back into our previous position.

He kissed my neck gently and said, "I loved you; do you know that?"

I didn't hear him correctly, so I didn't respond. My body felt heavy, and I wanted to sleep. With my eyes shut, I found peace in Sam's steady breaths, and his rhythmic heartbeat sang me into a satisfying slumber. I drifted back into the darkness, but I didn't feel alone this time.

CHAPTER 3

Over the next week, I woke up long enough to take more meds, eat something small, and then was back out again. I couldn't tell how many days had passed, but I finally reached the point where it didn't hurt to move. I sat up and examined my surroundings. The basement was still chilly but didn't feel as cold as it had. The two coffins hadn't been moved. Determined to put more clothes on and move, I pushed myself to a standing position. My legs felt as if I had tried to run a marathon in my sleep. After a few minutes, it seemed like some of my strength had returned, and I walked over to a pile of clothes. I grabbed my backpack first and dug out the baby wipes.

"Sam," I attempted to say. I cleared my throat and tried again. "Sam." It came out as a squeak. I had no voice.

I didn't see Sam anywhere. Quickly, I washed my body with wipes, noticing I no longer looked like a lobster. There was no pain when I touched my skin, either. It wasn't a shower or a bath, but I felt better than I had. I put layers of clothes on: thermal underwear, jeans, and sweats on my legs. Thermal, long sleeve shirt and sweatshirt on top, then added three pairs of socks.

The silence of the basement was broken by the movement above me. Could it be Sam's footsteps? I listened carefully, trying to make out the noise when I heard a loud *thud*. It sounded like something hitting the ground hard.

What if it was Sam, and he was hurt? I had to find out. I cautiously walked up the stairs, my legs protesting every step. The burning sensation in my muscles made it almost impossible to move. If I wasn't careful, I would fall down the stairs backward.

I peered out of the door. Heavy flakes were still falling from the sky. The sun was covered by thick clouds, making it difficult to see.

"Sam, is that you?" I asked, surveying everywhere around me. Everything I looked at had an undisturbed, thick, white layer. I thought I had imagined the noise, or maybe it was an animal running through. Deer were heavy in this area of town.

I couldn't go back inside yet. I needed to put my mind at ease and ensure there wasn't anyone or anything up here.

I ventured a few more feet west and saw something that I thought was a massive rock. My vision had been known to play tricks on me even on clear days, and I wasn't going to walk away when there was a possibility of it being an actual person. I cautiously approached it and saw it didn't have the same thick layer of white covering it. It hadn't been here long.

My mind told me to leave it and go back down where it was safe, but my heart screamed a different tune. If Sam hadn't saved me, I would be dead, and if that was Sam, I couldn't leave him here to die inches from safety.

"Sam?" I whispered one more time as I got closer to it.

"Sara," a weak voice uttered.

I grabbed the massive dark figure and rolled it towards me.

"Kyle!" I exclaimed.

I fell to my knees beside him. His breath was short, and I couldn't find his pulse. He was covered in dirt and snow. Streaks of ice ran down the side of his face, and the bit of his face that was exposed was a bright red.

"Kyle, I can't carry you. So, you have to help me," I fought to say.

He was out. I shook him with all my might and tried to get him to look at me.

"Kyle, look at me. Kyle, you have to open your eyes."

I repositioned towards his shoulders, hooked my arm under his, and pulled as hard as possible. He didn't budge. He was too big, and I was too weak.

"Come on, Kyle, you've come this far. Don't give up. Damn it, Kyle!" I tried to scream.

I bent down as close to his face as possible and pleaded, "Kyle, you have to get up. Just a few more steps, and then we can get you warmed up. You're home. Please don't give up now; I need you!"

I kissed his cold, dry, rough lips, hoping it would cause some reaction. Nothing. I shook him as hard as I could with no response.

"Damn it, Kyle. Once again, I have to save us," I cried.

My hand started throbbing from the bitter cold as it permeated through the bandage. How was I going to get him inside the house?

My mind was racing with ideas.

There is ice under the snow; I could probably sweep some of it away and use the ice to push him toward the stairs.

I removed the snow from below my feet. *That won't work; the ice is all but gone. I'll go get some rope. I could pull more with my entire body weight versus using only my arms or legs. That might work. Wait, no...How am I going to tie a knot with one hand? I'm not that skilled at a slip knot with two functional appendages, let alone one. Think, Sara. You're the one who has to save him.*

As the thoughts came and went inside my head, I heard the snow crunching, like someone was walking on top of old, hardened snow.

Something was moving closer to us. Without knowing what I was going to see, I prepared for the worst.

I felt along the ground with my good hand for a pipe or

something that could deal some damage. I touched a round hard object and swore it was a pipe. I pulled it closer and saw I was holding my daughter's favorite stuffed doll. It felt hard because it had gotten wet and then froze.

Who was I deluding? I couldn't save my kids; now I had to sit and watch Kyle die. What did I do to deserve such torture?

"Sara, what are you doing up here?" a familiar voice rang.

"I heard something, and I thought you might be hurt, but look—it's Kyle. Help me get him inside," I cried.

Thank goodness for Sam. Right when I was ready to give up hope, out of nowhere, Sam showed up, my knight in shining armor, to rescue me once again.

"Get the door open. I will grab Kyle," Sam said, rushing over to pick Kyle up.

They were about the same size, but Sam was a little taller. Sam had a more muscular build to his body, but I thought that came with his life as a bachelor.

Sam knelt a bit and threw Kyle over his shoulder like it was second nature. I watched him cautiously carry him down the stairs. He placed Kyle softly on the bed he and I had shared and started pulling his coat off.

"How long were you outside?" he anxiously questioned.

"I'm not sure, twenty minutes or so."

"Are you okay?" he asked, still feverishly working on getting Kyle out of his layers of clothing.

At that moment, I couldn't help but realize this was the first time Kyle and Sam had been near one another since the last day of high school.

"Sara, are you okay?" he urged once more.

"Yes, sorry," I responded.

"Take your clothes off," he replied.

"What?" It flew out of my mouth before I processed his request.

"If you want to save your husband, undress. We have to warm him up."

"Yes, of course I do," I answered in a hurry, not only to Sam but to myself.

I started the daunting task of undressing one-handed. As the blood flow returned to the injury, it began burning and hurting worse. I tried to contain my pain and worry about saving Kyle's life. I was down to the t-shirt in no time. I stood staring, watching Sam get every stitch of clothing off of Kyle.

"You have to lie against him with your bare skin, Sara. He is worse than you were, and I'm afraid we will lose him. Hurry and take that t-shirt off, your bra and panties too, and then get in close to him," Sam pleaded while undressing himself.

I wasn't going to argue with Sam's logic. He had saved me, and he would save Kyle as well.

I crawled into bed next to Kyle's naked ice-cold body and placed my searing skin against his. I understood more now why it burned so bad in my dreams. It felt like I was hugging a giant popsicle. I placed my leg on his and wrapped my injured hand across his chest. I tried not to touch Kyle with my hand. The throbbing and overwhelming heat was making it uncomfortable.

Sam bundled me in and came to Kyle's other side to take his place. I watched Sam climb into the bed and press his body against Kyle's. Although he said nothing and had no expression, it must have made him uncomfortable. With Sam finally set in his spot, I decided to ask.

"Where were you earlier? I woke up, and you were gone."

"I've been working my way around the neighborhood scavenging for supplies, looking for a better heating option than just candles and the one kerosene heater I found," he responded with a thoughtful look.

"How many of the neighbors have I lost?" I quietly asked.

"All of them," Sam plainly answered.

"How is that even possible? Someone had to have survived. We can't be the only three people left."

"I'm sure we're not, but as far as the houses surrounding

59

you, we are. I have been through six places that used to be homes, and they are either deserted, or the owners are dead," he calmly replied.

It was all authentic, yet I couldn't accept that so many had perished in such a short time. Why weren't we better prepared for this? I was staring at the ceiling when Sam interrupted my thoughts.

"We need to cover all the way up past our heads to keep the heat in," he said while pulling the heavy stack of blankets up and over us.

I laid my head on Kyle's chest and listened to his faint, slow heartbeat. Having my breasts pressed against his cold body made them hurt.

"Can I put something on my breasts, please? This intense cold is very discomforting," I whispered to Sam.

"I'm sorry, Sara. Clothing will block your body heat. I can place my arm in between you if you think it will make it hurt less," he offered.

It was a strange suggestion, to say the least, but the pain was too uncomfortable to stay close.

"I can't see you, so I'm going to bring my hand across, and you place it where you need it blocked," he softly said.

"I won't be able to guide you with my bad hand. I can't feel anything with it. You're going to have to reach, and when your hand grazes my nipple, you will know where to place your arm," I quickly said.

I had no other way of knowing where to have him place it, and I was already shivering from being next to Kyle. I didn't want to disappoint Kyle by not being able to stay near him to save his life. Yet, on the other hand, I needed to halt the pain.

"I'm not sure...." Sam started to speak.

"Please, this is the easiest way. Embarrassing, yes," I reassured him.

"Okay then, I'm coming over." He chuckled.

I waited till I felt the tips of his fingers tickle the side of my breast.

"If you follow down and hug Kyle's side, you will be in the perfect spot to block the cold."

I lifted high enough to allow his hand to follow the side of Kyle's chest. I rested upon his arm, and the warmth was instantly gratifying. It felt much better. It was a tremendous relief to keep my body next to Kyle because of Sam.

"Thank you, Sam."

"I told you we have to stick together. We are all we have. You, Kyle, and I will have to keep one another alive," he whispered.

"Still, thank you. I would still be there if you hadn't followed me into the tent and helped me bring my kids home."

Not just there. I was sure I would have been dead. While lying next to Kyle, I found myself wishing, praying, and hoping he would make it. He had been through more than I knew trying to get back to us. Despite all our past problems, this was going to be the time to reconnect and rekindle our love. A fresh start at remembering what it was like to genuinely be in love.

"Sara, you still awake?" Sam whispered.

"Yeah, Sam. I'm still up. Why?" I asked.

"You said you remembered me; is that true?"

"Did you know we planned on having six kids when Kyle and I got married? Can you believe we actually thought we wanted six kids?"

I didn't want to discuss high school. I refused to relive it or stir up old feelings that had long since faded.

"Six kids, I never thought of Kyle as a kids man. So why did you stop at two?" he snickered.

"Two reasons. One, we were crazy to think we could handle six. Two, I had to have a hysterectomy after I had Thomas. They couldn't stop the bleeding, and that's how the world sometimes goes. But the two I have, or had, I love more than anything else in this world."

"I remember the day Samantha was born. It was the happiest moment I had ever experienced and even topped the day I married Ellen. Don't get me wrong, Ellen was a vision in white, but Samantha was a baby dependent on me for everything. A little child who loved me no matter what, pure unconditional love. No judgment, no disappointment, just love." He sighed.

"The first day when you left to go find her, did you?"

I thought twice before I asked, but he brought them up, so I figured it was okay.

"Not yet. I'm waiting for the snow to let up before I make the trip to Ellen's house. Kyle proves why I don't want to try yet. I don't want my Sammy to find me like this, or worse, never find me at all."

"I will go with you next time," I mumbled.

"If you can, I would enjoy the company, but you may have to stay with Kyle. We have to get him healthy."

"How did you meet Ellen?" I questioned, trying to keep the conversation going.

"Believe it or not, she spilled her iced coffee on me one morning before I went to work. She was shocked that I didn't freak out from the cold or get angry with her. I just looked at her and told her I would prefer a hot coffee if she wanted to give me a drink. From there, we kept running into one another all over the place. It seemed God had a plan for us to be together." He sighed.

"How long were you married?"

"Not long enough. She said we fell out of love. The truth behind it was she fell out of love with me. I still loved her. The look on Samantha's face when we told her I was moving out is one I will never be able to erase from my memory. She was six, and all she could do was ask me why. I didn't have an answer that wouldn't have made her mom the bad guy, so I told her it was me. It had been almost six years, and she still looked at me with disappointment. I have to save her. I have to let her know I have always loved her and never wanted to leave."

"I'm so sorry, Sam. That must be very difficult to have to live with for all this time. I'm afraid I taught my kids it was okay to let someone who says they love you mistreat you. The way Kyle would talk down to me in front of them had to have impacted them in some way. I tried to laugh most of it off or pretend he was joking. I told myself they weren't old enough to understand, but I think, on some level, they did. I tried to never let them see me cry or hear the nasty, hateful things he said to me. I hope I sheltered them half as much as I tried to. It's funny, you know. Here I am, trying to save his life even though he was so mean to me for so long, yet the two complete angels are lying over there, unable to be saved. Not ha-ha funny, but still funny somehow," I said through watery eyes.

The tears were rolling down my cheeks, following the curves of my jaw to my neck. I could feel them sliding down my neck and across my breasts, landing on Sam's arm.

"Please don't cry," Sam whispered.

"I'm sorry, I'm tired. Goodnight, Sam."

"Goodnight, Sara."

I wasn't tired, but I was done with the walk down memory lane. Sam shared many intimate things, and I was glad he did, but I hated being an open book. The coldness of Kyle's body and my shivering were going to keep me from sleeping. I stared at Sam in the darkness and wondered if he was looking at me too.

What will Kyle say when he finds out Sam helped save his life? There was no love lost between these two men, or at least that's how it seemed all those years ago.

I moved my arm up and reached my hand on what I thought was Kyle's shoulder.

"Sara, is your hand wet?" Sam asked.

"What?"

"Your hand, is it wet?"

"I'm not sure. It stopped throbbing a little bit ago."

"Move your arm down, please," he requested.

I did as he asked.

"It's your hand. Sara, your hand is completely soaked!" He exclaimed.

"Oh, I can't tell. Is that bad?" I stuttered.

"It could be. Either your blisters have burst, or you had it in the snow. Did you have your hand in the snow?" His questioning intensified.

"I'm not sure. With everything going on, I wasn't paying much attention to where my hand was placed," I squeaked.

"Regardless, I'm going to need to re-wrap it."

"Can't it wait until we get Kyle warmed up?"

"Yeah, I'm sure it'll be okay, but if it starts hurting again, you'll tell me. Right?"

"Yes, of course I will."

Did I stick my hand in the snow while trying to save Kyle? Unfortunately, the question was more challenging to answer than it should've been.

My body either got used to the cold, or Kyle was warming up because I stopped shivering. My eyes were feeling heavy. How could I be tired? I already slept so much.

Hidden in the darkness behind my eyelids, a light was shining through. I stared till the glow cleared, and I saw Sam's face the day I told him I was getting married. All these years, I thought he was happy for Kyle and me. Now remembering his face, I saw the smile, but I noticed something I had never paid attention to before. I saw a deep sadness in his eyes. How did I not know one of my best friends wasn't happy for me?

The dream played out in real-time, but when I focused all of my attention on one aspect, it slowed to a crawl, allowing me to process things in a new light.

After I shared my excellent news with Sam, he gave me an overly tight hug. I rubbed his back slightly, thinking I was embracing someone truly happy for me. I never realized his pain.

Kyle pulled me towards a group of his friends to show off my ring. While I was preoccupied with them, Sam disappeared. Sadly, I hadn't noticed he had left. We continued our progression of sharing the great news. It never crossed my mind that he went so quickly. It was close to being the last day of high school, and between graduation and now our proposal news, my brain hadn't put much thought behind it.

Kyle and I were young and in love. We believed there wasn't anything in this world we wanted more than each other. Kyle looked happy; he appeared to be a man in love. He told everyone we came into contact with that I chose him.

A question ran through my mind: picked him over whom? It's not like I had multiple offers. Suddenly, everything clicked. He was gloating because I chose him over Sam, though I had no idea it was a competition. I was oblivious to Sam's true feelings. He had been a great friend to me. He was someone I could count on no matter what, and I could always depend on him regardless of the situation.

The dream shifted to graduation day. The principal had just presented to the class, and we moved our tassels and threw our caps into the air. I beamed at Kyle and then turned to smile at Sam, but he was already out of sight. I felt a need to see him. It had been weeks, and he wasn't returning my calls. I hurried outside and waited just past the doors, eagerly seeking him. I watched as my classmates and their families left the building. I was polite to those who stopped but kept my eyes searching for Sam. I stood there for an hour after the last person walked out. Finally, the doors opened once more, and my heart broke in my chest. Kyle wrapped his arm around me, telling me it was time to go. I didn't get to speak to Sam.

I opened my eyes and was bombarded with memories I had buried deep inside my mind. I didn't like remembering that he had abandoned me after all this time. The replaying thoughts collapsed in my chest as it rested on the look his mom gave me the day I searched for him. Two weeks after graduation, I had finally had enough. I went to his house to demand that he speak to me. His mom wouldn't let me in, saying he had left town for a while. She was hurt; I remember that now. Broken-hearted.

I swiped the tears from my face. He walked away from

our friendship, never bothering to say goodbye. He left me. How could I have forgotten that? How could I have blocked the memory of him turning his back on me without a single word?

I wanted to confront Sam and demand an answer, but it was so long ago. What did I expect to gain? Maybe he wouldn't remember it the way I did, and perhaps he thought we parted on good terms.

I placed my head back on Kyle's chest and felt his heart beating stronger. He seemed to be getting better.

Sighing, I listened to Kyle's heartbeat with a smile. I planned on lying there until he woke, but my body had other ideas. My stomach was growling for the first time in days, so much so it was causing physical pain. I guess you can't live off of painkillers and Gatorade for long. I tried to ignore it, but with every grumble came more pain.

Finally giving in, I slid out from under the covers. I tucked them back in to keep the heat inside with the men. A cold chill ran down my spine as I hurried to get clothes on. Then, donning a sweat suit, I walked over to the shelves of supplies.

While surveying the stock in the candlelight, I could see just how much Sam had acquired over the last week. There were bandages and alcohol—drinking and disinfecting. We had beef jerky, rice, and a ton of prescription and over-the-counter pill bottles.

I grabbed a bag of beef jerky and tore it open using my teeth. I pulled the bulkiest piece out and shoved it in my mouth. Not my brightest idea, but I was too hungry to think logically. As I chewed, I remembered Sam had said something about a new bandage. With all the work he had been doing, I didn't see any reason to wake him. This I could manage on my own.

I grabbed the antibacterial cream and a rolled bandage from the shelf. Placing everything on the box next to my beef jerky, I began unraveling my hand.

The bandage was wet and smelled funny, but the sooner

I changed it, the better I would feel. I pulled back layer by layer and realized Sam had done a great job wrapping it up. Once I finally got the last of the rolled gauze off, I pulled the little squares away and understood why my dressing was wet. The blisters engulfing my fingers had burst. Once again, I had five separate digits, not one giant one and a thumb. I took the cream, unscrewed the cap with my teeth, and squeezed lines out on my hand down each digit. Once every finger had some antibacterial cream, I placed the tube down, threw another piece of dried meat in my mouth, and started to rub in the cream.

"Stop that!" Sam yelled.

"What," I tried to say, but there was way too much meat in my mouth.

"Your hand is not clean, and you're going to infect the open wounds on your other hand," he huffed.

"Huh!" I said with a look of utter confusion.

"Let me do it for you."

"I'm getting it," I mumbled through my over-stuffed mouth.

"No, you're not. Trust me."

He pulled a bottle of antibacterial gel from the shelf and squirted it on his hands. After he meticulously rubbed it in, he walked to me and took over. I watched his caring and graceful movements as he repeatedly bandaged my hand, saying nothing to him while he worked. I shoved piece after piece of jerky into my mouth until the package was empty. I tried not to focus on his bare chest or the way the lounge pants hung low on his hips. He wasn't a sculpted Greek god, but his body would get many women's hearts fluttering.

"I guess I was hungrier than I thought," I chuckled.

"You're healing quite nicely. In about another week, you should be able to lose the bandages completely." He smiled.

"Thank you," I replied with a childish grin.

I sat there staring into his eyes, inwardly asking him why he had left me. Pleading for some answer as to what I did wrong so long ago. There were many times over the years I needed him. Didn't he know that?

He was the first to break our gaze, turning his attention towards the shelves.

"Kyle shows no signs of hypothermia. All his extremities are in great shape. He seems to be mildly dehydrated and exhausted."

"I didn't know you were a doctor?" I stated as I scoured the shelf for more food.

"I'm not. I sold insurance for a living but read medical textbooks to pass the time at night."

"That's a rather sad thing to share. I've never once thought, 'What shall I read tonight? Oh yes, *Intro to Terminal Diseases 101*. Yes, I think that would be riveting,'" I joked in my best male voice.

With a smile that took my breath away, he said, "It's not like that exactly. You remember my mom?"

I nodded as I dove into a pack of crackers.

"Well, she always had a home remedy for whatever ailed you, and I was working on putting all of her old fixes into a book. I was doing research and enjoyed what I was reading, so I continued."

"I see. How could I possibly think your passion for it was weird?" I laughed.

I didn't want to lock him down in another embarrassing gaze, so I focused instead on the pile of goodies in front of me.

I needed to clear my head of the painful memories that haunted me. I blanked my mind, and when I did, a thought came slamming to the front.

I have an emergency radio down here.

I got up from the box I had been sitting on and dug through the shelves of canned goods to pull out the old radio. I put new batteries in it and clicked it on. I scoured through the static-filled FM airwaves, but every station broadcasted the same thing on a loop.

The loud annoying alarm and a voice saying, "This is the Emergency Broadcast System. Everyone stay in your home until further information is available. The government has issued Martial law; no one should roam the streets. Looting is a crime, and anyone caught will be punished severely as Martial law dictates; punishment will be swift and according to the law. Stay in your homes."

"You believe this crap? The city has gone to hell, and they're worried about people stealing things. Give me a break," I huffed.

Once I had been through the FM stations three times, I flipped to AM. Again, most were saying the same as the FM broadcast, but two channels had different messages.

The first station had a powerful voice that was upbeat even though his message was anything but. His tone rang, "It is the time of Satan! The apocalypse is upon us now! God has chosen his children to take, and those of us who are left here are not worthy of entering his sacred paradise. Lock your doors, and board up those windows because the good people are gone! Only the foulest of the foul and the evil-hearted are still here. You may think I'm mistaken, but if you were pure, holy, and righteous, you are gone. If you have hatred, lust, evil, envy, or greed in your heart, you are still here. Welcome to the living hell—the worst is still to come. I do not preach at you; I merely give you a glimpse of what has been brought upon us all. I, too, have been left in this world because of my impure thoughts and actions."

I found myself drawn into his voice and listening to his every word. It was as if he was speaking directly to me, making sense of the devastation.

"Crazy ass people already. You need to keep searching," Sam interjected.

I wanted to continue to listen, but I didn't want to upset Sam, so I progressed in the pursuit of finding anything else. That was when I heard the second voice. This one was deep, but seemed to be murmuring into the microphone. "I don't know if anyone will receive this, but I will try and put it on a loop. It has been three days since the town was hit by more tornadoes than I can count. I've lost everything and every person who meant anything to me. I came to the small station hoping to locate people and perhaps salvation. Instead, I only found an empty building with an emergency broadcast message playing on a loop. No one has been in here at all today. My home was destroyed, and there was no sign of the government or help from the Red Cross. I'm going to wait for someone to show up with some answers about where all the assistance is."

There was a slight pause, and it started again, but it wasn't on the loop. It was an additional recording.

"I'm on day five, and still no sign of any kind of help, government or otherwise. The snow hasn't let up even a little, and I don't know how much longer the power will last at the station."

I looked at Sam. I had no idea what day we were on. Had it been five days since my babies died?

Sam could see I was trying to ask how many days, but I said nothing. A second pause followed, and then the same voice rang through, fainter this time and sounding exhausted. It was as if his hope was gone. "It is day 8, and no one has come."

I quickly looked at Sam, and he held up both hands. Ten days. It had been ten days since this all started. I turned my attention back to the voice on the radio and intently listened to his message.

"This will be my last entry. I have to leave and find food and a more permanent place to stay. However, I have to warn you all. I was a guard at the prison outside of town. I also worked weekends at Cerritus in the secure treatment wing. That's code for the area with the really messed up criminals. Both places were deemed maximum security facilities. Most of you were unaware of that, and those who did know probably didn't give it a second thought.

"All the stone walls and barbed wire fences were to keep in the worst of the worst. Our prison held rapists, murderers, and child molesters. Cerritus housed many of the same kind of people, but those were called patients and deemed criminally insane. It didn't make them any less dangerous.

"Eight days ago, the prison stood mostly firm when all the storms hit. It was not completely demolished like many other buildings in the area. Unfortunately, Cerritus wasn't as lucky; half of it was destroyed when I walked by.

"During the storms, the power went out everywhere, including the prison. Since then, the facility has been running on its backup generators. As of yesterday, most of the power was routed to keep the cell doors locked and the criminals in. In three days, the generators will stop.

"The warden has released the minor/misdemeanor criminals, grand theft auto, physical assaults, thieves, and so on, to keep the worst ones secured longer. But unfortunately, this only provided one additional day. So, when these doors open, those still here will be targeted.

"Be careful. If you don't own a gun, get one. Some of the worst criminals were held there, but you must be aware of two. These men are pure evil. Marcus Franklin DeMoss is a violent rapist and murderer. The District Attorney could only prove he raped and murdered six women, but he was suspected in twenty-four more. Don't let his baby face fool you. He may only be twenty-two, but he is a master manipulator and skilled killer. It is hard to believe there is someone worse than him, but there is. His name is Jonathan Paul Ellis. The media dubbed him Jon-Jon.

"The police found the remains of thirty-four people on his property. Male and female adults. When one victim's daughter begged him to tell her why he had taken her father's life, all he said was, 'because it was fun.' He killed and mutilated out of pure joy. If we were a state that believed in the death penalty, he would have gotten the needle, but since we don't, he will soon be a free man.

"If any of the numerous prisons throughout the state are all still standing, then God help us when the evil behind the walls gets to come out and play. If you cross paths with Jon-Jon or Marcus, do what's left of the world a favor and kill them because they will have no problem ending your life.

"I have this looping thing figured out and have pulled the power from everything but this machine. I will keep this repeating as long as it can. Trust no one until you know exactly who they are, and even then, I suggest you stay vigilant and never let your guard down. There has always been evil, but it has had good to combat it. The world is down on good and up on evil. The balance has shifted, and we all need to be prepared. God, help us all. My name is Kevin Marshall, and I pray for your survival. Just survive!" My eyes stayed fixated on the radio, waiting for him to say something else, but the loop started over.

Sam and I were silent, letting what we had heard sink into our brains. I lived on the opposite side of town and only thought a little about the prison or Cerritus. Suddenly it was real. No police, no government. We were on our own, with survival as our goal.

Heavy thumping passed across the top of our heads; I looked up, thinking about the numerous things that could make the sound echo through the basement.

"Deer," Sam answered before I could even ask the question.

"They love the fields out behind the house. It doesn't surprise me they are moving into the neighborhood. Should we worry about the coyotes, too?" I replied.

"Eventually, we will have to worry about all the animals roaming," he surmised.

Chapter 4

Fighting for survival scared the hell out of me. Now on top of the weather we had to deal with murderers and monsters that took pleasure in killing.

I grabbed a bottle of water off the shelf thoughtlessly and tried opening it. It only took a second to realize I wasn't able to open it.

"Please," I whispered as I extended the bottle out to Sam.

He opened it and gave it back to me. I placed it to my lips and chugged. I watched through the bottle as Sam turned and walked away.

I placed the now empty bottle back, wiped my mouth with my good hand, and headed to the men.

Sam was sitting in a chair next to Kyle's bed. His demeanor had shifted, and not in a good way. He always sat up tall with a firm expression, but now he slouched over with his elbows resting on his knees. His left hand was grazing his chin while his eyes were lost in thought. I studied his body language but couldn't decide if he was mad, sad, or plain terrified. He ran his hand across his chin once more, then up and through his hair, stopping at the back of his neck.

Kyle did the same when he was stressed, but I didn't get that vibe from Sam. He let out a huge sigh and stood straight up.

"Get back in bed with your husband. I will be back later," he huffed as he pulled on layer after layer of clothing.

"Where are you going?" I asked as I took the sweats off.

"Don't worry, I will be back," he replied before heading up the stairs.

I crawled back into bed and laid down beside Kyle. In the darkness I replayed the look on Sam's face. It took me a moment for me to figure out he was expressing sorrow. For the first time, he was giving me a look at the side of him he had omitted up to this point. The broadcast had shattered his hope and belief that help would come. His trust in himself was diminishing.

"Kyle, I hope you can hear me. I know what it feels like to be surrounded by darkness, but you're not alone in there," I softly spoke.

I chuckled a little to myself and continued, "Do you believe we are in this situation? After everything we have been through, this is how we end up. It's funny in an ironic sort of way.

"It wasn't all bad, our marriage I mean. We've had some really good times together, you and me. I can still remember the look on your face when the kids were born. Tina was our first, and when the doctor swooped her way after being born, I saw this worried look on your face. You stood by me and I'm sure you would've stayed, but I could see the concern in your eyes. She was in the corner with all those people surrounding her, and we couldn't even see her. You kept glancing around and finally I realized that you were scared for her. The look in your eyes told me somebody who loved her needed to be with her, not strangers. I released my grip and said, 'Go, Daddy, check on our daughter!' Despite all the bodies in the room, you managed to maneuver your way over to her and stood by her side."

I couldn't take the smile off of my face. It had been a long time since I thought about the day she was born. My memory was lacking some of the finer details, but the love we felt was imprinted on my heart. We were more than husband and wife; we were now a family.

"Thomas was a much quieter delivery. When the doctor showed you your baby boy, I could see how proud you were. This was your boy, your son, heir to your name, and nothing was going to change that. There were only a few of us in there, but the minute that nurse walked away from him you swooped right in and picked him up. I still remember spending the night watching you two as he slept on your chest. You even made sure he was close enough to you to hear your heartbeat. I wish the good outweighed the bad.

"What happened to turn you into who you became? Did I do it? Was I as bad as you always said I was? Did I turn you into the cold-hearted, controlling asshole you became? Could I have done things differently and changed what our lives turned into?"

The sorrow was bone deep, causing my body to be wracked with uncontrollable shaking. I could feel my heart beating faster, making my chest hurt. It felt as if it was going to explode out of me. Try as I may, I couldn't keep the sob from escaping my throat as I broke and big ugly tears rushed down my face.

"I wish the kids were still here, and I wish we were happy again," I whispered while wiping the tears.

I nestled my face into Kyle's neck and listened to him breathe. This was the first time in years he wasn't snoring, and that made me chuckle. I couldn't help but think back on all the occasions I'd yelled at him to stop snoring or to finally go and see the doctor. Lying there, I replayed everything that happened since the storm started. I wondered how many other people were going through the same thing. How many people were left trying to deal with the devastation that surrounded us all?

In the silence I heard stomps against the stairs. Sam must have been back. Given the fact that he refused to talk before he left, I doubted he would now. I didn't bother looking out of the covers.

"Sara, you wake?" Sam choked.

"Yes, I'm still awake." I yawned.

"Get dressed. We have to go."

"Where are we going? What about Kyle?"

"We won't be gone long; he will be fine. Trust me, just get dressed."

I did as he asked. As I stood beside him, I remained silent as he stared into his reflection shining through the highly polished coffins.

"It's time. We have to move them," he whispered.

Suddenly I was filled with rage. "What, no. Move them? Move them where?"

My blood was boiling. Nothing made sense, and now he wanted me to let him take my babies away.

"Listen, Sara. When Kyle wakes up, we don't want him opening these. There are some things in life that a father should never have to witness. They won't look like they did when I laid them in there. It will be a picture you will never get out of your head and one he will never forget. You don't want that, not for that to be the last image of your child," he warned with his hand resting upon Thomas' casket.

I tried to hold back the tears. I knew the kids were gone, but as long as they were close by, I felt an odd comfort. Now, out of nowhere, Sam wanted me to let him take them away from me.

Nothing was making sense, and I was in complete and utter denial. I stuttered, "Can't we just advise him not to open them?"

"Sara, think about this for one moment." He turned to face me, placing his hands on my shoulders before continuing. "Will he listen to you?"

The look on Sam's face was one of sincerity; he wasn't doing this to hurt me. I wanted with all my heart to say yes.

I wanted to be able to say we had that level of respect for one another, and he would listen. However, what came out was the truth. I bit my lip as the words flowed with disappointment. "Probably not."

Sam pulled me into him and gave me a slight squeeze. "Do you think you could help me take them out?"

"Yes, I can," I sputtered, wiping the tears from my face.

Sam squatted in front of Thomas' casket, and I patiently waited for his instructions on what he wanted me to do. With an elegant yet swift movement he had Thomas positioned on his shoulder and calmly said, "First get the door at the top of the stairs open, please."

I rushed over to the stairs and pulled the door free. I must have looked funny, because Sam chuckled as he walked by. I was in awe at his abundant strength. Glancing at him, you wouldn't have guessed it. I watched as he took the coffin to the back of the same vehicle he brought us here in. The snow had finally stopped, but I could see wet droplets cascading across my vision. It felt warmer than the last time I came outside. The mix of the wet-on top of the already fallen snow was making everything a sloppy mess.

"Are you sure now's the best time to do this?" I asked, concerned about our safety.

Sam secured the coffin and walked back over. He stopped in front of me and let out a sigh. "No, but the snow has finally stopped. It is a lot warmer than it was, and I have to find my daughter. It's been long enough."

Looking into his eyes, I could see the moisture pooling behind his lids. He ran his hand through his hair before continuing. "What if she's hurt, cold, or hungry? Not knowing is eating away at me. I can't calmly wait any longer. I don't have the strength to keep wishing and praying she's okay. I have to find her; I have to know. She hasn't been at any of the other places I've looked."

He ran his sleeve across his eyes and headed back down to

get the other coffin.

I waited at the top of the stairs for him to come out. Society had yet to return. It looked as if Sam's tracks were the only around other than what appeared to be paw prints. As I waited for Sam, I tried to follow the tracks with my eyes. When I saw they led to Ms. Johnston's house, I cringed. Another path circled my house, and I followed it with my eyes and could see it was looping the foundation of the house.

"It was a dog, looking for food. It trailed behind me to where the vehicle was hidden. I had some chips in the glovebox, so I gave it to him. I'm sure he will find his way back here, but I couldn't let him starve," Sam chimed in, noticing my concerned expression.

"And those?" I asked, pointing at the tracks leading next-door.

"Coyotes would be my guess, but I haven't found them yet. Perhaps the dog scared them off." He chuckled.

I thought about what he said, but only for a few moments. The sound of Sam shutting the rear hatch quickly brought my mind back to the task at hand.

Sam closed the door to the stairs and asked, "Are you ready? We need to get going."

I shook my head yes, walked around to the passenger side, and climbed in. Sam quickly found his seat, starting the ignition without saying a word. Immediately, I reached to turn on the radio.

Sam placed his hand over mine. "It is the same as before. I can't hear it again." The softness to his tone did nothing to hide his pain and sadness.

I understood his frustration and lowered my hand into my lap. I needed the hope that there was someone out there fighting to get the world back on track. Perhaps Sam had missed something.

"Maybe they have updated the emergency broadcast system," I pondered out loud.

"I listened to every FM station and every AM station all the way back to your house. Do you think I'm so incompetent I would have missed something so important?" he hissed.

"I didn't mean to..." I stuttered.

"Just forget about it."

Sam drove slowly through and around the mounds of snow. I knew buried under each and every pile was something horrible. A car, pieces of houses, bodies, or worse. The only tracks were the ones made by wandering animals and now our own.

I turned to look at Sam. I wanted to ask where we were going, but didn't want to upset him again. What kind of place did he have in mind for my babies?

My anxiety wasn't from mistrust because I trusted Sam enough. Strangely, all the loving feelings I had for him from high school were still warming my heart.

"Do you have some place in mind, or are we just driving till you decide to stop?" I asked, trying to be playful, but my tone made it come off as rude.

"I wouldn't be driving if I didn't have a place in mind. Without power, I can't get gas from the stations, and with most of the cars already syphoned, finding more gas is nearly impossible. I'm not wasting the gas, so please give me an ounce of credit. I haven't let you down yet, have I? I have a nice, quiet place for them. No one will disturb or bother them there. It's a peaceful place," he reassured as we continued to make our way down through an area that was not familiar to me. I couldn't tell where we were. Nothing was the same as before.

The clouds were thick, making visibility low. We didn't go faster than twenty miles per hour. I wanted to try and explain myself—tell him I wasn't questioning him, just worried about leaving the kids anywhere. I need him to see I was a mess; I wasn't thinking clearly, or perhaps I was, but didn't know how to express it without constantly coming off as ungrateful. I didn't mean to be confrontational; it was instinct to protect myself. I wanted to ask him to be patient with me, but I could tell Sam wasn't in the mood.

Before long we came to a place I actually recognized; it was the largest cemetery within the outer three towns. I knew they had many small outside mausoleums and one larger one as well. There was one I had forgotten about, an inside mausoleum, and it wasn't easy to find. Therefore, many people forgot about it.

Something felt off about it when we pulled up to the snow-covered glass doors. The outer perimeter of the entry looked to be solid oak, with masterfully carved fleur-de-lis in the inner corners to hold the mosaic glass in. The double doors had long, curved brass handles polished to a brilliant shine from constant use. It was a beautifully enchanting entrance to a place meant to be a haven of peace, yet it felt different. Perhaps it was my imagination. I could only conclude it was a consequence of the fear of leaving my babies behind.

I got out of the vehicle and walked over to the doors. A small section of the delicate glass had been broken, large enough for someone to put their hand through and unlock the deadbolt. I didn't think anything of it. I figured Sam had already been here to ensure we could place the kids inside. There were numerous footsteps in the snow, both animal and human, but even this didn't register with me.

I pushed on the door, opening it with ease. I turned to look at Sam, seeing he was out of the SUV.

The second set of doors I came to was just as magnificent as the first. This set was carved cherry wood and adorned with angels to escort your arrival. Small crosses made out of the same mosaic glass were close to the handles, with two more located closer to the top of the door. I bet when the sun hit the entry, the color that shone through made the room glow with heavenly warmth. On the right side of the door was a section of broken glass, like the first. This one was bigger, and someone had removed all the glass from the cross. I slowly placed my hand on the finely carved wood handle. The fine hairs on my arm stood up, and I felt extremely nauseous. My instincts were telling me to be on alert. Something was telling me not to open the door. I had to shake the fear I had of leaving my children.

I must persevere and do what is right for them and their father. If this is the best place for them to be during this devastating time, I will have to accept it.

Taking a deep breath, I opened the door. Once I walked through, my heart stopped. I could barely pull in any oxygen; the air was stale and filled with death, decay and a harsh chemical smell . The tears formed involuntarily. Who would do this?

Sam came in closely behind me, gasping at the sight before him. I took a few more steps and was overwhelmed with sorrow. I felt my remorse, and the pain of every person lay to rest there.

The once gloriously polished marble room was decimated. The beautiful sheets of white rock inlaid with flakes of gold and silver lay on the floor in a pile of rubble. Every cove that housed someone's loved one was broken. The coffins were thrown out with the bodies hurled around like pieces of discarded garbage. The vandals even went as far as dumping the ashes on the ground.

"Why would anyone do this, Sam?" I exclaimed through tears.

There had to be a hundred or more coffins and bodies strewn everywhere. The flowers were thrown from every pot. The deceased had been violently ripped from their final resting place.

I walked up to one of the plaques and ran my finger across the little kid's pictures that were taped onto the stone that read Grandma. *This is disgusting. The world is going to hell, and someone decided it was the time to vandalize and rob graves.*

"Sam, I can't leave them here! Look at what they did. My

children aren't safe here. Even in death, I will protect them," I whimpered.

He made it to me in two strides, wrapped his arms around me, and pressed my sobbing face into his chest.

"I didn't know, Sara. I'm so sorry," he muttered.

The grip around me was tight, and I could tell he wasn't oblivious to the vile destruction. I could feel the sorrow in this room. It was as if the spirits were weeping alongside of me.

"I can't be in here anymore. What could they possibly have been looking for?" I asked, drying my eyes.

"Numerous years ago, there was a big epidemic of people robbing graves. People would rob the graves for their personal possessions, gold, diamonds, and other things they could sell. The only thing I can think of is they did it because, with the world falling apart, they think gold and stones will be the only tradable things. I don't agree, but that is the only explanation I have. If I allow myself to think about it in any other way...No, I can't think about it any other way." He sighed.

"What now? Where can we take them that is safe?"

"I have another place, but I've never been there myself," he explained as we walked out together.

I turned around to face the disaster once more and quietly whispered, "I'm sorry this happened to you."

I took comfort in Sam's strong arms for as long as I could, then we walked quietly to the car. There wasn't anything I could say. The images of the grandchildren were burned into my eyes. I didn't take a breath until we cleared the entryway of the cemetery. Closing my eyes gave me no relief. My body wouldn't stop shaking—the fear was consuming me. *If this is what survivors are doing to the dead, what chance do we have?*

We drove up to a large industrial building. He parked the car, turned to me, and said, "Wait here, but if there's any sign of trouble, leave and don't look back."

He opened the door and headed out.

"Sam—wait, what are we doing here?" I tried to ask, but he

was around the building in a flash.

I felt like I was living in a constant state of confusion, with no one to answer my questions. Patience was always easy for me, but I had reached my limit. I waited as long as I could, but the anxiety and fear drove me to open the door. I started to get out.

"Don't get out. I got what we need!" Sam's voice echoed as he hurried around the corner carrying a box marked *hazardous*.

I got back into my seat, waiting to pounce on Sam the moment his foot stepped inside the vehicle.

"What is that?"

"Don't worry, it's something we need."

"It looks like something toxic. Why do we need something like that?"

"Just trust me."

"I think I have done well with trusting you and not asking too many questions, but now I want some answers," I huffed.

"Bear with me a bit longer and it will all make sense, I promise." He finished by touching my knee and gently squeezing it.

I let out a disapproving sigh and turned my attention outside, watching the lifeless scenery pass us by. I started to fall into myself, like I used to do with Kyle, not questioning and believing he was doing what was best for us both. It was irritating that he wasn't sharing everything with me. It was time to ask more questions, consequences be damned. I was tired of just going with it.

"Did your house survive the storms?"

He didn't answer immediately, and I thought he wasn't going to answer at all. I hadn't asked a difficult question.

"No, I brought what I could salvage to your place, everything except for the box in the back. My family photo albums, some loose things, extra pictures, and the other small things I could find are in there."

"Why not bring those inside, too?"

"Well, if Kyle wakes up and tells me to take a flying leap, I can leave without worrying about remembering to grab those things." His voice was sincere and solemn.

"I wouldn't let him do that," I urged bitterly.

"It's always better to be prepared."

I must have looked as dumbfounded as I felt. He didn't feel like I would stand by him in front of Kyle. He wanted to preach trust to me, but he didn't trust me. His words reverberated in my brain, but processing them was slow.

"I have never stood between you and Kyle. I didn't do it the first time, and I'm not about to do it now," he snapped.

"No, you ran away like a coward and never bothered to say anything to me. You didn't stand in anybody's way or by anybody or for anybody," I ranted.

"I gave you what you wanted." His voice was emotionless.

"You gave me what I wanted? You left me!" I snapped, feeling my face burn from the rising anger.

"You had Kyle. You didn't need me anymore," he retorted.

The second the words echoed throughout my ears, my heart broke, and I couldn't hold it in any longer.

"Didn't need you. Is that what you actually thought? You were my best friend. Do you know how many times I tried to call you? How many letters I wrote that came back to me? Do you have any idea how hurt I was? You were my closest friend, and you walked away from me. No, you ran from me, and here I spent more hours than I can count wondering why I let Kyle mentally beat me down for so many years. You were the first to think so little of me, to care so little, that you just...just..."

I couldn't finish the sentence; I was so enraged. I didn't want to relive this high school drama, yet here it was in my face like it was only yesterday. I had spent so many years hiding, burying all of those feelings and memories.

"Sara..." Sam moaned.

"Don't, I don't care anymore. It's in the past, and we all

84

know we can't change the past. All I care about is getting my kids somewhere safe. I'm so sick and tired of this mess, and I just want to have something finalized. Getting my kids to a safe place for them to rest is all I care about," I demanded.

I couldn't look at him. I'd let my guard down, and the flood-gates of emotions exploded. I swore to myself I was going to put my feelings for him behind a titanium wall. Why did they have to bust out now—why couldn't I keep them locked away?

Sam made a hard left, and the rear of the vehicle slid. I wanted to ask why we had to make such a dramatic change, but that would have opened the door to further conversation that I refused to have.

I could feel him looking over at me every few minutes, but I refused to meet his gaze, instead keeping my attention focused on the outside world. A world I didn't recognize. The path he was taking was reasonably clear of debris, which surprised me, but within a few feet, I could see awful things. A group of dogs was fighting over a human arm. Half houses dotted the side of the road, and businesses were nothing but rubble. A single car lay on its side resting against a pole, the driver still buckled in their seat.

The bleakness in front of me hurt my heart further. How many emotions can one person withstand before finally col-lapsing into a sobbing, blubbering mess?

We continued driving, the sun breaking through the clouds in the distance. It was a beautiful sign. I used to believe it was God's way of letting me know that even in these dark times, he was still there, and as long as the light shone through, we should have hope. But I wasn't feeling hope, love, or light anymore. Instead, it reminded me of more innocent days, and I was thankful for the memory. The light usually came and went as the clouds moved, but the beams remained fixed on something.

"Would you look at that?" Sam pronounced, sounding a bit stumped.

I wasn't going to fall for it. I kept my head turned and wiped under my eye, trying to clear the wetness before he could see it fall. I looked up, took a deep breath, calmed my mind, and regained some composure. *I won't let him see me cry over him. I won't give him the justification of knowing he still means that much to me.*

When I wiped my eyes, I lost sight of the rays, but it didn't surprise me. I knew they would be gone soon enough. Like everything else beautiful in my life, it would be taken away.

"Sara, just look at the windshield, please. You have to see this," Sam urged once more with a lighter, delightful tone to his voice.

Reluctantly, I turned to look out the windshield. We were in another cemetery. Toward the west, the rays of light I had lost were shining through. I leaned forward to get a better look at what it was glowing on, but with all the debris and broken trees, I couldn't tell.

"It can't be..." Sam whispered.

I wanted badly to ask what, but this could have been a trick to get me talking. That was a chance I couldn't take.

"In the box behind my seat is a set of old skeleton keys. Please get them out," Sam requested.

I leaned over and grabbed the small box located behind the driver's seat. It was no bigger than two shoe boxes stacked on top of one another and had a mishmash pile of stuff in it.

The first thing that caught my eye was an old cassette tape labeled 'to you from me.' I ran my fingers across the sloppy writing, recognizing it immediately. It was a tape of our favorite songs from the old days. Pushing it to the side, I kept looking. I came across photos of Samantha and her dad. She couldn't have been more than five or six years old. *Wow, she looks so much like him. They were happy.* I couldn't help but smile. Buried in the middle of the photos of Samantha was a single picture out of place. I saw it, but my mind didn't register it. I pulled it out and smiled. I flipped it over and read the back.

'Mom and Dad at her wedding. They said she looked radiant.'

"Your mom was so beautiful, and her laugh was so contagious. I remember her laughter the most." I giggled, looking at his parents and me in the photo. "It meant a lot to me having them there. Your mom was always so nice to me." I sighed before putting the picture back.

Sam never responded, but then again, why would he? I continued to flip through the last bits of Sam's life, or at least the memories he could hold in his hands.

"Did you find the keys?" he calmly asked.

I almost forgot what I was looking for. Seeing bits of Sam's life was a nice distraction.

"Not yet," I responded, with my head still in the box.

Buried at the bottom was a dingy old T-shirt wrapped as if it was protecting something precious. The item had once been bright yellow but was now just a nasty, dingy yellow. Quietly, I unrolled the shirt to find two old brass skeleton keys secured inside a plastic baggie. I placed the bag down beside me and opened the T-shirt. The design had long since faded and you could only see a bit of white and gray from whatever used to grace the front of it.

I stared at the T-shirt, trying to figure out its significance. It was beat-up and didn't seem to have been worn in years. *Why would he keep this?*

"We're here," Sam interrupted my thought process.

I gasped when I looked out the windshield. I could see the radiant streaks of light breaking through the heavy dark clouds and shining on an old building. "I had a guide. I didn't think I was going to find it," Sam stated.

He grabbed the bag with the keys and got out. I couldn't take my eyes off the brightly shining sunlight focused on this single building. I watched with warmth in my heart till the rays finally faded out. The architecture was unique. Nothing around it was even close.

"Where are we?" I asked as I stepped out of the vehicle.

"This is my family's mausoleum," Sam stuttered as he looked at the building and took a deep breath. "Watch your step," he urged as he proceeded forward.

You could see it had been a while since anyone had been here. The first sets of steps completely fell apart from the roots growing through and pushing them out. Two giant stone statues, one of a man in a suit with his hat pressed into his chest and his head lowered, looking towards his feet. The other was a petite woman holding a dainty handkerchief to her face as her face was also looking down. They graced either side of the sidewalk. The pathway past the first set of stairs had collapsed on one side.

The site looked out of place in the cemetery. It reminded me of the buildings you see in old Roman Empire drawings. When it was newly built, it must have been magnificent. The first things to draw my eye were the four perfectly uniform columns holding the front of the roof. They were made of granite, but time had caused them to crack and pieces to fall free of the forms. The overly large door was an odd greenish-blue color. Once I got closer, I could see the Alperstein family crest engraved on the door. Upon detailed inspection, I recognized the strange green color was due to oxidation on the copper-plated door. A large male lion head hid the keyhole from sight.

Sam walked up beside me and inserted the skeleton key. With a hard turn right, I heard the massive door unlock. Sam pressed his shoulder to the metal and pushed. It was stuck. I placed my back against the door and squatted down on my legs. I didn't wait for any command and pushed with all my force. Between the two of us, we managed to slowly open it with a low creak. It took every ounce of strength to help pry the door, but when I saw the inside, it was worth it.

There were eight long marble stones on either side of the building. They ran from ceiling to floor. The back wall had what was left of the window on it. There was a small piece of glass still wedged between the steel bars, but most of it was gone.

"My great-great-grandfather built this himself. He used to say even in death, we would be together. He and my great-great-grandmother are on the top. He had two sons, my great-grandfather and his brother. Great Granddad is over here on the top. Under Great Granddad are my grandpa and grandma. The bottom two were supposed to be for my mom and dad. Since they were never found, I had nothing to place here. I've only been here once. When I was a small child, my mom brought me here and showed me where they were to be placed. I never had a reason to return, and when my parents passed, I thought I would be placing them here. But like I said, they found nothing, so their tombs are empty. I want your kids in my parents' places." Every word echoed in the small building.

"Sam, are you sure?" I asked, worried that my previous outburst may have swayed his decision.

"Yes, I told you I would place them somewhere safe, and I can't think of anywhere safer than here," he finished before walking out the door.

Unlike the last place, I sensed peace here. I wasn't scared, worried, or upset over having to leave the kids. For the first time, I felt relief in knowing where they would be. I could feel his mother's warmth even though her body wasn't physically here. Kyle told me about the plane crash. Sam and I hadn't spoken in so long by that time, so it had been pointless to try and contact him. I thought I would be the last person he wanted to see at his parents' funeral. Then Kyle confirmed it was a stupid idea, so I never went. Never called, never made a single attempt to offer him condolences.

Sam came back in carrying Tina and placed her coffin down before walking over to the marble stone with a brass plaque that read 'mother.'

"I need your help. This is very heavy. I just need your help setting it down." He handed me one of the keys before finishing. "Once it unlocks it will slide forward. From there, we need to set it down and slide it over in front of this one." Sam pointed to the one that had 'father' on the plaque. I took my key and inserted it into the hole. "Go ahead and turn your key."

I did as instructed and waited for Sam to do the same. With a loud thud, it unlocked, and before I realized it, I was straining to get it placed down safely.

"You can let go. I have ahold of it," he whispered.

I let go and watched him slide the large stone over.

I turned around to face the mother-of-pearl pink coffin. I dropped to my knees and rested my head and arms on the top.

"You are my All-Star! I love you very much and I am so proud of who you have become. One day I will see you again. Until then, you keep your head held high. You are a spectacular person and the best big sis anyone could've asked for. I love you, my sweet baby girl," I cried.

I lifted up and moved out of the way. Sam came over and grabbed my baby once more and gently placed her in the opening of the wall. He pulled a pink rose from the inside of his coat and rested it on top of her coffin.

I smiled; the gesture was small but meant the world to me. Sam shot me a look of 'are you ready?' and I walked over with my key in hand. Sam helped me pull my side up and into place first, and I quickly locked the stone back where it belonged. Sam followed suit on his side, placed the key in his pocket, and walked out to the vehicle.

Closing my eyes, I listened. In the silence I could hear her laughing, and that small sound put me at ease.

A few minutes later we were removing the other stone. Once it was set out of place, I walked over to Thomas. His coffin sparkled a bit more against the marble stones, as if his personality were shining through. Placing my hand on his coffin, I softly spoke, "You've always made me laugh and gave so much love that everyone around you couldn't help but flock to you. I love you more than the moon and stars. Stay with your sister, and I will be there before you know it. Keep laughing and giving out all that love."

I dried my eyes and stood out of Sam's way. I watched him place Thomas in carefully. I waited to see what he would add with him, but he didn't have anything. He walked over to grab the stone cover. I wanted to ask why he had nothing for Thomas, but he must have read the question on my face because he answered before I even asked, "I put something in with him before I brought him in here," Sam replied.

We both worked to put the stone in place. I locked my side and couldn't let it go. I found myself asking, "What did you put in with him?" I had no idea what he was going to tell me or why he seemed to be keeping it a secret.

"I gave him his favorite SpongeBob blanket," Sam replied.

His words stunned me, and my heart dropped. The tears were filling my eyes faster than before. *How did he know? Where did he find it?*

"I...couldn't locate it after the storm," I pushed out behind the lump growing inside of my throat.

"You talked about it in your sleep quite often. You said one was in his baby trunk. I took it from the trunk before I brought up Tina. I knew you would want him to have it. You once said it was his safety," Sam said with his head down.

I stood in front of him, raised up on my toes, and gave him a soft kiss on the lips. Lowering myself, I said, "Thank you, Sam. You will never know how much that means to me."

I turned to leave but couldn't walk out yet. I was stopped by the feeling of my children giving me one last hug. I placed my hands on each leg exactly where my kids' backs would be. I lowered my head and whispered, "I love you both."

When I felt them leave, I made my way out the door. My heart was pounding hard it as if it would leap from my chest. I tried taking deep breaths, but that didn't seem to help. The overwhelming thought of never holding my kids again hit me harder than I realized it would.

Sam walked past me to the SUV, grabbed the box marked *hazardous* and headed back into the mausoleum. I couldn't go in, but I watched as he opened the case and pulled four-gallon size jugs out. He unscrewed the cap on each jug and placed them in the corners. *What is he doing?*

The label read "formic acid." I watched him come out with his face covered, then he pulled the brass door shut and locked it.

"What is the acid for?"

"The smell is just as toxic to the system as drinking the liquid. It should keep people and animals from entering," he stated as he walked by.

Looking at my surroundings, I could see paw prints in the snow, and multiple animals were lingering around—a rabbit, squirrel, raccoon, and I think a dog—not really in sight, but at night I bet this place was teeming with nocturnal creatures.

I crawled back into the passenger side and watched for Sam. The rain fell in big, fat drops, each fighting to get to the ground first. The sky was illuminated by the lightning dancing all around us. It was a gorgeous sight. I dove back into Sam's box, thumbing through more pictures. There were a lot of his wife and their daughter. She looked like a happy little girl. At the very bottom of the pile was an old, tattered Bible. I pulled it up to my nose and took a deep breath. I loved the smell of old books, I always have. Before returning it to the box, a small picture fell out; the image in my lap was no bigger than wallet-size. I flipped the paper around to see Sam and me.

I chuckled at the sight of our old selves. He was wearing a bright yellow shirt, and then it hit me. *How could I have forgotten?* I picked the dingy shirt back up and finally realized what I had missed. With the picture in hand, I returned to that day when we were seniors in high school.

We were goofing off outside of my house. Nothing was going on, and it wasn't any different than any other time he came over. The exact details were a bit fuzzy, but I remembered us ending the night with a passionate kiss. It was the first and last time we ever showed our affection in that way.

I placed my fingers to my lips as I recalled the heat and electricity that came from our short exchange. I couldn't believe I forgot all the passion and fire his kiss held. Back then I didn't appreciate the amount of fire his kiss had. Now I understood more than ever.

Quickly, I shoved the shirt and picture deep inside the box and practically threw it back behind his seat. *I don't need this crap.*

"Are you okay?" Sam asked as he joined me in the vehicle.

"Yeah, just ready to go home and check on Kyle. It's getting dark and it's been an exhausting day."

"Yes, it has."

He leaned over towards me and looked at my feet. I jumped, asking him in a panic, "What are you doing?"

I startled him with the aggressiveness in my voice, and he sputtered, "Looking for the box to put the keys back."

I let out a sigh. "I put it back behind your seat. Give me the keys, I'll put them back."

He handed me the two old brass keys, and I leaned over towards him to put them back in the box. I should have waited a few more seconds before leaning because we came face-to-face.

We gazed at one another, and every urge in my body told me to relive that moment we shared all those years ago. Everything tingled with delight at the thought of his lips pressing against mine passionately. I looked at his lips and unconsciously licked my own. I caught myself and moved my gaze back to his eyes. He knew what I was thinking.

He looked at my lips, slowly contemplating his next action. I wanted to lean in the last little bit and feel something other than sorrow. When his eyes returned to mine, they were smoldering intensely, and I couldn't ignore it; the promise his eyes held excited me and terrified me. I quickly threw the keys into the box and stretched all the way over to my door, fixating my attention on the window.

I exhaled quietly, trying to calm the excitement torment-
ing me. The entire drive home I kept repeating in my head, *'I
love Kyle, I love Kyle, I love my husband.'*

CHAPTER 5

There was so much of my life in high school I had forgotten. It was like my mind had cloaked all of those memories. The older I got, the less of my childhood I remembered. I was not sure if it was normal or if my mind was trapped from all the years of mental abuse by Kyle.

Even though I was facing the window, my eyes shifted over to Sam. *What is he thinking about? Am I losing my mind? Is the stress of everything causing me to believe I'm feeling more than I do, or more than I should?*

How many times had I passed Sam in the hallway at the kids' school and not noticed?

I found myself mindlessly spinning the band Kyle gave me. This band he bought me when I was pregnant with Tina, and my fingers swelled up horribly. He hated that I wasn't wearing a ring, and it was the last sweet gesture I remember him doing for me. I continued rubbing my thumb across the bottom of it and around the side.

"I see you still fidget when you're deep in thought," Sam said, breaking the long silence between us.

I glanced at him and smiled. Once again, he knew me to a T.

"I don't understand what just happened between us, but

I will leave when I get you home. I don't want you to be uncomfortable," Sam insisted as we turned down my darkened street.

I shifted my body to look at him. "What happened wasn't bad. I felt electricity that has long been gone from my marriage. It was like I was a schoolgirl again. If you leave, you will be breaking my heart for a second time, and I won't be able to handle that," I confessed.

I placed my hand on Sam's leg and whispered, "I can't lose you again. I need you more now than before."

I removed my hand and mentally prepared myself to see Kyle lying unconscious on the bed. Sam parked and hurried to open the doorway to the stairs.

I made my way down the stairs and walked over to the bed with Sam following close behind. I took my coats off and tossed them to the side before pulling the blanket down.

Jumping sharply, I screamed, "Kyle, where are you?"

"Dammit, woman, why do you have to yell so loud?" Kyle groaned as he came around the wall of shelves.

I ran and threw my arms up, encasing him against me. He was awake and was looking good. Sam stood off in the shadows, allowing us a quiet moment.

"Let go of me, Sara!" Kyle groaned.

After releasing my death grip, I whispered, "Sorry, I'm just so happy to see you're awake. I thought I lost you."

Kyle placed his hands along my shoulder and shoved, effectively moving me out of his path back to the bed.

I glanced over to the shelves and saw they were in complete disarray. My four erotic novels were torn to shreds on the floor. I let out a heavy sigh. This is why I always hid them from him before. He must have seen the one I placed back up on the shelf and dug until he made sure he found them all. He called them trash. I used them as an escape from life. They awoke a longing within me that he never understood.

"I heard more than one person come down those stairs

with you. So, who's with you and where the hell are my kids?" Kyle hissed in his hateful tone.

I walked over and sat at the end of the bed, ready to answer his questions.

"Don't sit down. I didn't invite you to sit there. Sit your ass on the floor and tell me what I want to know," he commanded.

I moved from the bed to the ground and softly said, "Sam Alperstein is with me."

"Sara, you need to speak louder. I can't hear you. Don't make me repeat myself," Kyle interjected.

Clearing my throat, once more I said, "Sam Alperstein is with me."

Kyle chuckled. "You mean that fat loser that used to follow you around school like some lost dog is in my house? This is too funny. Well, let's see ya. Step out of the shadows, fatty."

"Kyle, he saved my life and yours. He deserves your respect." I interjected.

I don't know why Kyle always called Sam fat; Sam was never fat. It was just another way for Kyle to try and make Sam feel bad about himself.

Sam took a few steps forward with a hard look of murder marring his face.

"Sara, how many times do I have to tell you to shut up? You are to speak when you're spoken to, and I wasn't speaking to you," Kyle roared while sending me a look of disgust that said, *'You should know better.'*

Shamefully, I cast my head down. This was the man I was worried about saving. This hateful excuse of a man. *How could he mean more to me than my own life? I am pathetic.*

Kyle grinned at his own little triumph over me. "Why are you here, Sam? Don't you have somewhere else to go? Don't you have someone else to bother? Because she is my wife, not yours. I won her over in high school. Even your sad attempt to talk to her at our wedding failed, so why are you here now?"

I shot Sam an inquisitive look. *He was at my wedding? I*

never saw him. If he was there, why didn't he talk to me or let me know he showed up?

"What's the matter, Sammy boy? Cat got your tongue?"

"Damn it, Kyle, leave him alone."

"Shut the hell up, Sara. This whole damned situation is your fault. So just shut the hell up!" Kyle screamed through gritted teeth.

Sam took a few more steps forward and bent down in front of me. He placed his hand on my chin and raised my head up. The concern he had for me was obvious, and I tried to not let him see the tears threatening to engulf me. Without taking his gaze from me, he quietly whispered, "I'm going to go and see if I can collect more gas, and then we will go find my daughter."

"Please don't go, it's late and dark," I cried through clinched teeth, hoping Kyle wouldn't see I was talking.

"I promise I will come back for you, but if I stay now, I will do something you will hate me for," Sam confessed, throwing a hateful glance at Kyle before walking away.

I couldn't watch him leave. I believed he would keep his promise, but for some reason I felt like I was never going to see him again. I heard the stair door shut, then the sound of Sam and his vehicle leaving me.

"What kind of hell have you made for me to come home to?" Kyle spat.

"I have tried my hardest to make this work. If you haven't noticed, the world has gone to hell, and I didn't do it," I demanded.

He sat up straighter on the bed, bellowing, "Well, you could have fooled me. Here I am damn near dying to get back to you, and I find you in my house with another man. Not to mention the fact that I have been over every square inch of this basement and can't find my kids. Where are my children, Sara?"

I stood up from the floor and paced. "First off, Sam saved both of our lives. Without him, we would be dead. He has not asked me for anything."

"Of course, he hasn't asked you for anything...*yet!*"

I stopped pacing, sat down on the bed next to Kyle, and looked him directly in the eyes. "The kids were at school when all the storms hit. When it was safe enough for me to leave the house, I went to the school, but they didn't make it. The tornadoes had ripped the school apart around them. When I found them, Tina was holding onto Thomas' hand. She had comforted him during the scariest moment of their lives. They were gone by the time I got to them, but Sam helped me bring them home. I took them to a mausoleum earlier today."

I wiped my eyes and reached over for Kyle with my good hand. He pulled away and stood up, a fire growing inside of him.

"You mean to tell me you were more concerned with your own safety than my children's? You hid down here like some scared rat while my babies were killed? You let my children die to save your own ass?" he yelled as he moved, throwing his hands in the air as he paced around the small section of floor by the bed.

"No, that's not it," I fretted.

"You bitch, you stupid lying bitch. I can't believe you valued your own life over *MY* children's." He continued to scream, working himself up into a frenzy, and the look on his face was scaring me.

His face was beet red, and the hate poured from every inch of his body.

I stood up to try to calm him and walked in front of him, stopping his pacing.

"I never would have thought you were capable of killing my kids," he hissed.

"Killed? I didn't kill the kids."

I couldn't have seen it coming—I watched in slow motion as he turned ever so slightly and brought his arm around with a full swing. Not completely understanding what he was about to do, I stood motionless as his meaty fist connected with the side of my face. I heard what sounded like a slap against my skin before momentarily losing sight in one eye. The pain radiated from above my temple then shot across my eye. I barely registered what he had done to me when a second blow hit the same side. I heard a loud pop, then felt my cheekbone and jaw shift unnaturally. *What the hell is happening?* Within a split second, I went from trying to help Kyle understand to being hunched over, holding the side of my face wiping blood from my nose and mouth. My knees were threatening to buckle. I was too shocked to cry. I could feel the blood flowing and the swelling start almost immediately. I didn't want to blink because it caused the skin to move and fresh pain to hit. I could feel my temples pulsing like a migraine on steroids. I was nauseous, confused, and very close to being taken to a dark place within me.

"I knew you were worthless—a useless cow—and you have proven me right. You're selfish, only ever thinking about yourself. You have to go get help. You have to find out what in the hell is going on in this world, and you have to do it now! Damn it, Sara, you owe me. You owe me because you killed my children," he snapped.

"Where is it that I am supposed to go?" I whispered through the pain.

"You're so stupid. Go to the God damned police station and find out what the hell is going on. Oh, and don't bother coming back until you have some real answers. Now get the hell out of my face."

I grabbed my supply bag and coats from where they laid. They still held the warmth of my previous venture out. I walked around to the front of the shelves, grabbing things I might need. After putting a few more bottles of water and a box of peanut butter crackers in my bag, I was zipping it up when Kyle yelled, "Get your fat ass going—you're wasting time. You don't need that shit, leave now!"

I walked back around. Looking at Kyle and softly crying, I somehow squeaked out, "I still love you."

"I don't love you. I haven't for years. If only I'd left you when I first thought about it, I could have saved my children."

"They were my kids too!" I gritted through clinched teeth.

"But I loved them more than you ever could; you've just proven it to me."

His rough exterior finally cracked, and I could hear the tears threatening his voice. He let out a loud scream as I made my way up the stairs. His pain echoed through me. I knew what he was feeling, and I left him crying in the basement. I secured the door, then bent over and grabbed a handful of wet snow, pressing it to my cheek. I couldn't hold it there for long before it made my bare hand throb. I dropped the snow, wiped my hand dry on my coat, then shoved it deep into my pocket.

The darkness was all-encompassing and threatened to swallow me whole. I had never witnessed a night I would have compared to death until that night. There was a flashlight somewhere in the bag, but it would have been pointless. My eyes would adjust. Fear reminded me I may not be alone out here, and I didn't need a light announcing where I was. The rain felt lighter falling onto my face than before, but it created a heavy mist. I couldn't help but think the point of sending me out was so I wouldn't come back. Perhaps I shouldn't come back.

I tried not to think about what transpired. Kyle had never raised a hand to me before, and his actions shocked me. The sting of the physical betrayal was nothing compared to the words he hissed at me. The thought of me doing harm to our kids was preposterous, but he blamed me as if I pulled the life from their bodies. *How could he think I didn't love my children as much as he did? I hope this wasn't how things were going to be between us now.* If it was, I had no reason to stay with him. I could walk away and never return, yet there I was on a wild goose chase because he told me to. The only thing holding me back was my own blinding love.

I had never felt so betrayed or worthless in my life. *How dare he think that I...I.*

Maybe he's right—it's my fault. I should have tried to get to the kids when I first heard the sirens. I'm a horrible mother who didn't save her own flesh and blood.

I dropped my head as the absurd thoughts clouded my mind. So, this is what he has made me. Someone who second-guesses every move she makes, doubts her intentions, and finally caves to the belief that he has to be correct. Why does he have to be right? The position kept the rain off of my face. My pace was slow as I tried not to replay the haunting truth regarding my choices in life. I needed to clear my mind and keep it blank, or I would fall to the ground, curl into a ball, and cry myself to death. Kyle had proved me wrong when I thought my heart couldn't break anymore. I would drown myself under more self-guilt than he had to feed me.

I walked through the devastation and destruction of the city. I lived outside of the city limits, but was still reasonably close. It took less than ten minutes to drive to town from my house, but I was on foot this time.

I walked by snow-piled mounds of junk. With the steady rain, there was still a good amount of snow covering the ground. The stench of death permeated the air. I'd never been great with remembering which way was north, south, east, or west, and it was more difficult with no GPS and unrecognizable terrain.

I walked in a daze for what seemed like hours before reaching the street on which the Public Safety building was. I wasn't far from the police station.

Staying lost in my own constant loop of previous events blinded me from the absolute horror around me. I walked past dead bodies half buried in the snow. Animals gorged themselves on human remains while the sound of coyotes filled the empty streets.

I stopped in front of the police station and stared at what was left of the building. Originally, it was four stories high, but now the top two were missing, and one side had been ripped off. There was no use trying the front door. It would be locked, plus I could see a massive hole in the side. Seeing no life inside. I walked through the side yard, finding a lower spot to climb in. Once I scaled the wall, I pulled my bag around and dug out the flashlight.

Even with the light, seeing inside the building was difficult. I continued to crawl and maneuver my way deeper into the structure. It was silent.

"Hello?" I asked cautiously.

I walked by broken chairs and desks lying on their sides. I crossed the room quickly, coming to a steel door. I pointed my flashlight toward the handle, but there wasn't one. Not just missing—it was utterly cut off. I pressed my hand to the door and pushed it open.

The area was pitch black, and the air smelled foul. I raised my flashlight to glance around. The desks in this room were still upright. At first glance, it looked like the department went home for the night and never returned.

I walked around the first desk, hit my foot on something, and fell forward. I tried to catch myself with my hands, but the floor was wet. I slid forward, and my face bounced off the cold, wet tile. The pain hit fast, and stars danced across my vision. It took me a few minutes to get my bearings and then a few seconds more to try to move.

I growled and cursed under my breath as I forced myself to my knees. I glanced left and then right. I had dropped my flashlight. After crawling forward a few steps, I saw the light shining under the closest desk. I stretched my good arm as far as possible to pull it out. I spun around and planted my butt on the floor, resting my back against the desk.

I can't believe I fell. Once I got the flashlight flipped back around, I shined it over where I lost my footing and saw a chair lying on its side. I'd caught my shoelace on the edge of the leg. Only I could trip so complicatedly.

I shined the light on my clothes and then my hand. Great, now I smell like coffee—rotten coffee, no less. The wetness that drenched my body was also on my face. I used the sleeve of my coat to wipe it off before dropping my arm and contemplating whether to move on or to go home. My face burned. I could only imagine what I looked like.

What the hell am I doing here? What did I honestly think I could accomplish by coming to this place? But I can't go home without answers, not just for him. I need them for myself.

I picked myself up off the floor, leaning against the desk to get my footing. I grabbed the light and stood it up on its end to get better coverage. It took a few minutes for my eyes to adjust to the new lighting.

The desk in the far-right corner seemed to have someone sitting at it. I knew my mind could play tricks on me, but I was positive it was a person at the desk with their head lying on it. Cautiously, I walked closer. I left the flashlight where it was. If this person was dead, I didn't need a brightly lit image of it seared in my brain.

"Are you okay?" I whispered as I got closer.

I placed my hand on what appeared to be their shoulder. I pulled the chair back and saw nothing. It was just an officer's winter coat and hat. I was relieved and upset at the same time. I didn't want the person to be dead—I just wanted it to be a person.

I walked back to the light and moved it down two more desks. Then I scanned the area from the center of the large room for any sign of life.

"Mmmm..." a faint voice moaned.

I froze. *What was that? Who was that?*

I quickly grabbed the light and began surveying the room. A chair sat in the far-left corner, back towards the door I came through. When I held the beam at it, it, too, looked like a coat

THE COST OF LIVING

and hat had been strategically placed on the chair. I wasn't sure whether to check it out or continue onward. With my light still securely on it, I watched the hat shift. I must have imagined it. I blinked repeatedly and stared. Again, the hat made a slight movement.

I started to shake. *Is there someone under the hat?*

I walked over to it, each step carefully placed to not fall again. Once I cleared the last desk, I could see the chair. I wasn't crazy; there was someone handcuffed to it.

I stopped outside of reaching distance and asked, "Are you okay?"

The hat moved once more, but this time it lifted to reveal a face. He was young, maybe twenty-eight. All the color had drained from his features, leaving him pale with dark bruises distorting his features. There was dried blood below his nose, trailing down the side of his lip.

"Run," he struggled to say.

Within a few seconds, my predisposed process to evaluate and understand the threat failed miserably. I gave it no thought before I bent down toward him. I had to help him.

"How do I get you out? Where is the key for the cuffs?" I inquired as I examined the area around him.

His shoes had been removed and each of his ankles was secured to the chair with handcuffs. The pool of blood surrounding him was tacky and dark. His arms were pulled back so tightly his shoulder blades were almost touching. The overextension of his chest had to make it difficult to get a full breath. I couldn't tell how his hands were attached to the chair, but they had to be for him to stay in the unbearable position.

His breaths were shallow but steady. The rattling in his chest was slight until he forced more air in to speak. "Run."

"Afraid not. If running was an option, I wouldn't be here now. I'm going to get you out of here."

I grabbed my bag, throwing it up on the desk. I dug out a bottle of water, held it in my arm, and twisted with my good hand. Luckily, it cracked open with my first try. I tipped his head up and slowly poured the water into his lips. I was going faster than he could drink, and it began trickling down his chin.

"I'm sorry," I stated, quickly stopping.

The young man allowed his head to fall forward but swiftly recovered it and lifted it back into place.

"Leave me, run. He could still be here," he said once more.

"You might as well give up on that notion, because I'm not going to leave you like this. There is no one here. This place is empty. I saw no one on the street coming in either. You and I are the only ones around here for miles."

I placed the bottle down and walked around to the first desk, opening the middle drawer. I began throwing the papers off to the side. Once I cleaned the first one out, I proceeded to the one on the left. There was a tray resting in the drawer with an array of keys in it. I plunged my hand in, closed my fingers around them all, and pulled them out.

I moved closer to the light and began sorting through the keys. I had no idea what I was searching for. I understood enough to know I wasn't looking for a normal key. The few keys left in my palm were unusual. One had a fat, round head to it with funny shaped prongs, reminding me of the end of a cable coax. There were a few smaller ones like my old diary key that I had as a young girl. Then a few more that I wasn't sure were keys.

"Are any of these the key?" I asked the young man while shoving the keys close to his nose.

"No," he breathed.

"Great," I huffed, then chucked the keys onto the desk then proceeded to walk around to the next station.

"Wait!" he exclaimed.

"If you're just going to tell me to run again, don't waste your energy."

"No, please come closer," he urged.

I walked over to him and stood in front of him.

His voice was still weak, but it had a bit more life to it. "The key is small, silver, and has a circle at one end with a small piece of metal just at the top. There are no markings on it, but at the end of the shaft is a small nodule that goes into the cuffs to unlock it. I doubt you will find it; he took any he could find before leaving me here to die. However, there is another style key that doesn't look like a key at all. It looks like a tool. It is black with diamonds cut into the handle. The tip looks like it could be removed like a multi-purpose screwdriver. It has a holder on it like a pen. If you unzip my coat, I don't think he took mine from my upper left pocket."

I reached forward.

"Wait, please do not be alarmed at what you might see."

I nodded my head in compliance and proceeded to unzip his coat.

His police uniform shirt was unbuttoned, and the t-shirt underneath was had long slices in it and was stained with blood.

I did as promised and didn't let his wounds distract me. I pulled his button-down shirt together and his body tensed in pain. I grabbed all of the pens out of his pockets and quickly stepped back. I placed my hand over the light and tried to steady myself as I sorted between the items. It took a moment to find the one he was talking about. He was right; it didn't resemble a key but a tool.

I bent down and unshackled his ankles first. The cuff was so tight that it had cut deep into his skin. Once it was unlocked, I slowly tried to open the first one as he screamed in agony. I held my breath as I moved over and did the same for his other ankle. The sound of his screams echoed through my head long after he stopped.

I turned my attention to his arms. Both of his shoulders had to have been pulled out of their sockets. You would expect the cuffs to be on his wrists, but instead they were around his upper arms just above his elbows. Like his ankle, the cuffs were tight on his arms. I wasn't sure if they were dislocated or if the tendons had been ripped apart by the force.

The hole that I needed to unlock the cuff was tucked into the backside of the chair, and I had to turn the cuff while it was attached to him. His screams were fading in strength, and I was afraid he was giving up. I unlocked it from the chair first then his arm. When the cuff dropped, it made a loud thud that echoed in the overly quiet room. The second arm wasn't as difficult, and I removed the cuff much quicker that time. It, too, made a loud sound once it hit the floor. I couldn't help but think the cuffs might come in handy, so I grabbed them and stuffed both them and the key into my bag. I turned back to help the young officer off the chair.

He had no control over his extremities, and when he slid off the chair, it felt more like he dropped from it. I positioned him on the floor with his back touching the cold surface. I gently moved my hand from his head, resting it on the tile. I needed to prop his head up. He was bleeding from his mouth and his nose was completely swollen. I doubted he could breathe. I got up, remembering the coat that scared me. It barely took a few seconds to retrieve it and place it under his head.

He was cold. The room was blocked from the rain and the snow, but it had no heat and there was a chill to the air. I needed to find a way to get some warmth into this place. I stood back up and walked around the open room looking for a metal trash can. I needed a way to start a fire, keep it contained, and heat him up. I checked every desk, but they were all plastic.

After exhausting all the possible spots in the room, I went out the large steel door and back into the crumbling part of the building. I started grabbing whatever I could find and digging in the debris for something that would work. I looked through most of the room and was ready to give up, yet I wanted to check one more spot to be sure. I reached down to grab what I thought was another trash can. When I pulled it up, I realized it was a small balcony grill. There was no lid, and it was dented, but it would accomplish what I needed it to.

I took my find and anxiously worked my way back. I pushed the desks clear and placed the small grill down.

"Shoot..." I mumbled to myself.

I needed something that would burn for a while. All of the chairs were metal, but I remembered seeing a wooden hat rack by the back of the room. I hurried to get it. I lifted it up over my head and slammed it into the ground as hard as I could. The shock radiated through my hands as it splintered everywhere. I gathered the pieces I could find, then scooped the papers off the desk closest to me and went to the grill.

I dropped the wood in first then the flat paper. I took a few sheets and crumpled them up and placed them in. I went back over and dug in my bag for my candle lighter. I clicked it a few times and it lit up brightly, setting the paper ablaze. I watched the fire for a few minutes to make sure it was going to keep burning. Once I thought enough time had passed, I grabbed my bag, used my foot to scoot the grill as close as I safely could, then went back to sit next to the young officer. I leaned against the wall by his head. I could feel a gentle warmth touching me, taking the chill out of the air, but it wasn't large enough to do any real good. I didn't understand how cold I was until I felt my body relax ever so slightly because of the heat.

I was at a loss. I didn't know what else to do. Pulling my knees into my chest, I rested my chin between them. *Ouch,* I was not sure which hurt more. I must have hit my knee when I fell. The pressure of my head against my knee sent a shock pulsing down my calf.

He was right. I couldn't stay, but I couldn't leave him there to die. Could I?

Scooting a bit closer, I whispered, "I don't know what to do. I'm not...uhm...knowledgeable, and I haven't met many living people these days. I don't want you to die, but I don't know how to save you either."

He looked over at me with a serene kindness.

"You have done more than I thought anyone was going to

do. Don't be upset. You can't save me. It's my time to die. I accept my fate. I'm proud of what I've accomplished in my life."

He wasn't scared or angry. He seemed to be at peace lying on the police station floor.

"How can you accept death so openly?" I questioned through the building tears.

"My family was taken from me at the beginning of all this destruction. In a single moment, I knew there was something more I needed to do. The moment consisted of me cradling my newborn daughter in my arm while holding the hand of the woman I loved more than anything, helplessly watching as they took in and let out their last breath. I was left for a reason, so I kissed them a final time and buried them together on my property. I put my uniform on and came here to see what my orders were. Needless to say, I was the only one here. I came in every day just like I would have if the storms had never hit. I came in and listened to the deadening static on the satellite radio waiting for it to break with someone in charge giving orders. Every day I sat at my desk just waiting, praying, and hoping for some sign of life.

"Then yesterday someone cut through the steel door, and I thought aid had finally arrived. Once the lock was gone, this figure emerged through the door with such grace and confidence. When I looked at the way they carried themselves, tall, straight shoulders, head held high, it led me to believe I was looking at someone high in the government or the military. You could feel the confidence radiating off of him. I approached him with excitement, extending my hand out to shake his, and he hit me across the side of my head."

I could empathize with his tragic start to all of the chaos. I also grasped the concept of needing something to hope for, a tad bit of normalcy during the unknown.

"I regained consciousness and tried to ask him what he wanted, but every time I opened my mouth to speak, he hit me. He broke bones in some sick order, starting with my feet, then the ankles, and every bone up both legs. Once he finished breaking them, he started to cut me with a razor. He was so mastered in his technique. Every slash was superficial, minimal blood with maximum pain. I was floating between consciousness and unconsciousness.

"He took my keys, and when I finally awoke, he was gone, but I was still here in the chair. He left me here to die. I have fought to hold on as long as I could. I knew someone would come to help me, but I admit I didn't think it would be a civilian."

He chose every word with deliberation, needing to say what had to be said before he couldn't talk anymore.

"Did he tell you what he wanted?" I was confused over what would possess someone to do this to another human being.

"No, he never asked me for anything and just smiled every time I screamed. A few times I caught him closing his eyes like my wife used to when she would listen to classical music. I think he enjoyed himself," he softly answered.

"Did you know him?"

"He carved his name into my chest, but I couldn't tell what it said from looking down. Can you see what it says, please? I want to know who he was."

"What's your name?" I was trying to distract from the request. I didn't want to know the name of the person responsible. It was easier to pretend this act wasn't committed by another human if I didn't acknowledge it. Naïve, yes, very, but I didn't want to think about what type of person was on the streets with me.

"I'm Derek Merrow, born and raised here. Now, could you please look? I think I deserve to know who is responsible for this," he begged.

I took in a deep breath and dug into my bag for a knife and the wipes. I leaned up on my knees, fought through the pain, and looked down into the baby face of young officer Derek Merrow.

I reached over him to finish unzipping his coat. Opening the pocketknife, I grabbed the collar of his under shirt and sliced in one quick motion. I set the blade down and ripped the rest of his shirt open.

I grabbed a baby wipe, reassuring him, "This is going to be cold and may sting a lot, but I promise to be gentle."

He nodded in compliance. I placed the baby wipe to his chest gently, but he still stiffened up in pain.

"How do you know he carved his name in you?"

He took in a quick breath and spit out, "Because he said every great artist must sign their work."

I couldn't imagine what he endured. Carefully, I removed the wipe and looked at his chest. Without thought, I reacted to the name with a loud gasp. "It can't be…"

I could feel his eyes staring at me widely in anticipation of what was carved into his flesh. "What does it say?"

"Uhm, it reads Jon-Jon," I answered cautiously.

He closed his eyes. "I don't know him. I remember hearing about the trial in the newspaper and on TV when I was a beat cop. I don't understand why he came after me. Maybe I gave him a ticket once when I was still new. I wanted to prove myself by cracking down on the speeders. Looking back now, I can laugh about it. I was determined to make a place for myself at this precinct. What did all the hard work get me?"

"I don't think it had anything to do with you personally, Derek. You were just in the wrong place at the most opportune time. He kills and tortures for pleasure, nothing more," I interjected.

The fire produced a soft glow, allowing me to see around the room with ease. I got up and pulled my flashlight from the desk then returned to my previous spot next to Derek.

"What's your name?" he moaned.

"Sara," I said plainly.

I placed the flashlight beside me and illuminated the area closest to us. I could see my bandaged hand. It was nasty, covered in dirt, coffee, and blood.

"You can't stay here long," Derek softly stated.

"I can stay as long as I like," I objected.

"No, the carbon monoxide being produced by that fire will consume this room without proper ventilation. You will die," he warned.

I stood up and grabbed the metal chair with both hands. Pushing through the pain, I rammed it into the window.

He chuckled as he said, "Bulletproof glass, Sara. You can't break it, but good idea."

I looked at the window. I hadn't even cracked it. Defeated, I dropped the chair and went back to my seat.

I sat there and sighed. The pain in my hand wasn't as horrible as I thought it was going to be. I wished I remembered to grab the first aid kit and lifted my hand over the light to get a better look at my bandages. They were stained, tattered, and in dire need of replacing. I placed my hand in my lap, even more defeated and confused.

"There is a first aid kit in the bottom drawer of the desk you took the keys from," Derek coughed.

I wasted no time in getting to the drawer and grabbing the kit. Quickly, I sat back down and began removing the disgusting wrap lacing my hand.

"What happened to your hand?" Derek inquired.

"Frostbite."

"Just your hand. Isn't that odd?"

"I was saved before any more damage could take place."

"What about your face?"

"I did this when I fell on your floor earlier."

"I may be dying, but I'm not stupid, nor am I blind. The person who saved you, are they responsible for the damage to your face?"

"No, Sam is a good man. The man who left his mark on my face is the man I promised my life to. It was my fault. I shouldn't have pushed him during a difficult time. He loves me; this was just an accident. This was a one-time lapse in his judgment," I explained while pulling the rest of the bandage free.

There were still a few raw and sensitive places on my hand. I looked through the first aid kit and pulled out the gauze pads and band aids.

"Rationalize it all you want, but if he hit you once, he will do it again."

I didn't respond. He wasn't telling me anything I hadn't already thought about, but none of that mattered. I loved Kyle and had to take the bad with the good. I didn't fear Kyle, though I was sure I should.

Silently, I continued to tend to my hand. I was able to keep it covered while still having full movement.

I found my mind focusing more on Jon-Jon than on anything else.

"What did Jon-Jon need your keys for?"

"I don't know. Maybe he thought the key to the armory was on it."

"Was that key there?"

"Yeah, but the first thing I looked for was bullets for my gun. The supply closet was empty. Even if he gets into it, he will be sadly disappointed." He laughed.

"What do I do now?" I solemnly asked.

"You leave me here with the fire going. I will fall asleep and just not wake up. I'm already dead. My soul just hasn't left this body yet."

"I can't leave you here to die alone," I whispered.

"My friend, I'm not alone. My wife is watching over me. She is here with us, waiting for me so we can go together," he softly spoke.

"Is anyone coming to help us?" I quickly asked, though I was sure I knew the answer.

"There is no one who will be coming to help. Sara, you have seen the devastation of just our town. It's like this in towns everywhere. Now is not the time to rely on others to save you. Now is the time to survive. Evil is lurking through the streets and countryside. Find it, destroy it, and then rebuild. You are meant to do more in this life. You have a destiny."

"Derek, I'm nobody. I'm just trying to hold on to the hope that someone can...save me!" I cried.

"You have it all wrong. You're not the one in need of being saved. You *are* the savior. Once you embrace it, you will understand."

He had me all wrong. I wasn't the strong hero type. I was the follower who never disobeyed the master. After putting everything back into my bag, I closed it up.

"Sara, before you go, and yes, it is time for you to go. Get into my back right pocket and take out my wallet, please."

I leaned over him and did as he asked. With his blood-soaked wallet in my hand, I waited for his next instructions.

"Take my driver's license with you. Once you have accepted your role in this apocalypse, go to my house. There is a shed in the backyard. It doesn't look like much, but know you're in the right place. Go inside and look at the dirt floor. You will see a small metal piece with a hole in it. Use the handcuff key tool to unlock the latch. Follow the ladder down, and you will find everything you need to take out the evil people lurking in this world like Jon-Jon. Don't argue, just take it even if you never go there. Now, leave before you start getting tired too."

I didn't want him to fight me on what he felt was right, so I took his license with no expectations of going there. I threw my bag on my shoulder, pulled my hood up, and slid his license into my back jean pocket.

"I'm sorry," I stated before walking around Derek and heading back to the steel door. I stopped at the exit, second-guessing my actions on leaving him.

"You're blessed by God, Sara!" Derek exclaimed.

Yeah, right, I thought. Pulling the door behind me, I headed out into the terrifying world. Clearly, the carbon monoxide poisoning or blood loss had affected his thinking.

I cautiously followed my existing trail out of the building and back onto the street. Then I again placed my hands in my pockets, tilted my head, and began the progression home.

Flooding my mind were images of a madman standing over officer Derek, laughing as he slowly carved his name into his victim's chest, laughing at the anguished screams from the young man.

Walking down a side street, I noticed a slight glow illuminating a window of what was left of a small house. I cautiously walked up to it and heard whispered voices inside.

"Hello," I stated as I stood close to the window. You could hear them trying to quiet each other.

"I won't hurt you; I'm just trying to figure out what's happening. My name is Sara. Can you help me?" I ventured.

"We can't help you. Go away," a female voice said.

"Do you know if the government has anything set up anywhere?" I pressed.

The window curtain moved, and a beautiful olive-skinned woman peered at me. "Please leave us alone," she urged.

"I will. I'm just trying to figure out what's going on," I pleaded.

She sighed, "We all are. I was working at the hospital when the first set of storms came through. We were working with the National Guard to get the patients moved when the ground began to shake and what was left of the hospital collapsed in. The Guard told us to wait and that they would return with more people to help, and then they left with the patients we had gotten out. That was days ago. I go back every morning to the sight of the hospital, but no one ever comes. The group I have here from the hospital will continue to wait until help arrives. They will be back for us all. Give me your address, and when they come for us, I will have them collect you too," she confessed.

"No, that's okay. I'll figure something out on my own, but

thank you," I cautiously replied while backing away from the window.

I continued on my way. I didn't want to be collected. I wanted to be rescued. So I picked up my pace, walking faster and trying not to look back over my shoulder to see if someone was following me. I noticed a few more lights in the windows and figured I should try at least one more.

I walked up to a small brick building with a single door and window facing the street. I walked up and knocked lightly. The lock clicked, and the door cracked enough to have a double-barrel shotgun pointing at my face.

I immediately threw my hands up. "Get the hell out of here," the calm voice ordered.

"I don't want any trouble. I'm just looking for answers," I quickly interjected.

"I ain't got no answers for ya, so keep walking," he stated while pushing the gun farther out.

Hands still up, I walked backward, "Sorry-sorry to have bothered you. I'll be going now," I uttered.

I didn't turn from him until he pulled his gun in and shut the door. What the hell is wrong with people. I pulled my bag straps up and continued on.

I got to the outer part of town and cautiously thought, I have no answers for Kyle or myself. He specifically stated not to come back without solutions and wouldn't take what I'd learned as a good enough response. I needed to go by the radio station that Kevin was broadcasting from. Maybe some other people heard the same message I did and went there.

I couldn't help but smile at the thought of others at the station waiting for answers or aid. People who were perhaps more humane than the ones I'd already met.

For a brief moment, I pulled my hood off to figure out exactly where I was. I'd been by the station before. I'd never actually gone in, but I knew where it was. I needed to go southwest. I turned, pulling my hood back up, and pushed on.

The rain was still trickling down, and with the moon covered by clouds, it was pitch black. I could barely see a few steps in front of my face. I walked, looking down to ensure I wasn't going to trip over anything. Hours must have passed since I started my journey. I couldn't shake the oddest feeling that with every step I felt I was closer to an answer. Yet, I could have sworn I was being watched. Moving faster, I increased the size of my actions in case my delusion was warranted. I turned the final corner towards the station and lifted my head to see if the building was visible. For the first time since this all started, I felt relief. An overabundance of warmth flooded my senses. What I saw gave me tremendous hope.

The windows were glowing through the frosted panes. There was someone in the building. Finally, I was going to get answers. The excitement built up inside me, and I was ready to explode. I took off at a dead run for the structure. I couldn't stop smiling. Finally, something was going my way.

The building was small, and it didn't look much like more than a single car garage. I ran up to the door closest to the street. After taking a calming breath, I turned the knob. It didn't budge. I tried again. Still, it wouldn't move. I pulled first, then pushed without hope. I wouldn't let this bother me. I made my way around the building looking for another way in and found a rear entrance. This time I didn't think; I grabbed and pulled. Success—the door flew open with such ease I almost fell from the force I put into it.

It took me a moment to re-gain my balance, but once I did, I headed into the station. The silence was ominous. If there were people here, they weren't making any noise. The brightness inside surprised me. It was almost too illuminated for such a small building.

There was a hallway that split in front of me. I could go left, right, or straight. There was a room to the left and the DJ's booth to the right. If I went straight, it would take me out the first door I tried on the front of the building. The walls of the small hallway were lined with candles. They were about six inches apart all the way down both sides and straight in front of me. This aided in keeping the room warm, but seemed to take something from the air. I couldn't help but wonder where everyone was. The hope I had recently experienced was quickly fading into fear. I could see the DJ's booth. There were numerous buttons glowing and the small sign read, 'on air.'

As far as I could tell, it was still broadcasting the same as it was days earlier. *Someone had to have been here to light the candles. There is no way they have been burning for days. Hours, yes, but not days.*

Every ounce of my body told me to leave, run out of the building, just go. Yet I couldn't go home without getting Kyle his answers, even if that meant my life.

I dropped my shoulders, held my head up higher than I ever had before, and went down the hall to the door on the left.

I placed my hand on the knob and pressed my ear to the door. Still, I heard nothing. I turned the handle and pushed. When I peered in, the first thing I saw was candles, too many, it was overkill. No one would need this much. Not for light, and I doubt this amount was needed even for warmth given how small the room is. Walking into the office, I headed straight for the desk covered with candles. The candles were pillars, but not encased in glass. Every inch was enveloped in wax from it flowing down as they burned. Most candles claimed they were dripless, but this mess proved otherwise.

As I stared into the dancing flames, I couldn't think of anything but the hell Kyle had in store for me. I understood he was upset, but his actions were deplorable. The candle heat helped veer my mind to Sam and his warm embrace. Could I open up to Sam about what I wanted? The type of relationship that would have my stomach fluttering and my body burning to be touched. I tried for years to get Kyle to see I needed more from him, a deeper understanding of each other. I wanted the type of marriage that blended two people in all the right ways, combining souls.

I shook my head violently to disengage the fantasy. But instead, I thought about the structure and the open flames. How had the building stayed intact? Why wasn't it engulfed in an inferno? The candles were not strategically placed to maximize light; they were just put as closely together as possible. I wouldn't let the station burn. Not only would it spread throughout the town, but the broadcast warning about the murderous inmates would be lost.

There wasn't much I could control in this ever-darkening world, but this was something I could prevent. I bent down and blew out the ones on the floor first. Then I worked on the desk. I hadn't surveyed the entire room, so the number of candles remaining was a mystery.

I finished the mass of candles in front of me and coughed lightly from the smoke rising. I cleared my throat before dropping my hand on my jacket to pat down the slow flame. I had gotten a little too close and almost caught myself on fire.

I glanced to the left. There was a small cabinet with about fifteen candles on it. I walked over and blew them out one by one, but out of the corner of my eye, I saw something. I didn't turn my head, nor did I stop what I was doing. Instead, I tried to look out of the corner of my eye for a split second to see what was messing with my vision.

My heart sped up in my chest. Blood flow became faster, causing me to not only hear it echoing within my ears but also feel it pulse within the veins along my temples. I wasn't alone—someone else was here. They were sitting against the back wall, watching me. Not speaking, not moving, and until this moment, not noticeable.

The door was close—*Could I make it to the exit before they got to me?* I darted toward the frame in my own clumsy way, but once I grabbed the doorknob, I glanced back at the figure. They hadn't moved.

I released the knob and turned to get a better look.

They were sitting with their back to the wall and legs extended straight out. I couldn't tell if it was a man or a woman. A black trench coat was draped across them, and an oversized cowboy hat rested on top of their head. I took a few steps closer. The style of the black work boots suggested a man, but a few female friends of mine had to wear boots like that to work.

There weren't any candles along this wall or anywhere near the person, and the ones that were still lit created a haunting glow around us.

"Hello," I stuttered before extending my foot to kick their shoe.

I pulled my foot back and waited. Nothing. *I don't think they are alive...*

I reached down and removed the large hat. It was wet with blood. I tossed it to the side. A man with cocoa skin sat before me. I squatted down and used two fingers on his forehead to push his head back to the wall so I could see what he looked like. His flesh was still warm to the touch. When his head rested against the wall, I saw the face of a man who had been tortured.

He had no eyes. All that remained were deep crimson holes. His eyelids had been removed, leaving behind gaping emptiness. As if that wasn't disgusting enough, his right ear had been removed. His chin was coated in a dark red substance, more than likely blood, and it ran down along his neck and soaked his clothes. Without looking to verify, I ventured a guess that his tongue had been removed as well. I moved from him and tried to hold back the dry heaves. The sight was atrocious, but I found myself wanting to know who this man was.

I reached around behind him and felt for a wallet. On the carpet behind his back but hidden from plain sight was an iPod. When I activated the touch screen, I saw that it was recording. I stopped the progression, saved it, and went back into it.

I debated for a moment, thinking about what I might hear and how I wouldn't be able to erase it from my memory. Call it curiosity, intrigue, or stupidity, but I had to listen to it. The battery life on the device was low, and I knew it wouldn't be much longer before the recording would be lost.

I moved back to the side that had been overly lit with hot, fiery candles. I sat down, making sure I was facing the door, then placed the device on the floor in front of me. With my legs crossed and butterflies wreaking havoc on my insides, I pressed play.

The voice started, and immediately I knew who the dead man was.

He began, "I left in search of food and a permanent shelter, but after days of wandering I have realized there are very few buildings still standing. I took food from a few of the houses nearby and decided this station was the safest place to be. It is small, but if anyone hears the broadcast that I have looping, there is a chance other survivors may come here, and I want them to know they're not alone in this. I've started this voice diary because when I talk into it, I feel like someone is listening to me.

"I have left the front door locked, but I'm keeping the back unlocked for any survivors who hear my voice and come seeking shelter. I'm not worried about the prison. Once those bastards see how bad this town is, they won't stick around. They need people to feed their psychotic impulses, and few people are left in town."

There was a brief pause before his voice started again. "I wanted to add to this daily, but the battery is getting low. There's still no one here but me. I'm beginning to think there are no survivors but the prisoners and the mentally ill patients that got outside the walls of Cerritus. I have not heard another voice in what seems like years. I miss the laughter of my children and even my wife's nagging. What was that? Thank God in Heaven, someone is at the front door. I'm going to wait till they come around to the back. Finally, signs of another living person. I can't tell you how relieved I am—there is hope."

At that moment, I knew I was going to hear the voice of the person who killed this man. I continued to listen to every word as it oozed from the recording.

"Hello," Kevin inquired. "No..." his voice tightened. The one that followed was gruff, calm, and a bit lower overall. It was a masculine voice that would bring images of a handsome man, but something in it made me cringe and feel sorrow.

"Officer Marshall, how lucky am I to find you here? I was beginning to think this damn place was nothing more than a ghost town. I can't tell you how happy I am to see you after all this time. You were one of the first to abandon us. I'm just glad the director didn't have the same stone heart as you do. For his gratitude, I killed him quickly. You, on the other hand, I'm going to make suffer before you finally gift me your last breath. I assure you it won't be quick, and you're going to beg me to finish."

"You don't want to do this. You have a chance to go anywhere you want and do whatever you want. You should relocate somewhere with more people. You could be someone different," Kevin tried to state forcefully.

"After that wonderfully descriptive way you defined me on the radio, I knew I had to find you. You're making me even more famous than I could ever have imagined. We have some unfinished business, you and I," he hissed.

"Get away from me, Jonathon!" Kevin yelled.

"The media calls me Jon-Jon. Kevin, you know Jon-Jon makes me seem more likable, and that's all I have ever really wanted. To be liked, admired, loved, and all the other crap the media said I needed to fill the void in my life." His tone was sincere.

"Don't take another step, Jonathon," Kevin demanded.

I heard a loud thud, the sound of exhaled breath and little grunts.

"Get off of me!" Kevin bellowed.

It was followed by a bone-chilling laugh. I could hear a loud pounding noise—once, twice, then a third time before the sound of rustling clothes and movement filled the air. I imagine it was him knocking Kevin out and moving him into place. The next sound left nothing to the imagination. Metal slammed into metal followed by a blood-curdling scream. It continued with additional pounding and more yelling.

Once the hammering stopped, there was a sigh. "There, I can't have you trying to run away on me while I work. That was more difficult than I remembered, but the sound of your sweet screams was like a grand crescendo in my own orchestra. I'm going to share a secret with you. I enjoy hearing a woman scream in ecstasy. Tantalizingly painful female screams produced by sliding my favorite blade across their skin, cutting just deep enough to bleed is hypnotic. Therefore, everyone thinks I prefer the screams women gift me, but I enjoy a man's scream on a completely different level, because I know it takes extreme pain to invoke a scream like you just did," he gloated.

"Piss off!" Kevin bellowed.

"Now-now, be nice, or I will cut your tongue out."

"Cut my tongue out. Go ahead. Then I will die quicker, and you won't enjoy your screams."

"Good point. Let's see how you do when I start with your finger nails, then we'll see how it feels to lose an ear. Maybe after that I'll pull your teeth out one by one, and finish by taking your eyes out. How do you feel about that, loudmouth?" Jonathan hissed.

The screams were heartbreaking. I couldn't stop the tears from flowing down my cheeks.

I quickly pressed the button to skip forward, it would only go in thirty-second intervals.

"Isn't this fun, Kevin? With this little experiment we have just proven you can still scream without your tongue. Plus, I didn't cut it all out—just the tip. Hopefully that will slow how quickly you bleed out. You don't need the outer part of your ear to hear, but I only took one because I said I would, and unlike you, I am a man of my word."

God, who would do this? I pushed the button again three times in a row.

"I do enjoy spending time with you. Are you comfortable?" he boasted.

Why am I still listening to this? I skipped three more times.

"In medieval times, the Chinese would torture someone by making numerous cuts all over the body, allowing the person to slowly bleed to death. If you didn't die the first day, they would come back and reopen all the cuts. This would continue every day until the person either told them what they wanted to know or died. If I had the time with you, I would make this last for days. As it is, I'm busy, so the cuts will be a bit deeper.

"Do you know what it felt like in that sealed room, wondering if I was going to starve to death before the power finally failed? What I'm doing to you is mild in comparison to two weeks of little food, constantly wondering if someone would come to help. The feeling of my body eating away at itself gave me a new appreciation for life. I could be like you and do devious things to you, making your mind break, and it would be as painful as a physical death. Instead, I have decided to make you my first beautiful piece of art."

I skipped more than six times. I needed to get to the end, find out if he told him anything about where he was going or what he would do next.

His voice made it clear he was trying to project a feeling of delight. He enunciated when needed, added inflection at the right moments, and even dropped his tone when the wording deemed it. He was putting on a show anyone would be proud to have recited. Yet, for some weird reason, I felt my heart ache for Jonathon and his idea of accomplishment. There was a sorrow to him; perhaps I felt as if I could relate to the person putting on the show. Years of always needing to be what Kyle wanted instead of who I was made me the perfect actress.

Gave feeling when I needed to, but most of it wasn't real. It was my own show, for one. It had to be close to over. Three more skips, and I was almost to the end.

I heard him sigh before he spoke, but when he did, he was still calm and in complete control.

"You know, I'm having so much fun with you, but I noticed a pig farm about a mile down the road. I bet they have a lot of fun utensils. Yeah, I think I want to go get us some new toys to try out. You stay here...Ha-ha wait, what am I saying? Where are you going to go? Don't die yet—I'll be back so we can finish this up."

The knives tinked as he placed them down. Kevin was silent. Jonathon hummed as he prepared to leave. I didn't know the tune, but it was sad and full of pain. *What kind of murderer hums something sad when they are doing what they claim to love?* Then I heard the door open and close. Every muscle in my body ached from sitting tensely. I mourned Kevin's death, but I found myself crying for Jonathan.

I didn't want to think about why I felt bad for such a horrible person. It had only been a few minutes of silence when I bent down to stop the recording, but I couldn't stop it just yet, as when I reached to turn it off I heard the door open on the recording.

My mind went straight to Jonathan's return. He was fast because the closest house was a few miles away. I thought I would be hearing more gruesome details of what fun he would be having with a corpse. I was done. I grabbed the iPod and activated the screen. Before I put my finger on the stop button, I heard it.

I hurried to my feet as I listened to the word "hello" echo through the iPod.

If you figure in the time it took me to blow the candles out and subtract that from the few minutes of silence, it came down to seconds. I missed him by seconds. I could have walked into this torture. *What if he didn't get that far and noticed the lights dimming? What if he saw my shadow cross the window? I've got to get out of here.*

I shoved the iPod in my pocket without any thought. There was no clumsiness this time. I was off the floor and out the door in seconds. I ran down the hall and stopped to grab my bag. I didn't try to secure it, only snatched it and went for the back door.

I reached the handle and felt it turning under my hand. Someone was opening the door. I froze and tried to twist the knob. I wasn't as strong as they were, and the door opened.

The force they yanked with pulled me through the doorway and I fell forward once I let the handle go. I landed half in the door and half out. My breath was knocked out of me and there was a sharp pain below my breast. If I managed to survive this night, I was going to be black and blue.

All I could see on the ground were dark shoes. My heart was racing, and I broke out in a fine layer of sweat and began trembling. I was terrified. I had witnessed two of Jonathan's works of art, and I damn sure wasn't going to be his third. I didn't need to kill him, just outrun him. A rock the size of my hand was on the ground next to me. I grabbed it and smashed it as hard as I could into his shin. I hurried to my feet and took off in a sprint. He pulled my hood, choking me and yanking me back. He wrapped one arm around my waist and the other around my mouth. I tried to scream, but nothing could get past his death grip.

Jonathan has me and I'm going to die. I know Kyle doesn't want me to return, but I don't need to die like this.

He lifted me up and carried me around the corner of the building. I wasn't ready to die, at least not without a fight. I started to kick as hard as I could, and he pulled me tighter into his chest. I could hear his breath by my ear when he whispered, "Sara, chill out. Someone's coming."

Sam.

Immediately, I relaxed, and he released his grip. I grabbed

his hand and pulled him away from the station and down into the small section of woods to the west.

I looked towards the station to see if Jonathon was who Sam heard. I wanted to get as far away from this place as possible. With a death grip on Sam's hand, I started moving backwards, never taking my eyes away from the station.

A twig snapped close to me, and I froze. *He can't be behind us; I've been watching, I would've seen him come around.*

I stood still, trying to analyze the likelihood of getting out of this alive when I felt the hot breath and heard a huff.

I squeezed Sam's hand as I turned to see who was behind me. I wanted to laugh at myself as I looked into the bulging eye of a large brown cow. The cow passed between Sam and I, breaking our hands free as it continued on its path.

I ran my hand across the heifer when she passed. It was a relief to see some animals were still alive. I secured my bag and whispered, "We need to get back home."

"I agree," Sam replied.

CHAPTER 6

A good chunk of the walk back to the house was made in silence. I didn't know what Sam heard and wasn't taking any chances that someone was following us. When we finally made it to my street, I stopped.

"What's wrong?" Sam asked.

"Why were you at the station?" I quickly questioned him.

"What?"

"Why were you at the station?"

I didn't look at him. I only stood still-hidden inside my hoodie, waiting for an answer.

"Uhm, I don't think I need to explain my actions to you," he said defensively.

"Sam, just answer the question please," I whispered.

"Okay fine. I need gas to go find my daughter, and I knew there was a pig farmer down from the station. I thought he might still have gas in his reservoir tanks," he sarcastically answered.

"Then where's your car?" I hissed. I couldn't help but think he was lying and following me, or worse. What if Jonathon and Sam were the same people? That thought left as quickly as it came. Technology would have made sure the justice system knew his real name. I was tired of being lied to, manipulated, and walked on. I deserved better.

"I'm only indulging in this accusatory line of questioning because of whatever hell you must have seen in that building to come out fighting. I didn't drive because I couldn't afford to waste what little gas I had left, so I decided to walk, and if there was anything left in the tank, I would drive back to fill it up. I saw a shadow in the radio station and thought it was the guy from the warning. I was going to ask if he knew anything, but when I opened the door, I was surprised by someone falling to the ground. Before I could recognize you, I was cracked in the shin with a rock. I only knew it was you by your bag. When are you going to trust me?" he finished.

"I...the things I've seen, Sam, they're horrible, and I feel like I can't trust anyone. Everything I thought I knew feels like it has all been a lie. The life I thought I was going to have has been destroyed, and I don't know who I am anymore," I softly said.

I turned till I was in front of him, and the tears covered my face before I could stop them. Then, fighting through breaths to not let him hear the anguish, I said, "Sam, I wish I was dead. Not in the placating way of being dramatic, but in the 'I can't do this anymore, and I want out' way. Will you help me? Please take me out of this world because I don't want to be part of it anymore. I'm tired of the struggle. I don't remember how to fight, and I don't think I want to. What exactly would I be fighting for? A life I don't want anymore, a husband who hates me? I have no friends, family, or anyone to call and check on me. I'm floundering and lost, so help me take the pain away."

He pulled me into his chest and whispered, "Never. I'm not going to let you die. I need you, Sara. I can't do any of this alone. I need you; do you hear me? I need you. Even more than my need is you needing to find you. Be the woman I know you are, show someone the side of you no one sees, and together we can figure out the rest."

"I don't want to go back to Kyle yet, not with me feeling like this," I admitted.

The street was covered in vehicles, both upside-down and upright. Sam released his grip on me and walked us to the nearest car. He pulled on the door handle. Nothing. He went down and tried the next few, but they were all locked. Finally, he approached me and joked, "It's the end of the world, and people still lock their cars; go figure."

He tried to make me laugh with the comment, and he succeeded. I let out a little chuckle. He grabbed my hand and walked toward an empty van in the middle of the field. It was upright and looked like someone had driven it there and parked it.

"I'm going to break a front window, and we can sit in the back till you're ready to go home," Sam stated as he began to look for a rock.

I walked up to the driver's door and pulled the handle. I giggled a bit to myself when the thing opened right up.

"Or we can try the door," I laughed.

"Well, it seems your day is already looking up," Sam chuckled.

I didn't wait for him before I unlocked the rest of the doors. Then, after closing the driver's door, I wasted no time getting into the far back seat of the van.

It had three rows of seats. The front two were bucket-style, and the far back was a bench. It was darker and easier to conceal my face.

Sam came in behind me, laughing as he said, "All the way in the back? Are you planning on trying to seduce me?"

His face lost all expression and color when I replied, "Of course I was; what else do you do in the back of a van during the end of the world?" I tried to hold a severe tone to my voice but couldn't. I finished with, "I'm cold. I can sit closer to you on the bench seat."

It was partly true, but the rest was the darkness I felt I was falling into. I had to shut off my emotions, or I wouldn't survive much longer.

I tapped the spot next to me to move him over. When he

got close, I lowered my head to hide my face in my hoodie.

He sat next to me and leaned forward to match my body language.

"Do you want to sit back?"

I held silent until the dome light went out. "Yes. Will you wrap your arm around me, please?"

I sat back, and Sam extended his arm out and around my shoulder. I moved in as close to him as possible, but he seemed tense.

"Sara..." he cautiously started.

"Yes?" I reluctantly responded.

"Don't take this the wrong way, but you stink. Really bad."

"Oh." I pulled away from him quickly. If he could have seen my face, the parts that weren't bruised would have been crimson.

"Your house is just a few blocks away. Let me go get you some clean clothes," he insisted.

"No!" I yelled. "Sorry, with Kyle awake, I don't want you to have to deal with him. Maybe not all of my clothes stink. I layered up before I left."

I yanked my coat off and shoved it into the seats in front of us. I pulled on my hooded jacket and to see if the stench soaked through. It felt dry, so I thought it was okay. Kicking off my shoes and the two layers of sweatpants, I added them to the clothes pile up front.

"Sam, will you put those outside? I think that should take care of the smell," I said.

"Yeah," he replied as he moved forward. He grabbed the clothes and went out the side door. Instead of throwing them down, he laid each item out neatly on the hood to dry.

He climbed back inside, and I quickly focused my attention on putting my shoes on. I couldn't let him see what Kyle did to me. He wouldn't understand.

Taking his place beside me, he motioned for me to move closer. Once more, I slowly fiddled with tying my shoes to avoid exposing my face to him.

Before I moved back over, he said with excitement, "Look at what I found!" He dug behind the seat we were in and pulled out a huge comforter. "No offense, but your hoodie still smells, so take it off and I will keep you warm with this."

Take it off? I guess it's still dark, so it should be okay. Hesitating slightly, I unzipped my hoodie and pulled it off. I balled it up and threw it up into the front seat.

"Here, I'll take it out," he offered as he began to move toward the front.

I couldn't let him open the door.

"No, I'm really cold. It can wait till later. Will you please sit with me so I can get warmed up?" I quickly begged, grabbing his arm.

"Okay," he replied.

He moved back into position, and I slid in closely to him. After he wrapped his arm around my shoulders, I rested my head on his and pulled my legs up and under the blanket with us.

The sound of Sam's slow, steady breaths relaxed me. I wanted to close my eyes and forget about everything that happened today. I could do without the feeling of sorrow for my children, the fear of knowing there was a crazy person hunting us, or the betrayal and worthlessness Kyle made me feel.

I knew I would have to explain things to Sam eventually, but in this moment of closeness, I wanted to forget.

Sitting in silence with him reminded me of a part of one of my favorite books, where the main characters are sitting in an old pickup truck waiting for a tow. The two look into each other's eyes and share a life-altering kiss. The kind of kiss you feel in every molecule, one you never want to end. The characters do more than a single kiss. They explore and touch until they can't stand being apart any longer. It's steamy and erotic and everything I've never had.

Sam rested his cheek on my head and softly asked, "Why

are you wandering outside?"

Crap, I will have to tell him about Kyle, and he will get mad.

"Why didn't I see you at my wedding if you were there?" I redirected the questioning back onto him. It was childish to change the subject. I learned this technique from Kyle—distraction and blame with a hint of shame to get out of answering anything you didn't want to.

"Is this how you want to play? There must be an idiotic reason for you being out this late. I mean, why else would you so obviously change topics." He sighed.

"I could say the same about you since you're not answering my question either," I replied without missing a beat.

"What did you get into that smelled so bad?"

"Fine, I see how this is going to go. I will be the bigger person and answer the first question. I tripped over a chair leg and fell into a mess of stale coffee and blood."

I could feel him holding back a laugh as he cautiously chose his next question. "You tripped over a chair leg at the radio station and landed in stale coffee?"

"You have my permission to laugh. It's funny. However, I wasn't at the radio station when I tripped. I was at the police station," I corrected.

Sam's body went from loose to rigid instantly, and I could feel him trying to sit up straighter.

"Sara, what were you doing in town at this time of night? You have no reason to be walking the streets alone. Do you have any idea what kind of people might be out there? Not to mention the wild animals that are roaming and taking advantage of the buffet of the dead. What could have possessed you to think it was a good idea? I was already ticked that you were at the radio station, but to find out you put yourself in more harm is extremely disappointing," he ranted.

In the midst of Sam's denigrating of my abilities, I felt like a switch in my mind flicked on and I finally started to see what Derek was trying to tell me.

The words exploded from my lips with confidence I'd never felt. "Sam, I am a grown woman. I'm not a scared little girl. I can take care of myself, and I will do what I can to help figure out what we need to do next." Holy shit, I just stood up for myself. I said what I felt, and I didn't regret it. I was mad that he didn't think I could do anything myself. I was getting really tired of being undervalued.

"I didn't mean it like that. Why didn't you wait for me?"

I felt his body slump a little as if defeated before he shifted beside me, trying to look me in the eyes. He always had been someone who believed eye contact made for much deeper conversation.

Now we were both out of the blanket and sitting up in place. I thought about my answer carefully. I needed him to see it was my choice; I couldn't tell him the truth.

"Screw this. I hate not seeing your face when I'm trying to have a conversation with you," Sam exclaimed as he reached above us and turned the dome light on.

I was a bug caught in the light of death. Once I got close, I was going to get burned, but I couldn't take my eyes off the alluring beauty.

The next few seconds seemed to move in slow motion. I tilted my head back down and looked directly at Sam.

He didn't say anything at first. His eyes drowned in a deep sorrow as they filled with tears. A single tear rolled down his cheek, and before it dropped from his chin, his eyes changed to rage. His face flamed red as he screamed, "I'm going to kill him!"

He jumped up and moved toward the door. I grabbed his hand, fell to my knees, and pleaded, "No you can't. He's not worth it. Don't let him do this to you."

He yanked his hand from my grip before heading out the door. Quickly, I grabbed my hoodie and bag, then ran after him.

By the time I got my hoodie on, he was out of sight, but I

picked my pace up to a soft jog. It didn't take me long to reach the house's stair entrance. I looked down the open doorway to the dark basement. It wasn't that way when I left.

"Sam, Kyle, where are you?"

I didn't wait for an answer and headed down the stairs by twos. At the bottom I was abruptly stopped by Sam.

"Where's Kyle?" I demanded.

"You can't come down here," Sam replied matter-of-factly, but with an overly calm tone. I knew that tone; it was what I would use when my kids were having a meltdown, and I needed them to see me remaining at peace so they would gravitate towards a more tranquil disposition.

"Like hell I can't! Move!" I warned. I was pissed. I was unsure if it was over not being allowed into my home or because of the placating tone.

I glanced around Sam's massive figure to see five candles lit and what appeared to be someone standing toward the top beams of the basement.

Then, it hit me.

I pushed Sam aside; why didn't he just move? I crawled through under his arm. I ran to the candle circle, threw my bag off, and quickly grabbed Kyle's waist.

"Help me, Sam!" I screamed as my eyes burned through the tears. "Sam, damn it, get him down!" I frantically cried. I knew he was already gone, but I couldn't accept it.

Sam walked over and cut the rope free from the beam and quickly grabbed Kyle before he fell to the ground. I dropped to the floor and went straight into CPR training mode. I titled his head back and opened his mouth. I bent down and blew air into his chest, lifted up, and started compressions.

"Don't just stare at me, Sam, help me!" I screamed. "Two, three, four, five," I counted out loud on the compressions, then moved to give him another breath.

Sam grabbed my hands as I positioned myself to start on his chest again. "Sara, he's cold. He's been dead for at least two hours. You're not going to bring him back."

How does he know how long he has been dead for?

I shot Sam a hateful look and shoved his hand away. "One, two, three, four, five," again I whispered and repeated. I tried not to think about what I was doing. I needed to stay focused.

Sam sat along the wall watching as I continued to breathe and then resume chest compressions. I was going to fight for us even if Kyle didn't want to. I wasn't sure how long I worked on him before my eyes began to blur from the tears welling up. I took in a deep breath and tried to stay focused, but the harder I concentrated, the worse it got.

I leaned back against my feet to take the pressure off my knees. For a moment I sat silently, then moved forward and rested my head on Kyle's chest. He was stiff. I no longer heard his heartbeat or felt any life pulsing through him, and his skin was chilled to the touch. There was a piece of paper shoved into his pocket. That wasn't like Kyle; I was the note-taker, always with a reminder in my pocket. I pulled out the crumpled paper and smoothed it open. Slowly, I read the letter addressed to me.

Sara,

I'm not a cold, heartless bitch like you! I can't bear living in this Hell knowing you killed my kids. Your selfish, self-preservative actions have caused the dissolution of my family. I hate you more than words can express. My first thought was to kill you, but I won't give you the gratification of an early out. Instead, you get the pleasure of living knowing that you killed everyone you claimed to love. This is your fault. You may not be the one standing here with a gun to my head, but you are the controlling factor in this forced decision.

Somewhere along this marriage, you shut down and closed me out. Your words said you loved me, but your actions were that of a mindless zombie. You doomed

our lives together years ago, and I finally stopped try-
ing to love the cold shell you've become.

I'm sure you will find it gratifying to know you
were the last thing on my mind before I hanged my-
self, but only rejoice in knowing I was thinking about
the woman I married and not who you have become.
I will not tell you I'm sorry because I'm not. I tried
my hardest to forgive and forget, but the image of my
children won't get out of my head. You've done nothing
but cause me heartache and grief for more years than
I could count. I hope you are proud of yourself. As I sit
here and finish this letter, I realize I have hated you for
more years than I ever loved you. I hope you burn in
Hell.

Your husband,
Kyle

My eyes stung as I re-read the last two lines again. Drop-ping the letter, I hid my face in my hands.

"Sara?"

Sam's soft voice echoed in my ear, but I couldn't respond. My mind was reeling over Kyle's written words. I looked at Sam still resting against the wall.

"That bastard never wrote me a single damn letter all the time we were together. Not even when we were in school, and the one time he chose to was to write this shitty-ass suicide letter. It's written haphazard and almost like by force," I spat.

Grabbing the letter, I crushed it into a ball and threw it at Sam. My face was heating up and the growing aggression coursed through my veins.

Sam leaned forward and picked up the letter. He unrolled it and began glancing over it.

I couldn't watch him read the hateful things written to me, looking down at Kyle's cold, lifeless body, I began burning with a new hatred. I balled my hands into fists and pounded on

Kyle's chest as I screamed, "You stupid bastard, I loved you. You treated me like shit, and I still loved you. You made me hate myself, and I still loved you!"

I couldn't see through the tears searing my cheeks. The flesh along my fingers took the brunt of the hits. Each blow slashed at my tender meat, bruising and ripping my bare hands open, but I never gave up. I hit him for all the names he called me, the hateful words he spoke, and every tear he made me shed. I hit him for the years he made me love him and then for yanking it away.

I pulled back to start another round of blows when I was yanked into Sam's chest. "Enough, Sara."

But it wasn't enough; it would never be enough. I fought Sam's hold. He didn't get to "check out" and left me with more pain. What right did he have to make me feel worse? The harder I fought, the tighter Sam's hold became. My heart was splitting inside my chest, and the pain radiating throughout my body only made me want to hit Kyle even more. I had been so stupid, thinking we would be better after all of this, that he would like to try rebuilding with me. How could I still fall into his trap? Amid all the destruction, I thought we would learn how to love each other again, and like he always did, he took that dream from me.

With a quick spin, Sam had my back pinned to the concrete wall with his weight. He crossed my arms over my chest and leaned into me. I couldn't move. I lowered my head and tried to stop my mind from replaying his last words over and over on a steady repeat. I had to convince myself this wasn't my fault.

"Sara, look at me," Sam quietly requested.

I was a mess. With the tears, sweat, and snot running down my face, I couldn't look at him. I shook my head no and continued to glance at the ground, hoping my hair would cover the worst of it.

The rage slowly began to subside despite my desperate

need to keep fueling it. Anger and hate were easier to deal with. Having to think about everything happening wasn't something I wanted to do.

"Leave me alone, Sam," I whispered, defeated once more.

"Sara," he sighed.

"Don't you get it, Sam? I ruin everything; I'm destructive to be around. I kill those I love and bring down everyone who comes in contact with me. Save yourself by getting as far away from me as possible." At this second, I believed exactly what I said; I had ruined everything.

Sam said nothing, but he didn't release me. Instead, his body continued to press into mine as if he would never move. I lifted my head to look at him; his eyes were closed, and his face tilted slightly.

I should have seen it coming. He was disgusted with me and couldn't bring himself to look at me. I pulled off of the wall to free myself of his hold. The leer of disappointment wasn't something I wanted to see. Not from him, not when I was already at my lowest. My movement pulled his attention back to me. I tried to lower my head before he noticed me, but I was unsuccessful. He placed his palm on my uninjured cheek and used the pad of his thumb to wipe some of the tears away.

I still couldn't look him in the eyes, and his gentle touch brought more tears. He leaned into me to place his forehead against mine. Then, slowly, he lowered his lips to my injured cheek and gave me a feather-light kiss. Something I would have done to soothe one of my kids' injuries.

"I'm sorry."

The two little words whispered with such heartfelt sorrow drained me. The pain radiating through my chest increased, and I swore my heart was ripping apart. Soon, there wouldn't be anything left of it. What was he sorry for, abandoning our friendship, watching me crumble? Was he sorry for what was left of my pathetic life? It was physically impossible to take in a full breath. The few quick inhales I managed to pull in were shallow and increasing in speed. An anxiety attack was approaching swiftly.

"Sam, I can't breathe!" I frantically spoke while trying to push him away from me.

He took a step back to give me room. "Slow down your breaths before you pass out."

I wanted to scream 'no duh,' but instead I slid down the wall and placed my head between my knees. I had to get away from everything. I needed to breathe.

Sam turned to face Kyle's body, presumably trying to figure out what to do with him.

I stood up on unstable legs mumbling, "I need to breathe, I need air."

I sprinted to the stairs, taking them in three quick leaps. After pushing the door open, I ran as fast as I could. I could hear Sam yelling for me, but I didn't care. I wasn't going to stop until I had to. I needed to be free, if only for a fraction of a moment.

The debilitating sorrow weighing down on my chest was replaced with a different type of pain, one from pushing myself beyond my physical limits. I ran past the houses, through the yards, and to an open field. I pushed my legs into the remaining snow and mud, the earth grabbing hold of my shoe with every step. In the darkness I felt free, but I was alone. My leg cramped, locking up my knee, and before I could slow down, I was falling face first to the ground.

I didn't care. I lifted up, resting on my legs. I raised my head toward the sky and tried to catch my breath. Once I was able to I pulled air deep into my chest, and screamed as loud as I could. The pain came pouring out of my throat. It wasn't screechy, but it was deafening and carried more emotion than any word could. I screamed until my chest was empty and then I did it again. I continued until my throat was ripped and sore, until nothing would come out. I closed my eyes briefly, but with them shut all I saw was Kyle's handwriting.

Soaking wet and staring into the clouded sky, I didn't attempt to move from my spot. There was a faint sound in the distance, but I didn't take my focus off the sky. I needed to see the stars and wasn't moving until I could look at them. It was probably Sam coming to get me, anyway. Why was he here? Why did he continue to stick with me through all of this? I didn't want to be like Kyle and wonder about his motives, but why would he show up after all these years and act like he wanted to be friends again. Was it all an act? If it was a joke, it was on him because I had nothing to take. Sam would have to wait.

After what felt like an hour, the clouds finally parted slightly to reveal the moon shining brightly. It was an inspiring sight, but I wanted to see the stars. I used to wish on them when I was a little girl, and it brought comfort to think this blazing light in the night could grant wishes; I missed the innocence of youth. But, unfortunately, the clouds only opened for the moon. I glanced away in despair to find Sam and froze. The person staring at me wasn't Sam.

The moon caressed each of his features in an angelic glow. He was truly breathtaking, standing at least 6'4" with a lean, muscular build. He wore his hair long, shaggier in length and style, enhancing his face wonderfully. It was a dark blond color or perhaps a light brown. It was hard to tell. He wore a hip length leather coat, accentuating his broad shoulders, jeans, and boots. After looking down his figure, I refocused my attention on his face. I could barely gaze at his features. He was beautiful, and I wanted more than anything to look into his eyes. I was overwhelmed with an odd need to see what color they were and if they were as transfixing as the rest of him.

He began walking toward me with strides that were long, confident, and determined.

I should have been scared, but I wasn't. I felt calm and centered as he made his way toward me. I didn't try to hide my apparent interest in him. I was intrigued, captivated, completely lost in the movement of his body.

He stopped less than a yard from me, seeming to re-think coming toward me. My shoulders dropped from the rejection. I shouldn't have expected anything less. Kyle always made sure I knew how unattractive I was.

"I don't do this."

His voice practically sang to me. I lowered my head and let the sound of it bounce around my mind.

"Your screams drew me to you. Your pain pulled me. I ran as fast as I could. I had this fierce need to find the person who was giving the world the gift of their pain."

The passion lacing his words confused me. I looked up at him, perplexed.

"A gift? How could you think of it as a gift?" I rasped.

He took the last few steps toward me and squatted in front of me. I tried to keep my gaze on his shoulders to avoid looking in his eyes. He placed his warm fingers under my chin and slowly raised my face to meet his. Just as I was about to make eye contact, the clouds covered the moon, encasing us in shadow. The lack of the light didn't stop his words.

"It's a gift because we live in a world where no one truly expresses their emotions. We bottle them up or pretend it doesn't hurt as bad as it does. Then you have those who over-act and seem like they are giving you a heartfelt answer, but they are only trying to play on your sympathy. People harden their hearts or just don't give it all like they say. The pain you shared was pure, true, and completely gut-wrenching."

He paused, taking my hand in his and placing it on his chest before continuing. "I felt it here as if it was my own pain pouring out of me." His heart was beating erratically. Listening to him I would have never known how rapid his pulse was, and it was exciting to feel how I affected him.

I was mesmerized by him. His voice was soothing, but there was a pull between us. I felt as though I could just wrap myself around him. It was electric and animalistic, and for the first time in my life, I wanted to throw caution to the wind and kiss this stranger. I wanted to feel his lips pressed against mine. I wanted him to pull me into him with the same need I was currently feeling. He felt like love, hope, and home all mixed into one. How could a stranger pull this feeling from me?

The silence between us wasn't awkward. Instead, it was comfortable, as if this was where I was meant to be. Before I filtered my thoughts, I spoke softer than a whisper, "My name is Sara. Are you an angel?"

His chest vibrated as he chuckled. "No Sara, I'm not an angel. My name is Adam."

I was mortified, and he laughed at me. I quickly realized I was being ignorant. He wasn't any different from any other man in my life. I didn't try to mask my feelings; I wanted him to see exactly how I felt about being laughed at. I registered his surprise as I pulled my hand from his chest. I stood up, needing time to process, so I did what seemed to be my standard response this night. Taking a step back, I tried to clear the rasp from my voice before saying, "Adam, you shouldn't be out here. There are some killers on the loose. It's not safe to be out alone. Be careful, one of the murderers killed someone a few miles from here at the radio station, and I don't know where he is now."

"What do you mean there are killers on the loose?" he inquired softly.

I ran my hand across my throat, rubbing at the pain. "Killers from the prison, someone named Jonathon and another named Marcus. Kevin, the guy at the radio station, was killed by Jonathon. Kevin's still there. You can go look if you like. I left him there."

I sighed heavily, flinching at the pain as I rubbed my eyes.

"I'm so stupid, thinking I could actually find someone to give me answers and help me." I tried another deep breath in and out to calm the tears. I'd already embarrassed myself in front of him; I don't need to add crying.

"I cried for him, cried for his pain," I softly confessed.

"You cried for whom, the man killed? Did you know him?"

He tried to keep his tone level, but I heard a slight elevation.

Finally, taking a small breath, I replied, "I cried for the killer. The man pretending to be something he wasn't because that was who the world deemed him to be. It was nice meeting you, Adam."

I didn't allow him to ask me why I would cry for a murderer. I couldn't handle seeing the look of disgust my confession would create. So instead, I walked away as fast as my legs would carry me, not wanting to explain to this angelic man how I could hear more than just the words the killer spoke. I couldn't tell him I had felt the overwhelming pain beneath the confidence of the murderer's voice.

I genuinely am losing my mind.

I should have gone back, but I didn't. So instead, I walked until I could see the place I called home, but instead of continuing, I stopped at the end of the block and sat under a tree. It was still too dark to see clearly, so I waited until the sun broke the horizon.

Maybe I'll get lucky, and Sam won't search for me. I could close my eyes and wait for death to take me. I felt nothing— not coldness, sadness, happiness, or pain. Finally, I'd become detached from everything. I succeeded in shutting it off and becoming numb. It only took meeting a person way beyond my reach.

I leaned into the trunk, relaxing in my numb cocoon. It didn't take long for my eyes to close, and I refused to fight the draw of sleep. I was ready to be done with it all.

Again, I found myself alone in the darkness. I should have tried to locate where I was, but I didn't have the energy. I sat down on the cold stone floor, trying to disappear into the dark. The pull to be one with the emptiness felt like the right move.

"Mom, you need to get up. Wake up, Mom!"

The soft sound spoke against my ear. I jerked my head to the side before swinging around.

"Mom, wake up. It's not your time!"

I whipped around the other way to the ear she was whispering into.

"Tina, honey, where are you? Why are you in this dark, lonely place?" I frantically cried.

"I'm not here, Mom. You are, and you don't belong here. Please wake up," she softly cried.

"I miss you," I whispered.

"Now, Mom. Wake up now. Please, please, wake up!" she frantically cried.

I didn't want to. I was too tired, the dark too comforting, but hearing the fear in her words made my mind up for me. I tried to open my eyes, but they felt heavy and dry. One eyelid wouldn't even crack, the side Kyle struck. I tried forcing my eyes open, but all I managed to do was flutter my eyelids. A dark figure was in front of me.

I tried two more times to open my eyes, but my body fought back.

"Back away from her," a strong voice echoed.

"She's mine."

The tone was confident, but it wasn't Sam.

"Adam," I moaned, not realizing how much my body hurt. Finally, I pulled my eyes open and saw two blurry figures a few feet away.

"I don't know who you think you are, but I found this ripe treasure all alone sleeping under the tree. She belongs to me," the other voice spat.

"She's not alone. I'm here, so take off before I do something you will regret."

"Adam," I whispered again.

"Adam huh, what kind of lame ass name is Adam?" the other voice sarcastically spat.

He moved towards me. I tried to scoot away, but it was useless with how sore, cold, and tired my body was. It wouldn't obey.

"Don't worry, honey. I won't mark you up like Adam did. Tisk, tisk. I like my women soft and unmarred. You'll like what I have planned for us. You'll be calling me master in no time, but for now you can just call me Marcus." Pride rang through his voice as he pronounced his name.

The fear at the mention of the rapist's name helped me focus on the threat in front of me. I tried to move my legs, but my ankles were tied together.

"Untie me," I croaked; the pain burning my throat had only lessened slightly.

"Sara, stay calm," Adam said steadily. When I moved my hands toward my ankles, I discovered my arms were secured to my sides.

"Untie me," I hissed.

"Oh, she's a feisty one, isn't she?" Marcus grinned.

"I'm going to make you wish you were never born, Marcus!" The venom in my words surprised Adam as much as it did me.

"Ha-ha, like I said, feisty. Mmm, just thinking about you fighting me before I enter your wet..."

Adam planted his fist hard across Marcus' jaw before he could finish his sentence. Marcus stumbled slightly, but quickly regained his footing.

In the blink of an eye, the two were throwing forceful punches at one another other. They didn't stay in eyesight, and I struggled to free myself. It was pointless—I was stuck.

"Damn it, Sara. What the hell have you done?" Sam cursed softly into my ear.

"Oh, Sam, thank God you're here. Untie me," I begged.

I was so absorbed in their fight and the fear of what if Marcus won that I didn't even hear Sam approach me.

"Quiet—I don't know where those guys went or when they

will be back, so we need to hurry." Sam removed the ropes. "Where did this coat come from?" he asked while lifting the leather off my chest.

No wonder I was warm. Sam tried to throw the coat to the side, but I grabbed it before he could.

"Don't," I whispered.

Standing, I gently placed the coat across the lowest hanging limb. I would have kept it, but I didn't want Adam to get cold or sick. I wished I could tell him thank you. I looked at my hand and decided to leave him the only thing I could, slipping the ring from my pinky. It was yellow gold with a small stone in the center of a heart. It was the only thing I had from my dad. Since he gave it to me when I turned thirteen, I'd worn it every day. When I first started wearing it, it fit on my middle finger. After all the years it only fit on my pinkie. I slid it into the inside pocket of the coat before I stepped away.

Sam quickly grabbed my hand and pulled me towards the house. The pace he set was too fast, and I didn't get to look for Adam.

I could feel Sam's agitation like a cloud of guilt. Before I could understand why I felt guilty, he was pushing me in front of him and onto the stairs. I stumbled with the first few and feared I would fall down the rest.

Righting my footing, I spun to yell at him. He was close when I turned, making me forget what I wanted to say. Forcefully, he moved me so my back was against the wall. We hadn't made it all the way down the stairs yet. As I opened my mouth to protest, he covered it with his hand. He pressed his body into mine, pinning one arm in between us and the other behind me. No matter how much I fought, I couldn't move.

I licked the palm of his hand. It was childish, but he had no right to be mean to me. I hurt everywhere, and he wasn't helping. The glare I received from him told me he thought it was childish as well. I opened my mouth to bite him when I heard someone walking above us.

His focus shifted to the footsteps. I closed my eyes, trying to calm my heart. The steps stopped short of the opening, and my body trembled. Sam's eyes darted back to me. A tear slipped down my cheek and landed on his hand.

Things kept getting worse. Sam needed to leave, find his daughter, and let nature take its course. Nothing good ever came to the people around me. I had brought this danger upon us. The tears were falling more freely, one after the other. Sam pressed his forehead to mine but kept his hand against my mouth.

I couldn't tell who was above us. Sam looked at me, silently pleading with me to keep quiet and not to give our location away.

"Please don't worry about Marcus. He won't bother you again. Sara, you are precious. You're all three of the Algea wrapped into one, but I will call you Ania. Eris would be proud to call you daughter. I will not forget what I experienced last night nor the words we shared, and I will keep your gift next to my heart," Adam quietly stated with passion I didn't deserve, then his descending footsteps echoed around us.

How much more can my heart take? He may have laughed at the thought of being an angel, but he had to be one. There was no other explanation for why I was pulled so fiercely towards him.

Sam's expression asked questions I didn't want to answer. Better yet, ones I couldn't answer. He lowered his hand from my mouth slowly, grabbing the zipper on my hoodie and pulled it down. I couldn't get my shaking under control, and the tears weren't showing any sign of letting up.

He eased himself away from me enough to pull my arms free. He opened the jacket and slid his arm around my waist, making sure his hand was touching the bare skin of my lower back. Pulling me into him, he moved his other arm around my back and placed his fingers on my base of my neck. He tugged me tighter to him, forcing my lips millimeters from his. Time felt as if it stopped, and I was trapped in his gaze. He looked as if he wanted to devour every inch of me, but the glare held hate.

I wrapped my arms around him and placed my head on his shoulder. He bent into my neck, and I felt his lips graze my skin.

"You had me so damn scared," he confessed, tightening his hold.

It felt good being held by him even if I didn't deserve it, and I realized I had stopped shaking.

"I can't go in there. I can't see him," I whispered.

Sam's hand climbed my neck to caress my scalp while his other rubbed softly against the skin on my side.

"He's gone. I took care of it."

His breath on my neck caused a shutter of delight. He lifted me up and took us down the rest of the steps. In a matter of seconds, he had my coats shoved down, freeing my arms. He kept me against the stone wall, not giving an ounce of separation. We were only embracing, but it felt as if we were caressing every inch of each other's body.

My rational side tried to break through the fog consuming my mind. *Didn't I find my husband dead last night? Shouldn't I be mourning?*

The sensual fog responded, *Didn't he hate you? When did he last kiss you or hold you? Six months? More? The last time he was intimate with you was well over six months ago, when you woke him with a gesture most men wouldn't discourage. Do you remember how pissed he was when he realized you wanted more than to pleasure him?*

Sam continued to press his face to my neck, not moving. He only breathed, inhaling faster than before. I tilted my head to expose my neck to him. I wanted to feel his lips on my skin. He didn't disappoint, placing feather light kisses along the lower part of my neck. If I hadn't been so sensitive to his presence, I may not have felt the delicate placement. I moved my hand up his back, around his bicep, and into his hair. Grazing my nails along his soft waves, I tried to make him intensify his kisses. His chuckle vibrated through his chest.

"Why are you torturing me? Let me go, you obviously don't want me," I whispered.

"You think I don't want you?"

Before I could respond, he pulled my hips into his, allowing me to feel how much he wanted me. At the same time, he drew his teeth across my neck and bit slightly. I moaned and rubbed myself against him.

My mind was finally at peace. If I could describe blind bliss, it would be this. Sam's sensual assault was all I could think about. Once Sam took my lips into his nothing but devouring everything he was willing to give mattered. He guided me toward the bed while he continued tasting and exploring my mouth. The backs of my legs touched the edge of the bed and I lowered myself onto it. Sam pursued with growing confidence.

His kisses hurt my bruised lips and the shadowing of his beard stung along my sore jaw, but I refused to let him see the pain. He kept most of his weight on his elbow to keep the pressure of his body off mine. He ran his hand up my outer thigh toward my knee, guiding it up and around his waist. When his hand closed around my knee, I flinched at the pain it caused.

His hand stilled, and he began withdrawing his lips from mine. Not wanting to stop, I tried to pull him back to me, but he slowly shook his head.

He moved up onto his knees and looked down at me. He blew out his breath as he ran his hand over his mouth and closed his eyes.

Shit, I knew this would happen. He's ashamed of what we were doing. I ran my tongue over my bottom lip, tasting the familiar tinge of metal. I touched my swollen lips, pulling my finger back to see the bright red blood lining it. I tried to position myself up on my elbows, but the small movement sent pain shooting throughout my side.

"Damn it," I moaned. It was the wake-up call I needed; I really couldn't believe I was about to be so reckless. Was I so starved of attention that I would jump into sex with Sam? The honest answer was yes, I was.

Sam's eyes opened suddenly, focusing back on me. He grabbed my foot and quickly removed my shoe, never taking his eyes off me. When he picked the other one up, I let the breath out I hadn't realized I was holding.

Placing my foot back down, he continued moving his hand up the outer side of my calf, past my knee, and up my thigh. I anxiously waited to see what he would do next.

"Relax," he whispered while unbuttoning my jeans.

I closed my eyes, trying to control my breathing and my overactive imagination. I felt the cool air on my skin as he slowly slid the jeans off. The jeans were heavy with water from the night, and the feel of his warmth made me shiver. Sam inhaled sharply before moaning, "Sara."

It wasn't a sensual sound of lust, but more an admission of fear. I opened my eyes to see Sam looking at me like I was dying.

"Fuck, Sara, how the hell have you been able to move?" he hissed.

The last of my lust quickly took a nosedive and was replaced with acute anger.

"Don't look at me like I'm the worst person on the planet," he interjected.

"Why wouldn't I? Who the hell half strips a woman and then makes a comment like that while she is laid out beneath him?" I growled.

"Once you cried out from me touching your knee, all thoughts of doing anything went out the window. My intention was to see how bad your knee was."

I gasped as I registered what he said. *How dare he?* He was no better than Kyle! Kyle used to act like he wanted to be intimate, and the minute I was undressed he would start telling me how I let my body go, or I wasn't sexy, or how no one would ever want to be with me. It was an irrational thought to have, but it consumed me none the less.

"I'm fine, no need for your concern," I hissed.

"You're not fine. Don't even pretend you are. Damn, Sara, your thigh and knee are purple. Sit up and let me see your side. Take off your shirt," he commanded.

"Go to hell, Samuel Eli Alperstein." My voice was laced with sarcastic sweetness.

He sighed, relaxing a little. Maybe he thought our little argument was done. I hated him in that very moment, and I hated myself too. I didn't know how to be intimate with anyone other than Kyle, and it scared me. I was embarrassed and hurt, and I wanted to hurt him too.

"Give me my jeans so I can get dressed and we can pretend this never happened. You should have left me alone instead of torturing me when you don't want me. It's cruel, Sam; even Kyle didn't stoop that low."

With a quick motion, he was hovering over me. I heard his jeans unsnap and the sound of his zipper lowering. He grabbed my hand and wrapped it around his hard length. I felt the warmth from his body immediately and gently closed my fingers around him, absorbing the feel of his arousal. It was like soft velvet encasing hard steel. He hissed as I tried to move my hand on him, then tightened his fingers around mine.

"This is how much I desire you. I have thought about being inside you more times than I can count, constantly dreaming about what it would feel like having your body take me into its wet warmth. I think about the smell of your skin as I kiss every inch of your flesh—the taste of your lips pressed against mine. The sounds you would make as you found release. I'm consumed with thoughts of you allowing me to make love to you after all these years, knowing it will be my name on your lips as your orgasm consumes you. I want you more than any man could ever want a woman, but I want to savor you. I want to kiss you from the top of your head down to your toes and everywhere in between. I want to taste all of you and explore every inch of your luscious body. I want to worship you and then make love to you for hours, days, weeks even."

Each whispered word was an erotic caress across my skin. His eyes closed, and he slowly moved his hips, causing me to stroke him. I was not sure he even realized what he was doing, and I was not about to stop him.

"When you let me make love to you, I want to touch you everywhere."

Opening his eyes, he moved our joined hands, placing mine on my stomach and quickly covering himself. He left his jeans undone and leaned back down onto me, running his hand lightly over my injured side.

"You're hurt, and I won't take advantage of you like this. I need you to want me now and still want me again tomorrow. I'll not have you upset or distant because a fear-induced lust drove you to make a decision you wouldn't have made otherwise."

I lifted my hand and smoothed his hair from his face. "Not fear." I smiled.

"Fine, grief-filled lust. Either way, it's not the right time. Besides, you still stink from the coffee," he cautiously joked.

He knew exactly what to say to kill the mood. He grinned at me, kissed me once more, and moved to the edge of the bed. With a subtle grace, he stood.

Slowly, I crawled off the bed, trying to figure out a way to wash myself. I walked over to the shelves and pulled off an empty bucket, grabbed a few old towels, a bottle of shampoo I didn't recall putting there, and finally dug through my tote of clean summer clothes. I noticed some sports bras and new panties and grabbed them too.

Sam's intense gaze burned into my back as he watched my movements. *What is he looking for? Probably to see if I limped because of my knee.* I didn't before, and I was not going to start now.

Once I had everything in the bucket, the last thing to grab was some water. I reached for the jugs I stored in case the water got shut off so we could still wash. One of the many times Kyle overdrew our account led to a bounced check to the water company. They waited until Friday evening at 4:50 to shut me off. By the time I realized it had been turned off, it was too late to get it turned back on, so I spent the weekend without running water. I ended up purchasing multiple gallons, and ever since I kept water on hand. I walked around into the room where the water heater and sump pump hole were. I stripped out of the last of my clothes, opened the door a crack, and threw them out. I heard Sam laughing.

The water sent chills down my spine, causing my flesh to rise and the little hairs on my arm to stand at attention, but I didn't have much of a choice and tried to keep my mind on other things while I washed quickly. I needed to insist Sam go and see if his ex-wife and his daughter were safe. It would be nice if one of us managed to have some good luck.

"Who is Derek Merrow, and why do you have his driver's licenses?" Sam asked from the other side of the closed door.

Shit...He's going to be pissed, but oh well.

"He was a young officer I met when I went to the police station. I told him I would keep his license in case I found his wife, so I could tell her he had passed away."

The second part was a lie, but I didn't want to tell Sam the rest. It would only make him angrier.

"When were you at the police station?" he asked, trying to sound calm, but I could hear the anger hiding in his voice.

"The same day I was at the radio station. I tried to tell you about it last night. I went to the police department first. It was mainly rubble, so there wasn't anything there to help us, and I didn't want to argue over why I left in the first place. You should also know there are survivors around. I saw lights glowing in windows." I finished, trying to sound firm.

"He made you go, didn't he?" he whispered.

"It doesn't make any difference now. I did what I did by my own choice regardless of who gave me the initial suggestion."

"He's damn lucky he's already dead. How did you see to get to the police station with your eye swollen shut?"

"Sam, please stop. I don't want to talk about it. Just let it go," I sighed.

As I scrubbed the shampoo into my hair, I found holding my breath lessened the pain. My entire scalp felt bruised, but I knew it was just the pain radiating from the side of my face and head. I dumped the rest of the jug over my hair to rinse it and squealed, "Oh shit!" It felt way colder doing it like that.

Sam pulled the door open suddenly. "Are you okay?"

Straightening up quickly, I flung my hair back from my face and tried to reach for something to cover myself with. He walked towards me and pulled the towel from the shelf then wrapped it around my waist, leaving my chest bare. My body was shaking uncontrollably, and I felt my teeth chattering involuntarily, but the way he looked at me made me shiver for different reasons.

"Sam, I need to get dressed," I whispered.

His warm hand glided slowly up my stomach to just below my breast. "Does this hurt?"

As soon as he asked, I sucked in a breath and held it. Closing my eyes, I nodded as I tried to step back from him. I couldn't move; he still had hold of the towel.

"Breathe, Sara," he stated. Slowly, I released the air and felt the towel close around my shoulders. "When you're done, don't put a top on yet. We need to bind your ribs. I think you bruised one or two."

I opened my eyes and watched Sam walk out the door. I tried to think of when I would have hit my side that hard, and the only thing that came to mind was when I fell out the door at the radio station. *I am a walking accident.* I heard Sam go up the stairs and out the door. *Why is he mad? It's not his body that's battered and bruised. I don't understand men.*

After dressing as quickly as I could in a t-shirt and shorts, I returned to bed. I sat down, placed my elbows on my knees, then rested my face in my hands, sighing loudly. *Everything is messed* up. I ignored the steady ache radiating from my body. Chuckling to myself, I thought of all the times Kyle told me I was fat. Shouldn't some of it have protected me? Unfortunately, that was not the case. More fluff just meant more to bruise.

The decision to wrap my knee was pressing in my mind. I got up, grabbed what I needed, and sat back down. With mechanical precision, I wrapped my knee, ribs, and elbow. I'd never admit how the pain in my side decreased slightly from the binding, because that would mean Sam was right in how bad I really was.

I hated feeling weak, as if I couldn't make decisions for myself. I'd had too many years with Kyle constantly making me feel less than human. I was confused and still feeling very lost. I wanted to go back to life before this, perhaps not Kyle.

I didn't think I was in love with him anymore. I still loved him; he was the father of my kids, but I wasn't in love. I stayed lost in the fantasy of my erotic novels when it was he and I because my life had been missing something for many years. Desire, drive, and want were things I needed to discover and pull myself out of this disrespectful state in which I had been floating through life.

Finally, I downed four Advil and a full bottle of Gatorade.

Allowing my body to fall back onto the bed, I was going to close my eyes for a few minutes. Once they were shut, the image invading my mind was Adam. Who was he? Why did I have this unnatural drive to follow him anywhere? What was it about him that pulled at me with such fierce need? Why did I give him the only thing I had left of my dad? The question I had asked echoed in my mind, *'Are you an Angel?'* His deep baritone laugh caressed my every memory, as if I still had my hand on his chest as he chuckled.

I looked at my hand in my dream, and when I glanced back up, I was sitting at a table in a darkened restaurant. Music played softly in the background. None of the other places were occupied. The colors in the venue were mute. Nothing stood out, and it was odd to see everything and blandness at the same time.

"Would you like desert first?" the sensual voice asked.

I looked across the table into Adam's beautiful face.

"I find I would rather have my desert first," he stated matter of fact.

I couldn't speak. Instead, I nodded and glanced down at the table. It had a deep purple cloth. The only reason I knew it to be purple and not black was because of the glass center piece. It was cracked but crystal clear. The single tea light cast a large luminescent ring that extended out.

"Is cheesecake still your favorite?"

I looked back across the table at Adam, but it wasn't Adam sitting with me. It was Sam. *What the hell?*

"Yes," I whispered, while I looked around to see where Adam went.

"I ordered it just like you used to eat it. I hope it's still the same," Sam quietly reflected.

I was still lost in thought when the waiter cleared his throat. I moved my arms, scooting back into my chair and sitting a bit straighter. I smiled up at the waiter, but he was already turning to leave.

"Thank you," I quietly breathed.

The waiter had brought me New York cheesecake, with cherries on the side and a dark chocolate sauce in another dish.

"This is the only way to eat cheesecake," I mused.

I watched his hands as they went to work, placing cherries onto my serving first and then drizzling dark chocolate over the entire slice. I gazed up to smile at Sam and found myself looking at Adam. This was way too weird.

"This is exactly how I eat it." I smiled as I took a large bite, closing my eyes to savor the explosion of flavors on my tongue. I moaned softly; the taste was absolute heaven.

"There are a lot of things about you I never forgot."

I opened my eyes and smiled at Sam once again. The whiplash from this dream was making me queasy. I didn't engage Sam and instead continued to enjoy my dessert. Between bites, my dinner partner changed four more times. It was funny not knowing who I was going to see each time I looked away or closed my eyes.

The conversation was light, then Sam excused himself before leaving the table.

"I ordered us both steaks, I hope you're alright with that?" Adam asked as he came back into view and sat down with me. "Sara, can I ask you something personal?"

"Sure, anything, Adam," I reassured him.

"Have you ever replayed something in your mind and wished you would have taken advantage of a missed opportunity?" His face fell, and he looked at the table shamefully.

I thought about what he was asking and wanted to say yes, but that was not what came out of my mouth.

"There will always be times in our lives when we wish we could have a do-over, but if we did, what kind of a person would we be? We learn from the things we do wrong and the things we wish we would have done but didn't. We can only hope to correct the mistake or missed opportunities the next time and then cherish the knowledge gained from it."

He continued to look at the table, and I suddenly felt uneasy about my answer.

"That's probably not what you wanted to hear," I whispered.

When he quickly looked at me, I wished the light was brighter in this place, because I still couldn't see what color his eyes were.

"It was honest and from the heart. It's exactly what I asked for."

A mouthwatering aroma tickled my nose. The steak smelled as if it had been grilled. I turned, anxiously trying to find the waiter. I felt my mouth salivate with anticipation. The smell was so strong it seemed real, not like a figment at all.

As I started to awaken, I touched my lip. When I quickly wiped at my mouth, I heard a faint chuckle. I was drooling in my sleep. I never do that.

"You're lucky I don't have my phone on me, because it would have had your face as my wallpaper," Sam chuckled.

"I don't normally drool in my sleep, but I smelled something wonderful in my dream." I yawned.

I sat up and looked over in the direction of Sam's voice. He was huddled near a small charcoal grill.

"Is that steak?" I asked skeptically.

"Yes, this weather is working in my favor. The meat store is still standing, and the cold is keeping the meat in the big freezer from spoiling."

We ate in companionable silence. It was the best piece of meat I could remember eating. Once we were finished, I finally said what was weighing on my mind.

"Sam, I think you need to head to your wife's house and check on your daughter," I calmly said.

He cleared his throat before replying. "She's my ex, and I already checked her house. The next place to check is her sister's. It's where we are going today."

"Is it far?"

"A few towns over, roughly a forty-five-minute drive. We will drive as far as we can and then walk. Get your stuff ready," he finished before standing.

"I'm just going to slow you down, so you should probably leave me here," I confessed.

"No."

He didn't elaborate. He took the trash from the food and made his way toward the stairs.

Well, crap. I guess I don't have a choice. Who am I kidding?

I'm glad he's still including me.

I couldn't help but smile as I dressed in warmer clothes. He would find his family today, and then I would return to the house with the people from the hospital. Together we would figure out where to go, and for once I was going to try and be helpful and a better person.

Chapter 9

It didn't take long to organize what I needed. A few bottles of water, some protein bars, and a bottle of Gatorade. I quickly downed more Aleve before meeting Sam on the stairs.

"All set?"

I nodded, suddenly overwhelmed by the task before us. We walked over and got into the SUV in silence. Way too many questions were running through my mind that I didn't want to think about the answers to. *What if we don't locate her? What if we do find her and she is fine? Will I be able to handle Sam having his child alive while mine aren't? Can I keep it together if we find her already gone?*

I glanced over at Sam. His profile was the epitome of strength and determination. The silence was threatening to suffocate me, pulling every breath out without the chance to fully draw in another.

Looking down at the middle console, I found an anchor to redirect my thinking. I cleared my throat and tried to force the words out of my mouth. "You're still charging your phone?"

He was utterly focused on the road ahead; I wasn't surprised when he didn't answer.

I returned to my vigil of watching the destruction pass the window in a slow, steady motion. There was a slight movement in some of the mounds; you could see a tail of a dog or coyote. I saw a few cats sitting on top of cars, watching the world move around them. The snow covered most of the ruins, but occasionally you could make out a body. A few houses were left untouched from the front, and I hoped the people in them survived. Eventually, the road opened up, and there was nothing for miles, no debris, cars, or people.

"I do just in case we come into a place that might have service, but what's plugged in now is your iPod. I found it in your jean pocket and, uhm...I don't know, I thought you would like to listen to your music. The license you had is in there too."

I looked over once again. *My iPod? I don't have an...Oh, wait. He must mean Kevin's. I forgot I put it in my pocket.* Things kept stacking up, and I was beginning to think my mind was fracturing. I opened my mouth to tell him whose it was and why I had it, but he interrupted.

"Why did that guy call you Alegena or Annia? Who is Airiss, and what did you do to make him proud?"

There wasn't any sarcasm or malevolence in his tone.

I was trying to think of how much to say when Sam's whispered words hit my ears. "What did he experience that night that he was never going to forget?" He exhaled before speaking a bit louder. "Don't lie to me, please. I deserve that much from you."

Omission wasn't lying; at least that's what I told myself before I spoke.

"Uhm, his name is Adam. He found me in the field about a mile from the house last night after I ran from the basement."

"What the hell, Sara."

"Please don't talk. You wanted to know what he meant, and I'll tell you. Just don't ...don't judge...don't overthink it... don't worry. You asked about it, and I will tell you my experience, but you don't get to diminish it in any way." I sighed, proud of myself for setting a boundary.

"He found me in the field. I thought it was you when I heard him, so I didn't try to hide. I hadn't seen anyone out in this area since everything started. Yeah, I saw bodies and said goodbye to people on the verge of death, but you were the only other living, breathing person in this area. I mean, really, who can fear the unknown when it seems the world's gone? When I finally decided to confront you, I was frozen to the ground by emotions too raw to describe. I'd been screaming. I screamed for so long and so loud, I wasn't thinking about anything but death. My death was what I thought he was bringing me. He had to be the angel of death. Confident, beautiful, and full of something I still can't describe. Briefly, we talked about pain, sorrow, distress, and grief. This is what he experienced last night with me—raw, passionate, uninhibited pain."

Turning away from him, I looked up towards the clouded sky.

"I left him standing in the field. I ran away from him, just like I do everyone else. I sat beneath the tree hoping when I fell asleep I wouldn't wake up. I didn't want to wake up. Every second since the storms hit has caused another tear, gouge, or rip in my heart. The school kids, my kids, the neighbors, Derek, Kevin at the radio station, Kyle, Adam, you all have had some impact on me. I lost myself long ago, tried to change to fit into a world I wasn't wanted in, and in the process, I disintegrated. I don't know who I'm supposed to be. I'm no longer a mother, wife, daughter, sister, or neighbor, so what am I? I've spent so much time fading into the background. Hiding from everyone until the day came when no one even remembered my name, protecting myself so I couldn't hurt anyone else or be broken anymore. The one man who vowed to love me lied. Instead, he continued to rip at my soul until I didn't recognize the person in the mirror. So, yes, I sat down under that tree and prayed for death to take me. What I found was darkness and my daughter saving my life. She was the reason I woke up when I did."

I gently wiped the tears from my eyes, still not looking at him.

"He called me a daughter of Eris. Eris was the Greek Goddess of strife. If I remember correctly, she had three daughters called the Algea, meaning the personification of sorrow and grief. Ania is sorrow; her sisters are pain and distress. Marcus was the name of the guy who was trying to take me. Adam was the other man. He stopped Marcus from kidnapping me. Before you ask, I don't know for sure, but I think Marcus was the same one Kevin tried to warn us all about on the radio.

"Next, you showed up and helped me get free. I could feel your aggression. It permeated the air around us so profusely it made me feel guilty. You know the rest."

I secured my hands under my legs so Sam wouldn't notice them shake. I don't know what bothered me more, the thought of him seeing me raw and emotionally bare or the silence that had once again taken hold of the air.

The scenery passed until there was nothing I recognized. I didn't know where we were or how much farther we needed to go. The interstate was slowly becoming more littered with debris; however, so far it wasn't anything we couldn't maneuver around.

When I couldn't stand the silence anymore, I decided to try and get answers to things from long ago.

"Were you really at my wedding?" I softly asked.

"Yes."

I waited for more information, but he didn't say anything else.

"Why didn't I see you?"

"I was refused entry into the church. They wouldn't let me come in with my parents, Kyle stopped me. I snuck in after the ceremony started. I got to see you just before you walked down the aisle with your dad."

There was no emotion in his voice, just stating facts.

"Oh. I didn't know."

Great...This makes the silence much better, I thought sarcastically. *Wait, he tried to sneak into my wedding?* I didn't know if it was the stress, the pain, or the lack of a good night's sleep, but the thought of him trying to sneak into my wedding made me giggle. Before I could get myself under control, I was laughing hysterically.

Between laughs, I breathlessly tried to say, "You...all 6 feet and 6 inches tried...my wedding...No wonder...caught you... You were...practically...a sign."

Sam laughed in the middle of my sentence.

"Yeah, I guess it wasn't the brightest idea, but I needed to see you."

This stopped my laughing.

"Why? Why then after almost a year and a half of no contact? What was so important that it had to be said on the day I was getting married and not before?"

I was back to looking at his profile, waiting for answers.

He ran his hand across his mouth and jaw. "You know why."

"Obviously I don't, or I wouldn't be asking," I replied sweetly, but I think it came out sounding childish.

"I had to tell you...that I loved you and wanted you to pick me. I wanted you to choose me over Kyle. I don't know, I think I wanted you to run away with me. To hurt Kyle the way he hurt me. I wanted—no, I *needed* to rip his heart from his chest and claim it as mine. I should have been the one to have you— body, mind and soul," he scoffed.

I laughed in my throat, but a dark, hateful chuckle resonated from me.

"You had all of me and chose not to do anything about it."

A look of shock ran across his face, followed by confusion.

"What, Sam? No witty remark regarding that one? Let me break it down for you."

I turned to face him as I finally told him what I wanted to say all those years ago.

"By our sophomore year, you had my heart. We spent all of our time together, and I felt like you understood me. We were as close as two people could be. There was nothing going on in my life you didn't know about. You encompassed all of my thoughts; you had my mind.

"When we started our junior year, I thought you felt the same way I did, but I was too nervous to try anything. Next thing I remember you had a girlfriend. Not just someone you went to the movies with a couple of times but a real one, Becky Minerson. The girl you gave yourself to, the one who took you away. She broke your heart. I'll never forget the look in your eyes when you found out she was cheating on you. I held you and we talked for hours about everything. You captured my soul that night.

"It didn't take you long to move on to Brittany. It wouldn't last. Neither did Marsha, Carol, Mia, Lynn, Tia, or Chloe. The whole time I thought, 'After this girl, he will see me as a female and not just his friend.' I had to watch as you kissed, hugged, and doted on each and every one of those girls. Hand holding, make out sessions in the halls, and numerous lonely walks home because these girls were jealous of our friendship. How do you think that made me feel? I ached every time one of your girlfriends broke your heart. Yet, I didn't really matter—I was in the background for all of it. Then it finally happened late one night senior year. I saw you look at me like you did all the other girlfriends, as if something had changed and I was the one you wanted. I melted when our lips touched, and my body felt like it belonged in your arms.

"The kiss ended too quickly, and before my eyes opened, you turned your back on me and practically ran away. The pain of being rejected by you..." I shook off the thought before continuing. "After that I realized it was childish to think we would be together. Then Kyle showed up and asked me out. I never imagined one date would turn into anything more. When he kissed me goodnight, he looked at me and did it again. He wanted me and it felt glorious. In the back of my mind, I still thought you would be the one I gave my virginity to. I waited for you until I couldn't wait any longer, and then I gave myself to Kyle.

"Don't you see, Sam? You had all of me and did nothing about it. I told you I loved you so many times I lost count. Every time I said it you would place both of your hands over your heart and say, 'Aw, right back at ya.' Never once did you say it, but I convinced myself you loved me too. Oh, the foolish hopes of a teenage girl.

"In one fast swoop I was engaged and losing my best friend at the same time. The best way for me to describe it was you died the day I told you about the engagement. You died because I never talked to you after that day, I never saw you, and as I waited for you after graduation, a piece of my heart ripped. When I went to your house and your mom told me you left town, the part of my heart that belonged to you turned black and died. I spent more hours crying for you than I want to admit. I went by your mom's twice, sometimes four times a month for updates. She never told me anything other than you were fine and would be home soon. Eventually, I stopped checking in. Over time you became a faded memory of a love who never loved me back. I rationalized it as you being the nice guy who had to deal with an overly-obsessed teenage crush."

I sighed and moved so I was sitting properly in the seat, then I let my head drop back onto the rest. I felt drained. I could hardly move. A deep, dry laugh escaped through a distraught face.

"At one point I pictured telling you all of that in an angry voice with my hands gesturing wildly, throwing you all the compassion and pain I felt at the time. It's funny to see I can say it to you now so calmly, but the pain is just as fresh as if it happened yesterday. Oh well, we can't change any of the past, so I guess it really doesn't matter. Not any of it—not the what-ifs or the whys, they're all moot."

I rubbed my face hard, trying to erase the images dancing behind my eyes. I wasn't going to break down, not now. Not when there was something more important to be done. After I left Sam with his daughter alive and unharmed, then I would finally let go of it all.

I sat back up and glanced around. Sam pulled over and stopped. Were we even on the road anymore? When did things get so bad again? In front of us sat a shed in the street like it had been deliberately left there.

"We have to walk from here. I can't get through on the main path and the field is too littered to chance it. We still have a way to go," Sam stated before getting out.

He moved so fast I didn't register what he said until he was pulling my door open. It was sweet of him to do that for me, or at least I thought that was what he was doing. He waited for me to get out then reached in and opened the glovebox to pull something out. I didn't wait to see what he was doing. I got my bag out of the back seat, shivering as I pulled it on. It was still chilly but not as cold as it had been.

I ducked behind the door to conceal the painful expression marring my face while I stretched my knee out, and then my side. I wasn't going to let him see me in pain. If I worked out the stiffness, I would be fine. I closed the door just as Sam was checking the mechanism of a gun. He slid it into a holster and then tucked it in the front of his jeans before fixing his shirt. He opened an old-style map, glanced at it a few times, and then folded it up to stash into his coat pocket.

What the heck is going on? Why does he have a gun? Where on earth did he find it? Does he know how to use it?

I patted the side pocket of my bag to reassure myself the Swiss army knife was there. I had a larger hunting one in the bag, but the little one was sharper and easier to grab. It calmed me a bit.

When I opened my eye, Sam was standing in the same spot, patiently waiting for me to get into gear. I walked toward him, but he started heading out before I caught up to him. I let out an exasperated sigh, not looking forward to the long walk ahead with more awkward silence. The cold wind blew, and the ground crunched under every step. The chill eventually permeated my clothing, but the numbing effect was glorious for my aches.

"A little farther," was all Sam said over an hour later.

"Where did you get a gun?"

"My dad gave it to me."

"Oh, okay. Why?" I rushed to catch up to him so I could walk next to him.

Without acknowledging I was beside him, he said, "It's a Colt 1911a1 made in 1943. It was my grandpa's. It's the one the military issued him in WWII. He died before I was old enough to ask questions about it. My grandma is the one who gave it to my dad with the understanding that I would get it on my twenty-first birthday. When Dad gave it to me, I went to see Grandma about it. She told me Grandpa had been riddled with guilt over everything he did in the war. The only reason he could bear to live with it was because deep down he knew what he did had to be done. He told her he kept the gun as a reminder of how easy a life could be taken away and how after they're gone, you're left paying for your actions. He told her he was reminded every night when he closed his eyes of all the lives he cut short in the name of freedom. The gun was an anchor to remind him of why."

We continued on once again in silence. Talking had become a burden. If we talked any more it would lead to more emotion—emotion to worry, worry to panic, and panic to irrational behavior. The less we said, the easier it was to appear strong.

Sam stopped to re-check the map. He unfolded the papers and tried to hold it still in the constant flow of wind. He didn't say anything while he studied the paper. He folded the map back up, put it away and pointed. "On the other side of that hill is Ellen's sister's house."

I nodded; glad we were close. I was starting to ache but wouldn't tell him. While we made our way to the top of the hill, a familiar odor tickled my nose. It was one that before the disaster I had never experienced, but since then I'd smelled it more than I ever cared to. It was the stench of rotting flesh. Immediately, we understood someone was dead on the top of this hill. One would think with the cold weather a body wouldn't decompose, but it still does, and it smells. I didn't want to think about how rank the odor would be if it was warmer. I walked a bit faster, trying to catch up with Sam. I didn't want him to be alone when he reached the top. The closer we got, the worse the smell became; it was physically taking my breath away. I stopped pulling in air through my nose and used my mouth instead, but the air was so tainted I could taste the death. Choking back the urge to vomit, we finally reached the top of the hill, and it was far more devastating than I had imagined.

About four-hundred yards away was the start of a driveway lined with rows of massive oaks. The trees drew my attention—not because of the immense size of them, but because there seemed to be something inside of them. Beyond the trees was what was left of Katy's home. It had been a two-story house, but the second story was completely leveled. The windows had been replaced with boards covering about half of the gaping holes.

Sam started down the hillside. "Wait up, Sam. I'll walk with you," I urged, but his pace didn't slow. When he got to the driveway his legs gave out, dropping him to his knees.

"Sam, are you okay?" I yelled then tried to get down the hill a bit faster.

I jogged over to him, but before I could reach him, my eyes played a horrible trick on me. After rubbing my eyes, I gave myself a second to refocus.

I took the last few steps to Sam.

"Sam, they can't be real," I uttered, placing my hand on his shoulder.

They can't be real...It's a joke, has to be. This monologue repeated through my mind.

"Don't be stupid, Sara. Of course they're real, and there are hundreds of them," he spat without lifting his head.

Real. The word echoed through my brain like a bad song. We had come here for a reason, and I wasn't going to give up until I had the answer I knew Sam needed.

I pulled my hand from his shoulder and walked around him. I was going to see if there were any children here.

The display before me was something I never would have imagined possible. I approached the first tree and gazed at the lifeless bodies hanging from the limbs. They hadn't been thrown into the trees by the tornadoes; they had been placed there. They were hanging from wires and hooks attached to their bodies and had been dead for some time. The bodies were bloated, flesh was hanging off in places, and you could see many had duct tape around the joints, my guess would be to keep them together. They reminded me of old marionette puppets. Every person seemed to be positioned. Many looked like they were flying, and others were seated on the branches. Every male had a female companion; luckily, there weren't any children. Each tree had this type of display. The closer I got to the house, the more people I could see. There were picnic tables full, over two dozen tables I would guess, and multiple lawn chairs, more than I could count—all with bodies occupying them.

"Hello, visitor, how are you? What brings you to our home? Okay, friends, say hello!" I heard from across the lawn. Jumping, I quickly turned to see a man walking toward me. He was tall, thin, and covered in filth. I could smell him before he came next to me. Unwashed skin, body odor, a tinge of some kind of alcohol, and of course the smell of rotten flesh were clinging to the clothes he wore. The fact that I could pick out his stench over the decomposing bodies shows how rank he truly was. He had a big, bright smile on his face.

"Quiet down, everyone. I will find out who this is. She will meet each and every one of you, be patient," he stated then waved his arms around as if to calm a large crowd.

Without moving my head, just my eyes, I looked to see if I had missed someone.

"My name is Chris. And you are?" he questioned with a smile and a hand extended.

I looked at his blackened fingers and hugged myself instead of shaking his hand.

"Uhm, I'm Sara. Who are you talking to?" If Sam's family wasn't here, I wasn't about to stick around any longer that I had to.

"My friends, of course. They have all come to me in a different way, but they each have their own place in this home." He smiled and pointed to the dead filling the yard.

I placed my hand to my mouth and pulled my thoughts together so I could ask the hardest question. "Are there any children here?"

"Oh, of course there are! The mothers have them in the backyard. The kids just love all the swing sets and sandboxes I have found," he answered without a second thought.

"So, they're around back?" I stated as I started heading toward the corner.

"Yep, just around there." He pointed to the side of the house.

Quickly, I walked backwards around the side—no way was I giving him my back.

Before I got clear of him, he turned from me and said, "She's off to see the moms and the kids. They're going to enjoy that. She seems very nice, you know."

Devastation affects everyone differently, but that man is screwed up. I hoped the children were alive, or at least there weren't as many of them as there were adults.

When I cleared the side of the house, my knees buckled under me. I quickly found myself face down on the grass, holding back tears.

One, two, three...No, it can't be...Seven, eight, nine. Nine

wooden swing sets full of children. I wiped my eyes and counted again—still nine, and at least a dozen small sand boxes with
kids everywhere. For every three children there was an adult
female. *These must be the moms he spoke of. What kind of
sick, sadistic fuck are we dealing with?* A dozen kids per swing
set plus six more per sandbox. I had to look for Samantha
before Sam saw this hell.

I ran around past the front of the house and met Sam in
the middle of the drive. Chris was hot on my heels, following
me like a lost puppy.

"Stay here and let me have a picture of Samantha, let me
look for her. Please don't go any farther," I cried.

"She is my daughter; I have the right to look for her," he
growled.

"I don't doubt that for an instant, but I'm trying to save
you from the nightmare lurking behind this house. If you have
no reason to see it, you shouldn't. Isn't this what you told
me at one time? Once you see it, you can't un-see it, and if
your daughter isn't there, I don't want you to think the worst.
Please, please let me look first. If she is here, I will come get
you, but please let me help you!"

"I should be the one to find her," he stated forcefully and
walked toward the house.

"Please, after everything you've done for me and my children, at least let me help you look for her. What's around the
back of this house is horrific, and I want to get as far from here
as soon as possible."

"Fine," he stated as he reluctantly pulled the picture from
his wallet.

I glanced at the picture and reached for it; he pulled the
picture farther away, letting me know he wasn't going to let
me hold it.

"They are very pretty girls. She is on the slide, and her
mom is sitting next to the first sandbox," Chris chimed in
calmly as he glanced over Sam's shoulder.

"They're here, I knew it...Samantha?!" Sam exclaimed then sprinted away.

"Sam, no—don't!" I screamed as I tried to keep up with him.

I knew all too well what it felt like to lose a child; however, the thought of some maniac killing all those kids and then posing them like trophies sickened me.

"They're very sweet girls you have, very polite!" Chris yelled as we ran.

What the hell is he talking about? These people are dead.

Sam was already around the back of the house before I could get to the side.

"No, Samantha, no, no—not my little girl...Sammy, no, nooo!" Sam bellowed through tear-rimmed eyes.

I was too late. I couldn't save him from the last image of his little girl. This vision would be seared into his memory, forever haunting him.

Having finally made my way around to the back of the house, I watched as Sam knelt down at the feet of his daughter's body. She was propped up as if she was just getting to the bottom of the slide. She wore a pink Hello Kitty shirt, jeans, and sparkling purple shoes. There was dirt on her face, clothes, and arms. Dried blood was under her nose, a large dark spot on the side of her shirt and jeans at her waist. Her eyes were closed, her hair made up in wild pigtails, and her skin was a pale bluish-purple.

"I see you found her," Chris said with a huge smile.

Sam was sitting at her feet with his head resting on her thigh, shattered. This strong, beautiful man had crumbled at the sight of his daughter. I watched the pain play across his face.

With every second he broke further until I finally could see not sadness and understanding, only anger. I looked at Chris standing off to the side with his arms crossed at his chest as his face wavered through the tears forming in my eyes. Before the tears fell, Chris' dirty face turned into Kyle's.

I turned towards him, making sure I was in his line of sight. "What kind of stupid, sadistic, perverted asshole are you? How could you kill all these children, all of those people out front?" I demanded through gritted teeth.

He looked at me with absolute shock and stuttered, "Kill, kill...me, you, you, you...think I kill, killed all these wonderfully friendly people?"

"Yes," I hissed impatiently. I dropped my bag to the ground but held firmly to the knife.

He took a step back as if I slapped him. "No, I didn't kill anyone, I rescued them. I found each and every one of these people. I brought them here to be part of our family."

"They're all dead, that's disgusting," I spat.

"Just because your mind's eye is blind doesn't mean mine is," he stated matter-of-factly.

My confusion must have shown on my face.

"I know you see death, but I see rebirth and life. Just because the body doesn't move anymore doesn't mean they are no longer in there. I see past the inactiveness of their bodies and see the people. I missed being around people."

I could barely get the words out. "What the hell are you talking about?"

"My old home had many people living in it until the big wind took out some of the stone. I tried to be good and wait, but I got lonely, so I started to walk until I found this place."

Wonderful, yet another prisoner. This nightmare just keeps getting worse.

"Where exactly was home?" I pressed.

"Cerritus was my home."

Cerritus, that explains a lot. The most secure asylum for the criminally insane.

I never saw Sam move, but he was standing in front of Chris with the gun pointing at his forehead.

"Where did you find his little girl?" I questioned quickly,

trying to get the answers I needed before Sam killed him.

"She was in the field beside the house and her mom was in the tree all the way in the back," he stated while looking in the direction he had found them.

"How did you know they were mother and daughter?" Sam growled.

"There's a picture of them together in the house." Chris shrugged. "They look alike. If they weren't mother and daughter, then they were sisters," he whispered.

I took another step towards Sam cautiously to not startle either of them.

"Chris, how did you become a resident of Cerritus?" I asked as I heard Sam growl the word psycho.

"I protected my family," Chris proudly stated, puffing his chest out.

I shot Sam a look of bewilderment.

"How exactly did you protect your family?" Sam sneered.

"It doesn't matter how I did it, only that I did it. I protected them like I'm protecting all of these people, my new family." Chris motioned his hand around again to encompass his collection.

Bodies, you idiot. They are the shells of people, nothing more than rotting flesh and bone. Psycho doesn't even cover this moron.

I placed my hand on Sam's shoulder. "We should take care of your little girl. This is not how she should be."

I spoke so low I was afraid he didn't hear me. I wouldn't let my emotions take over. He needed me to be the strong one just like he had been for me. I wouldn't let him down. We would get through this together.

Sam lowered the gun. I quickly looked back at Chris to see the relief on his face a second before Sam's fist connected with his jaw. He hit the ground hard, knocked completely out.

When I turned my attention back to Sam, he was kneeling in front of his daughter. Head down, shoulders moving slightly, he needed a minute alone to grieve.

I looked around the yard for anything we could use to re-move her and perhaps a shovel to bury her with. Having no luck, I made my way back over to Sam. He was unsuccessfully trying to pull the boards free that attached Samantha to the slide. I bent down beside him, placing my hand on his arm.

"Sam, let me help you. It's been many years since I worked with tools, but I used to help Dad all the time. I'm sure it will come back to me," I pressed.

"Leave me alone, Sara," he painfully moaned.

"No, I'm not going to leave you. I'm here to help. What do you need me to do?"

"Damn it, Sara! Kyle was so right about you. You're dense and utterly worthless. Leave!" he shouted into my face.

"This isn't you; you're upset about the situation. I know you don't mean what you're saying. It's okay, I understand." I rushed to confirm, placing my hand to his cheek.

"I mean exactly what I'm saying! Kyle was right. Here you are on your knees begging me like a whore pleading with her pimp to give her one more chance to make it right. Should I whip my dick out and let you show me exactly how helpful you can be?" he spat as he shoved my hand from his face.

I didn't consciously mean to do it, but my eyes shifted to his pants. I quickly brought them back up, but it was too late. The look on Sam's face said it all: a mix of burning need and malevolence.

He gave a forced evil laugh. "If you want it that bad, baby, I'll gladly let you suck my dick when I'm done with this."

My face burned with embarrassment. "I..."

"Just go away, Sara. I've carried you this whole time, and I'm sick of it. I'm tired of worrying about your fragile mind. Take your 'woe is me' self to someone who cares because I'm done. Get the hell away from me," he hissed.

There was nothing I could say to him. Dumbfounded and utterly shocked, I walked around the structure. I must have been a glutton for punishment, because instead of moving away, I went into the house hoping to wait him out.

I watched from a broken window as Sam removed his daughter from the slide before working to free his ex-wife.

When Chris regained awareness, he was wise enough to stay on the ground and quietly observe. With Sam digging the graves for his family, I took a moment to look around the small room. There was a breakfast nook, slightly off from the kitchen.

An array of photos was scattered on the table, including the one Chris mentioned of Samantha and her mom. Tucked under the pictures was a worn-out book. Opening, it I expected to see more images of Ellen and her family, but instead it was a newspaper article with the headline 'Local man and his demon obsession.' A few minutes into scanning the article, I understood how Chris protected his family. He believed demons were actively trying to possess them. He murdered each and every one of them to save their souls before trying to end himself. He was the only one to survive. He killed his three kids with an overdose of a prescription narcotic and then strangled his wife with his bare hands. He told the judge it was the only way; he had to send them to God, so the devil didn't win. Sighing, I said a silent prayer for his family.

Turning my attention back to the window, Sam was tapping down the last of the dirt on his family's graves. He strode over to the garage, disappearing into the half structure and coming out with a gas can. With a determined tilt to his face, he poured gasoline on all the kids. Chris jumped to his feet and let out an inhuman scream, but Sam ignored him, making sure all the children were coated before chucking the empty can aside. He had his lighter out before Chris could get close enough to him.

With the bodies going up in flames, Chris continued to curse Sam. "You bastard, they were my friends! I brought them here; I promised them peace. You're a monster. I'm going to kill you and the girl, and then I'll start collecting again.

I'll find more friends."

Sam casually walked up to Chris, gracefully pulled the gun from its holder, took aim, and within a blink fired directly into Chris' skull.

I thought I should scream, but my body froze while my ears rang.

Sam raised the gun, moving to place the barrel under his chin, and my stillness disappeared.

As I ran through a large hole off the kitchen, I prayed I'd make it in time, screaming as loud as I could, "No!" I ran up to Sam and threw myself against his chest, frantically crying, "You can't do this—don't, Sam, please don't do this!"

I looked up into a set of eyes lost with despair. It stole my breath and physically pained my heart.

I whispered as the tears pooled in my eyes, "Sam, no."

I moved his arm down from his chin, the strain in his muscles not wanting to yield. Leaning up, I placed a soft chaste kiss on his lips. I held my lips there, not really kissing—just keeping a connection and praying he'd understand my unspoken request.

He placed his hand on my shoulder and gently pushed my body back, but he let his forehead rest against mine. I knew in that moment I'd lost him.

"I have always loved you, and I always will," I whispered before turning from him and running to the front of the house. I wasn't going to watch him or try to convince him life would be okay. I guess it was because I didn't think it would be okay. I couldn't make him understand what I didn't comprehend myself. He didn't see me, so lost in his anger, but even if he did, I had no clue what he would have seen because I didn't know who I was anymore. Perhaps it was better this way. A huge part of me wanted to go back and ask him to kill me first, but a small amount of self-preservation kept me moving away. I grabbed my bag from the porch then continued to run down the drive. When I crested the top of the hill and heard the shot, my knees buckled, sending me rolling down the opposite side of it.

Just when I thought there was nothing left of my heart to break, I learned that even a broken heart will continue to break, and it hurts more with every new gouge. I couldn't breathe from the pain encompassing my chest. Everything flooded my heart again as if the thin scab trying to heal it was violently ripped away.

"Damn it!" I screamed into the air as I tried not to hyperventilate.

I sat with my face buried in my hands, crying until my eyes burned and my throat was sore. It was all my fault; I should have never let him help me. I was numb; I didn't ache anymore because I couldn't feel anything. The sun was almost set, and I needed to get somewhere for the night. I decided to walk away from the setting sun. *Perhaps I can find my way back home.*

I walked until my knee hurt too bad to take another step. After trying several different cars along the stretch of highway, I finally came up to one that was unlocked. I crawled into the back seat, grabbing more Advil and downing them with an Aleve chaser for the pain and swelling.

What am I going to do? After making sure the doors were locked, I lay down on my side and curled myself into a ball to conserve heat, wondering if I would survive the cold night. Debating as to whether I wanted to. Why did everything have to be so messed up? I wanted to let the hateful things Sam said replay in my mind. That was how I was trained, to think about what I did wrong.

That was how it had been for years, but this time I didn't. He was angry and said untrue things to hurt me. For the first time in years, I didn't dwell on the negative or how it was my fault. I just closed my eyes and let my mind stay blank.

CHAPTER 8

Mental exhaustion gave way to oblivion and then to deep sleep. I had no idea I was shivering until I felt a warming sensation flood my body, something wrapped around me. I snuggled into the heat, taking in every ounce of the freely given warmness. Finally cozy, I drifted back under the spell of sleep.

A slight jarring sensation forced me to wake quickly in a hazy flash. Opening my eyes to darkness and feeling the vehicle's subtle movement beneath me scared the cloud out of my sleep-drugged brain. I shot up before I could think through the multiple implications.

"Adam?" I croaked out as I stared in shock at the driver.

He looked up into the rearview mirror, making an attempt to see me as he said, "Lay back down, Sara. We're almost to the place I call home. You'll be warm and safe there."

Too exhausted to argue and in too much pain to care, I laid back down and drifted away to the rocking motion of the car, picturing I was sitting on my grandma's old porch swing in the summer.

The next movement was one I recognized without having to open my eyes. Adam was carrying me closely, protected in his arms. At this second, I wouldn't have cared if he was bringing me to my death. *The people around me always got hurt. I should enlighten Adam, give him the chance to run before he ends up dead as well.*

"I can walk," I whispered, letting Adam know I was awake, but I didn't open my eyes and curled farther into his neck.

He let out a chuckle as I placed my nose on his skin and took a deep breath. He smelled phenomenal, clean like newly-washed laundry and fresh rain. I'd never encountered the combination anywhere else before, but I liked it tremendously.

He didn't attempt to put me down once we made it into the house. He continued to hold me as he carried me down a hall, then onto several flights of stairs. It seemed like he was carrying me down into a dungeon, and I glanced around. The stairwell looked like the stairs in buildings, with a little light shining close to the floor. After taking the last few steps he continued down another hall and walked through an open steel door into the largest bedroom I had ever seen. Still comfortably draped in his arms, he went straight to the bed and sat me on the side. I adjusted my clothing and looked up to find him watching me. He knelt down beside the bed in front of my legs and began taking my shoes off. Nothing was said, yet the silence was comfortable. The feelings I had when I first saw Adam hadn't changed or lessened. The air seemed electrically charged, and I was too shocked to say a word.

My husband had never taken my shoes off. This small action made me feel more vulnerable than I had in a while. My stomach dropped, and I couldn't help but seem unsatisfactory in his eyes.

I was the first to break eye contact, hoping he didn't sense the self-doubt plaguing me.

When he finished with my shoes, he slowly ran his hands up the outside of my thighs until he grabbed my hips, then pulled me closer to the edge of the bed. I had to widen my legs to accommodate him still kneeling in front of me. He unzipped my coat and helped me remove it completely. He moved just enough to throw the item in a chair behind him. When he turned back around, I held my breath, not understanding his

183

look of adoration. I was scared but calm, worried, yet I knew I would keep letting him undress me.

Just when I was ready to move away from him, he wrapped his arms around my waist and placed his head against my chest, nestling between my breasts. He held me tightly. Feelings I shouldn't have been having were coursing through me, completely unnerving me. I wanted to push him away. *No, I should shove him off.* But I needed to run my hand through his hair, kiss the top of his head, and wrap myself around him. I could feel the way he made my heart beat, faster than even Sam ever had. I didn't know how long we sat there before I finally wrapped my arms around him, but when I did, he let out a sigh of contentment.

When he released me, I immediately missed his warmth. He placed his hand along my jaw and rubbed his thumb across my bottom lip, causing me to shiver uncontrollably. He licked his lips, and my stomach did a somersault; he was going to kiss me. I needed him to taste me, and when I thought he would he lowered his hand and took a step back, then another. He turned from me, moved over to a different door, and without looking at me walked out.

What the hell is wrong with me? Damn, Kyle was right. Sam said he wanted me but didn't, and now I would have sworn Adam desired me, but he walked away.

I removed my hoodie, throwing it onto the chair with my coat, and followed it with the extra pants I wore. I stretched out on my side before curling into myself. I needed to decide what to do and then leave this place. I couldn't hear any sound until the door Adam went through opened. I didn't look at him, silently hoping he wouldn't say anything to me and would let me wallow in my self-pity.

The bed dipped behind me, and a second later, he picked me up again. His scent flooded me once more when my face rested against his heated flesh. I placed my hand flush with his bare chest and slowly ran it across, feeling the light dusting of hair tickle my palm. I was still hurt, but something pulled me to him. It was a raw feeling, almost a primal need to be with him. It was unnerving to seem like I had no control over my body. With those feelings running rampant within me, it was freeing not to have to second-guess every decision. At this moment, I wanted to be reckless and carefree. I wanted to do what I wanted and not worry about consequences or what else might go wrong. I needed to feel desired and wanted and all the things you think when someone wants you more than they want to take their next breath. Decision made, I was going to explore this burning desire I had for Adam.

We walked into the room he had vacated, and he placed me on the countertop. I heard the water in the shower running and was stunned to see the mirrors around me fogged over. He had a working shower with hot water. I turned to him and finally noticed his hair was wet and he had a towel wrapped around his waist. He was every bit as delectable as I thought upon our first meeting. I slowly took in his features. Strong muscular shoulders extending down into equally robust arms.

His chest was well-defined but not overly buff. His abs were well sculpted. I followed the dusting of dark hair running down his abdomen that disappeared below his towel with a curiosity and yearning to see more.

I glanced back up to his face and got my first real look at the most entrancing set of silver eyes I had ever seen. *How did I miss it in the other room?* The lighting in here was better, and some of the fog encasing my brain had started to clear.

My mind was going a thousand miles a second. I reached out to Adam, and he immediately took my hand. Still keeping my focus on his eyes, I pulled him towards me. Once he was between my knees and as close as the counter would allow, I took his face in my hands and pulled him close. I was in absolute awe with the color of his eyes. They were gray, but they seemed to be emitting a glow towards his retina.

"They can't be real," I whispered. "Absolutely breathtaking," passed my lips as I continued to examine Adam.

Eyes had fascinated me for as long as I could remember. I think it's because you can't always hide who you are when you look into a person's eyes. It's said they are the window to the soul, and many people laugh at this. Yet if you ever looked someone in the eyes for any length of time, and I mean truly gazed, you would see things others might not.

Under my perusal, Adam's eyes dilated, and lust stared back at me. I unconsciously moistened my lips, and they dilated further. *He is definitely thinking about sex.*

Our lips were almost touching. I could feel his breath caressing my face. I straightened my back, allowing me to press against him. The feel of his soft lips exploring mine sent a euphoric tingle through my entire body.

With more confidence than I had ever had in my life, I pressed into him further, wrapping my hands around his neck and running my fingers through his hair, wanting to taste every inch of him. His hands tightened around my waist and pulled me into his chest. Gently parting my lips, I slipped my tongue out to taste him. The moan he expelled as he opened his mouth to me encouraged me, allowing me to explore the inside of his mouth until I felt his tongue caress mine. Immediately, I was engulfed in an intense burning need.

I remembered the butterflies in my stomach I'd felt when I was aroused and expected it. This wasn't anything like that; his sensual onslaught went directly to my core. This burning need hit straight to my clit, causing it to twitch in anticipation.

My hands roamed his back, raking my nails along his flesh as I went. Hard, defined muscles twitched under my exploration. We kissed until I had to come up for air. My lips tingled with a wonderful sensation. When I opened my eyes to look at Adam, there was an aggressive need in his expression. He was asking permission for what we both knew was going to happen. In the few seconds I looked at his open need for me, every other thought I'd ever had left my mind. I didn't concentrate on anything or anyone.

I couldn't speak, so I gave a slight nod. Without a second to re-think any of it, he grabbed the collar of my shirt and ripped it all the way down the front.

He took in the sight of my bandaged ribs and froze.

"Did that guy you were with do this to you?" he calmly asked.

His hand was almost touching the end of the binding but hovered, unsure of what to do.

"No, I'm an accident on two legs," I chuckled.

His attention went back to my face as he placed his hand on my sore cheek and whispered, "And this?"

I lowered my eyes so he wouldn't see the guilt I still felt as I said, "Given to me by someone who doesn't matter anymore."

I wasn't going to let Kyle ruin this for me. I removed the remnants of my shirt and grabbed the edge of the binding on my elbow. Without looking back at Adam, I uncovered my arm. After moving it around and making sure it was relativity okay, I put my hands under the edge of my bra and pulled it over my head. I didn't try to tease or be seductive; I just removed it completely. I went to grab the bandage when Adam stilled my hand. I couldn't control my reaction to him stopping me. I was once again stung by the foolish notion that I could actually have what I wanted.

"Oh, okay," I whispered before turning to grab my bra back.

"No," he growled when he saw what I was reaching for. He let out a sigh and said, "Let me."

I pulled myself together enough to lift my head and see his attention was riveted on my bandage. He ran his hand along the binding lightly, making sure his fingers brushed the underside of my breast. The subtle movement caused my nipples to harden almost painfully. My body anticipated every small touch he made. He grabbed the end of the binding finally, removing it from my ribs. The pain was less than before but still altered my breathing. I held perfectly still as he lowered his head toward my chest, anticipating his lips. He kissed a path down between my breasts and then tenderly pressed light ones along my injured side. It was overwhelmingly sweet, but at the moment that wasn't what I wanted.

I pushed Adam back enough for me to get off the counter. Once I got my footing, I proceeded to unbutton my pants and pull them down. The shower was teasing me, and I wanted under that hot water just as badly as I needed to be one with Adam. I bent over and took the wrap off my knee, and before I could straighten back up, he was in front of me looking at the nasty discoloration of my knee and thigh.

He once again peppered my injury with feather-light kisses. This kind of affection was not something I was used to, and I was at an absolute loss as to what to do. I didn't have to do anything; Adam kept kissing my leg until he got to my panties. He placed his nose between my thighs and inhaled deeply. After being married for as many years as I was, I didn't think there was anything anyone could do sexually that would embarrass me, but Adam managed to make my cheeks burn as I blushed like a teenager.

His hands moved up and pulled my panties down my leg, bringing a shiver from my body. He retreated long enough to get the panties out of the way. Once they cleared my feet, his face was between my thighs, kissing softly. He pushed me back again until I rested against the counter, lifted my injured leg and placed it over his shoulder. Looking up into my eyes he took his tongue and licked me. I gasped at the feeling of him exploring the most intimate part of me. It didn't take long for the orgasm to build within me.

"Adam, you've got to stop. I'm too close," I moaned.

I didn't want him to, but I needed to feel him inside of me as I peaked. He wouldn't stop. Instead, he slid a finger into me and then a second, followed by him taking my clit between his teeth and slightly nibbling on it.

"Adam," I sighed as my body convulsed around his fingers. As my mind returned to the present, he was still running his tongue across my sensitive clit. I could have let him keep pleasing me, but we had wasted enough of the hot water. Lowering my leg from his shoulder proved to be more work than I had expected, but once my legs were firmly planted, I grabbed Adam's towel and pulled him behind me towards the shower.

His deep laugh brought a smile to my face, but he wasn't moving. I looked over my shoulder, trying to give him my best 'come get me' glance and regretted my brashness immediately.

Shaking his head no, he said, "Shower's all yours. You need to let the warm water work its magic on those bruises. I'll be in the bedroom when you're done."

Without another word, he left. I looked back at the shower and had to do a double take. This was the largest, most luxurious shower I'd ever seen: eight heads, and a bench big enough to lie down on.

I made my way to the middle of the shower, melting at the first touches of the warmth running over my aching muscles.

I wanted to lose myself in the water's rhythm, but I couldn't get my mind to stop replaying all of my faults. What Adam did felt like rejection. Too many years of Kyle's venom flooded my thoughts; all the hateful things he said to me about my body made the brush-off real. Adam must have felt sorry for me or something but didn't want to truly be with me.

I tried to hold off the negative thoughts, but they kept swirling around my mind like a hurricane. The physical differences in the guys I'd tried to be intimate with meant nothing when they all reacted the same way. How blind was I to miss that something about me was distasteful to the opposite sex? The tears ran down my face unchecked. I was trying to find myself, and all I keep seeing was a loser no one wanted. The burn of rejection hurt more than the wounds covering my body. The two people who loved me for me were gone, and I was too chicken to take myself out. The reality check was that I deserved everything I was getting, not only because I was taught I was a waste of space, but I had been trained to see that I was too weak to change it. What was the point of fighting the truth? It only made things harder.

I put my head under the water to drown out the sound of my tears, needing a few more pitiful minutes to pull myself together before I went out and faced Adam. *I'll stay tonight and leave early in the morning. There is no reason for him to feel like he has to help me. I refuse to be his burden too.*

With the water rushing down my head, I didn't hear the shower door open or close or the sound of Adam's feet on the tile. Nor the sharp intake of breath he took as he heard me quietly asking God why he made me undesirable. No, I didn't realize I wasn't alone anymore until I felt the washcloth across my back. I tensed immediately, chastising myself for being too lost in my own world to notice the simple things going on around me.

Adam stepped into me; his larger frame made me feel small. I couldn't move past him, and it felt as though he wanted me to stay exactly where I was. He began caressing my sides with the cloth and working his way towards my front—washing my stomach first then gently moving over my injured ribs before making his way up one side then back down my arm. Meticulously cleaning every square inch of my body. The cloth ran over everywhere but where I truly wanted to feel it. I felt him step closer to me, leaving no space between my back and his chest. The resounding thud from the saturated washcloth landing on the soaked tile floor tightened my body in anticipation.

I tilted my head to expose the column of my neck, hoping he would understand my unspoken plea. Adam didn't disappoint. He kissed below my ear then trailed down my neck. When he got to where my shoulder met my neck, he ran his teeth across the skin, causing an involuntary shiver—reading my body better than anyone else had, he followed the graze with a light bite. The moan passing my lips couldn't have been stopped even if I wanted to. I felt him smile against my neck before he bit down a little harder, turning my legs into jelly.

He continued to lick and kiss the tender flesh he'd bitten, working his hands down my body, bringing me to a heightened bliss. If he maintained his rhythm, I would be climaxing again, but I wanted him inside me when I did.

Turning around in his arms, I eagerly sought his lips. I needed to taste him again. Devour the angel sent to save me from loneliness and despair. There was nothing subtle in our kiss; it was lips, teeth and tongue all working in overdrive, consuming one another. He broke the connection this time, breathing heavily but still gliding his lips over my neck. My body was on fire, and I felt every inch of his hot skin pressed against mine. His cock pulsing along my stomach told me he wanted this as bad as I did.

Without any separation, he walked me back till I felt the tile wall with the bench slightly over to the side. I reached between us and lightly wrapped my hand around his hard flesh. I wanted to please him as he had me. I tried to move so I could sit, but he growled, "No," against my flesh. My body tensed from the rejection. I thought all men liked it when a woman went down on them; once again, it must have been me. With my mind processing at ninety miles a minute about what was wrong with me, I didn't notice Adam had stopped kissing me and was instead watching me. I shrugged my shoulders at him, but before I could berate myself both his hands were on my face. Looking directly in my eyes, he said, "I would love to have you suck my cock, and I plan on you doing it later, but if you get those succulent lips anywhere near me, I'm going to explode, and then I'll be done. I would rather be inside your wet, eager..."

I didn't need to hear the words and pressed my lips to his. Within the next second, three things happened rapidly. He lifted my injured leg, placed my foot on the bench, and bit the side of my neck. Before my other leg failed me, he gave a forward thrust and was buried deep inside of me. The rapid succession was all it took; I erupted into the best climax of my life.

He held still, but I felt him pulsating inside of me. His movements were subtle at first—testing how well we merged. The soft, breathless sighs and minor moans he made were music to my ears. I'd never been with anyone who verbally expressed their enjoyment, and I was finding out how much I liked it. It made me wetter, which caused him to moan more. Finally, I couldn't take the soft, shallow thrusts any longer and tried rotating my hips to force him deeper. He had me pinned tightly, so I wasn't able to. I pleaded breathlessly, "Please."

He kissed me hard on the lips before whispering, "Never beg me, Sara. I'll give you whatever I have that you want, but don't ever beg."

Could I tell him what I wanted? Would he listen? Kyle never did.

"What do you need, Sara?" he spoke against my neck.

"Harder, deeper, faster. I need it harder, Adam. I won't break."

If I thought too long on the words I spoke out loud I would have turned at least three shades of red, but Adam never gave me time for embarrassment. His thrusts immediately became long deep strokes.

It was amazing, but before I could get lost in the bliss, he changed his movement again. Digging his hands into my sides, not only was he going in as hard as he could, but he was moving faster, and I was awash in sensation. It was too much and not enough; I wanted him to keep going, but I think I mumbled slow down. I was on the verge of a climax unlike any before, but I wasn't sure. It was building too fast, drowning me in the intensity. My climax was on the edge, but my body refused to let go. It was starting to hurt, and I began to shake in his arms. He pulled my clit between his fingers and pinched. It was what my body needed to finally release. I'm not sure what I said when the waves of pleasure crashed into me, but it was loud.

My heart was beating harder than ever before. I opened my eyes to look at Adam, who was still deep inside of me, lightly running his fingers in circles around my sensitive clit.

Adam let me ride my orgasm without thrusting. Once he noticed I was coming down from it, he continued with a few more hard thrusts, pulled out of me and stroked himself from the base to the tip while his juices were expelled from his body. We were both panting, worn out and a little sore, but it was a good kind of soreness.

"You didn't have to do that, I can't have kids," I said without thought. Why did things keep pouring out of my mouth around him? "And I'm clean. I've only ever had one lover, and it was my husband." Again with the word vomit. *Damn it, I need to stop.*

I looked down at the tile floor, picking out little specks of blue and gold to calm my heart and my mouth. Adam's hand brushed past my shoulder as he stopped the water, and in silence he walked out of the shower only to return straightaway. When he came back, he was wearing a towel and carrying one for me. He tried to help me dry off, but everywhere he touched caused me to wince.

"I don't mean to hurt you, and I'm clean too. I haven't had a lover in a very long time," he whispered while letting me take over drying myself.

Why did he sound sad? I wrapped the towel around my body and chanced a glance at him. He was looking at me like I was special; there was awe on his face. No one had ever admired me like he did. I detoured my eyes again back down to the tile floor. Fidgeting with the towel gave my mind something else to think about in the silence that now sat between us. It wasn't awkward or uncomfortable, just quiet.

He reached for my hand, and I gladly placed mine in his. He led us out and back into the bedroom, turning off the lights as we left the bathroom, but not once trying to collect my clothing.

My steps were slower than before, and I couldn't hide the excruciating pain from playing across my face with each step.

He quickly dropped my hand, going back around the other side of the room. Before I could think of questioning him, he was in front of me holding out a glass with a dark liquid in it.

"Drink this all in one gulp," he insisted.

I sniffed the liquid and recognized it as alcohol, but I was not sure what kind. I downed the entire drink in one gulp and then shuddered from the burn running along my throat. He took the glass away while I struggled with the tears filling my eyes and the incessant need to cough from the strong drink.

He returned and proceeded moving me until I stood at the bed with the back of my knees pressed against the mattress. I placed my hands on either side of his waist just above his hip bone, and slowly ran my thumb along the indentation created by the design of his body. The feel of his skin pebbling under my fingertips made me smile; he was ticklish. I continued working my fingers along his side and then around to the front of his chest. I followed the curves of his muscles, feeling the softness of the hair covering him as I explored his body. Lightly I touched the scars I noticed, ones that told a story of a difficult time. My heart tugged viciously in my chest at the thought of all he must have endured in his life. With this tugging came the stark realization that I didn't know this man standing in front of me. I had no knowledge of his last name, where he was from, or even his age.

A slice of fear closed around my heart. My brain had finally decided to join the party and was screaming for me to run.

"Don't. We can get back to reality tomorrow. Let's enjoy each other's bodies for the night and then worry about the rest later," he softly spoke.

The vulnerability in his eyes floored me. How could someone like him worry about being rejected by me, a plain, ordinary, plump, unattractive woman? Here he stood, the sculpted image of a Greek God, and he was worried about being denied by me.

I slowly dropped my towel, letting it pool at my feet, sat

down on the bed, and pulled myself to the middle of it. Looking directly at him, I motioned him to join me with the crooking of my finger. He dropped his towel, climbed onto the bed, and didn't stop until he was on top of me. I pulled his head down and whispered, "Take me," biting his earlobe lightly. I felt him physically sigh with relief.

The rest of the evening went by in a blur of sweaty bodies, exhilarating bliss, and sounds of pleasure until we drifted off wrapped around one another.

I awoke with a start, sitting straight up and grabbing my throat to make sure there wasn't anything choking me. I wiped the sweat from my face and tried to control my shaking. I chanced a glance at Adam sleeping soundly beside me. *What the hell was I dreaming about?* I couldn't remember it exactly, but the terror resonated within me. I slowly maneuvered my way out of Adam's arms and off the bed. My body ached in places that hadn't been used in a long time, which made me smile. The injuries hurt horribly, telling me I hadn't taken anything for pain other than the alcohol for over eight hours.

I struggled to walk to the chair to grab my extra clothes and my bag, which was sitting on the floor. Adam must have gone and got it after I fell asleep. I cautiously made my way into the bathroom, and with robotic movements I re-wrapped my injuries, got dressed, and took more pain medication.

My mind, heart and body were all fighting an internal debate. My head said *run far and fast,* my heart requested that I give this vulnerable man a chance, and my body was screaming *hot damn, did you count how many orgasms he gave us?* I splashed water on my face, pulled my hair back into a sloppy ponytail, and turned to leave the bathroom.

I stopped at the end of the bed and admired Adam. He looked peaceful lying half under the covers with his arm thrown up over his head. I grabbed a pen from my bag and took a book off the nightstand. I tore out one of the blank filler pages and wrote:

Adam, thank you for saving me.

Sara

Was it a bit dramatic? Possibly, but this is what my heart, body and mind agreed was the best thing to say. I placed it on the pillow I had used and quickly turned and left.

The first few stairs were hard to maneuver, but eventually my stiff muscles loosened up, and I was able to get up them quickly. At the top, I opened the door to the house and found myself walking into a large pantry. I roamed over the food, selecting a few power bars, trail mix, and three bottles of water. I glanced once more back at the door leading towards the bunker, still questioning my decision, but I left the pantry. I didn't look at anything in the house as I made my way towards where I thought the front door would be.

Not finding the way out started to frustrate me. I walked into the closest room and was standing in an office, so I decided to look out the window to get my bearings. The sun was on display in all its vivid glory—there wasn't a cloud in the sky. I could see the road out the window and knew I was going in the correct direction. I turned back towards the desk, noticing a bottle of aspirin sitting on top. As I passed the desk, I grabbed the bottle and shoved it into my bag.

I saw a set of keys sitting on the table by the front door. I reached out to grab them but decided not to. Without knowing if they were Adam's or someone else's, I chose to leave them. I opened the front door, took a step out into the sun, and silently cursed. It was still freaking cold out. The sun could be deceiving at times. I pulled my hood up and proceeded forward toward the large open gates.

Standing at the end of the drive staring down the street, I sighed. *Wonderful, I have no clue where I am.* Even as an adult there are times when finding the correct answer seems unattainable, and you have to resort to old school logic. Taking in another deep breath I thought, *Eanie while looking left, meanie turning back to the right, minie left again, moe back right, this will be, turn left once more, the way I go.* Looking to the right, I started walking. I had no idea what street I was on, not to mention whether I was in my town or another.

I should have been looking at my surroundings, but I was lost in thought. A nagging feeling in my mind was telling me my dream was important, but I still couldn't remember anything about it. Shortly, I made my way to the large gates closing off the rest of the world from the community. I grabbed the bar and tried to push with no luck. They were locked up tight. I looked on either side only to see a ten-foot-high brick wall running as far as I could see. At the bottom of the gate was a gap about two feet tall, so I shoved my bag under it before lying on the concrete and sliding below the gates.

I wiped some of the dust off but gave up quickly and found myself walking again without direction.

When the sun was blazing over me, I saw my first indication that I was going in a good direction. I strolled into what I thought was the town's main street. Located on either side of the road were stores devastated by the storms and others almost entirely untouched. Had the tornadoes meandered their way through town? I approached the scene with extra caution, not wanting to get caught off guard. The debris looked maintained. It was moved off of the road in places and contained within large masses. It seemed like some of it was sorted through and more organized. Someone was trying to clean up the city.

One store stood out from all of the others because it had the word 'open' painted over the glass window. I tried to look into the building but couldn't tell if anyone was inside. I glanced around once more before deciding to go in.

As I pushed the heavy door in, I heard a ding as I entered. Dozens of mannequin heads were placed around the large room wearing a variety of colorful wigs. I recognized the basic design of a salon. This shop was empty of patrons but full of body-less mannequin heads. I listened for any sign of anyone.

Was this someone's idea of a joke? Everything you would expect to see in a salon was on display, except for the clients. I took a few more steps towards the closest vanity.

Trying to understand why there were so many mannequin heads caused words to reverberate a memory. *"My friend, my new family."* Deciding it wasn't a good idea to be there, I took a step back. As I was about to turn and leave, a calming voice entered the room. "I'll be there in just a moment."

I looked around quickly but couldn't discern where it came from, and then she was flowing into the open room from somewhere in the back. She was beautiful, wearing a long, sleeveless burgundy dress with a large rhinestone covered belt cinched in at her tiny waist and matching sandals. She had straight black hair down her back, accentuated by the healthy glow of her skin. Where I was a large version of a woman, with too much weight everywhere making me look odd and pudgy, she was the perfectly formed kind: her chest and hips measured the same with a little tiny waist between. Stopping in front of me, she politely said, "My name is Naomi, and I'm so pleased you came to see me today, but as you can see, I'm completely booked. You can stay if you'd like, and I can see if I can work you in, but I can't promise anything."

Impulsively, I looked around before turning my attention back to hers and observed that although her emerald green eyes sparkled like a finely polished jewel, they were lacking depth, feeling almost as if there wasn't a soul within her. Yes, she was articulate, poised, refined and kind when she spoke, but something was missing. She didn't wait for me to reply. Instead, she moved to the closest mannequin and began asking it how she would like her hair done.

I stood dumbfounded, watching her for I don't know how long when a voice behind made me jump. I turned quickly to see Adam standing in the doorway. *Why didn't I hear the ding when he came in?*

"Naomi, I have a few new clients for you," he stated with a flat smile.

She gave him a large grin with perfect white teeth and said, "Marco dear, you may show them to a seat." She'd added a fake French accent to her dialect.

Adam carried in four mannequin heads with short wigs attached. I watched as he tried to find places to put them on the increasingly full surfaces.

What the hell is going on? I wanted to ask a dozen questions, but nothing came out. Instead, I stood with my mouth slightly open, unable to voice my thoughts.

Naomi turned to me once more and sighed. "Candace dear, even though it seems we are swamped today, I'm not going to need your assistance. I can handle it myself," she beamed with a Southern accent.

"Okay..." is what came out of my mouth.

Adam laced his fingers into mine and pulled me out the door. Once the cold, fresh air hit me I spun on him, yanking from his grip to hiss, "What the hell is going on? Why did she call you Marco?"

Calmly he replied, "For the same reason she called you Candace."

Even though he gave me an answer, it wasn't what I was looking for. "Will you come with me? There are things I must do, and I can explain as we go."

He motioned towards a cherry red SUV parked in the middle of the road with a large flatbed trailer attached. There was something on it covered up by a massive tarp. I looked back at Adam, trying to determine the best option. When I had left that morning, I had intended to leave him behind, and yet here he was.

He sighed and ran his hand along the back of his neck. I could see my own torment reflecting in his eyes. He didn't know me any more than I knew him, yet he opened his home and his body to me. I was ashamed of myself for what I allowed to happen last night and needed to be alone to sort out what I was feeling. If I was honest with myself, I wasn't processing anything. I didn't want to think about how right he felt or how my upbringing made me think it should be wrong. I couldn't go into the underlying issue of why; my brain refused to see past feeling and embrace logic. It seemed the emotional woman I had become was hiding behind an 'I don't give a damn' wall.

Decision made, I walked over and got into the passenger seat of the SUV. I took a quick glance at Adam to see his jaw was slightly slacked and his eyes opened wider in surprise. He moved around the front of the vehicle and got into the driver side. He started the car and proceeded forward at a snail's pace.

"Who is she?" I asked with less force as my mind tried to block the past images of Kyle and his many women. I knew Kyle had one mistress after the other, and I had turned a blind eye to all of them. I obviously wasn't giving him what he needed, so he had found it elsewhere. I couldn't allow them to replay in my mind, or it would destroy more of the wall I tried to erect to protect myself from my self-loathing.

"I found her wandering the grounds of Cerritus in nothing but a nightgown a few days after the first heavy round of storms. She wouldn't talk to me at first, but I convinced her to stay inside what was left of the asylum for another day. When I went to leave her in her room, she said her name was Naomi and she didn't belong there. I went into the office and looked through the files. It took me most of the day to find her file, and once I did we packed her few things and I brought her here to the Expression's Cosmetology school. She was elated and began working on the wigs that were there. When I go out, if I see any, I bring them here to her." He smiled faintly.

"Why?" I asked, completely confused.

Instead of answering, he questioned, "Haven't you ever wished you could be somebody else?"

Yes, I have on more than one occasion. Instead of tearing open that wound, I said, "Why would I?"

"Because sometimes people just need the chance to escape and be who they truly want to be instead of being who others deem them to be," he answered in a defeated breath. "Her real name is Jennifer Pickett. She is forty-seven years old and responsible for killing her entire family."

I inhaled sharply but didn't say a word as I waited for him to continue.

"She and her family were on their way home from a celebration honoring her husband's achievements at work. Things were stressful at home, and she hadn't been sleeping more than an hour or two at night. She decided to have a glass of wine with dinner to relax, enough to calm her frazzled nerves, and it allowed all the sleepless nights to catch up. When it was time to go home, she insisted she was exhausted and shouldn't drive, but her husband laughed at her, telling her she was just being paranoid. Instead of standing her ground, she did what was expected of her and got behind the wheel. She ended up falling asleep and drifted into oncoming traffic." He put the car into park and turned to look at me.

"What burns me the most is any of her three kids should have been able to drive them home, but her husband kept their oldest son who was twenty-two constantly filled with liquor and let his nineteen-year-old twin daughters have two glasses of wine with dinner. Between all of them she was the only one sober enough to drive, but even without the alcohol she was the last person who should have been driving; she was on too many nights without sleep. The screams of her daughters woke her, and she tried to swerve back into her own traffic lane. As she hit the intersection, she ended up hitting an oncoming truck. If that wasn't bad enough, a young kid out joyriding in his parents' Navigator ran the red-light seconds after she hit the truck and t-boned into the passenger side of her vehicle. Her file said she told the doctor the worst sound in the world wasn't the sound of her daughters screaming but the infinite quiet that followed seconds later. She said before she passed out all she wished for was to hear her children screaming because then she would know they were still alive."

I didn't say anything or wipe the tears from my face. I just continued to listen.

"She attempted suicide four times before her sister stepped in and had her committed. She tried twice more in the asylum. The notes say one day she came to the doctor and told him her name was Naomi and she was a world-renowned hair stylist with a list of clients that would make anyone proud. The eight physicians sat down and decided that her development of another personality was her mind's way of trying to heal all of the hurt that had been thrown onto her. They chose to allow her this mental freedom. Although she was never a hairdresser, that didn't stop her from proclaiming it. She would brush and style other patients' hair and was allowed to schedule haircuts, but they never allowed her to actually cut anyone's hair."

He took my hand from my lap, pulled my fingers open and placed my palm on his cheek, leaning into my touch.

"Marco was Jennifer's son, but to Naomi he is the sweet boy who helps her clients find seats. Candace is Jennifer's sister, but to Naomi she is her assistant, always by her side when things become overbearing. Even though we are not standing there with her, Marco and Candace are still in the studio with her because they are always with her, inside her mind. I could have left her at Cerritus to figure things out on her own, but if I had she might be dead—or worse, one of Marcus' catches. I couldn't let her get hurt when there was something I could do to help her."

"How long ago did she lose her family?" I whispered, more a question to myself.

"She has been at the asylum for six years and lost her family two years before that. She has been Naomi for four of the six, and I don't think she has any idea of who she used to be anymore."

My heart broke for her and everything she had endured. "She became someone completely different from who she used to be out of necessity, and now she is who she is because she knows nothing else," I whispered.

"Others are living in the upstairs apartment. A gentleman named Hank is a schizotypal personality disorder. He is twenty-six and pretty harmless. He believes he has the power to heal people, but his anxiety won't allow him to actually get near anyone to heal them. Then you have Clarissa, originally diagnosed with pantophobia eight years ago when she first came in. It has recently been changed to generalized anxiety disorder with severe panic attacks. This means everything scares her; the only person she talked to at Cerritus was Hank. I tried to save as many as I could." He sighed.

Looking back at Adam, I asked, "Are you who you were before the storms, or are you someone different?"

"Aren't we all different?" he absently questioned, lost in his thoughts. "The person I met in that field showed me heartbreak and sorrow. The person in my shower gave me the desire and want, but the woman sitting next to me is cynical and guarded. Which one of those is the real you? You gave yourself freely to me but were pissed when you thought I had somehow lied to you. You are looking for the wrong in every situation to explain why you shouldn't trust or believe me. I haven't lied or misled you in any way, so I ask again, aren't we all different?"

He closed his eyes briefly, pulled my hand away, and lightly kissed my palm before getting out. Sighing to myself, I looked around the open field and noticed row upon row of wooden crosses. *He's right, I am guarded and looking for a flaw so I don't have to try and sort out what I'm feeling. I'm scared and confused. I don't know how to be someone other than who I have been. But I do know I don't like who I used to be.*

I followed his lead and got out. Walking to the back, I saw Adam messing with the trailer. I watched him unfold the tarp to reveal about twenty bodies stacked, one on top of the other.

I hadn't smelled them before, but I did now and cringed at the thought that I was getting used to the horrid odor.

"What are you doing?" The question blurted out even though I could see the answer in front of me.

"Tending to the dead. Someone has to, and I've yet to find anyone else willing or able to do it," he replied as he worked to uncover the bodies. Once the tarp was free, he neatly folded it and tucked it under a group of bungee cords tied at the front of the trailer.

I tried not to interrupt him but felt as if I was watching with a sick fascination as he went into the large barn and pulled a flat cart from inside. Maneuvering it to the back of the trailer, he silently worked the body from the top of the pile onto the flat cart. The corpse had its hands and ankles zip-tied together. Glancing into the trailer, I saw they were all tied like this.

Adam must have noticed my intense look. "It's easier for me to move them if they are tied."

After placing the first male down, he rolled him slightly and patted his back pockets, then went around to the front until he found what he was looking for. Adam pulled out the man's wallet and gently rolled him so he rested on his back.

I grabbed the wallet from Adam the moment he started to open it. "You can't steal from a dead man," I hissed.

"Wow, Sara. I wish I knew the man who made you so cynical of all males. I would gladly give him a lesson of my own," Adam growled as he pulled the wallet back.

"I'm not cynical of all males," I denied loudly, though I knew he was right.

"The passion you extrude whether you're mad, upset, or in the throes of ecstasy continues to astound me. This is why I'm so drawn to you, why I can't stop thinking about you—why I want nothing more than to wrap my arms around you, kiss you until you're lightheaded, and then pull you into the building and take you hard."

"Flattering me is not going to make me turn a blind eye while you take that man's money. It's wrong and you know it," I stated, standing my ground.

Adam chuckled at me, and I could feel my face burn with anger. He had no right to laugh at me. I turned around, yanked my bag out of the SUV, and started to walk away. I'd had enough of men laughing at me like I was some twit who knew nothing about life.

"Stupid, arrogant man thinks he can be an amazing lover at night and treat me like a dumb doll during the day has another think coming," I mumbled as I stormed off.

I practically jumped out of my skin when Adam wrapped his arms around me from behind and rested his head on my shoulder, stopping my movement.

"Sara, Sara, Sara, we need to retrain that brain of yours, and your heart. Stop jumping to conclusions and start asking questions. How will you ever learn anything about anyone if you walk around like a horse with blinders on?" he sighed in my ear.

Once he figured out I wasn't going to try and run, he let go of me and moved to stand in front of me. The first thing I noticed was his bare chest.

"Adam, where is your shirt? It's too damn cold out here for you to not have one on," I huffed.

He unzipped my hoody and slipped his arms inside to wrap around my waist, buried his head in the crock of my shoulder, kissed my neck, and without releasing me, said, "My shirt, jacket, and gloves smell like the dead, so I had to take them off before pulling you into my arms. I swear to you, Sara, I don't steal from the dead. I need the wallet to get an ID to mark the grave. Not everyone has IDs on them, but I try to make sure everyone has their own name, not just John or Jane Doe. Even with the help of the tractor, it is still hard to dig into the frozen ground, but I will keep pushing because when I leave them, they attract scavengers."

He pulled me tighter against him. "Damn, you smell good and feel spectacular," he husked.

Giving in, I wrapped my arms around his waist. "I smell like you, so you obviously enjoy your scent a little too much. And as for how I feel, well, I have a few extra layers of fat, so I guess it's making me softer."

I could feel his laugh before I heard him.

"Go put your clothes back on before I have to put you in one of those graves, too," I scolded.

He pulled me back towards his vehicle, giving me the most breathtaking smile, I'd ever seen.

"I can't believe we've never crossed paths before now. You are who I have been looking for most of my life," he whispered.

I couldn't help but cringe as I remembered when another man told me I was everything he was looking for. Kyle once said to me I was his soulmate. When we got married, we decided to write our own vows, and I still remember what he said to me: "I, Kyle Travis Lister, take you, Sara Renea Tolson, to be my lawfully wedded wife. I promise to kiss you goodnight even when you're angry at me. I will listen to you no matter what you want to talk about. You will always be my best friend, the person I will turn to no matter what life throws at us. I will wipe your tears when you cry, stand by your side when you need my strength, and let you stand on my shoulders when you need a lift. I will love you today, tomorrow, and every day after, for as long as my heart continues to beat. Oh, and I promise never to intentionally eat the last bowl of ice cream."

I didn't realize I'd closed my eyes until I opened them to see Adam still shirtless in front of me.

"Where'd you go just now? I lost you for a bit," he whispered, hesitating before taking another step towards me.

"Adam, I..." I tried to speak, but the words wouldn't come. I needed to let him go before I turned him into Kyle. I had to be the reason Kyle became who he became, and even though I always thought I did what was best for us all, somewhere along the way, I created a monster in him. As he made a monster of me. Here Adam was working to be something better for those of us left, and I couldn't destroy him. The harder I tried to compose myself, the more it felt like my sorrow was radiating from me in a continuous beat.

I looked down at my body to see if the pain was physically pouring from me. When I glanced back up at Adam through tear-filled eyes, I was so consumed in my grief that I couldn't see what he was feeling. I could barely tell where he was or how far away he was.

Within seconds, he was against me, kissing me like it was the last time he would ever see me. His touch told me more than words could have said: he didn't want to lose me, but he knew he'd already lost me. I had been so starved for love, attention, and desire that I kept clinging to anyone who showed me even an ounce of it. First Sam and then Adam. *Am I capable of loving, or am I just using those who get close?* A kiss that should have set my heart and body on fire only made me want to cry more.

He pulled away from the kiss but continued to hold me while pleading softly, "Please don't leave me; please let me show you I can be who you need me to be. Please don't break me—you've just started to heal me. Please don't."

I pulled him tighter. "Were you ever married?"

"No, I never found the person who made me feel whole, not until..."

I couldn't let him finish. "How old are you, Adam?"

"What does it matter? Age is only a number."

"Please," I pressed.

"I'm twenty-eight years old," he reluctantly stated.

I squeezed my eyes tighter, hiding my face on his shoulder, trying not to let him feel me tremble from the tears.

"I'm poisonous to your soul, Adam. I kill everything and everyone who attempts to get close to me. It permeates in my every cell, and I can't watch you die the slow, agonizing death that will come from your attempt at loving me. I need you to know that no one has ever made me feel like you do. You are safe, compassionate, and light. You make me feel like the most precious thing you have, and for that alone, I won't let my poison consume you too. I was married and had two wonderful kids that I loved completely. I'm thirty-eight, and it's my fault they are dead. My friend you saw me with before, I killed him too. So, you see, Adam, I can't stay. I can't hurt you too."

"Don't I get the choice?" he pleaded.

"No, please see I'm doing this for you," I whispered.

"Will you let me show you what I'm doing before you go?"

I didn't trust my voice, so I nodded. He guided me towards the barn while I wiped the tears from my face. When I cleared the door, it took my eyes a few seconds to adjust to the darker interior, but once it did, I could see it was designed more like a studio apartment than a barn for farm equipment. One wall was covered in cork boards with organized rows of pictures on it. Adam pulled my bag from my arm and sat it on the floor by the door.

I walked closer to the board and could see they weren't pictures but driver's licenses.

"I pin them up in the order that I bury them so I'll remember what name to put on the marker. When the other cities get to us, people will be able to find their families."

It was overwhelming and sad to see how many people he had buried.

"How many have you buried, Adam?" I asked without taking my eyes off the multitude of faces.

"I've buried one hundred eighty-nine in the lot out here and forty-seven in the garden at Cerritus."

He's been surrounded by so much death since the storms tore through the world. No wonder he's drawn to me.

He stood about a foot behind me with his hands fisted at his sides so he wouldn't touch me. He looked vulnerable, and I'd be damned if it didn't remind me of me. I needed to feel him once more. I wanted to have the moment of ecstasy wrapped in his arms. If I was better and sound, I would keep him and work on being who I was supposed to be, an improved version of my old self. But instead, I would use him to feel what I had been missing.

I turned to him and asked, "Is there a bed in this place?"

Confusion marred his brow. "Yes, up in the loft." He pointed to a ladder on the right side by the kitchenette.

"Lock the door and join me up there."

I didn't wait to see if he would do it. Instead, I turned and made my way up the ladder. Even though the area was open and exposed to the rest of the building, it was still fairly dark. I kicked my shoes off and quickly removed my clothes and bandages. By the time I got them off, I knew Adam was in the room watching me. It got darker after he shut the door.

"I don't know where the bed is, and I'm worried I'll fall off the side," I chuckled.

I jumped when I felt his hand run along my hip. He pushed me forward and spun me towards the bed. I removed my underwear and bra before climbing under the covers and waiting for Adam to join me. After a few seconds, I began worrying about this being a stupid idea.

"Adam?" His name was all I spoke, but I poured every ounce of my fear and my need into it.

I felt the bed dip, and then he was under the covers with me lying at my side.

"At this moment, I need it to be about you and me, as we are this very second. No past to weigh us down, no future to distract our thoughts, just you and me connecting. Can you do that?"

I don't know how much time passed, but he didn't say anything, and I felt like a fool. He knew I was using him, and he chose not to let it happen. It was idiotic of me to think I could do this to him without him figuring it out. I turned to my side, away from him, so I could leave the bed.

Adam's arm came around me, pulling me flat on my back. He climbed on top of me and kissed me like he had outside, with every ounce of his emotions saying goodbye. I tilted my head silently, encouraging him to kiss me deeper. He slid his knee between my thighs to separate them slightly until I opened my legs wide, inviting him in. He let out a deep groan once he lowered his weight onto me.

He fit me perfectly, not overly heavy or too bulky. His body mirrored mine in a sensual way. I placed my hand on his firm behind and pulled him into me. It was my turn to moan when his swollen shaft rubbed against my overly sensitive lips. He worked his way into my body with slow, shallow thrusts, letting us become one. Taking every second to unite us a one, letting me be awash in the sensation.

All thought of my future departure was gone. I knew what I would do, but I didn't want to taint this with sadness. I wasn't prone to sappy moments in life. Those types of things, living happily ever after, were fairy tales told to little girls to mask the fact that men are cruel, demanding creatures who take whatever they want and don't think twice about what it may cost anyone else.

"Stay with me in the moment, Sara. Stop overthinking all of it," Adam whispered.

How did he always know what I was doing it? His movements never hurried; it was as if he was pulling every ounce of pleasure from our connection.

With my climax coming to a boiling point, I couldn't think of anything but him deep inside me. I was close when he stopped moving and lifted up on to his knees, still buried in me.

"Adam, I'm so close. Please don't stop."

"I need a minute, Sara. I don't want this to end so soon."

I continued to work my hips along his shaft. I was too close to think straight. I groaned in frustration when he placed his hands on my hips to stop my momentum.

While keeping me immobile, he pulled my legs over his forearms, and before I could contemplate the change in positions, he had withdrawn from me and had his hot lips over my swollen clit. He wasn't gentle with his passion as he sucked me into his mouth and grazed his teeth over me once, twice, and by the third time I was panting and clawing at the sheets so close to exploding it was borderline painful. He released the suction of his mouth and lightly licked a few more times before once again sucking me in hard. I was lost to the sensation as I came on his mouth. He continued to lick me lightly, bringing me down from my high.

Lowering my legs, he then thrust back inside, causing me to spasm around him. He leaned down and kissed me. I could taste myself on his lips. I moaned and sucked his bottom lip into my mouth, biting softly. His thrusts became erratic, a few shallow, then harder but barely coming out, some were long and deep. By the time I thrust my tongue into his mouth, he was growling his release. He rested his head beside mine, taking in deep breaths to calm his heart. I wrapped my legs around his waist, knowing he was going to pull free of me, but not wanting to let him go yet.

He wrapped one arm around behind me and lightly squeezed my butt cheek. With his breathing under control, he nipped and kissed my shoulder. He hit a particularly ticklish spot and I couldn't help but squirm and giggle.

"Once more, please, but this time take me hard and fast," I whispered.

He lifted his head to look at me. I couldn't see his expression, but I could guess he was questioning whether he heard me correctly.

"Last night we explored and learned one another's bodies. What we just did I can't put into words, but I know you're holding back."

"I don't want you to think about me later and assume I used you," he whispered.

I giggled. "Used is not a word you will find in my vocabulary to describe what you do to my body. Mastered would be a better word."

"What you're asking of me, is that how your husband did it? Did he fuck you hard and fast?" he hissed.

Why is he mad at me? He is still inside of me, and he's angry?

"No, my husband took his pleasure and only cared about his own. Used is a better word to describe his love making, but I never realized it until I was with you," I admitted.

"Then how do you know you want it like that?"

Because that was what my novels always asked for, I spent too many lonely nights pleasuring myself to the thought of someone who couldn't get enough of me. I craved the feeling of what had been described repeatedly in the books, but I couldn't say that. I sighed out loud; this was a waste of time. "Last night, you said you would give me whatever I wanted that you could give. Stop holding back and show me what you enjoy."

"I can't," he finally whispered.

Well, don't I feel idiotic. "I understand."

I didn't, but I wasn't going to let him drown me in self-loathing the way Kyle always did.

I untangled my legs from him and released my hold.

"Adam, I have to go," I softly urged.

"I know." He crawled out of bed and turned on a battery-operated lantern.

He sat on the side of the bed with the sheet tucked around his legs, watching me as I got dressed. While pulling the last few things on, I glanced at him. He had his elbows on his knees and his hands on his face. It was a position of defeat.

"When you figure out who you're meant to be in this new world, will you come find me?" he asked so softly I almost didn't hear him.

I sat down beside him trying to understand his question.

He pulled his hands from his face and ran them around each other in a silent show of nervousness.

"We are connected in a way most people are not. I know you feel it too. You can deny it to yourself all you want, but you can't hide it from me because I feel it in every breath I take, every touch of your skin to mine, and every unspoken word that passes between us."

"I won't deny there is something in me that recognized something in you. This part is foreign to me, and I don't understand why I'm pulled to you so strongly. It's as if you own a part of me so deeply. I can't shake it no matter how hard I try."

"Yet you still feel the need to leave me?"

"Yes. Don't you see, Adam? I have to leave to keep the poison from consuming you. Besides, I don't know you, and your unwillingness to talk about who you were before the storms leaves me with too many variables."

I stood to leave, and he grabbed my hand, pulling it to his mouth and kissing it lightly.

"Promise me you will come back to me," he pleaded.

"I'm not sure I could find you again even if I tried. I've never been good with directions, and having the world gone to hell and destroyed makes it even harder," I admitted.

He laughed loudly. "Lucky for you, that is something I can help you with."

He dressed quickly and motioned for me to head down the ladder first.

Once we both were back down, he walked over to the file cabinet and pulled open the third drawer. I watched as he grabbed out an atlas and a few other maps. He unfolded one of them and began marking different areas in a kaleidoscope of colors.

Glancing over his shoulder, he motioned for me to join him. Standing beside him, I looked at the map and smiled at his attempt to make it as easy to follow as possible. He pointed to a route marked in purple. "This is the clearest and most direct way from your house to mine. I also tagged the directions to the prison and Cerritus so you can avoid them."

He folded the map back up and handed it to me before walking over to my bag and stuffing the atlas and other maps into it.

I took my bag and gave him my best smile, although I felt it was lacking real emotion. I was numb, and this alone scared me. *I've always felt things so deeply, and now I feel nothing.*

After adjusting my bag on my back, he handed me a set of keys.

"I can't take your vehicle. Won't you need it? And I've walked before."

"You're an hour and a half from home. You need a vehicle, and this is to a Jeep parked on the side, not the one I'm driving, so you're not taking mine."

"Oh," was all I could think to say.

I followed him outside and stopped in front of a deep wine colored two-door Jeep. It looked as if it was designed for off-roading with a grill bar in the front and it sat up on a larger set of tires.

Opening the passenger door, I threw my bag in and tucked the map safely under it before turning back to Adam.

"Please put a shirt on." I giggled.

"If I did, then I couldn't do this," he said as he pulled me in for a final kiss. "Promise me, Sara," he whispered into my hair.

"I promise," I heard myself say.

"Until we meet again." He sighed then walked away.

I got behind the wheel, started it up, and drove for ten minutes before stopping to look at the map. I was going the wrong way, but it only took me a few minutes to get back on the correct course.

He had really worked hard to clean up the main roads in town. There was a clear path all the way out of town. When I had gotten outside of town, it seemed like an excellent place to re-check the map and get my head together. I pulled over and got out to walk a bit. I wanted to clear the nagging thoughts telling me to turn around and let Adam show me how I could be an improved version of myself.

About one hundred yards from where I was standing, I could see something hanging in a tree. I wasn't too far away; I could still turn around and have Adam come get the poor soul out of it. At least I thought it was a person. I walked with long, swift strides towards it.

One look at the decomposing disfigured face brought back a flash of memory. I knew him but couldn't quiet place it. Then I read the sign tied around his body. 'Rapist, Murderer.' It hit me and I turned, practically running away. That was Marcus, and I was pretty sure Adam placed him there. I damned near ran to the Jeep, stopping at the rear long enough to throw up what little I had in my stomach. Did Adam murder him?

The answer was obvious. Why else would Marcus be hanging from a tree with a noose around his neck?

I couldn't let myself dwell on the life or death of one evil man. I drove towards home with a new nagging in my brain. *Will I go back to Adam knowing he's a murderer too?*

Once I got into town, I recognized more of my surroundings. I flashed back to Adam's board of driver's licenses and recalled I still had Derek's. I pulled over and dug through my bag until I found it.

After spending way too much time locating the address on the map, I made my way to Derek's house. The sun was already setting, leaving a kaleidoscope of colors on the horizon, and before long it would be too dark to see well enough to drive.

As I turned onto his street, I noticed his neighborhood fared better than mine. There were more houses standing here, less were collapsed or demolished. Three or more houses were lit up from the inside, but after my last experience, I wasn't going to try and talk to them. If I found anyone in charge, I would remember to send these people help. The farther down the road, the worse the houses got. They were less whole and more pieces.

215

Driving almost to the end of the dead-end street did nothing to calm my nerves. At the end of the road sat half of a house at the address on his license. I pulled into the front yard and got out, thoughtlessly.

Stepping over dead branches and debris made it harder to get to the backyard. Once I did, I could plainly see the small shed, but there was a fallen tree in front of the door. I tried to get between the debris and the door, hoping it would swing in, but there was no room to spare, and I couldn't push it open.

Taking a few minutes to move around the structure proved there was only one way in or out. The frustration of the day was starting to add up, and I refused to leave feeling defeated.

The idea that sparked in my mind wasn't the best, but damn it, it would work. I returned to the Jeep and dug into the back for something to use to remove part of the tree. Lucky for me, whoever owned it must have done a lot of mountain climbing because there was a long blue nylon rope in the back. I moved the bits and pieces of other people's lives from the path as I went around to the driver's side of the Jeep. Climbing in, I quickly threw the Jeep into reverse and drove up the yard for the rear. That tree was going to move one way or another.

After parking I jumped out to put my plan into action. Finding the most secure place to tie around the tree was more trouble than it was worth, so I fastened it to the branch blocking the door and then tied it around the Jeep's bumper.

I reconsidered where I had secured the rope and moved it to the trailer hitch. I didn't need to be picking the bumper up off the ground. I got into the driver seat and slowly accelerated until I could feel tension in the line. With a slight smile I gunned the gas and sent the Jeep into a slide. I kept at it, pressing down on the accelerator until I felt the ground slide under my tires, and the motor began to whine in frustration. According to the dash, my rpms were topping out, and if I continued to push I would blow the motor.

After a few more seconds I called it quits. If I hadn't moved that branch by then, I wasn't going to.

I killed the engine and climbed out to see my handywork. I'd accomplished two things in all that "pedal to the metal" action. The back tires were buried into the ground, and the large tree branch had rotated and pulled about six inches from the door. It was still going to be a tight fit, but I was getting into that shed. Turning back to untie the rope led me to understand that if I released all the tension caused by the vehicle, the tree might roll back against the door. *Screw it; I'll remove the rope before I leave.*

I snatched my backpack out of the passenger seat then walked back to open the shed door. I placed my bag down, grabbed the handle, turned to the left and pulled. Nothing. I tried moving it right, but it wouldn't budge. I turned and pulled again and again and yet again, becoming progressively angrier.

Tired and frustrated, I leaned against the door and messed with handle again. After turning it as far to the left as I could the door swung open towards the inside and I landed hard on the ground, jarring my senses for a moment.

I laid there stunned for a few seconds, groaning at the pain radiating out and tried to figure out why it wouldn't push open before. No answer came, but as I looked at my pack sitting on the tree outside the door, I couldn't contain the giggle that erupted from me or the hysterical laughing that followed, or the tears that fell silently at the end. This was my life, and none of it made a bit of sense.

Sitting up, I rubbed the tender spots on my shoulder, then crouched over to grab my bag. It was getting darker, and if I wanted to explore, I needed to get moving.

Locating the handcuff key was easier than getting it to work. I don't know how long I fought with it, but when it finally unlocked, I could have jumped up and down like a little kid. Once the lock clicked, the handle moved to the left, and the latch opened. It swung out, leaving a dark hole. I hooked my flashlight to my pant leg and made my way down the ladder. I should have counted the steps but could only concentrate on the dark surrounding me. There was no sound or light, and the lack of two main senses did weird things to my thinking.

At the bottom of the ladder I found concrete. Turning from the entrance, I took a cautious step forward and was momentarily blinded by a flood of light. I must have triggered some sort of auto-light system.

It looked like I was in a silo of some kind. Tentatively, I touched the walls and felt cement. A few feet in front of me was a door. Steeling myself for what might be on the other side, I took a deep breath.

Without giving myself a chance to overthink what might be behind the door, I moved towards it. The area was underwhelming. It was a large open room used for multiple purposes. There were shelves full of supplies, well-thought-out rations unlike mine at home, and a few beds set up in one corner covered in colorful quilts. The crib brought fresh tears to my eyes. There were simple accommodations, but what drew my attention the most was the wall with the monitors, computers, and other electronics.

I could hear a generator running but couldn't see it anywhere. There wasn't anyone in the space, and it didn't seem like anyone had been here for days or weeks. I looked uncertainly at electronic equipment but decided it wouldn't hurt to try. I turned on the Chromebook first, hoping to connect to something on the internet, but it wouldn't. I kept getting an error message saying the site was down. I turned it off and moved along the counter to what looked like a complicated walkie-talkie. Surprisingly, it wasn't on, so I pushed the power button.

Deflated, I slumped in the closest chair and tried to decide if I wanted to attempt to go home or stay the night. The room wasn't cold, but it wasn't where I craved to be, and after everything I wanted to be at home. Suddenly I was drained, both physically and mentally.

Decision made, I stood to turn off the radio when it crack-led to life. "Damn it, Derek! Where the hell are you?"

I froze, listening to the voice yelling out for the young, dead officer.

The radio crackled to life again. "This was your idea, Derek, and we haven't heard from you since all this shit went down. Where are you? It's been weeks, and the rest of the group says I should just stop trying, but I can't."

I felt bad for the young male voice on the other end but refused to answer the call. After quickly turning the radio off, I made my way out of the bunker and out to the cold. The Jeep eased into reverse and made the job of removing the rope a quick action. With the rope back into the Jeep, I drove home in a mental fog.

Chapter 9

A few blocks from home, I parked the Jeep haphazardly and walked the rest of the way. The weather had soured. The moon was no longer visible, hidden behind black clouds, and the snow began falling again with fat flakes at a faster speed. It would soon be whiteout conditions.

I stopped in front of the door and stomped off as much of the snow as I could before going down into the dark basement. I wished I'd taken the time to enjoy another hot shower before I left Adam. I placed my bag on the ground once I cleared the stairs and continued making my way over to the bed in the dark.

Before I reached the bed, strong arms clamped around my waist and over my mouth. I tried to buck the intruder and battled with all my strength. Finally out of options, I rammed my head back, cracking the trespasser in the face and giving myself a splitting headache. The arms around me loosened, and I took the opportunity to turn, pulling my fist back and releasing a close punch to his jaw. Then I kicked out blindly hoping to connect with something sensitive.

My kick missed, and before I could formulate another plan, I was on the bed with my hands pinned above my head and the weight of his body caused the mattress to give under me, pushing me farther into it, making me feel as if I couldn't escape. I could smell the alcohol permeating off of him.

I started shaking violently as the fear swallowed me whole, and through tears I cried, "Please, don't hurt me."

He placed his head in the crook of my shoulder and neck, forcing me to turn my face to the side. He breathed in deeply along my neck, and I closed my eyes tightly, trying to control my whimpers.

"Damn it, Sara, you scared the hell out of me," he exhaled in my ear.

The tears of fear changed to ones of confusion, pain, and joy.

I gave a dark chuckle. "I scared you?"

"Yes," he hissed, still not letting me go.

"Are you real, or did I fall asleep at the wheel and crash?" I cried.

"What the hell kind of question is that?"

He didn't attempt to move, but he let my hands go, and I wrapped them tightly around his chest, crying into him.

"I heard you fire the gun, and it felt like you ripped a chunk of my heart out with it," I whispered.

He rolled over, taking me with him, and settled my head on his chest. I could hear his heartbeat slowing from its frantic pace.

"Where were you?" he whispered while running his hand through my hair.

"An angel helped me when I got lost on my way home. I was cold and alone thinking someone I cared about had just taken the shitty-ass way out. I probably would have frozen to death otherwise," I murmured, trying not to let my anger show.

He stopped messing with my hair. "I thought the only choice I had was to end it all. My whole world crumbled when I found her. I was at peace with my decision, but then you ran to me whispering something I never thought I'd hear from you ever again. You looked so lost and utterly broken that it made me take a moment to think. I thought about all you've been through and the fact that you were still standing with me despite the despair you were fighting. You chose to help me even though there was a chance we would have found her alive, knowing you would have to watch me connect with my child when you could no longer connect with yours. I'm not sure I would have been as strong as you if our roles were reversed. I don't think I would have been able to help you look for your kids if I had just buried mine. I would have been pissed because you still had a chance with your kids and mine was now gone. I would have resented your ability to hope.

"I shot the last bullet into the ground to take the temptation away. Stayed and controlled the fire, then headed out to find you. I didn't find you on the way back to the car and figured you'd already made it back home. But when I got here it was cold, dark, and empty. I went back out and looked for you. I looked for hours before coming back, hoping you had arrived while I was out."

His voice went whisper-soft. "I...thought I lost you too, and my heart hurt so bad that it felt like it was ripping apart. I couldn't stop the pain. Things have a way of changing what you once believed you needed to do. I'm sorry for what I said to you. I chose hateful words to put distance between us. I didn't want your pity or your concern. I thought my plans were irrevocable until I decided to let those last things go."

He was absently rubbing his hand over his heart.

"Sam..." I whispered.

"Yeah, Sara?"

I didn't say anything, unsure of *what* I could say. The entire situation was too raw and painful to get into. Sam felt like the same man lying next to me, but I was different; torn apart and not yet reformed. I still loved him, but he let me think he would rather be dead than lean on me.

Even if it was a brief amount of time, he still picked any other option than me. How was I supposed to act—like nothing had happened?

"Never mind," I stated.

"I am sorry I hurt you, Sara," Sam whispered with his face buried in my hair.

"I know."

I understood, but it didn't make the betrayal any easier. I needed to decide whether or not I could forgive and forget. *Can I move forward knowing at any moment he could pull a Kyle and check out?* That was not a fair comparison. Not everyone was going to treat me like Kyle did, not everyone was going to be heartless, and I needed to stop expecting the worst in people, just like Adam tried to tell me. Good thought, but I didn't know if I would ever be able to actually put it to practical use.

Sam's breathing evened and I could tell he was asleep. I pulled myself free to sit up. With my head in my hands, I let out a long sigh. *What am I going to do? My body still remembers feeling every inch of Adam, and here I am with Sam.*

I was at a major crossroads. Should I stay with Sam and move forward with whatever he chooses? Should I join Adam and work with him cleaning and rebuilding the town? Should I go back to Derek's and see what could happen with the group on the other side of the radio? Should I introduce Sam to Adam? Could I trust them both and show them the bunker? Every ounce of me wanted both of them in my life. With Sam, I was comfortable in his presence. With Adam, I felt invigorated and more alive than I had in years.

Why does the decision have to be so hard? Shouldn't it be an easy selection? These aren't life or death decisions.

I stood up from the bed and made my way to the stairs. I needed air—fresh, cold air to clear my mind and hopefully make my choice easier.

As quietly as I could, I went up the stairs and out into the dreary night. I looked up at the dark clouds covering the sky and took a few deep breaths.

"Still staring up trying to find those stars?" the low rumble of Adam's voice said.

"Always," I chuckled.

I could feel him standing behind me. The heat radiation off of him was inviting, like coming home. He didn't embrace me or touch me, and I missed his closeness. I turned and wrapped my arms around him, taking his scent into my lungs.

"I've missed you," I whispered, shocked that I admitted it out loud to him.

It took a few moments before he relaxed into me. Something was off; he was acting different. It was almost like we never shared any of our intimate moments. *Does he regret being with me after all? Is he here to tell me goodbye, to rescind his invite of being with me?*

"Is everything alright?" I hesitated as I asked.

"You make me want more than I should have," he replied with a strain in his voice.

"What does that mean?" This was a weird conversation given I had spent the entire evening wrapped in his embrace.

"I want to be someone else for you."

"You don't have to, just be yourself."

"You wouldn't like me nearly as much if I was myself." No emotion came from his voice; it was a blunt answer.

I wrapped my hand around his head and pulled his mouth down to me, feeling his lips pressed against mine. The moment our bodies touched he pulled me in closer to him and kissed me like he'd never done it before. This was different, but I couldn't place why, and I didn't care. He felt good. He was the first to release. We were both breathing heavy, and when he stepped away, I shivered from the loss of his heat.

In the moonlight his features were hidden. He was messing with something on his chest. When I stepped back into him I noticed for the first time the necklace hanging from his neck and the ring attached to it. My ring was around him, the one I gave him days ago. Why did he wear it now but not before?

I reached up and placed my hand over his heart. It was beating erratically.

"Are you okay?" I asked, concerned over his reaction to me.

"I want to take you away from here and have my way with you," he groaned.

I looked up at him and smiled. "You can have me whenever and wherever you want me."

His gaze held a look of confusion for a moment before turning to pure lust.

"Adam?" I moaned.

"I have to go," he replied before turning and walking away.

What the hell was that all about? What is wrong with these men today? I stood staring in his direction for a few more moments before going back inside.

Dumbfounded and confused, I made my way to the bed and took my place next to Sam.

I fell into a deep, heavy sleep for a few hours before I woke suddenly, covered in sweat with my heart pounding. I tried to sit up but couldn't. A hand was on my chest holding me down.

There were three possible responses to this situation. I could try and run, fight with all my strength, or I could have done what I did. Freeze. There I was, heart pounding, labored breathing, and completely frozen in place. I couldn't see anything. I opened my mouth to scream or yell something, I wasn't totally sure. It didn't matter either way because as quickly as I opened my mouth a hand was covering it too. I knew it wasn't Sam; I could hear him snoring next to me.

"You're safe, I needed to see you," a whisper moved across my cheek.

I immediately relaxed. Pulling my arms up, I removed the covering from my mouth and stood up. I could feel Adam close to me. I grabbed his hand and guided him back towards the door.

He pulled me up short. "Not outside."

I walked to the far corner of the basement and lit a candle.

"What's wrong?" I interjected.

"I needed to see you," he whispered as he reached a hand up to touch my face.

I leaned into his caress as I giggled. "You just saw me a few hours ago, and you walked away from me, remember?"

"I'm trying to give you space, but I don't want to let you go. I want to spend all my time with you. I'm addicted to the way I feel when I'm with you. I'd even agree to keep your friend close if it meant spending more time with you," he interjected.

I could feel his sincerity and didn't know how to handle it.

"It'll be light in a few hours, and this will be a very awkward conversation with Sam, but we need to figure out how to move forward, all of us." I sighed.

"I'm glad your friend isn't dead. So, you must not be as poisonous as you think you are?" he interjected.

"No, I guess not," I replied, trying to determine whether I believed it.

Not waiting for his invitation, I walked into him and wrapped my arms around him as I asked, "Why did you leave so abruptly earlier? What happened?"

I felt him tense. "Earlier?"

"Yes, when you saw me looking for stars. You said you wanted me; I told you that you could have me whenever you wanted. Then you just walked away. Do you regret having sex with me? I want to try and be a better person, and I think you are a great example of someone I would like to emulate."

"You saw me earlier?"

"Okay, Adam. This isn't funny anymore. If you just want to be friends, I'm okay with that, but you've got to be honest with me." I tried to sound casual, but I wasn't sure I accomplished it.

"Fuck, Sara. How many times have we met?" he asked with concern.

I laughed, thinking he was joking until he pulled me out of his arms and looked at me fearfully.

"When did we first meet?" he questioned quickly.

"In the field, you heard me screaming," I replied.

"You were unlike anyone I'd ever met. I just wanted to wrap you in my arms and never let you go. Then we met a second time when I pulled you from that cold car," he reassured me.

"No, remember, you saved me from Marcus."

"What?" he cautiously questioned.

"I saw you again the next morning, after we met in the field. Marcus had me tied up. I gave you my ring for saving me," I answered, reaching out to touch his chest where my ring would rest. "Why aren't you wearing my ring? You had it on earlier."

Why does he keep taking it off?

He placed his hand over mine, and I could feel his heart rate increase. The fear was still in his eyes, and I knew something was very wrong.

"I don't even know where to begin. I never in my life thought that once I finally found the person who called to me, that they would be the one who called to him too." He sighed.

I could tell whatever he needed to say was weighing on him. I grabbed a blanket from the stack, threw a few more on the ground near the wall, and motioned for him to sit. I draped the blanket around his shoulders and sat down on his lap, letting him wrap us both up in the warmth.

"Start at the beginning and I will try not to interrupt," I stated as I leaned into him.

"You're going to hate me," he whispered.

"I promise you I won't. Like you said, it's a chance for us to be more. We are no longer who we used to be. This new world demands we be better, that means we have to leave all our old demons behind. I have to learn this just as much as you do. My demons are mental, and it will take me a long time to expel them, but because of you and Sam, I will learn how."

This was the truth. I needed to stop letting the horrible things Kyle used to say to me determine who I was now.

"I'm a twin," he blurted.

I waited for him to say more, trying to stay true to my word of not interrupting. Instead, I snuggled in closer and pulled his hand into my lap.

"I did meet you in the field. I felt your pain as if it was my own. I wanted to ease your pain but didn't know how. I've never been able to understand people, and when they are fake and hide who they really are it makes it difficult for me to connect with them. I've tried to read books, hypnotherapy, shock therapy, intense counseling, and everything in between to get that part of my brain to work the way it is supposed to. Nothing helped, and eventually I learned to read people in a way most can't. I look for subtle movements. The shift of the body, a twitch in the face and unconscious signs within their eyes." He tilted his head back against the wall.

I ran my hand up his neck, along his jaw, and slightly pulled his head down to meet my lips. It wasn't a kiss of lust, just reassurance that I was still there and listening.

He rested his forehead against mine for a moment before he lifted his head and sighed.

"My twin brother started the same as me, but after the shock therapy he chose a different way to understand people and their emotions. He felt he could force them to show him exactly what they were feeling and thinking. I couldn't get him to see that when you force an emotion you rarely get what you're looking for. It's usually hate, anger, frustration, contempt, or any of the raw, fast-burning emotions. Not real ones but forced reactions."

My heart ached for what he had to deal with. I couldn't image trying to navigate life without the basis of emotion, or having to be poked, prodded and shocked to help 'cure' you.

"I know you saw my scars. They are from him; he would trap me, tie my hands, and cut me until he got what he called a true reaction. Finally, I reached my breaking point when we were seventeen years old. I went into my dad's closet and took out his gun. I placed it on my head and was ready to end the torment. Jonathon saved my life. He yanked the gun away a second before I pulled the trigger. I will never forget the sound of the bullet leaving the chamber. When my parents walked in, Jonathon had the gun in his hand. I was on the ground, bleeding. The bullet ricocheted off the steel beam in my room, shattered, and a piece was embedded in my head. My parents thought he was trying to kill me, so they sent him away. I tried to tell them the truth, but they didn't believe me. I owe my brother my life, even if he doesn't see it that way. The piece is still in my brain. It was unremovable, but it only affects my life a little. There are times I lose time, and a few times that I've had to be put into a medically induced coma due to it shifting in position."

I couldn't fathom having lived through what he had. It made me think there was hope for me yet. If he could experience so much tragedy and come out stronger from it, perhaps I could too.

"We both continued separate counseling, and I learned it's okay to be me and that others will accept me more if I'm honest with them. Yet even with that, I've learned to hold a part of myself from the rest of the world. People are cruel, especially when they are scared, confused, or feel like they are powerless. He learned to embrace himself as well, but he chose to try to teach people how to stop hiding their emotions or overreacting to things and give a genuine reaction to the situation. He has made it his life's work to pull people from their own thoughts and force them to accept who they are."

I wanted to think he was doing this in a typical way, like becoming a psychologist or counselor, but in my heart I knew what Adam was going to say next.

"Promise me you will stay away from him. He's been lost for so long I don't even know my brother anymore," he pleaded.

"Tell me his name, Adam," I urged.

He sighed. "His name is Jonathon, but the media called him Jon-Jon."

My stomach dropped and I began to shake. No wonder Marcus was now dead. The guard at the radio station, the young officer Derek—all killed by the man I offered myself to a few hours ago.

"Is he going to kill me too?" I whispered.

"If he wanted you dead you already would be. The fact that your friend is still alive is very surprising. That must mean he really likes you."

He tightened his grip on me, urging me to silently trust him.

"What am I going to do, Adam?" I half cried.

"I won't let him hurt you. I promise I will protect you."

The decision as to whether or not I was going to show the guys the bunker had been made for me. This place would never truly be home again. It was full of pain and sorrow. It was time to move forward.

I don't know how long I sat wrapped in his arms before sleep finally claimed me, but it was the most peaceful rest I'd had since before the storms.

I woke a few hours later relaxed and ready to face the day. There were multiple things to discuss and worry about later. At the moment I wanted a few more seconds of the peace I experienced in Adam's arms.

Keeping my eyes closed didn't ease the sound of Sam's vomiting. Even after I had the kids, the noise people made when they were getting sick had always triggered convulsions of my own.

"Damnit, Sam, go outside before you make me puke!" I yelled.

I glanced up to see Adam looking down at me completely startled. I shouldn't have yelled without seeing if he was awake first. He looked as if he had been scared awake. I started laughing and straightened myself up.

I placed my hand on the side of his face. "Sorry," I managed between giggles.

"It's alright. I just had a major flashback to when I was a child and my mom would get tired of us ignoring her and break out her pissed-off mom voice." He shook his head to clear either the ringing in his ears or the image it provoked.

"Are you ready to officially meet Sam?" I asked hesitatingly.

"If this is what you want, then this is what I want, too." He smiled.

I was not sure it was what I wanted as much as it needed to happen. I had to stop pretending, living in the past, or not caring about the direction the future would take. I needed to move forward and figure out how to live again. Before standing, I pressed my lips lightly against his, barely brushing them, but enough to feel the softness of his lips touching mine.

"I should go check on him. I'll be back in a few minutes," I stated, while grabbing a bottle of water and one of the pain relievers.

How much had Sam consumed over the last day and a half? I proceeded up the stairs to follow his footsteps. The door was still open and he hadn't moved far, sitting with his hands encompassing his head. Every few seconds, he spit.

"Are you done?" I asked before venturing any closer.

"Yeah, I think so," he replied pitifully.

I sat with my back against his. I reached around and dropped the aspirin in his lap and then tapped his shoulder with the water. It took him a few minutes to respond, but I waited patiently. After all, I had nowhere else to be and was about to drop a bomb on him. I leaned back, making sure he would feel the pressure from me, and sighed.

"I truly am sorry," he mumbled.

"I know," was my reply. I knew he wasn't trying to hurt me, but that did not erase the pain. It didn't dull it, and I knew when I told him about Adam, I was going to cause him even more pain.

"When you're ready, there is a lot we need to discuss," I said.

"He's here, isn't he? The guy from the other night?" he asked, though I could tell he knew the answer.

"Actually, no he's not, and that is a big chunk of what we need to discuss. The person you saw was his brother. You haven't met Adam yet, but you will, because he is here." I tried to keep my tone light.

"I've lost you, haven't I? You're going to choose him, aren't you?" I felt him deflate against me.

"I thought you were dead. I've seen so much death already, and you were the final breaking point. I'm ecstatic that you are alive, but you are very selfish, and I have spent years with a selfish man. I'm not going to go through that again. I put myself out there for you. I helped you look for your daughter even though I just buried my own kids. I've never asked anything of you until that moment I was asking you to stay with me, to choose us, and you couldn't even do that little thing for me. You hurt me with your words and then with your actions. I won't be another doormat for anyone ever again. Adam hasn't asked me for anything. He shows me that he cares about me. I felt like I chased you for years, tried to be everything you wanted me to be, but it was never enough. Then I did it again with Kyle. I gave him every ounce of me, and he just took and took and took until I lost who I was. I was fighting to figure out who you wanted me to be as your lover, but I was destined to always be your friend," I finished.

Oh my god, I just sounded like Kyle. I put him down for the choices he made and turned it around like he was doing them to intentionally hurt me. I should have apologized, but I couldn't because there was a ringing of truth for me; the feelings of hurt were true, but I didn't have to be so harsh.

"Now we need to look towards the future and decide what we are going to be in the new world. I don't think any other town is faring better than we are, and we are going to have to do more than just survive. Are you with us, or am I moving on with Adam alone?"

My heart wasn't ready to give him up, and I hoped he wanted the same as me.

"I need a few minutes. I'll meet you downstairs," he sighed.

His shoulders were slumped in, his head lowered, and he seemed to be pulling himself into a defeated ball. An outward sign of self-loathing and hate.

I stood up, ran my hand along his shoulders, and walked away from him, hopefully not for the last time.

Adam was waiting at the bottom of the stairs for me. "How'd it go?"

I shrugged, and he immediately wrapped his arms around me. Just the feel of him surrounding me gave me an immense sense of calmness.

"I will walk away if you want me to," he sighed.

"No, I want you with me. I'm choosing you," I spoke into his chest. I was picking him before Sam, over anything or anyone else that came into my life from here on out. I knew I was making the correct decision because I felt peace within Adam's embrace, a sensation I hadn't had in many years. "We still have to tell him about your brother and the danger he poses to us."

"I don't think he will hurt us." Adam sighed.

"He's hurt you before, so what is to stop him from doing it again? Just because he hasn't touched you in years does not mean he won't. I've learned people can be unpredictable and only do what makes them feel good. Love isn't strong enough to keep you safe. Just because you share blood doesn't mean you are untouchable. Love doesn't protect you, nor does it guarantee you'll not get hurt," I solemnly replied.

He pulled me tighter into his chest. "I hate that you have grown to feel that way. Love should be enough to protect you from so much."

"Not in the real world, Adam," I finished as I pulled away from him.

Sam was making his way down the stairs. He looked horrible. His eyes had dark rings encasing them but were bloodshot in the middle, and his skin was pale.

"Are you sober enough to have a serious conversation?" I asked.

"Nope," he replied. As he walked past me, I couldn't help but laugh at him. He moved over to the bed and dropped onto it face first.

"I could sleep longer myself," I giggled.

"No, it's fine. Just give me a minute or two, and then we can talk about whatever you want," Sam groaned.

I grabbed Adam's hand, gave him a light kiss, then proceeded to resupply my book bag. I wasn't doing anything other than trying to keep busy.

"Are you avoiding me?" Adam asked as he wrapped his arms around me from behind.

"No, just lost in thought," I sighed as I leaned into him. "So much has changed in my life. There is a lot to get used to and even more to learn," I said more to myself than to Adam.

"I get it. We will figure it out together," he responded.

I pulled the folded picture from my bag and showed it to Adam, "This was my family. Tina was my oldest, and Thomas was my baby. That man was my husband, Kyle. He is the one who helped shape me into who I am. I can't fully blame him because I went along, but he controlled everything in my life. Made me feel bad about being myself and the one behind my bruised face.

"He killed himself here in the basement. The storms killed my kids," I whispered with tears clogging my throat.

Adam ran his finger over my face in the picture. "You look happy."

I chuckled, "There were times when I was, and this day was one of those times. The photographer did a fantastic job, and the kids and I had a lot of fun."

I smiled, remembering how much fun the kids had, jumping and playing so the photographer could capture different expressions. Then, I noticed something new on the shelf. I walked over and pulled my photo album off the shelf. You could see where it had gotten wet, and there was mud streaked through some pages, but it was family photos. The world usually did everything digitally, but I still liked to have at least one album to thumb through. I knew Sam was the one who found it.

"I take it you didn't know this was over here?" Adam questioned while he watched me flip the pages.

"I thought I lost it with the storms. Sam must have found it," I sighed.

"He's a good man, isn't he?" Adam surmised.

"Yeah, he is," I confirmed.

"Alright, let's get this over with," Sam yelled across the basement.

I didn't want to leave the comfort of Adam's arms, but I knew I couldn't continue to ignore life. I closed my eyes, enjoying his embrace a second more before stepping out of his arms and placing the album back on the shelf before walking toward Sam and the undeniable future. I plopped down on the bed next to him. He sat at the edge of the bed, nursing his bottle of water.

"Sam, this is Adam. He is the person who saved me from freezing to death the night I thought you were dead," I stated.

I know it was unfair of me to keep bringing it up, but damn it, I was still pissed. Sam didn't say a thing in response to my introduction. It may have been better that way.

Adam didn't wait for me to say anything more he grabbed a stool and sat down with us.

"I'm going to give it to you straight. Jonathon, the killer, is my brother and has grown an attachment to Sara. I don't think he will hurt her, but I haven't spoken to him in years, so I don't know his agenda. Jonathon and I are twins, so he has used this to his advantage." He sighed.

I could see he was waiting for Sam to explode or blame him for bringing harm to our door.

Sam took a deep breath and said, "I guess this means we

are moving to keep our girl safe. Any suggestions as to where we should go?"

Adam shrugged as I said, "I have an idea."

"Jon knows about the house I'm staying in. It used to be our parents' place," Adam said.

"Good to know, but I have a different location in mind," I interjected.

During this conversation, Sam kept his head down, but at the mention of some new place, he raised it and gave me a questioning look.

I looked more at Adam as I spoke because once Sam heard what I had to say, he would know I omitted some critical information when I told him why I had Derek's license.

"I was sent to the police department to get answers. What I found was a young officer in desperate need of help. There was nothing I could do for him, but even as he lay dying, he helped me, or I should say, us. He has a fully stocked bunker out on the edge of town. I checked it out the other day. I think we should go there."

"You went by yourself?" was Sam's reply at the same time Adam said, "Why didn't you take me with you?"

I put my hands up in frustration. "I thought you were dead! I barely knew you and was conflicted about how I should feel about you. I'm not completely worthless. I can do some things on my own. Besides, I knew it would be empty," I huffed.

"I would have gone with you just so you had an extra set of hands," Adam whispered.

"I believe you, but have you ever heard the expression 'too good to be true'?" I didn't wait for his response and continued on. "Nothing in my life has worked out the way I wanted it to, not even a little bit! I lost my kids; my husband committed suicide and cited me as his reason. I've been called a whore, told I wasn't good enough, and for the second time in this life I lost someone I loved more than myself. If you look at what I have recently lived through, you would see two things. One, I don't feel worthy of you, and two, I am terrified you're just stringing me along. The bunker was somewhere that I had hopes for a new start, or at least a place I could hide from life until I was ready to try living again. I now understand by keeping it a secret from you I'm not helping myself or the two people I care about. I never intended to be so selfish. I was just trying to protect my own heart for a change and not let someone else take another piece of me." I finished with my head down, eyes closed, while trying to fight back the tears of failure.

I felt his hands on my cheeks before I noticed he was in front of me. He raised my head to look at him. I opened my eyes as a single tear escaped down my cheek.

Adam looked lost as he stood before me. "I had no idea. You should know I too have my own demons I'm fighting with. One of which is feeling like I'm not good enough for you. It sounds like we are going to have to learn how to figure out our own self-worth together."

Sam sat silently watching our conversation. He didn't interject or try to defend his own actions towards me. I reached over and grabbed his hand. I needed to let go of the pain of the past and start looking towards the future. One that I was fully expecting would include both of them.

"Let's pack up the essentials, and you can take us to our new home." Sam smiled.

"Yes, let's go see our new home," Adam agreed.

I liked the way the guys said 'our new home.' It told me they were both on board with my craziness. *Let's hope they stay this enthusiastic after they hear the voice on the radio and they see what the world truly has become.*

In silence, we all got up and started to pull together the items we deemed important. I went to collect the few pieces I still had to remind me of my old life—pictures and things. Adam was grabbing the medicine, and Sam went for the batteries and candles. Eventually, I was sure everything would make its way to the bunker, but for now we had what each of us thought was most important.

"I was thinking that we should take one vehicle. We can get the others there later," I suggested.

"I can't. I still need to check in on Naomi and the others," Adam interjected.

"Right, of course. I forgot—you can follow Sam and I," I quickly added. I dug into my bag and handed Sam the driver's license. "We are going here."

"Sounds good. Let's load up and head out," Sam replied before walking up the stairs.

I took one last look around. This was a final goodbye for me. I wasn't coming back. The boys could collect the rest. It was a final goodbye to the old me. I pulled the album close to my chest, turned, and walked out, leaving all that I was with Kyle behind.

The drive to the house was awkward and tense. I could sense Sam wanted to say something to me, but he never did. I should have probably interjected, but I didn't feel like answering the questions brewing within his mind. Before too long, we were pulling into a familiar driveway.

"It's all the way in the backyard," I stated before Sam could park.

He nodded and went into the backyard—not as far as I had, but it gave Adam plenty of space to pull in behind us. Once the car was turned off, I got out and went to Adam. I grabbed his hand and led him to the shed.

I opened the entry to the building and dug the key out of my pocket. The only sound was the hydraulics on the heavy blast door working to let us in. With the hatch open, I immediately descended into the dark. I remembered the feel of the ladder from last time and managed to get down it faster. At the bottom I waited for the men to join me.

"Which door?" Sam asked, looking around the small interior space.

Which door? That is an odd question. There is only one, I

thought before looking around. I was in such a hurry last time I hadn't noticed there were three doors.

"This is the one I went into last time I was here. I don't know what's behind the other two," I replied as I pulled the door open.

This was the same bunker, but it seemed different. I guess it was because I was seeing the space with more clarity than before. The crib still sat in the corner mocking me. I quickly turned from it as the guys made their way into the bunker. Neither said anything at first; they were looking at everything but not focusing on any one detail.

"Who did you say set this all up?" Adam asked.

"Derek, a police officer. It was meant for him and his family. His wife died in the first round of storms with his baby clutched in her hands," I stated before turning back to take in the room.

Under the wall of monitors was some kind of metal cabinet that ran almost the entire length of the space. I could see a box attached to the wall with pipes coming out of it. I couldn't read the brand, but I could tell it was an air filtration system. In the corner past the cabinet was a refrigerator.

I kept looking around the room, hurrying to glance past the crib towards the opposite wall with the two single beds along it. You could tell there was storage under the beds; they had handles that pulled out the bottom sections. Growing up I had a bed like this, but you could pull another bed out from below mine.

I walked over and bent down in front of the bed closest to the corner. I pulled the trundle bed out and was knocked on my ass. I had expected adult clothes, but instead I got infant clothing and a few picture frames of Derek and his family. I pulled one out. The baby had to be a few hours old given that the mom was still wearing the standard-issue hospital gown, and everyone who has had kids would have recognized the standard-issue hospital blanket.

Looking at the photo of this happy little family brought tears to my eyes. They were never going to grow old together. That baby would not get to experience anything. They were happy in this photo. Their life was perfect, if only for a little while.

I placed the picture back and pulled out the baby book. It was homemade, a scrapbook turned into a treasured memory. I opened the first page to see a picture of Derek as a baby. Below his was his wife's photo, and below it one of their little girl. She looked more like her mom, but she definitely had her dad's eyes.

"Sara, you need to close that drawer," Sam stated plainly.

"Sam" is all I got out before the tears came out more freely.

He pulled the baby book from my arms and placed it back in the drawer before shutting it.

"Why can't she look at that?" Adam asked more forcefully than needed.

"Because her kids haven't been gone very long, and this is going to trigger feelings she thought she had in check. Feelings that both of us need to keep under control, or the grief will eat us alive, consuming our every thought and overtaking the basic need to survive. It will encompass every ounce of her until she can't breathe or function," Sam stated before offering me his hand.

Instead of taking it, I scooted over to check the second drawer. I know I shouldn't have, but we needed to have a visual inventory of what we had. I swiped the tears and pulled out the drawer. I laughed when I saw it was full of washable diapers, formula, toys, and some wipes. I quickly shut it and stood up, wiping the remaining tears from my face.

Above the beds was a large picture of the solar system. It was captivating; the colors in the planets were vibrant and drew your attention. The only problem was that it was out of place. The rest of the walls were set up for efficiency, and this seemed like wasted space.

"Does that picture look odd to you guys?" I asked.

"It looks hand-painted. Perhaps his wife painted it, and it's up for sentimental value," Adam replied.

"Look around, there are no other art supplies. If his wife painted, there would be other supplies," I mumbled.

"That is odd, and why just one painting? There should be more," Sam interjected.

My eyes moved past the picture to the metal shelf full of bottled water, large containers of multi-vitamins, and multiple boxes of something called MRE.

"What's in those?" I asked while pointing to the MRE.

"Meals ready to eat," Sam answered.

I placed my back against the edge of the shelf and leaned as I took in the room. I felt the shelf shift and barely got my footing before it swung in to reveal another space. I walked into a smaller room with more shelves and a little kitchenette along the back wall—complete with a sink and stove. There was barely enough space for the three of us to be in the room at the same time.

"What a clever way to disguise something in plain sight. Derek was very thorough," Adam admired.

"Yeah, so then why the monster size painting?" I asked no one in particular.

"Perhaps it's also to hide something in plain sight," Sam hypothesized.

"Possibly, but what exactly would they be hiding?" I retorted.

"Guess there is only one way to find out," Adam said as he went back to the painting. By the time Sam and I got to the main room Adam was standing on the bed running his fingers along the underside of the frame.

"Bingo!" Adam exclaimed as we heard a clicking sound before he pulled the painting down from the top. There was a gun rack in the wall. Once it was fully opened, I could see knives as well, so a better term would be a weapons cabinet.

"I hope one of you two know something about those, because I have no clue," I blurted.

"I'm going to go see what's behind the other two doors," Adam explained a little more excited than I had seen him before.

I watched him walk out and thought about joining him, but Sam grabbed my arm. "Are you sure we can trust him?" he fretted.

"You don't trust my judgment?" I hissed.

"It's not that. I just worry about you," he confessed.

My anger subsided. "He is one of the good guys, just like you. This is a step in the right direction."

"If you say so," he whispered.

Sam walked over to the monitors and began messing with them. I could have warned him that they didn't work, but some things are best learned on your own.

Adam walked back in. "There are a bathroom and a generator in the other rooms."

I walked over and wrapped my arms around Adam, pulling him close. I don't know how long we stood like that, but it felt right. I released him first, but still kept my body close to his. I placed my hand in his and walked him over to the bed in the corner, sitting down and pulling him with me.

"I have a favor to ask of you," I pleaded.

"What do you need, babe?" he inquired.

"I want to go back to the police station and get Derek's body so he can be buried with his family. However, I can't do it myself. Will you please help me?" I begged.

"Absolutely. When would you like to do it?"

"Go now before it gets too dark, and while you guys are gone, I'll see if I can get something working on this wall," Sam interjected.

"I'm ready if you are," Adam assured before standing, pulling me up with him because we were still holding hands.

"Okay, then. We will see you after a bit, Sam. Good luck

with all the electronic stuff," I said before making my way out of the bunker.

At the top of the stairs, I stopped Adam. "We need some things before we leave. A tarp and some rope to tie around him would be helpful. I don't think he will be in the best of shape when we get there. It's been a bit since I left him."

"I have everything we will need in the SUV. What are you really worried about?" he asked.

"Adam, I left him there to die. He told me he was dead and that I needed to leave him there. I did, and I never returned to check up on him. I should have gone back, checked on him," I fretted.

"I'm sure he knew his body was dying and didn't see any reason for you staying just to watch him die," he stated plainly and rationally.

"I'm sure it is all true, but that doesn't make my heart feel any better," I said.

"It's not your fault, Sara. You couldn't have done more. There wasn't anyone to call or even medical service available to help him," Adam reassured.

"That's true, thank you."

With my hand still in his, Adam urged me, "Let's get going."

Once we were secured in the vehicle, I looked over at Adam. How could someone so kind, caring, and wonderful pick me? Would he regret it?

"Do you know where the station is?" I asked.

"Yes, don't worry. We will get Derek to his family." He squeezed my hand reassuringly.

It didn't take long to get to the station.

"Stay here and wait for me. You don't need to see him in this state," Adam said.

I didn't have the heart to tell him I'd seen and smelled worse. If he thought he was protecting me, so be it. What would it hurt? I sat in the SUV as he went in to take care of Derek.

The biggest change since the world stopped was the quiet. I missed the noises of life. Not necessarily the cars, but the kids playing and laughing. Every time my children giggled, I couldn't help but snicker with them. They both could light a room up. The silence reminded me of everything I'd lost. I tried not to fall into the chasm of despair that still surrounded my heart, but sometimes it was inevitable.

How long would it be before I couldn't remember the sound of their voices, the smell of their skin, or the smiles on their faces? The way they would say, 'I love you Mom.' How long until they began to fade? I didn't want to forget anything about them, yet I knew that wasn't realistic. Time would eventually rob me of them too.

The noise of the trees moving in the breeze was interrupted by the sound of shifting gravel; something was moving along the rocks. I tried to look out the mirrors without drawing too much attention but couldn't see anything. The steps were light, almost delicate, so I took a chance and got out. A few feet behind the vehicle was a cute little kitten sniffing around as it walked about. It didn't have a care in the world. The kids had always wanted a cat, but Kyle was allergic.

I bent down and waited for the little guy to notice me. It didn't take long before it was rubbing around my legs, purring loudly. It made me smile.

"You should keep it," Adam advised when he came out of the building carrying Derek effortlessly.

"Really, you think so?" I inquired.

"Of course, he can keep us company in the bunker." He smiled.

It didn't take much to convince me, and I wrapped the black and white bundle in my arms. He immediately nestled against my neck. I stood up, but before I could leave I heard a tiny cry and felt something crawling up my pant leg.

Adam grabbed the orange fur ball and chuckled. "I guess he doesn't want his brother to leave. Hope you can handle both."

"We will manage," I boasted as I snuggled into the kitten. "Are we good to go?" I asked.

"Yes, all set. Let's get our new family members home," he responded.

We both got in the vehicle with smiles on our faces. "My kids loved all animals, but they would have adored these two," I giggled.

"What should we name them?" Adam laughed.

"I'm not sure, let's wait and ask Sam too," I suggested.

"How long have you known Sam?" Adam cautiously asked.

"We used to be best friends, but we grew apart. I just found him again after the first round of storms, or I should say he found me." I sighed.

"Why did you grow apart?"

"He decided he loved me on my wedding day. He chose to walk away instead of watching me marry someone else."

"I imagine that had to be difficult, watching someone you love marry another."

"Adam, I don't want to talk about it anymore," I whispered.

"That's fine. I don't mean to pry. I was only trying to get to know you a little better," he admitted.

"You're fine. I understand why you are asking the questions, and eventually I will answer everything, but not now, okay?" I whispered.

He placed his hand on my thigh and squeezed it lightly. It was an unspoken acknowledgment of my request.

The silence between us was broken by the loud purring coming from the back seat. It felt good to laugh over something so small. I covered his hand with mine, content in this moment of partial normality.

To say Sam was surprised at the addition we brought with us would have been an understatement. He shook his head and laughed at me.

"What are your new friends' names?" he mused.

"I don't know. I thought perhaps you would have a suggestion." I smiled.

The kittens were making themselves at home, running around the room, getting into everything. Sam sighed. "How about the black one can be Chaos and the orange one can be Discord?"

I knew he was joking, but I liked them. "Perfect." I smirked.

Sam chuckled to himself and continued typing on the computer, trying to get the password-protected software to activate.

"Have you had any luck at all?" I inquired.

"No, not really. I need to get into these cabinets under here. There might be something in them I can use to help reach the outside world," he said more to himself than me.

I leaned down to look at the lock to see if perhaps I could find a usable key. The lock was the same as the entry, and I had the key in my bag. I looked around before it dawned on me, I had left it in Adam's vehicle.

"I'll be back," I muttered.

"I'll be here," Sam joked.

To my surprise I came out of the bunker and heard, "Damnit all to hell, son of a bitch, stupid piece of shit!" I walked behind the shed and over to Adam, who was pacing and swearing.

"Hey, what's wrong?" I hesitated.

"The damn ground is frozen solid! I can't even get a single shovel of dirt. I need the tractor to get him in the ground with his family," he fumed.

"Is there something else we could do?" I questioned.

"I put him in a large freezer in the house to keep the animals away from him. Looks like he will have to stay there until the ground thaws out, or I go bring the tractor here. I didn't mean to fail you."

"Adam, you haven't failed me. I understand there will be things that we are unable to do even with the best intentions. He is home, and that is another step forward in reuniting him with his family. I'm very proud of what you have accomplished for me. Could we light fires and unthaw the ground some so we can dig in it?" I leaned over and kissed his cheek.

"I should go check on some things first. Perhaps I will try that when I get back later," he said.

"I'm going to get my bag out of your car, and then I'm going back down." After grabbing my bag, I stopped in front of Adam and gave him a hug. "Don't be gone too long. I'll see you when you get back."

I walked a few feet before turning around. "The cats' names are Chaos and Discord."

You could hear his laugh reverberating around the yard, so I smiled.

I strolled into the bunker, observing both kittens sitting on the cabinet annoying Sam as he was trying to work. He either didn't see them or didn't care, but either way, it was funny to me. I couldn't hold the giggle in.

"Yeah, laugh it up. Did you find me the key to the cabinet?" he asked.

"I think so. It looks like it should take the same as the door to get down here," I replied while digging into my bag to get the handcuff key.

I unlocked the left side first, then the right. The door on the left slide opened to reveal a crate full of folders, each one labeled with a different person's name. Farther over we found blueprints of the prison and insane asylum. Even father down were maps of the town, outlining areas of the city and smaller towns still located within the state. They had places marked, but I didn't know why. Finally, at the far end were more file folders.

I leaned back, sighing. "Where do you want to start?"

Sam ran his hand through his hair, a motion I'd seen him do hundreds of times since we began our friendship again. He exhaled deeply. "I don't know. This isn't what I was hoping for."

"I know, but there has to be something useful here, or Derek wouldn't have it. You know that man did everything for a reason. We just have to figure out what it is," I explained.

"You're right, but I'm drained. I need to rest, or sleep, or do something to calm my overstressed nerves," he confessed.

"Okay, how about we try one of those MRE things on the shelf?"

The next few hours passed by in a blur of jokes and sharing funny things our kids used to do. It was good to talk about them again and learn who Samantha was. She would have been someone great to this world.

"Is this it for us?" Sam mused.

"What do you mean?"

"I mean, is this all there is to life now? We just sit in this bunker and hide?" he murmured.

"No, we find Jonathon and we dispose of him so he's no longer a threat to anyone. Perhaps we can find others that are a danger to society. Maybe look for other survivors...I know we aren't the only ones left," I confessed.

"How do you know this?" he asked.

"I heard someone on the fancy walkie-talkie last time I was in here, plus I have seen windows lit up and spoken to a few other survivors," I stated.

"Wait, what? Why didn't you tell me earlier?" he prompted.

"Until this moment, I didn't know if I was even going to tell you. The man on the walkie was younger, and he was worried about Derek. I couldn't tell him that Derek was dead. I turned it off and walked away. The other people are just staying to themselves and waiting for rescue."

I walked out of the kitchenette area and back into the main room. I felt drained and was more than ready to go to bed. "We will figure it out tomorrow. We have lots to go over to decide how we are going to proceed in this life. Goodnight, Sam," I whispered before crawling into one of the open beds. I knew when Adam got back he would join me. Sam nodded and moved over to the other bed to get comfortable.

"I hope you sleep well, Sara. Goodnight," Sam stated before he laid his head down.

I closed my eyes, hoping sleep would come easy, but it didn't. I couldn't shut off my mind. *Am I going to be able to do what needs to be done? Are you a murderer if you are only killing murderers? Will I be able to live with myself if I do take someone's life? How could I kill a man who looks exactly like Adam?*

When sleep finally claimed me it was the quiet oblivion I needed.

PART 2

SAM

Chapter 10

As I settled down to go to sleep, I reflected on everything that had led me to this place. All of the pain and suffering that brought me full circle back into the arms of the woman I swore I would never love again. How could I ever think revenge was going to make me feel better? I sought to mete out justice for those I loved. Is justice what I got? Closing my eyes, I embraced the sleep that screamed for me.

Many years ago...

"Sam, look, he asked me to marry him, and I said yes," Sara beamed as she shoved a ringed finger in my face.

"What? You're only seventeen. You can't get married," I retorted.

"Not this year, silly. We have to wait until he graduates, and by this time next year, I will be eighteen," she filled in.

"Why rush into anything?" I deadpanned.

This can't be happening; she can't really be marrying him. He will dull her shine. He's not what she needs. He's not good enough. This is ridiculous. Her mom won't let this happen.

"We aren't rushing anything; he loves me, and I love him. We are going to get married and start our lives together." She smiled.

"If that is what you want, then I guess congrats," I mumbled.

Wow, those words were harder to say than I imagined. How could she possibly want him? I thought she loved me?

"I know it's not exactly what you would call normal, but as long as my mom doesn't have a fit, I want you to be my maid of honor or at least one of Kyle's groomsmen if the thought of being my maid bothers you," she rushed to ask.

I could see she was holding her breath, waiting for my reply. She must have thought I was going to tell her no.

"Aren't you afraid I'll take the spotlight? I look mighty fine in a gown. No sweetheart neckline, though. I hate the way they look on me," I jested.

She laughed so hard she snorted, hitting me like a ton of bricks. If I was going to be at the end of the aisle, it wouldn't be beside her. It would be in front of her, asking her to be my bride.

She'd been my best friend for as long as I could remember. So why now did things have to change? Who was I kidding? I had wanted her since the night we kissed, but I waited too long, and now Kyle Lister would be her husband. Thinking of his name turned my stomach sour.

I gave her a hug as her other friends started to gather around. Then, I slipped out without saying anything else to her.

A week had passed since she showed me the ring. We were a month away from graduation, and I tried to keep my distance. I was putting space between us, and I could tell she didn't understand. Hell, I didn't even fully understand. I was a little disappointed when she called to tell me her mom said I couldn't be her maid of honor, but knowing her family as well as I did, I expected it.

A Month later...

"I am proud of each and every one of you. As you go into the world, think..." the principal droned on.

Come on, already, I have to get the hell out of this gym. I know she is looking at me, but I'm not going to look back over at her. Finally, we are all standing, throw the caps, no thank you, and I am out of here. I rushed and shoved past everyone to get to my mom and dad.

"All done. Let's go," I quickly said as I was removing my robe.

"Sam, wait, I want a few more pictures," my mom urged.

"No, we got enough. I'll turn my robe in and meet you at the car." I hurried.

"Wait, don't you want a picture with Sara?" my dad yelled.

I was already gone, past the chairs and halfway down the hall. I had to turn the gown in, get my diploma, and head home. I had effectively avoided talking to her for the entire month. I should have owned up to my feelings and told her why I'd been distant, but it wouldn't do any good, so why bother?

I was waiting in the car when my parents finally arrived.

"Is Sara coming to your party? I would like a picture of the two of you," Mom inquired.

"I didn't invite her, so no, she won't be there," I whispered, ashamed of my actions.

"What do you mean you didn't invite her? She is your best friend," Dad accused.

"Not anymore, Dad, just leave it," I mumbled, praying they would drop the subject.

A year later...

"Hello, Mrs. Alperstein. Is Sam home?"

The sound rang out strong and confident, a tone I'd known for years, the very voice I heard in my dreams.

"No, I'm sorry, dear. He isn't," my mom replied.

I knew she hated lying for me, but what choice did she have? I suppose she could have told her the truth. It was petty of me, but I was mad at her, even if she didn't know why.

"Okay, I wanted to drop off your invitations and make sure that Sam got his. I really hope you can all come," Sara bubbled on.

"Come in and sit down for a few minutes. It's been a while since you've come by. The last time I saw you was months ago." Mom ushered her into the family room while I stood hidden out of sight. I could see them from my spot in the kitchen, but they couldn't see me.

"It has been a bit. I've just been busy, and I didn't know when Sam was supposed to be back in town. I guess I thought he would come find me when he returned." Sara sighed.

"Men are stubborn creatures. They have to figure things out in their own time, which is usually twice as long as women take." Mom grinned.

"Sam has always been a bit stubborn; that is nothing new. I would love it if you guys could make it to the wedding," Sara said.

"I can't speak for Samuel, but Eli and I will definitely be there. Sara, are you happy?" my mother inquired.

Mom was never one for mincing words. She knew how much I cared about Sara and exactly what this marriage was doing to me. Sara had no clue, and I know my mom thought it only fair to tell her everything before it was too late. In my mind, it was already too late. Sara had made her choice, and it hadn't been me.

"Of course, I'm happy. If I wasn't, I wouldn't be marrying him," Sara chuckled.

"Dear, sometimes the heart doesn't know exactly who it needs until it has settled for someone else," Mom clucked as she grabbed Sara's hands in hers.

"I have a feeling you are talking about Sam. I've loved him

for years, and he never felt the same. Here is someone who loves me and tells me he does every day. If Sam was in love with me, he had his chance to tell me. I do still love him, but I'm no longer in love with him. I've moved on, and he needs to do the same, if that is what you are getting at." Sara sighed.

I knew she still loved me. I could hear it in every ounce of her denial, and I didn't know who she was trying to convince more: my mom or herself.

"I understand, and I will be happy to join you on your wedding day, Sara." Mom smiled.

Sara stood up and gave my mom a hug before turning to leave. As she reached for the door, she said, "I really want you there, Sam. I miss my best friend."

She never turned around or waited for a response; she just left. I thought I was far enough out of sight that she wouldn't have noticed I was there. I'd used this spot to spy on my parents multiple times over the years. I was wrong, but she didn't call me out or make a huge scene.

"Are you going to come in here and talk to me now or just stay standing there like an idiot?" Mom glared.

"What do you want me to say?" I sighed before coming into the family room and sitting beside my mom.

"I want you to go tell that girl that you love her and have for a very long time. I want you to be honest with yourself and her. I want you to man up and go after what you want instead of waiting for it to fall into your lap," Mom ordered.

"Mom, I love you, but you know I can't. She made her mind up, and her choice is him," I confessed.

"Did you ever tell her she had another option? Did she know you wanted to be more than her best friend? Did you give her any indication that you wanted her to be yours?" Mom stood forcefully, stiffened her upper body, and balled her hands at her sides.

"You know I didn't, Mom. I never found the right time. There was always something happening. Life got in the way.

Before I knew it, I was out of time. That's on me, but I'm not going to destroy her love for him by telling her I want to keep her as my own. It's my bed I've made, and I will just have to lay in it, alone," I surmised.

"Are you going to the wedding, son?" she coaxed.

"Yes, Mom, I will be going to the wedding. If I can't have her as my wife, then I refuse to lose her as a friend," I breathed.

Two months later...

"Gladys, how much longer are you going to be? Poor Samuel is sweating to death in his suit," Dad chuckled.

"I'm fine, Dad. I'm just a little bit nervous," I confessed.

"There is nothing to be nervous about. You have known this girl for years. Be happy for her and show her you can still be a good friend," Dad interjected.

"That's the plan, Dad." I smiled.

My entire body felt like it was going to implode, my hands were sweaty, and my heart was racing ninety miles a minute. All I could think was it should have been me standing up there waiting to see her walk down the aisle. Instead, I would be a spectator. I wanted to throw up. Perhaps I should have so I could have told my mom I was sick and couldn't go. No, that was the coward's way out, and I was no coward.

I sat down and tried to focus my breathing and calm my nerves. I had finally gotten relaxed when Mom walked in.

"Why are you sitting? It's time to go. We're going to be late as it is," she warned.

I stood immediately and followed them out the door.

The drive to the church was a blur. I kept replaying a scene where Sara would run into my arms and tell me she loved me more than him. I knew it was wishful thinking, but it calmed me in a way nothing ever had. She was my other half, and I let her slip through my fingers because I had been too blind to see it.

We pulled up to the church, and I quickly got out to help Mom from the car. Mom chuckled as I gave her an over-the-top bow before taking her hand and helping her out. I always knew how to make her laugh. I hooked her arm into mine and made my way up to the doors.

With Mom secured on my arm, I waited for our turn to go in. I hadn't gotten to the door before I was approached by Greyson, Kyle's best man, and from what I knew his only friend.

"You're not supposed to be here," he forcefully spat.

"I am. I have an invitation. I was invited by the bride," I calmly replied.

"I'm under strict orders not to let you in. You are not welcome here," he reiterated.

"Says who? Where is Sara? She is the one who invited me," I replied, starting to get agitated.

There was a commotion in front of the doors before they were shoved open.

"You are not welcome here. You can either leave, or I will have you physically removed by the police," Kyle hissed.

"Sara is expecting me and my family today. We already told her we would be here," I tried to rationalize.

"Your parents can come in, but you can't. I don't know what game you are trying to play, but I'm not allowing it. Do you have any idea how upset she was when you left without so much as a goodbye? Do you know how long she cried for you, her friend who was ignoring her, and she didn't know what she did wrong? Do you have any idea how long she has loved you? You will not ruin today for her. She picked me, not you! You can either leave on your own, or Greyson and Tommy will help you to your car," Kyle seethed.

"Now you listen to me, son..." Mom started.

"It's fine, Mom. I don't want to ruin her special day. I'll go home," I advised before kissing her cheek.

I walked away from the church with my hands in my pockets and my head hung low in defeat. I wanted them to believe they won, but I owed it to Sara to be there. I waited until the ushers left the doors as the ceremony began. I couldn't sit in the church because Kyle probably had someone on standby to call the police, but I could get into the atrium and hopefully see her before she walked down to him.

I slowly opened the door and crept inside and saw her waiting at the end of the aisle. She took my breath away. She was beyond beautiful. I could see she was shaking and tightened her hold on her dad's arm. He leaned in and whispered, "We could just turn around and go out those doors, no explanation needed. I'll send someone back for your mom."

I hadn't understood how much I missed her until I heard her laugh at her dad before throwing her shoulders back and saying. "I'm good, Dad. Let's go."

Then she was gone, one foot in front of the other, making her way to him. I wanted to run up to her and stop her. Freeze the whole thing and tell her how I felt. I took two steps before a weight pressed on my shoulder.

"It's too late, son. She's following her heart," Dad whispered.

Why did those simple words make me want to rip my own from my chest?

"It's not fair, Dad," I sighed.

"Life rarely is, son," he said.

I watched as she moved to him and took his hand in hers. I'd seen enough. I turned around and walked away from her again. The only difference was this time she never knew I was there.

One year Later...

"Mark, I can't thank you enough for this opportunity," I stated.

"Think nothing of it. You are doing me a favor. It's all yours now, son, enjoy," Mark concluded.

With a final handshake he was gone, leaving me in charge.

"Rebecca, I'm going to go get a coffee from the shop across the street. Would you like something?" I asked my administrative assistant.

"Mr. Alperstein, I can go get your coffee," she offered as she stood from her desk.

"No, stay and work. I'll get it. Did you want anything?" I chuckled.

"No, sir, I'm good, but thank you." She blushed.

Her reddened cheeks made me smile. Seeing that I could make the almost fifty-year-old blush like a teenager made my heart feel good. Life was finally moving in a positive direction.

The walk to the coffee shop was uneventful, but as I opened the door to enter the woman whom I thought I'd never see again walked out. She didn't see me, and chirped, "Thank you," with her hands full and her husband beside her.

How can you thank somebody and not look at them? I was so stunned by her nonchalance that I hadn't noticed someone else was trying to exit the shop. I went inside even though I was still watching them walk away. The next thing I felt was cold liquid running down my chest. I looked at my not-so white shirt then into the shocked eyes of a pretty brunette.

"I'm so, so sorry," she stuttered.

"Your eyes are very unique. What color are they?" I mumbled.

What am I thinking? I'm standing, blocking the door, covered in some sticky caramel-smelling iced coffee, and I'm asking her what color her eyes are? I need a swift kick in the a...

"My mom calls them topaz; my dad argues they are amber. So, take your pick," she chuckled as she moved a stray piece of hair out of her face.

"I'm Samuel, but everyone calls me Sam," I said.

"Ellen. I will pay to have your shirt cleaned; I am so sorry I wasn't watching where I was going." She blushed.

"Don't worry about it, Ellen. I am just as guilty as you for not watching where I was going. My head was somewhere else," I mused.

She quickly dug into her purse and pulled out a business card. With pen in hand, she scribbled something on it.

"Here is my number. Call me when you take your shirt to the dry cleaners. I insist you let me pay for the cleaning," she firmly stated.

"How about you let me take you out to dinner instead?" I countered.

I looked down at her card with a picture of a ballerina on it. She was a dance instructor. I could see it. She was about 5'7", athletically built, and carried herself with a power most people could only wish for.

"My mother would have a heart attack if she knew I was even contemplating this, but sure. When do you want to go out?" she responded with what I took as a bored tone. Her posture was relaxed. She didn't seem to be in a hurry, but I got the vibe she wasn't completely into the idea. Heck, she didn't exactly have the enthusiasm I was hoping for, but she had said yes, and that was a start.

"How about tonight? We could meet at the steak house, or if you'd prefer, we could go to Sofia's Diner. Your pick," I proposed.

I was a Sofia's kind of a guy. You could get some nice home cooked meals there. The steak place was expensive, not very good, and had its reputation because one blogger stated it was romantic. Sara and I used to go on Saturday nights and chuckle at the guys our age trying to win over their latest conquest with expensive, crappy food. The potato soup was good—our standard order back in the day.

"Don't take this the wrong way, but the steak house is overpriced, and I don't like the food. I'm a Sofia's kind of girl," she said hesitantly.

"Finally, I found a woman after my own heart. I will meet you there tonight at seven if that works for you?"

"That works for me." She smiled, glancing at her watch.

"Oh shoot. Sam, it was nice meeting you, but I'm going to be late for my morning class. See you tonight."

She turned and hurried down the street. I looked at my ruined shirt and chuckled. When I went in and ordered my coffee, my stained shirt drew everyone's eyes. My state of dress should have upset me, but it didn't because I met someone who I hoped would help me move on.

When I walked into the office later, Rebecca's eyes told me exactly how bad it looked.

"Mr. Alperstein, what happened to your shirt?" she inquired.

"I wasn't paying attention to where I was going and walked into a cold cup of coffee." I chuckled.

"Your mom has told me for years you spend too much time with your head in the clouds," she jested.

"Imagine how boring life would be if we were all grounded all the time," I kidded.

Walking into my office, I went to the small closet Mark had installed years ago. I was glad I listened to him and put a few changes of clothes there. I stripped out of the sticky clothes. My skin was tacky, but after a few minutes of cleaning, I was back to looking put-together.

The rest of the day flew by. Who knew insurance could be so time-consuming? I did enjoy the job, and I think that helped pass the day.

"Goodbye, Mr. Alperstein. Have a great weekend," Rebecca called from her desk.

I walked out to see her shutting her computer down. "You too, and don't tell my mom about my shirt at book club tonight, please," I begged.

"I may work for you, but your mom is my best friend. I make no such promise." She smiled.

She collected her things and was gone in a moment. I chuckled, thinking about the phone call I'd be getting either later that night or first thing in the morning.

I went back to my desk to finish up. The work came easy to

me, and before I knew it, it was six thirty. This meant I didn't have time to go home before meeting Ellen. I shut down the program and turned my monitor off. Glancing in the mirror, I made a few minor adjustments to my hair and straightened my shirt. It was now or never.

I got to the diner fifteen minutes early and was surprised to see Ellen there sitting in a corner booth. The exact same booth I picked every time I went there. She had a cup of coffee in front of her and an order of nachos.

"Decided to eat without me?" I joked.

She jumped a little, not seeing me approaching her.

"Okay, confession time. I can eat a lot. I have a very healthy appetite and have been told it's un-ladylike. So, I usually come early, order an appetizer or two, and eat it before my date arrives so I don't eat so much in front of them." She blushed.

I slid in the seat across from her. "Who says its un-lady-like?"

"Previous dates, my mom, my best friend. Actually, a lot of people have said it, now that I think about it." She chuckled.

"I don't care what they say. I say if you're hungry, then you should be allowed to eat." I looked over at her, and she blushed. It was cute, and I found I liked making her cheeks glow a light shade of red.

"Do I get one of your nachos, or are you stingy with your food?" I ventured.

"Help yourself. I also have stuffed mushrooms and an order of spicy wings coming. Janice should be coming back at any moment," she beamed.

I wanted to laugh but didn't want to offend her. She reminded me so much of Sara it was kind of scary, but in a good way because unlike Sara, there was a chance Ellen could be mine.

"How long have you been waiting?" I inquired instead.

"I've been here about fifteen minutes now. They're usually faster than this. I had hoped to have a clean table when you got here," she admitted, and again her cheeks flared.

"I always try to arrive early. I'd rather be too early than late. My mom is an arrive-exactly-on-time or fashionably late kind of person, and I guess I don't want the attention of being the last one to arrive. Yet, here I am, the last one to arrive." I smiled.

She ducked her head so I couldn't see the color returning to her cheeks. She was adorable.

"How was class today?"

"It was good. I wasn't late, thankfully. The house rule is if you're late you have to do a double pirouette in front of the class and then the class gets to critique you. Let me tell you, dancers are not nice when it comes to critiquing. I'm lucky I have the younger group and they are still learning the basics, but they would have had to try and perform the dance move if they were late. I follow the same rule because I want the kids to understand just because I'm adult doesn't mean I don't have to follow the rules too," she finished before stuffing a chip into her mouth.

"That's actually a really great way to look at things. Most adults have the mindset of 'I'm the adult and I don't have to if I don't want to.' I think you are teaching your students a life lesson," I stated.

"Some of my students were born with golden spoons in their mouths, so I doubt the lesson will resonate with them, but it won't be for a lack of trying." She smiled.

"You have a beautiful smile."

"It's just a smile, Sam. So, tell me about you. Do you have any brothers or sisters, secret wives I should be leery of?" she joked.

"No siblings. I was an only child. I'm just fresh off my third divorce. Mail order brides are nothing like they claim to be on the brochures," I said.

The look on her face was priceless, and I couldn't tell whether she was offended, worried, or a little scared of me.

I started laughing in earnest. "I'm joking, Ellen. I've never been married."

"Oh, well, you never really know about people," she chided.

"Don't be angry. I was just joking. Perhaps it was in poor taste," I concluded.

"No, it's me. The last guy I was with told me he was single, but I found out three months into our relationship he was married and had four kids. It was a real blow to my self-esteem because how could I have not known?" she queried.

"Did you love him?"

"I thought I did. I'm not so sure now, but that could be because I've convinced myself he didn't deserve my love. Sometimes people only show you what they want you to see. He was the first guy I'd dated since my fiancé died. I think I trusted him more than I should have because I was lonely. He reminded me of Jack so much I was blinded by the love I had for Jack," she theorized.

"That's understandable. How did your fiancé die?" I inquired.

"He got hit by a drunk driver. He and the other driver were killed instantly. They told me at the hospital he felt no pain, but how could that be? You would think as the other car hit his, he would have had to register some form of pain before it all stopped." She sighed. "I'm sorry, I'm taking us down a dark place I shouldn't go down."

"It's okay. I find myself questioning things that most people wouldn't think twice about, so I understand. How long ago did you lose him?"

"Almost two years ago now. I know I should be able to move on, but it's hard to move past your first love," she reasoned.

"I agree. Do you have any brothers or sisters?" I asked, trying to change the subject to something lighter.

"I have a twin sister, Katy, but I'm the baby by three full minutes. And no, I'm not spoiled. However, my dad might disagree on that one." She laughed.

"Why do you teach instead of performing?"

"Not every dancer has the drive to perform in front of a large group. I always thought I would be a grade school teacher, but I loved dance too much to give it up. The solution was a no-brainer for me. I would teach dance and then I could do both of the things I loved. There was never another option for me. I followed my passion, and it led me here."

"I commend you for following your dream," I offered.

"What about you, Sam? What do you do for a living?"

"I sell insurance."

"That sounds really boring." She giggled.

"To some I'm sure it is, but I enjoy it and it comes easy to me," I interjected.

Right on cue, her face turned that radiant shade of pink. I was starting to enjoy seeing the color on her cheeks.

Janice came over to take our orders, giving Ellen a nice break to collect her thoughts. She wasn't kidding when she said she could eat a lot. She ordered more than me, and that's saying something because I was no lightweight when it came to food. I was enamored by her. She had delicate features but definitely wasn't fragile. She could hold her own in the conversation and never backed down from any question I threw at her. It didn't take long for our food to arrive.

"What about you? Have you ever been in love?" she asked before stuffing a fork so full of pasta you couldn't even see the tongs into her mouth.

"Yes, it didn't work out. I was young and stupid. Lessons learned and all that mumbo jumbo," I replied.

I know I was being vague, but Sara was a memory I didn't want to share. Nor did I want the look of pity or the hundreds of questions. I could tell Ellen knew there was more to the story, but luckily, she didn't pry. She just smiled and continued to eat.

The banter between us for the rest of the evening was light and jovial. Ellen was smart and quick-witted. When she giggled it was full belly laughs, and she couldn't care less about what the people around us thought. There was a comfort between us, as if we had been friends for years. I wasn't immediately sexually attracted to her, but I knew with more time spent together that those feelings would develop as well.

I paid the bill and walked her to her car. "That was a lot of fun. I can't remember the last time I laughed so much," I declared.

"I had a really great time, Sam." She smiled.

I leaned in and kissed her cheek. When she didn't pull away, I moved to her lips. It was a light, lingering kiss. There was no spark of lust or driving need to take the connection further, yet it was nice and sweet.

"I say we do this again," I coaxed.

"I would have to say I agree," she breathed, leaning in for another kiss.

I waited for her to break the connection since she initiated it and opened her car door for her.

"I will call you tomorrow," I stated, watching as she slid into the driver's seat.

"You better," she joked.

I watched her drive out of sight and decided instantly that she was what I needed in my life.

I drove home in silence, trying not to compare her kiss with Sara's, but failed miserably. Sara's lips were thinner than Ellen's, and Sara was full of unexplored passion. Sara moaned when I kissed her like it was the best thing she had ever felt. Ellen didn't show that much enthusiasm. I should have never walked away from Sara that night, but the feelings she pulled from me had scared me. I wanted to make her mine so badly, but I was afraid I would hurt her. I knew she was a virgin and needed soft loving, not the inexperienced fumbling of an overly horny youth.

Even though I was thinking about her, she took it as rejection. Why was I so stupid? I should have told her how much I wanted her. I should have showed her, and I could have helped her tap into her passionate side.

There was an easy camaraderie between Ellen and me. We would be happy with one another. Perhaps not completely fulfilled, but there was a mutual respect that needed no explanation. She was safe and would be a wonderful mother. I was going to do everything in my power to make sure she stayed in my life.

Over the next few months we were inseparable, and before I knew it, we were moving into our own apartment. She was exactly what I needed to ease the memory of Sara.

Life flew by in a flash, and before I knew it, I was waiting at the end of the aisle for my bride to join me. Ellen was breathtaking to me, dressed all in white, with a smile only for me, and I would spend the rest of my life making her happy. Sara was nothing but a memory locked away in my heart.

My future wife was about to make me the happiest man alive. We were going to live happily ever after. It was not exactly a fairy tale, but whose life was? What we had meant much more. We had love and respect for one another. Yes, we fought, but we made up and learned from our mistakes.

Two Years Later...

"Sam, we have to go. My water broke!" Ellen yelled.

"We have time, dear. We will get to the hospital, but we need your overnight bag and the car seat," I calmly replied.

It was time. I was nervous, and if I thought about it too long, I would throw up. *No overthinking, just action.*

Fourteen long hours later, I finally got to meet my sweet little girl. She was six pounds, four ounces of perfection. While she was small and delicate, like her mother, she had my eyes and nose. I never thought I could love someone I just met so much, but I did. She had stolen my heart right out of my chest.

"Good job, Momma. She is perfect, and so are you," I whispered to Ellen.

"She is, isn't she?" She smiled, staring into my eyes, and within the next breath she slumped back against the bed, her head rolling to the other side, losing consciousness.

That wasn't normal. "Nurse, help me!" I frantically cried.

There was blood all over the bed. *What is happening?* She was so pale and drawn in.

"We need to get her to the OR immediately; she is hemorrhaging," the doctor demanded.

They wheeled her out of the room and left me standing there so confused, still holding our baby girl. A nurse came in a few minutes later. "Let me take her back to the nursery. You can head up to OR and wait for the doctor."

"What is happening?" I pleaded.

"If they don't stop the bleeding, she will die, but your doctor is the best. He will save her. Give me Samantha, and I will take care of her until you and Ellen are back in this room."

I was confused and torn. Should I stay with my daughter like my wife would want, or should I go to be with her? I needed her to know I would be there for her, so I handed my child to the nurse and went to find my wife.

I waited for what felt like days before the doctor came out.

"She is stable and will recover completely, but due to complications we had to do a partial hysterectomy. This means she can't have any more children, but hopefully she won't suffer menopausal symptoms," he stated.

"She's only twenty-three, and you gave her a hysterectomy?" I was baffled.

"We had no choice, Mr. Alperstein. We did what we had to in order to save her life. She is in recovery, and they will move her back down to the maternity ward in an hour," he forcefully stated.

The doctor turned and walked away with a huff. I hadn't intended on questioning his methods, but I hadn't been expecting any of this. I went back down to the nursery and asked the nurse to bring Samantha to the room.

When I reached the room, my mom was waiting with a confused look on her face. I had to explain it all to her and watch all the emotions play across her features. Ellen was too young for this, but life doesn't always go the way we plan.

By the time they brought Ellen down I could read in her face she knew what had happened.

"Hey, it looks like we are continuing the family tradition of having only one child," I joked.

She chuckled slightly and then started to cry. I sat on the edge of the bed and pulled her into my arms. I held her as she cried. I didn't tell her it was going to be okay or that our life was great as it was. I let her cry because she needed to feel all of the emotions and accept what life had thrown our way.

After two days in the hospital, both of my girls were released. Ellen was given strict orders to start seeing a counselor since the surgery could cause depression. I offered to go to counseling with her, but she told me it was something she had to do for herself.

The routine with a newborn was difficult to get used to, but we both worked at it. We were parents, and that meant we shared the load. Eventually, things got easier, or we got used to the extra chaos. Life was wonderful; everything was as it should have been.

Days turned into weeks, weeks into months, and months into years.

Chapter 11

Six Years Later...

It was a little after seven when the phone rang. I wasn't expecting anyone but Ellen; perhaps she was calling to say she was going to be late. She was already late, but that was normal. When she went to her folks, she tended to lose track of time.

I picked up the receiver. "Hello?"

"Mr. Sam Alperstein?" the soft female voice asked.

"Yes, may I help you?"

"Your wife Ellen and daughter Samantha are at the hospital. They were in an automobile accident," she stated.

I moved quickly to get my keys. "What hospital are they at?"

"They are at Mt. Zion off of Market Street, sir. They are both in ICU. You will need to bring identification to be buzzed into the wing," she explained.

Those words were a sucker blow to my stomach. I stopped moving; I couldn't breathe. Surely, she hadn't said what I thought I heard. Intensive care unit—that meant they were in critical condition.

"I will be there as quickly as I can."

The drive was a blur; I was at the hospital in minutes. I ran through the doors and quickly sprinted up the steps. The ICU was on the fourth floor. I stopped at the desk outside, showing them my ID.

"Go through to the next nurse's station, sir" the nurse behind the desk advised.

I walked as fast as my legs would carry me around to the other desk.

The nurse was on the phone, so I had to wait. I heard a familiar voice. "Man, you are lucky to be alive. What were you thinking? I thought you said you were sober enough to drive? I knew you were lying."

"Kyle, man, lay off. I'm fine. It was just a minor accident," Greyson stated.

I barely recognized Kyle. Greyson looked the same as he did at Sara's wedding, minus the tuxedo. His eyes where swollen and starting to show bruising, the bridge of his nose had dried blood on it as well as under his nostrils, and he was handcuffed to the wheelchair he was sitting in.

"You could have died. Those people in the other vehicle could die, and it will be on you," Kyle stated.

"I didn't do anything wrong. She was in my lane. Whatever happens to her and her brat is on her head, not mine. Besides, Dad can fix anything. He always has," Greyson chuckled.

"Man, that's not funny. Can you be serious for a minute at least?" Kyle sighed.

I turned back to the nurse when I heard her hang the phone up. "I'm here for my wife and daughter, Ellen and Samantha Alperstein."

"Mr. Alperstein, please go sit in the waiting room, and I will let the doctor know you're here." She motioned towards another door.

I left Greyson and Kyle bickering in the hallway and went into the waiting room. I didn't get a chance to sit down before the door swung open.

"Mr. Alperstein, I am Dr. Shaw. I'm sorry to have to tell you this, but your family didn't make it. We did everything we could, but the damage was too extensive. We lost them both," he stated. I could tell he was sorry, but he was already turning from me, too busy to give me more time.

"I'm sorry, what?" I questioned, knowing I heard him but still questioning my own ears.

"The nurse can take you to the room your family is in. Again, I am sorry for your loss," he finished before turning and walking away.

Behind the doctor stood a young nurse. "If you would follow me, I will take you to them," she whispered. She looked at me briefly then moved on. I wanted to ask her if the doctor was sure it was my family, but that seemed stupid. My feet moved, feeling heavier than normal. Each step forward was harder to take than the last.

We passed Greyson as the cop was moving him. "We need to go to the station once you get discharged from the doctor."

The nurse quietly opened a door at the end of the hall and ushered me in. "I will give you some time alone. Pick up the phone and dial nine if you need me," she murmured.

I walked fully into the room and watched her turn and leave like she was on fire. I looked away from the door and saw both of my girls lying on hospital beds with white sheets pulled up to their necks. This had to be a joke. They looked like they are sleeping.

I walked over to the beds. They were close enough together that I could touch both my daughter and my wife. I placed my hand on the side of Samantha's face as I bent down to kiss her on the forehead. There was little warmth left in her, and that radiant glow of life was no longer present. I leaned my head into hers and whispered, "I love you, little bug."

The tears were threatening to fall, and I was trying to stay strong, but here I was looking at my wife and daughter, dead.

It took a moment to connect the dots. Greyson had to have been the other driver. He said it was her fault. I didn't believe that for a moment. He seemed drunk or on drugs to me. How did he walk away from an accident that killed my girls with a head injury and a few scratches? I wanted to look and see exactly what killed the girls but couldn't bring myself to lift the sheet.

I laid my head on Ellen's shoulder and cried. I had to tell her parents and mine. I was going to have to deal with the police investigation. Was this an accident or something more?

"Sweetheart, I love you so much. I won't stand by and let him get away with this. Greyson will be punished to the fullest extent of the law. I know you and our daughter are together. I love you both. Why did you have to leave me? Life was perfect, baby. Why couldn't it have stayed as it was?" I cried.

I don't know how long I sat with them. Long enough for someone to come in and ask which funeral home I wanted the girls sent to. I sat with them until the director came to collect them.

"Mr. Alperstein, my name is Lori, and I am a grief counselor with the hospital. It's time for them to be moved, but I'm here if you want to talk about anything," she said.

"No, I think I'm just going to go home," I whispered.

"Take my card with you. Call me at any time." She extended her hand to me.

"Thanks," I said, taking her card.

I shoved the paper in my pocket and drove home in a mental fog. As soon as I walked in the door, I went to the phone.

Blowing out the breath I pulled in, I dialed Ellen's parents slowly. It was one of the most challenging calls I had to make.

"Hello," Catherine answered.

I took a deep breath in and tried to control the modulation of my voice. "Catherine, it's Sam."

"Hi dear, did the girls make it home?" she asked, fully expecting me to say yes.

"There was an accident on the way home. The girls were in a car crash and didn't make it," I whispered.

She didn't say a word. I heard the phone hit the tile, and

then I heard her scream, "Robert, they're gone. Our girls are gone." She was sobbing, and I didn't know if I should hang up.

I heard the phone being jostled and then, "Hello, who is this?" Robert demanded.

"It's Sam. The girls died this evening as a result of a car crash. I don't know any other specifics. I have to make more calls, Robert; I'm sorry," I finished before hanging up.

The second most difficult was my own mom. The phone rang twice before I heard her voice. "Hello."

"Mom" was all I got out of before I started crying. Then, finally, I couldn't keep it in anymore.

"Sam, what's wrong, hun?" she calmly inquired.

"Ellen and Samantha are dead, Mom. They died in a car accident. What am I going to do?" I cried into the phone.

I couldn't breathe a lungful of air as I hung up and fell to my knees. I don't know how long I rocked on the floor before I felt my mom's hand on my shoulder, and then I was up and in her arms. I cried more than I ever had. My world had just fallen apart.

Two days later we sat in the funeral director's office picking out caskets, flowers, poems, and many other things no one would actually think about, but each detail served a purpose. After seeing the casket my daughter was going to be in, I shut down. I couldn't handle it anymore. Too much, too fast, and it still hadn't hit me that they were truly gone. Thankfully, Katy and mom took care of the rest of the arrangements. I was there physically, but mentally I was fighting a daily battle to keep involved. I wanted to check out.

Three weeks after the funeral service there was a knock at my door. I went to answer it and was surprised to see a detective standing in front of me.

"Mr. Alperstein?" he inquired.

"Yes, and you are?" I questioned with little to no care of his answer.

I knew how I looked. I hadn't shaved since the service,

couldn't remember the last time I took a shower, and had been living in my pajamas for days. I smelled bad and looked worse.

"I'm Detective Thomas Mackaby. I need to talk to you regarding the investigation into your wife's accident," he offered.

"Come on in. Don't mind the house," I deadpanned.

"I don't care what your house looks like. I am fairly certain I've seen worse," he responded.

We walked into the living room; I threw the covers from the loveseat to the chair. Since Ellen's death, I hadn't been able to sleep in our bed and instead camped out on the couch. I motioned for him to take the seat I had cleared.

Detective Mackaby sat down and pulled out a small notebook. I could feel his eyes taking everything in, observing my every movement and mannerism.

"I am sorry for your loss. I won't even pretend to understand what you must be going through. I just want to clarify a few things, and then I will be on my way," he stated.

I nodded.

"Has anyone told you anything about the accident?"

"Nope, every time I call the station, they take a message and no one calls me back."

"We believe your wife was hit by a drunk driver. We have done all we can, and now it's up to the state's attorney to prosecute the accused. I came here as a courtesy to your dad; no one knows I'm here. There has been a mistake made by a rookie, and because of it we lost the breathalyzer results. The hospital never did a blood draw, so the state's attorney is fighting an uphill battle," he declared.

"You mean Greyson could walk away from this a free man even though he killed both of them?" I hissed.

"That is a possibility, but I need you to keep a level head about all of this. I wanted you to be prepared, so when the trial starts next week you have some idea of what you will be hearing. I have also heard that Greyson requested a trial by judge, so there will be no jury to determine his guilt or innocence," he said.

"It is scheduled to start next week?"

"I'm sure the message is on your machine, which seems to be pretty full. If I were you, I would be the man I know you are and pull yourself together. Take some free friendly advice from another husband and father. You need to help find justice for your family. It is your job as a father and a husband to make sure this guy gets what he deserves. If you need anything, have your dad call me and I will come back over. In the meantime, take a shower, change your clothes, and go sleep in your own bed. It's time to deal with the pain instead of hiding from it."

He stood without another word and left. I wasn't hiding from it; I felt the pain every waking second of every day. I didn't want to dive into it, dwell on it, or lose myself to the grief.

As I stood in front of the answering machine, I realized wallowing in my own self-pity was exactly what I had been doing. There were others who were hurting, and I made it all about me.

I pressed the play button and listened to concerned friends, my parents, Ellen's family and even Rebecca from the office. All worried about me. The last two messages were the most important. The first was regarding the headstone I had ordered and when it would be set on the girls' grave. A place I'd thought about but hadn't been to since they were deposited there. The last message was the state's attorney Blake Stanton. He wanted to talk to me before things went to trial. He left his number, but it was too late to call. I would have to try him tomorrow.

I looked around at the cocoon I had created for myself and my life. I finally saw what Thomas saw. I picked up the mess and made for the shower. Once clean and smelling much better, I took a few moments to shave the overgrowth of facial hair. Looking in the mirror, I saw the man my wife had married.

I went to the bed we shared, pulled her pillow to my face, and breathed deeply. Taking in her scent brought a fresh round of tears to my eyes. I didn't let them fall and instead climbed under the covers and fell asleep with her fragrance invading my senses like it used to. I didn't sleep well, but I did doze, and for the first time in a month I felt a small measure of peace.

The next day, I dressed and decided it was time to get back into the office. Work needed to be done, and if I wasn't going to do it, they would reassign my clients.

Rebecca greeted me with a warm smile as she wrapped her arms around me, giving me a hug of understanding and compassion. Seeing her was the hardest part of my day. After a few hours I was back in my comfort zone and time flew by. I called the attorney, but I got the machine and left a message.

When I got home, there was another message from Blake telling me to be in court Monday morning at 8am for the start of the trial. I blew my breath out and contemplated calling my mom but decided I should wait to see how Monday played out.

I walked into the den and decided to open the bottle of whiskey Ellen's dad had given me at the wedding. Knappogue Castle, a sixteen-year single malt that I had never tried. I was not much of a drinker, but I needed it. I hadn't planned on overindulging, just drinking a toast to Ellen and Samantha getting the justice they deserved.

I went to the kitchen in search of a glass and ice, replaying what Ellen's father said to me before he walked his daughter down the aisle.

"You will take care of my little girl. You will love her uncon-ditionally, and you will protect her as I have all these years."

Tears burned the back of my eyes. I had told him 'yes sir,' and then didn't fulfill the promise. The ice cubes made hollow thuds as I dropped them in one by one. I uncorked the bottle and watched in a fog as the amber liquid slid over the ice into the glass in a single fluid motion. I placed the glass under my nose and could smell the oak from the barrel. I touched my lips to the rim of the glass and took my first taste. The elixir burned going down, but had a rich flavor. The smoky undertones set off the overall taste. He did have a good palate when it came to whiskey. A second sip and my eyes closed. The image of Ellen's smile the day of our wedding permeated my mind.

I took my glass and hunted for something to eat. My mom had been over, and my fridge looked like a Tupperware party exploded inside of it. After all these years, she was still taking care of me. I grabbed the closest container and opened it to find homemade chicken and noodles that would definitely hit the spot.

I placed some on a plate and put it in the microwave. As it cooked, I called Mom.

"Hey, Dad. Is Mom home?" I asked when Dad answered instead.

"Nope, bible study group tonight," he replied.

"Oh yeah, I forgot. Will you tell her thank you for all the food, and thank you both for sticking with me during all of this?" I mumbled.

"You're our son. Where else would we be? Gotta go, son. Game's on," he reported before hanging up.

I chuckled at my dad. No matter how old he got, he was always the same. It was a fresh thought. Not everything had to change.

I sat down and ate in silence, alone with my mind, but nothing came to focus. For the first time in forever I wasn't thinking about anything. It was a nice break. With my dinner done, I ventured to the other room in the house I had been avoiding.

I opened the door and could have sworn I heard her say "Daddy" and giggle like she always did when I would come home. I walked around the toys and sat on her unmade bed.

"She doesn't have to make her bed every day. I don't make my bed every day," Ellen would say whenever I approached the subject.

"*No, you don't, because I do. I get up and make our bed every single morning,*" I would huff.

"*And I tell you every day not to waste the time because we will just be crawling back into it,*" she chimed.

It was a standard argument with us. One I never won, but one I missed so much. I hugged her favorite bear Suzi Q and smiled at the memories flooding my mind. One day, I would come in and clean everything up. Then eventually I would pack it up, and when the time was right, I would give it away. One day, but today is not that day. I placed Suzi back on the bed and made my way out of Samantha's room, lightly closing the door behind me.

My heart still hurt as if someone stuck their hands inside my chest and was squeezing. I knew it was all mental, but it felt real, physical. The simple movement of breathing tightened my chest cavity and sent a heavy pressure along my lungs, but I had to keep going for my girls. Thomas was right; I needed to be the man they expected me to be.

Sleep came easier. I might have gotten a full six hours before my alarm went off.

The weekend was dedicated to following up with all the phone calls I had been ignoring. If I heard, 'time heals all wounds' or 'you should be happy because they are with God now' one more time I was going to scream bloody murder. I thought about outsourcing the rest of the calls to my mom. I couldn't handle more 'sorry for your loss' or 'it will get easier every day.' Those people were full of shit. Only the ones who had lost someone close gave any real advice, which was usually to take it day by day and block out stupid people.

The trial was going to bring out more ignorant humans with their own idiotic opinions on how justice should be served.

Monday morning arrived quickly, and I found myself more nervous than I should have been. I believed in the court and our justice system. I knew the law was on my side, and Greyson would get what he deserved.

When I pulled into the parking garage, I was surprised to see it empty, but having never been to court, I thought perhaps it was normal.

The courthouse was buzzing with activity. Different people were moving through the metal detectors and chatting with council. I glanced around for Blake but had no idea what he looked like, so it was a lost cause.

I interrupted one of the security guards to ask, "Excuse me, can you tell me where I might find Attorney Blake Stanton, please?"

The guard pointed to a man in his mid-forties, no more than 5'10" with a prominent belly. He was wiping sweat from his forehead like it was ninety degrees. I took a deep breath and tried to remember my mom counseling me on never judging a book by its cover.

I walked over to him and extended my hand. "Mr. Stanton, I'm Samuel Alperstein, but everyone calls me Sam."

He looked at my hand, but between his sweat rag and his briefcase, he opted not to shake.

"Good morning, Sam. This should be an easy win. I have all the confidence in the world that this will be an open and shut homicide case."

He sounded more confident than I felt, but he was the one representing the state, so he had to be a damn fine lawyer.

We sat in silence, waiting for the bailiff to call us in. I was surprised there was no media around. You would think that a court date involving Greyson Richard would cause some stir. After all, his dad was the mayor. Before I could ponder this too much, they called us in.

I sat in the courtroom and listened to Greyson's attorney, one Mr. Robert Williams, ask the judge for a continuance, as he needed more time to prepare for the case. I silently chuckled to myself; surely the judge wasn't going to allow it.

Two minutes later, Judge Daniel Weston slammed his gavel down and announced we would reconvene in six weeks.

What the hell happened? I have six more weeks of waiting to see justice done. I took a deep breath and followed Blake out.

"What was that?" I demanded.

"It happens. I didn't think Robert would pull this, but it just shows me he has nothing to defend his client with. It's actually a good thing, Sam. If I need you, I will call." With that said, he walked away without another word.

I needed to go see my parents and explain what happened. The drive to their house was uneventful, but I didn't remember most of it; I was replaying the short court scene in my mind.

I pulled into the drive and luckily saw both of them were home. That wasn't always the case. I walked in the front door, inhaling the scent of bacon frying on the stove and some kind of strudel baking in the oven. I went into the kitchen and smiled. "Good morning, Dad."

He turned to look at me from the stove. "You know you're late for work, right?"

"No, I'm not. I took the morning off to go to the courthouse. The trial for the girls was supposed to start this morning," I deadpanned.

"Supposed to, what does that mean?" he inquired.

"Greyson's lawyer asked for a continuance and the judge granted it. Now we are looking at six more weeks of waiting. I feel like Greyson is a groundhog who saw his shadow and now needs six more weeks to prepare to face the world. I think it's unfair, but I'm the grieving widower and father, so nothing but swift justice would be fair." I sighed.

"Do me a favor and don't tell your mom they asked for a continuance. Tell her they finally set a date six weeks out. I don't need her getting one of her groups together to storm the judge's chambers. I'm not sure I have enough money to bail her out," he snickered.

"You got it, Dad." I winked.

"Good morning, honey." Mom kissed my cheek. "What brings you here so early? Shouldn't you be at work?"

"Like I told Dad, I went to see the state's attorney and found out they have scheduled the trial to start in six weeks. I don't expect you guys to go, but they were your family too, so I thought you deserved the choice," I clarified.

We made small talk over breakfast. I could tell my mom was trying to read my mood and gauge how I was doing. In all honesty, I was pissed-off, but the anger wouldn't help, and I did not want to hold on to it.

I needed someone to talk to, that one person who would actually listen. I needed Sara.

When I got to work, I hopped on the internet and did a quick search. Where was she? She had a Facebook page that hadn't been touched in years, but other than that she was invisible. I took a shot in the dark and searched through the company database, and sure enough there they were: Kyle and Sara Lister. *Why can't I shake this woman? Why is she buried in my heart deeper than I ever thought?* I wrote her address down and stuffed it into my pocket. Was I seriously contemplating going to her house? Yes, I was. I wanted to see her. I needed to see that she was happy. I had an overwhelming urge to check on her, talk to her, get an idea of who she was now. I wanted my friend back, but I also would have liked to call her mine; she could make me happy again.

I left the office and drove to the address. The house was quiet. All of the doors and windows were closed as if no one was home. Then, something went flying across the backyard. I stretched my neck to see what it was. An adorable little girl in her swimsuit came running after it, and when she picked it up, I could see it was a beach ball. Sara wasn't far behind her. She had put on some weight, but it looked good on her. But of course I didn't think she would ever appear bad in my eyes.

I wanted to stay and watch her with her kids. The file said she had two, a boy and a girl. I couldn't bring myself to get out of the car. Instead, I headed back to work. Would she recognize me or want to see me again after all these years? She looked good, happy, and that was all I wanted to know. At least, that is what I kept telling myself.

The weeks flew by one after the other. Every night I would go into Sammy's room and put one toy up. I never did touch her bed. I left it a complete mess because that was her. Going into her room did get easier; everything I touched brought a happy memory with it.

Chapter 12

The day was here. We walked into the court room as a group. I sat behind Blake's side and watched as Greyson and his lawyer made their way in.

"All rise for the honorable Judge Daniel Weston. Docket number 453268-763, State verses Greyson Richard for two counts of vehicular homicide," the bailiff's voice rang out strong and true.

The gavel came down hard as the judge said, "Please be seated. Mr. Stanton you may begin whenever you are ready."

"Good morning, Your Honor. The state will show that Mr. Richard was intoxicated the night of September 17th. It was his diminished capacity that caused the horrific accident that took the lives of Ellen and Samantha Alperstein. He willingly got behind the wheel of his car knowing he was well over the legal limit of alcohol. None of his friends stopped him, and as a result he ran Ellen off the road and to her death," he stated blatantly as if he was reading a boring passage someone else wrote.

His opening argument was cold. I had expected more from him, but I guessed he was trying to go with logic instead of emotion.

Mr. Williams was a different force to be reckoned with. He was about six feet, had a lean frame, and carried himself like he was the most important person in the courtroom.

"Your Honor, this was simply an accident. My client is only guilty of being in the wrong place at the wrong time. Yes, he clipped the side of the Alpersteins' vehicle, but the amount of damage he caused would have never led to their deaths. The real blame needs to be placed on the city for the faulty guardrail. If they had made sure it was up to code, it would have held the vehicle instead of breaking and sending them over the steep embankment. The crash from the hill is what ultimately killed the family, not my client. This is a witch hunt to get something from the town's most influential family, one that for generations has put this city above their own personal gains."

You have got to be fucking kidding me. He's going to blame the city and any other person he can pull from the damn sky. I wanted to yell, and it took all of my willpower to stay seated. I couldn't risk getting kicked out of the courtroom.

"The state can call its first witness," Judge Weston calmly proceed.

"We call Officer Kevin Marshall," Blake announced.

The man walked in and made his way to the witness stand. The room was quiet, eerie.

"Officer Marshall, I only have one question. Did Mr. Richard contribute to the Alpersteins' deaths?"

"Yes, if he had not hit them, they never would have swerved," he stated.

"Thank you. Nothing further, Your Honor." Blake sat down.

"Your witness now, Mr. Williams," Judge Weston stated.

"Are you a psychic, Mr. Marshall?" Williams spat.

"No, I'm not," Marshall chuckled.

"Then how can you sit here and tell us that without a shadow of a doubt Mrs. Alperstein wouldn't have swerved to miss a rabbit and driven off the edge?" he questioned.

"I was not asked about the what-ifs, Mr. Williams. I was asked about something that happened. The facts are if Mr.

Richard had not hit Mrs. Alperstein, she would not have reacted and ended up at the bottom of the embankment. If Mr.
Williams had not been intoxicated, perhaps he would have
stayed on his side of the road and we wouldn't be here today,"
Kevin deadpanned.

"Fair enough. Then answer this: would Mrs. Alperstein
be dead if she went over the side due to swerving to miss an
animal?" he inquired.

"I don't know, I'm not a doctor. I am an officer of the law."

"Nothing further, Your Honor." Williams walked away.

"You may step down, Officer Marshall. Call your next witness, Mr. Stanton," Judge Weston requested.

"The state calls Officer Derek Merrow to the stand."

When the doors opened and the officer came through, I
was shocked to see a young man walking to the stand. There
must have been a mistake. There was no way this guy was
an officer of the law. He was nervous and sweating heavily.
There were already stains developing under his arms, and he
fidgeted with his shirt, pulling it from his body as he made his
way in. This must have been the guy Detective Thomas said
made a mistake.

After he was sworn in, the questions began. "Could you
please tell us what you witnessed when you arrived on the
scene?" Stanton requested.

"I came upon a truck that had crashed into a tree. When
I first approached, it looked like a single car accident. I went
to check on the driver, but he was unconscious, so I called for
an ambulance. I did smell alcohol permeating from the truck.
As I turned to take in the scene, I noticed tire tracks going to
the edge of the embankment. When I looked over the side, I
could see an SUV had landed upside down against a tree along
the river. The tree was the only thing keeping the vehicle from
the water. I called for backup. Officer Marshall showed up and
climbed down to the other vehicle. I stayed with Mr. Richard
until the ambulance took him away."

THE COST OF LIVING

I could tell he had rehearsed that over and over again. It was to the point, and well-articulated.

"Nothing more, Your Honor," Stanton finished.

What the actual fuck is Stanton doing? Only asking one question like that summed everything up. Mom patted my knee, feeling my agitation rising.

"Your turn, Mr. Williams." Judge Weston motioned as he continued to take notes.

"Mr. Merrow, did you administer a breathalyzer?" Williams inquired.

"How could I? He was unconscious. As I said, I did smell alcohol in the truck, but was unable to find any open containers."

"Did you request for a breathalyzer or blood work from the hospital?"

"No, I did not. After Mr. Richards was released from the hospital, I escorted him to the police station where I administered the breathalyzer." The young officer shifted in his seat.

"Did the results show my client was over the legal limit?" Williams prodded.

"No, it said he was under the legal limit, but multiple hours had passed since the accident, and the body could have metabolized the alcohol by then," he quickly added.

"I'm sorry, Mr. Merrow, are you a medical professional as well?" he snickered.

"No, sir, I'm not," he huffed.

"Then you don't know for a fact that his body would have metabolized it that quickly, do you?" he countered.

"No, sir, I don't," Derek stated.

"Nothing further." Williams sat back down.

"You may step down, Officer Merrow. Next witness, Mr. Stanton," Weston advised.

"The state calls Miss Kayli Bronson." Mr. Stanton articulated.

The young woman walking in looked more terrified than

Derek. How was she going to help the case? So far, Stanton had been doing a horrible job. Where was the proof of culpability? I watched her take her seat and be sworn in.

"Miss Bronson, could you please tell the court what you do for a living." Stanton smiled.

"I'm a waitress at the Boarhead Bar," she said.

"Were you working the night of September 17th?" he asked.

"Yes, I was. It was dollar draft night. It's one of our busiest nights."

She kept glancing at Greyson. It was unusual. These weren't fearful glances but seemed more like she was enamored by him. As if she was putting on an elaborate show for him.

"Was Mr. Richards there that night?" Stanton questioned.

"Yes, Mr. Richards comes in every night after work." She winked at Greyson.

"How many drinks did you serve him?" he asked with a flat tone.

"Not more than his usual of two." She giggled.

"It says here that you told the police when they interviewed you that you served him six. Are you now saying you lied?" he spat.

"No, I told the police I served six to the table. Mr. Richard wasn't alone. His friends were with him," she clarified.

"That seems to be a big discrepancy from what the police say you said and what you are telling us now."

"I can't be responsible for the police not understanding me correctly. You'd have to ask them why they wrote it down wrong," she complained.

"Did you see Mr. Richard leave the bar?" Stanton scrambled to ask.

"No, I didn't."

"Nothing further." Stanton sat down.

"Your witness," Weston proceeded.

I didn't know much about court proceedings or how things were supposed to go, but that witness was pointless. How exactly did Stanton think she helped the case? She was obviously in love with Greyson and would say whatever she needed to protect him. I was trying to let Stanton do his job, but I was seriously doubting his abilities.

"We have no questions at this time for Miss Bronson," Williams replied.

Of course, he didn't. My lawyer had done a damn fine job of supplying enough reasonable doubt. Stanton had to be the worse lawyer ever. How did this man become the state's attorney?

"You may step down. Next witness, Mr. Stanton," Judge Weston prodded.

"The state rests at this time, Your Honor," Stanton stated.

I felt my dad's hand on my shoulder as I went to stand. This was bullshit. He can't rest—what was he thinking? Was this shit-show what passed as justice?

"Stay calm. I'm sure he has his reasons," Dad whispered.

"He better, or I'm going to kill him," I fumed.

"Let's break for lunch and reconvene in one hour," Weston stated as his gavel came down.

I waited for Stanton to exit the room. I hurried from the court, anxious to get clarification.

"Tell me you have more than that," I pleaded.

"Trust me, Mr. Alperstein, things are going according to plan," he stated, before slapping my shoulder.

Before I knew it, we were back in the courtroom waiting on the Judge to resume this circus of a hearing.

"All rise for the Honorable Judge Daniel Weston," the bailiff called.

"Please be seated." The gavel echoed in the silent room. "Call your first witness, Mr. Williams," Weston stated.

"The defense calls Miss Claire Sanchez to the stand," he supplied.

The woman that came through the door was stunning. She had long dark hair, glowing mocha skin, and carried herself with poise and grace. I had no idea who this lady was, but she took command of the room with little to no effort. This woman could lie through her teeth, and everyone in here would believe every word. I could feel the shift in the courtroom. The bailiff swore her in, and Williams slowly walked up to her.

"Miss Sanchez, would you please tell the court what you do," he cooed.

"I am a sommelier. I consult with patrons of the restaurant to pick out the perfect wine for their meal," she explained.

"Do you remember helping the McPherson family on the night of September 17th?" he continued.

"I do. They come in every Friday evening, but that night they had Ellen with them and her adorable little girl. It was the first time I had seen Ellen in years, and it was my first time meeting Samantha." She smiled.

Her smile should have calmed my heart, but it didn't. I had a feeling this woman was not going to help the case. It was like I knew her, but I couldn't place her. She struck me as a wolf in sheep's clothing, doing what she must but following her own agenda. It was wrong to feel this way about someone I didn't know, yet I couldn't shake it.

"Was there anything unusual about that night?" he nudged.

"Yes, Mr. McPherson only ever orders one bottle for the table, but that night his daughter insisted he order an additional bottle to go with dessert. The McPhersons rarely finished a single bottle. That seemed off to me, but who am I to argue with the client?" She batted her eyes.

"Is that all?" Williams persisted.

"I don't mean to cause gossip, but Ellen was very short with her daughter. She was snapping and yelling at her, and everyone in the restaurant could see Ellen was agitated."

"Objection, how can she testify to what everyone else in the restaurant thought?" Stanton huffed, snapping to his feet.

"I am merely providing evidence of Ellen's state of mind at the time of leaving the restaurant," Williams quickly added.

"I will allow it, but you are walking a thin line, Mr. Williams," Weston stated.

"Are you saying you thought she was agitated?" Williams coaxed.

"Yes, she was slurring her words and not making much sense. Her dad offered for her and Samantha to stay with them, but she said she had to get home," she continued.

"Objection, Your Honor. It's hearsay, and Ellen isn't here to defend herself," Stanton stated.

"Sustained. Miss Sanchez please stick to things you were a part of," Weston reprimanded.

"I saw her stumble when she tried to stand up, and I watched her push her daughter in front of her as they walked out. She walked out clearly having difficulty putting one foot in front of the other," Claire huffed.

"Nothing more, Your Honor," Williams stated.

"Your witness," Weston motioned.

"How long have you been at the restaurant?" Stanton questioned, never leaving his table.

"Six years," she replied.

"Did you know Ellen before you started working at the restaurant?" he continued.

"Yes, we went to high school together."

"And didn't you used to compete against her when you were both younger in dance competitions?" he countered.

"Yes, we did," she responded.

"And didn't Ellen beat you every single time?" he pressed.

"I'm sure I won a few, but who really keeps track?" she chided.

Finally, Stanton stood and walked over to her carrying pieces of paper. He placed a copy in front of Mr. Williams, another in front of the judge, and then one in her view. "Is this your Facebook page?"

"You know it is," she fumed.

"And could you please read what that sentence says?" He

pointed at the paper.

She sat up straighter, leaning forward a bit with both hands straight at her side. It looked like she was fighting the urge to tear the paper out of his hands. Her tone of voice rang with loathing and anger as she read the words to the court.

"It says, 'Ellen McPherson died last night, and I can't even pretend to be sad about it. I never liked her and am glad to see she is gone,'" she admitted.

"Nothing further, Your Honor." Stanton returned to his seat.

"Your Honor, I deleted that. It wasn't up for more than a few minutes before I removed it. It was a childish response to all the years of me losing to her at everything," Claire tried to clarify, frantically looking at the Judge for some sign of acknowledgement.

"Please step down, Miss Sanchez. Next witness, Mr. Williams," Weston ordered.

Finally, things were shaping up. This was what a lawyer should do on behalf of my family.

Three more witnesses from the restaurant later, and I was pissed. Obviously, my wife had had a difficult night that I knew nothing about. Regardless of her evening, she never would have put Samantha in harm's way. The next witness was one I had been expecting.

"The people call Kyle Lister to the stand," Williams announced.

Kyle came in as if he owned the world. I barely recognized him. I remembered seeing him at the hospital, but I guess I was too into my own head to actually take in any of his features.

He must have gained at least a hundred pounds, and he had a receding hairline; the top of his head shined with sweat as he made his way forward. By the time he sat down to be sworn in, he was completely out of breath. We had to wait for him to regulate his breathing and the bailiff brought him a bottle of water. Drama queen.

"Mr. Lister, where were you the evening of September 17th?" Williams jumped right in.

"After work me and a few buddies went to the Boarhead for some beers."

"Is one of your buddies here today?" Williams prodded.

"Yep, my best friend is right there, Greyson Richard. We have been friends since we were five, and he is very important to the company we work for. As the lead engineer, he oversees everything that happens," Kyle answered.

"How many beers did you guys consume?"

"I know I had four. I only saw Greyson drink two."

"Was he diminished in any capacity before he left the bar?" Williams asked.

"No, not even a little bit," Kyle reassured.

"Nothing further," Williams finished as he sat down.

"Your witness, Mr. Stanton," Weston commanded.

"What does four beers mean for you, Mr. Lister?" Stanton queried.

"I don't understand your question," Kyle huffed.

"Were you drunk, buzzed? Did you feel like you hadn't drunk anything?" Stanton clarified.

"I had a good buzz going, but I wasn't incapacitated, if that is what you are asking. I was sober enough to know I needed a ride home and shouldn't drive. I called my wife. She came and got me about five minutes after I called her, and Greyson left. He offered to take me home, but I had already called Sara, and I knew she was on the way," he stated, as if it was the end of the questions.

"So, you had no problem calling and waking up your wife, who then had to wake your kids up to come get you, instead of driving home with a perfectly sober Mr. Richard?" Stanton accused.

"Objection!" Williams hollered.

"No need, Your Honor. I withdraw the question," Stanton interrupted, trying to hide a smug smile.

"That's okay, Mr. Stanton. I would like to know the answer to that question," Judge Weston replied.

"Your Honor, I live on the other side of town. Greyson would have had to go way out of his way to take me home," Kyle snidely commented.

"And then maybe a mother and a daughter would still be alive," Stanton interjected.

"Objection!" Williams bellowed.

"Nothing further, Your Honor." Stanton returned to his seat.

"You may step down. Next witness, Mr. Williams," Weston proceeded.

I had to give the judge props. He was moving us along quickly. I would have loved to be done with this by the end of the day.

"Your Honor, my next witness won't be available until tomorrow," Williams replied.

"Very well. Court is adjourned until 8am. Each of your witnesses better be here, because I will be making a decision by the end of the day with or without them," Weston stated before his gavel hit down hard, resonating loudly throughout the court room.

Blake put his hand on my shoulder as we walked out of the courtroom. "See you in the morning. We are going to win this."

He was confident, and I wished I felt the same way.

As soon as I got home and walked in the door, I called Ellen's mother and asked her about the night of the accident.

"Did she order a second bottle of wine?" I knew I was being unreasonable, but I needed to know.

"Yes, she did," her mom sighed.

"Why?" I questioned, deflated.

"They were talking about replacing her at the studio. She was taking it very hard and didn't know how to tell you." She sighed again.

Sliding down to the floor with the phone still pressed to my ear, I whispered, "She loved teaching those kids. Losing that would have devastated her. I would have been there for her. Why didn't she just talk to me?"

"She just found out that day and was still processing it herself. You know we would have never let her drive if we didn't think she could, don't you?" she responded.

"Yes, I do. They also said she was mean to Samantha. Is that true too?" I begged.

"She was firm with Samantha. Nothing out of the ordinary, but Samantha was very whiny that night and was picking a fight with her mom, or at least she was trying to."

"So, in a certain light everything they said today was true, but they got the context wrong. Figures they would paint the picture in their favor," I grumbled.

"How did today go? I'm sorry we didn't come. I don't think I could handle it," she surmised.

"Honestly, I'm glad you weren't there. They are blaming it all on Ellen and the city for not maintaining the guardrail. It's difficult to just sit and listen to it all," I lamented.

We said goodnight, and I went to my room. I put on the DVD of Samantha's last recital and watched my baby dance her heart out. and fell asleep to the sound of her mom's praise. I slowly sipped the scotch and faded into sleep.

I repeated the same morning ritual as the previous day and was in the courtroom at eight, waiting for the judge.

I sat through another day of craziness. There wasn't one thing that stood out, just the same nonsense. They tried everything in their power to blame Ellen. I was in a daze, letting all the information flow over me, nothing sticking, until I heard, "Court is adjourned for two hours, and when we return, I will have my verdict." The gavel hit as Weston began to head to his office.

The room filled with quiet murmurs and bodies shifting as they began exiting. "Come to the house. We will wait together," Mom insisted.

"There is actually somewhere I have to go. I will meet you

back here." I kissed her cheek before leaving.

I left the courthouse and drove to the cemetery. I hadn't been here since they were buried. It was too difficult. I pulled over and walked to the girls' headstone. I had ordered them a ballerina. She was molded out of concrete but finished to look like marble. It showed a woman in a tutu, standing on her toes, feet crossed, arms above her head also crossed and a slight curve of her upper body towards the part of the stone that read my girls' names. It was exactly what Ellen would have wanted. I ran my hand along the arm and sat down in front of it. My parents had offered to place the girls in the family crypt, but this was where all of Ellen's family was. I knew she would have rather been here.

"I'm sorry I haven't been here. I couldn't bring myself to come. We've been in court for the past few days, and it doesn't look good. I promised you justice, and Greyson is making it out to be your fault. Why didn't you tell me you were upset? Why didn't you ask me to go to dinner with you? Why did you take the back roads home? Why did you leave me all alone?" I cried.

I heard a twig break and looked up. "I told your mom you were going to come here. You don't have to do this alone, son. We are here for you," Dad stated.

"Why didn't she talk to me, Dad? We were partners, and she didn't include me. Why did she shoulder the burden on her own? Why didn't she trust me to take care of her? Why didn't she love me enough to include me?" I raged.

"How could she do this to me? We were meant to grow old together. To have grandchildren running through the house, playing and screaming. I should get to see my only child graduate high school and then college. I should get to walk her down the aisle at her wedding. Instead, she is here lying in the ground suspended in time. How do I move on from here?"

He sat down beside me and wrapped his arm around me. "You move on one second at a time, one minute at a time, one hour at a time, and one day at a time. No one can tell you how you should grieve."

We sat in silence until it was time for Dad to get Mom and head back to the courtroom.

I pulled into the parking garage, taking a few minutes to get myself together. I closed my eyes and listened to the faint sounds of the traffic passing by. I practiced some breathing exercises to try and calm my racing heart. Deep breath in and slow exhale. I was anxious and nervous about what was about to happen. After a few moments, my body calmed enough for me to go in to hear the verdict.

We all sat waiting once more for the judge.

"All rise for the honorable Judge Daniel Weston," the bailiff echoed.

We watched the judge enter the courtroom, and immediately I could tell this wasn't a choice he completely agreed with. His shoulders were slightly lowered, and he didn't look at anyone as he made his way to the bench. His mannerisms showed he hadn't come to the decision lightly, and my heart sank.

"Be seated," he started.

He took a deep breath and placed his hands together in front of him.

He said lots of things, but all I heard was "not guilty." I was sure he had an adequate reason, but I couldn't figure it out. How did he come to that? Greyson killed my family.

"Son, we need to go." I looked up to see my dad and mom waiting for me.

The courtroom was empty. There was no justice for my girls. I slowly stood and followed my parents out of the courtroom.

I drove home, still trying to process everything that had happened. We lost, and Greyson had walked away a free man.

I got into the house and sat on the couch. There was only one logical explanation for that verdict; Greyson's family had bought his freedom.

I grabbed the scotch and didn't bother with a glass; I drank directly from the bottle.

Chapter 13

Two months passed. Then three, then four. Life was moving on without them, and I came home wishing they were with me every night. Instead, I'd spent more time with my folks, joining them for dinner multiple times a week. I found reasons to drive by Sara's before heading home every night. Afterward, though, my comfort was the single malt liquor. I replaced the Knappogue Castle after each bottle I finished. My evening routine was the same, come home, sit in the chair and drink until I passed out.

Katy kept calling and asking me to join them for dinner. I should have gone, but I didn't think I could look at Bethany without weeping. She was the same age Samantha would have been, and they looked more like sisters than cousins. I didn't need that reminder yet, on top of Ellen and Katy being twins. I hadn't been able to look at Katy since the accident. They were identical but enough differences that you could tell them apart. The similarities still got to me.

I'd been sitting in my parents' driveway for almost ten minutes. Thinking about what I could do to correct this injustice. Nothing came to mind. I would have loved to remove them all from this world. Let their families suffer as I was, but I was no killer. I wouldn't have been able to do it.

Could I?

I walked into the smell of fried chicken, one of my favorite foods and one of the few things my dad made.

"This smells wonderful, Dad," I said while sitting at the island.

"Thanks, it was my mom's recipe. That woman sure knew how to cook." He smiled, looking off into the distance, as if lost in a memory of his mother.

"Hey, honey. How was work?" Mom whispered before kissing my cheek.

"It was a good day, Mom," I replied.

"Have you told him yet?" Mom questioned Dad as she walked into the kitchen and started working on the potato salad.

"He just sat down. I haven't even had time to think about it. We can talk while we eat?" Dad concluded.

Watching my parents work in the kitchen was like watching a dance. Neither of them got in the other's way, and they moved fluidly as one. You could see the years of togetherness showing through. Ellen and I had never gotten to that point. She had the grace and beauty of a dancer, but when I was in the kitchen with her, I always got in her way. She never kicked me out, though. There are many big things I missed, but lately I found I the little stuff I missed as well.

Dad handed me the chicken, and I carried it to the table. I helped my parents set the table like I had for many nights prior. I knew where Mom wanted everything. We sat in the same seats we would sit in when I was growing up.

"Okay, spill it," I interjected once everyone was seated.

"Your dad is finally taking me to Tuscany. We are going to Italy!" she exclaimed.

My dad grabbed her hand and gave her the brightest smile. "She has been nagging me for years. I figured it was time to throw her a bone."

Mom giggled; I mean actually giggled like a little girl.

"When do you leave?" I inquired around a mouth full of food.

"Monday" Dad declared.

"So soon?" I gasped.

"We've been putting it off for a while, and to be honest, dear, we need a break," Mom muttered.

"I get it. You can't put your life on pause for me. I wouldn't expect you to. I want to see lots of pictures, and ship me some good wine." I chuckled.

"Of course, I'll be shipping you all kinds of fun things," Mom beamed.

"Will you drive us to the airport Monday morning?" Dad inquired.

"Sure thing, Dad." I smiled.

The excitement in my parents' voices kept a grin on my face the rest of the evening. We discussed Mom's itinerary and all the fun places she wanted to go. We talked about the food and the wine, and Dad jokingly complained he was going to be coming home ten pounds heavier. The feeling of family was strong, and I was lucky to have them in my life.

The weekend was gone before I could breathe, and once again, I found myself sitting in my parents' driveway. I smiled when my mom came bouncing out the door with her arms loaded with bags. Dad followed with multiple suitcases.

"Mom, it's a ten-day trip. What is up with all the clothes?" I laughed.

"I don't plan on doing laundry, and you never know what you might need. I have no idea what kind of weather we will have. I've always told you it's better to be overprepared than under." She handed me her bags, smiling.

"Do you need help, old man?" I joked.

"I may be old, but I'm not that old yet." He laughed.

Driving to the airport with my parents behaving like new lovers was a definite change for me. It was nice to see them this happy and excited. They deserved some happiness after all the loss.

I pulled up to the drop off zone and helped get the bags.

Mom grabbed a cart, and we loaded them up. We worked quietly and efficiently.

"We will see you in two weeks. Take care of yourself. I left food in the fridge for you. Make sure to get out of the house once in a while, and remember we love you with all our hearts." Mom dabbed her eyes. She always cried at goodbyes.

"Call me when you land," I urged.

Dad shook my hand. "Will do, see you when we get back."

With that, they were gone. I got back in my car and drove home.

I was sitting in front of the TV a few hours later when the phone rang.

"Hello" I mumbled.

"We made it to New York and are getting ready to board the next flight. I'll touch base when we get there," I heard Dad's voice, then he hung up before I could respond. My father, always straight to the point.

I fell asleep in front of the TV and awoke to a special broadcast. It was so loud I couldn't ignore it even if I wanted to.

"It is with a sad heart I bring you the news of Flight 4983. Somewhere over the Atlantic Ocean last night, the plane experienced a mechanical malfunction. Pieces of the wreckage have been located, including the black box, but all three hundred and seventeen passengers and crew have perished. We will bring you more information as we receive it," she concluded.

I muted the TV, jumped from the couch, and ran to the fridge to get Mom's flight itinerary. I scanned the page quickly, looking for the number of their flight from New York. Highlighted on the second page was 4983.

No, no, that can't be right. There has to be a mistake. Dad is going to call me any minute and tell me their flight was changed and they are finally in Italy.

There was a knock at the front door. When I opened it, every single inch of me went numb.

"Detective Thomas, what can I do for you?" I inquired,

knowing with every fiber he was here to deliver bad news.

"Can I come in, Sam?" he countered.

I stood back and let him pass me.

"Ah hell, Sam. I had hoped to get here before you saw it on the news. If I hadn't stopped by your office first, I would have made it." He sighed.

"I overslept this morning, or else I would have been there," I whispered.

I could see his eyes glossing over as he shifted his weight from one foot to the other and shoved his hands into his front pockets. He looked uncomfortable, sad, maybe even a little lost.

"I'm really sorry, Sam. The international authorities notified me less than an hour ago. Your parents are on the list of the confirmed dead. Your dad and I served together. He was one of the best men I have ever known, and I know he was damn proud of you."

"Thanks, Thomas. You can go," I mumbled, lost to the numbing reality.

I didn't walk him to the door and refused to look up when he left. I said nothing until his car drove away, and then I screamed, "FUCK!"

There was no one to call, no other family to alert. I was alone. It hadn't even been a year since I lost the girls, and here I was losing the rest of my family in one final blow.

I grabbed the pillow on the couch and screamed into it. *How much can a man take? How much pain can one heart handle? This shouldn't have happened. They should have never left. They only went because of the trial and the girls' deaths.*

Greyson had taken my entire family. How didn't I see this coming? What the hell did I ever do to Greyson Richards? It was not just him though—the judge, attorneys, and police where all in on it. It was a huge cover up. The Richards were lining every one of their pockets, and someone had to do something about it.

Me, I'm the one who has to do it.

I refused to allow them to live any longer, and they would pay for all the devastation that they had brought me.

Who should go first? I don't want it to lead back to me—I need to get creative accidents.

Judge Daniel Weston, honorable my ass. Attorneys Robert Williams and Blake Stanton. Those dumb ass cops, Merrow and Marshall. I would save Greyson and Kyle for last. Greyson would die a horribly painful death, and as for Kyle, I would dismantle everything he had ever loved. I would destroy them all.

Judge Weston had to be the first to go. One of the most frequent accidents was falls within the home. Daniel was going to have an accident. I needed to get to the office and look up some addresses. I had a new purpose in life, and once I made them all pay, I would end my own suffering and join my family.

I went to work with a lighter step and felt like finally a weight had been lifted from my shoulders. My girls were going to get justice after all.

One year later...

Patience was the key. I'd waited and watched every single movement the judge made. I knew his entire schedule by heart. He had finally made a small change in the routine, and it was enough for me to ultimately serve him justice.

Judge Weston had loaded up the family vehicle and left a little over an hour ago. The construction workers started the renovation two days prior. If my source was correct, they would lay the carpet for the stairs in the morning. When the workers left for the day, I was going to adjust the design slightly. I would extend the top stair, a little longer than it needed to be, so when he tried to step down in a hurry, he would lose his balance. If that didn't work, then I would push him. Either way, faulty steps would be to blame. After all, why would anyone want to hurt the wonderful Daniel Weston, the town's favorite judge?

The last construction truck pulled away, and it was time to get to work. I made my way behind the house, and as promised, the sliding glass door was unlocked.

Finally finished, I went home. It looked good. No one would know who did it, and the construction crew wasn't scheduled to return until Monday morning. Daniel wasn't due to come back until then as well, but I had a way around that. The next night was a vigil for the twelve people who died in the plane crash last year. I was going to call the mayor and suggest Judge Weston be the person who spoke on behalf of the town. If I couldn't convince the mayor, then it would be a waiting game. I didn't want his family to get hurt, but maybe that would be better. He could have the same emptiness in his heart as I did.

The call to Mayor Richard was quick, and he loved the idea. I think he felt it was easier to pass the responsibility off to someone else.

For the first time in years, I went to sleep with a smile on my face.

The following day flew by in a blur.

The vigil started at 6 pm sharp, and though there were three hundred and seventeen people killed that day, we were only honoring the twelve that had come from our sleepy little town. Four of which were crew: one pilot and three stewardesses. Then there were two retired couples, including my parents. Lastly there was a pair of newlyweds heading to their honeymoon and two recent high school graduates looking for adventure across the ocean.

I joined the crowd that had gathered in front of the only church in town. I ran through the most plausible outcome for the dear judge. He would enter his house and go up the stairs in the kitchen angrily because he had to leave his vacation early. He would dress and quickly make his way down the front steps, where he would overextend because of the first drop off and fall to his death. Clean, efficient, simple.

I was dismayed to see the Judge step up to the podium. Well shit, maybe he hadn't gone home first, but there was still hope. He began to speak, but I wasn't listening.

"He is so full of himself. If he could, he'd kiss his own ass," a voice next to me declared.

I turned toward the voice. He was almost as tall as me, and I was taller than most. His brown hair was a shade lighter than mine. His arms were crossed over his chest, but I could tell they were strong. His presence was commanding, and it made me stand up a little straighter.

"Relax, Sam. I'm not here to rain on your parade. I'm here to help you," he replied without looking at me.

"How do you know who I am?" I inquired.

"You sell insurance. Your face is on a giant billboard in the center of town. Your parents were very well-liked in the community, and we were both athletes in high school. A few years are separating us, but you had coach Burns, and I had him. He showed me a video of all the matches you won to help me improve. So, my picture hangs in my high school in the same place of honor as yours does in your high school," he answered.

"You know me, but I don't know you. What's your name?" I questioned, almost thinking this young man could read my mind.

He stuck his hand out for me to shake. "Jonathon Ellis, at your service." His shake was firm and confident. "The stairs were a nice touch, but all it managed to do was cause him to slide down a few stairs. He tweaked his knee; you could see his limp when he walked up the stage," Jonathon said.

What the actual fuck? How did he know? My heart was racing, and my hands started to sweat. Could he prove any of it, and would I end up going to jail? I turned to deny it, but I couldn't bring myself to it.

"What is this, some kind of blackmail?" I hissed instead.

"Not even a little bit, man. I want to help you get the justice your family deserves," he reassured.

"How do you plan on doing that?"

"We can't discuss it here, but I have set a few things in motion to help with the Judge. I don't know who else you have on your list, but I am here for you. Someone has to do something. This town deserves better than the people in charge now and needs a stiff wake-up call on how the world really works. It's been in the dark for too many years," he interjected.

"How do you know about any of it?" I demanded.

"I'm part of the construction crew working on the Judge's place. I heard you talking to the maid about needing to get into the Judge's place after the guys left. I did some research and found the articles on your wife and daughter. It's a real shame Greyson got away with two murders."

His eyes were still locked on the podium, and he had yet to turn to me. It was if we were making small talk while waiting on our wives. I didn't know how to take him. Was he serious, or was this some kind of trap?

"The Judge will get his tonight, and then you will see I mean what I say. I will meet you tomorrow at the spot next to the lake. The one you and Sara always went to," he finished before turning and leaving me standing utterly dumbfounded.

A part of me was scared. I could go to jail for conspiracy to commit murder, not to mention all the other charges that could be added on.

I went home with a pit in my stomach and a new ache in my heart. If I went to jail, nothing would ever be resolved.

I slept restlessly, and the next day I did what I'd done every morning for years. I turned the TV on and went to make a pot of coffee.

"Last night Judge Daniel Weston was shot down in his own home. The assailant was twenty-seven-year-old Tia Smith. Tia had just been released Friday after serving eight years of a twelve-year sentence for her part in an armed robbery. The jewelry store robbery left one clerk dead and two additional bystanders injured. Although Tia swore she didn't know what her boyfriend was doing and stated she was told to wait in the car; the Judge felt she had working knowledge of the plan and was in fact the lookout. Judge Weston was not lenient towards her and had given her the maximum sentence.

"Tia had a difficult time in jail and spent most of it in isolation for her own protection after multiple suicide attempts. It is uncertain what was going through her mind when she entered the Judge's home. Although the details are being withheld from the press, it's been surmised that she waited for him, ambushed him, and shot him twice in the chest. After a brief standoff, Tia was taken down by the police when she tried to fire on them. It is a tragic day for the Weston family and the city as a whole," the reporter finished.

They painted that girl as a criminal. Where were the condolences for her family? Now, I understood that Jonathon had meant what he said. I was going to have to meet him. So, coffee forgotten, I headed out the door to a spot I hadn't been to in years.

The location was way off of the beaten path. Sara and I found it one summer day while driving, playing a game of left and right. Once we were good and lost, we stumbled onto a small clearing next to the water.

When I pulled up, he was standing there looking out at the water, and I couldn't help but feel the confidence radiating from him.

"What the hell happened last night?" I urged, while walking up next to him.

"Weston died. Isn't that what you wanted?" he inquired.

"I wanted him to die because of me, not someone else," I stated, and even to my own ears, it sounded like a child throwing a tantrum.

Jonathon sighed. "Look, Sam, I'm sure you have a lot of

people on your to-kill list, and if you get tied to any of them, it takes away your chances of finishing. I merely gave you a helping hand. Tia wasn't very bright. She truly did nothing wrong with the robbery. Weston was too blinded by thinking everyone was a liar with something to hide that he didn't see the truth sitting in front of him."

"How do you know her?" I asked.

"Irrelevant. They will never tie me to her, and that's all you need to know," he deadpanned.

"What's next?" I asked.

"Well, that's up to you. Who else do you have on the list? How close do you want them to die? Do you want accidents, or do you want them to suffer? You decide the when and the how, and I will make it happen for you," he reassured.

"What do you get out of this?"

"If I answer you truthfully, don't look down your nose at me!" he hissed.

"I won't," I promised.

"I enjoy the thrill of the kill. I prefer to use my bare hands, but I'm fine manipulating people to get the desired result. I'm doing what I was created to do while maintaining control of the desired outcome. One day I will ask something of you. When I do, you will give it to me with no questions." he stated.

"Okay."

He openly admitted to enjoying the kill. I could scoff or laugh and act disgusted, but I realized I was just as bad as he was. I wanted these people dead and took pleasure from knowing they would soon be gone. Regarding wanting something in the future, I didn't plan on sticking around, so he could think whatever he wanted.

"You need something else to consume more of your time so there is no way of connecting you to any of this. Any chance you want to take on a girlfriend?" he chuckled.

"No," I stated. I wasn't ready to have a girlfriend. I wasn't ready to share my bed with anyone else. Eventually I would get there, but at the moment I didn't have the desire to be with anyone. My head screamed *liar* and Sara's face flashed through my memory. I shook my head to dislodge the image.

"The attorneys should be next. We need to wait about three months before we take one of them out. I don't care which. The fire house is always looking for volunteers, so I will become one to placate your need for me to look otherwise engaged. Greyson needs to hurt—I want him to suffer before he dies. Kyle, you leave to me. I have big plans to ruin his life. The two cops are on my list as well, but they are at the bottom. I want them to feel safe after all the others have died, and then we will plot their demise," I supplied.

"Very well, leave it to me. We will meet in this spot the day after any of them dies," Jonathon said.

"Agreed. How will I get ahold of you if I need to?" I asked.

"I work for Morrison Construction Group; you can always find me there. Otherwise, I will be around," he finished as he started walking away.

***

Life went back to normal. I did as I said I would and joined as a volunteer fire fighter and actually enjoyed it. It was hard work, but it kept my mind busy. I sold my parents' house and continued to live in the one I'd shared with Ellen. Months went by, and I was starting to think that Jonathon had duped me and played on my need to seek revenge.

Six months after our meeting, I got the news I had been not-so-patiently waiting for. I turned the TV on late one evening to hear the same fake sorrow in the reporter's voice as before. "It seems two of our finest attorneys have died in a freak accident last night. Blake Stanton and Robert Williams were found dead in their hunting cabin just north of the city. The two often went hunting together, and Williams' wife said this was their monthly trip. It appears an old kerosene heater is to blame with carbon monoxide poisoning listed as the cause of death. It is a sad day for our city. Our thoughts and prayers go out to the families in this time of loss. In other news..."

I clicked the TV off. Damn, he had managed to get them both in one shot. I was impressed. The fact that they were ruling it an accident meant no investigation. I shouldn't have been happy about death, but I was.

The phone rang. "Hello?"

"Hey, Sam, it's Katy. I just saw the news. How are you doing? I can only imagine what you must be feeling. He was your lawyer, after all."

"I feel great, Katy. He got what he deserved. Fate is stepping in and correcting all the wrongs done to us. Aren't you excited to see justice being served?" I smiled.

"Sam, you can't mean that," she pleaded.

"Why not? Don't you think what happened to your sister and niece was an injustice, or are you fine with the judgment?" I hissed.

"No, I wasn't happy with the decision, but we must follow the law. We did everything we could. It was a horrible accident," she tried to reassure me.

"To you maybe, but Greyson stole my wife and my child from me! That may not mean anything to you, but it means a hell of a lot to me!" I yelled.

"I didn't mean it like that, and you know it."

"I have to go. Goodbye, Katy," I said before hanging up on her.

She didn't get it. She couldn't understand the pain I lived with daily because she still got to tuck her little girl into bed every night. I refused to feel guilty about them receiving what they deserved.

The next morning, I met Jonathon at the lake.

"Color me impressed," I chuckled.

"I thought you would like that one. I'm sorry it took me longer than we discussed, but it's an art, and you really can't rush perfection." He shrugged.

"Oh, I understand. You got it done, and that was what I needed. Greyson is next. How soon do you think we can take care of that asshole?"

"I would love to make it on the anniversary date, but the cops would get suspicious. It's not like you've kept your feelings in check. Everyone in town knows how much you hate him. Which means you will have to make sure you are seen in public on the night we do it. Buy a movie ticket and then sneak out the back. Go to the old theater, the one downtown. The owner hasn't fixed the security system, so the cameras are out," he explained.

Jonathon was wider in the shoulders, more defined in his biceps, and thicker along his upper chest. His confidence was still as firm as before, if not deeper, but he was physically stronger.

"Meet me at the old barn back on the Abernathy property in two months. Let's get this list finished up sooner rather than later. I have things I will need to get back to. We will meet at 8 pm, so buy a late ticket and make sure you can get back into the building, so you can leave out the front with everyone else. Leave the rest to me. This one is going to be fun!" He was chuckling as he walked away.

Damn, that laugh sent chills down my spine. For a brief moment, I second guessed my alignment with him. He could have been more dangerous than I thought. But the ultimate goal of getting justice meant more to me than my own self-preservation.

Two months later...

The few months took forever. The night finally came, and I did as I was instructed. I went to the Times Theater and bought a ticket for the 7:30 showing. I got some popcorn, making sure to have small talk with as many town folks as possible without looking suspicious. I entered the theater, taking a seat in the back, and waited for the lights to dim. Once the show started, I got up and left out the back door, making sure to place a piece of folded business card over the latch.

The drive to the farm was farther than I expected, but I made it in record time. I had to go through the driveway around the rear of the property and down the dirt road to the old pole barn in back. I turned my lights off before approaching, coasting past it before parking about a block behind it, and then doubled back on foot.

I stepped through the side door to find Greyson hung up on a beam. His arms were extended above his head, and he was perched on his tip toes. This had to be putting extreme pressure on his shoulder joints. *Good.* I wanted him in pain. Jonathon nodded to me before picking up a bucket and throwing the water on Greyson to wake him. Shaking his head, he slowly opened his eyes.

"Good evening, sunshine." Jonathon smiled.

Greyson's eyes went huge "You!" he exclaimed.

I could see the terror in his expression. I don't know what had happened before I got there, but he was absolutely terrified of Jonathon. You could not only see the fear but also smell it as the urine ran down Greyson's thigh. An interesting development.

"I'm sorry, whatever I did, I'm sorry! I didn't mean it!" Greyson was babbling.

"It's too late for saying sorry, you asshole. You took so much from me, and now it's time to make you pay," I hissed.

"You don't want to owe this man anything. I am sorry for what happened to your family, Sam, but this isn't the guy you want to owe a debt to, trust me," Greyson hurriedly added.

"Are you ready?" Jonathon asked.

I nodded and watched Jonathon lay out a large array of knives and other sharp implements.

The time to listen to Greyson's excuses had passed. All I

could think about was getting justice for the girls. This guy was a liar and would say anything to save himself. I would pay anything to finally get some peace, so whatever Jonathon asked for, I would give him.

"First the clothes have to go, they get in the way," Jonathon said more to himself than to anyone else. He methodically cut everything away from Greyson except his boxer shorts and shoes. "How old was your daughter?" Jonathon asked as he switched one knife out for a smaller scalpel.

"Six," I hissed.

"We will start with six slashes. I think three on each thigh is a nice start." Jonathon nodded before he rested the blade on Greyson's inner thigh.

He cut into the left one first, making a long incision from inside his groin down to his knee, and he counted as he cut. The cuts weren't deep; it seemed more for pain than for damage. Regardless, the effect was exactly what I had asked for. Greyson was experiencing extreme pain.

Greyson was screaming and begging, "Don't do this, please don't do this. I'm sorry, so sorry. Ahhhhh!"

"Oh, you can scream louder than that," Jonathon coaxed as if he was trying to pull a stray kitten to safety.

After the six in his thighs, Jonathon moved to cut Greyson's arms from his elbow up to his armpit, but he didn't stop there. Continuing, he cut through his armpit, down his ribcage, past his hip bone, along the outer thigh—cutting along his knee and calf until he finally stopped just above his ankle bone. Two perfect cuts from elbow to ankle, only skipping over the part of his flesh covered with his boxers.

I should have been disgusted, and the logical aspect of my brain was screaming to stop this before it got too far. Yet the other part of my brain assured me this was mild compared to what I felt when I opened my eyes and remembered my family was dead. The heartache every night I crawled into bed, knowing my daughter would never again experience the gift of living. He was getting off easy because, at the end of this, he would be dead, not dealing with the reminder day in and day out. By the twelfth slash, Greyson had passed out from the pain.

"I don't think so, buddy," Jonathon hissed while throwing another bucket of water on his face.

In the distance I could hear a police siren. I didn't know if they were coming to us, but this was the only residence for miles.

"Go, I'll finish and meet you at the spot tomorrow," Jonathon urged.

I stood in front of Greyson and spat at him. "This is because of me; you are getting all of this because I wanted it. You will die because I planned it."

I nodded to Jonathon and proceeded to leave.

"The price he'll ask for in return will be steep. I hope it was all worth it," Greyson stressed before screaming as Jonathon pressed the blade against him once more.

I got back to the theater and was happy to see no one had moved my paper. The end of the movie was playing as I slipped inside. I was in my seat as the lights came up, waving at a few people as they passed me to leave the theater. I stood in front of the building for a few minutes more making small talk with a few of my clients.

The man who ruined my life was dead.

I went home that night and slept better than I had in years. Waking up with an extra bounce in my step and finally feeling like things were working in my favor, I headed to the kitchen to make coffee and clicked on the news.

"The state's most prolific serial killer has been caught. The police and FBI have been tracking this man for the last four years, seeking his identity. Jonathon Ellis was caught fleeing the murder scene of Greyson Richard. We are all no strangers to Greyson, the only son of Mayor Richard, who has had numerous run-ins with the law. When police asked Jonathon why he killed Greyson, his response was, 'Because it was fun.'"

Oh, shit! I dropped my mug, and it shattered on the floor. Rage had blinded me. If he sold me out, I would go to jail too. How could I trust someone I barely knew?

The doorbell rang and my heart dropped into my stomach. I took a deep breath and went to see if the devil himself was knocking. I opened the door. "Hello, Thomas. What brings you by so early?" I inquired.

"I wanted to come by and tell you that Greyson was murdered last night," he stated.

I motioned him in and walked to the kitchen. I grabbed the broom to sweep up the glass from the floor. "I heard."

"I see the news was just as shocking to you." He looked at the broken mug.

"You could say that," I chuckled.

"The guys at the station think I'm being paranoid, but I can't help but notice four of the people involved in your wife's case have died," he said.

"Yeah, I've noticed it too. I just figured fate was correcting the injustice. I wouldn't wish the pain that I went through on those guys' families, though."

I threw the broken cup away and grabbed two more from the cabinet then filled them both full before offering one to Thomas.

"Do you take anything in your coffee?" I inquired.

"Straight up is good for me," he replied before taking a sip.

"Thomas, you don't think I had anything to do with any of those deaths, do you?"

"I don't think so, but it seems too much of a coincidence to not raise a flag for me," he remarked.

"Understandable, but I swear to you I didn't kill any of those men. I've been trying to rebuild my life and move on. Physically killing them would be counterproductive," I explained.

"I figured as much, but really needed to hear it from your

own lips. Thanks for the coffee." He finished his final sip before setting the cup down and rising to leave. "Take care, Sam. It was good to see you," he said, smacking me on the shoulder as he walked out.

I watched him get into his car and leave before shutting the door. I didn't entirely lie; I hadn't actually killed any one of them, but I was not sad they were dead. I don't think he really suspected me, and if he did, he would have arrested me. I needed to lay low for a while and think through what I was going to do to get back at Kyle. I couldn't end up in jail; otherwise, I wouldn't be able to take what I wanted from Kyle: his wife and his kids. I would make them mine, and then I would destroy her and turn his kids against him. I would make every day a living hell for him.

Chapter 14

One year and three months later...

What the hell is going on with the world? The sirens were blaring from every corner of the state. Multiple twisters had already raged through, how many more were to come?

Sara, I needed to check on her. I'd been watching the family for a while and noticed Sara was broken and not at all the strong woman I once knew. I didn't think it would affect Kyle if I took her. He had more girlfriends and one-night stands than any married man should.

Despite the sirens, I drove to her house. It was almost completely gone, and my heart sank. I jumped from my car and ran up to the rubble yelling her name. There was no answer, and as I dug through the debris, throwing things off of the largest pile, I didn't find any sign of her. *Where could she be?* It only took a minute for me to realize where she was. She was at the school looking for her kids. I jumped back into my vehicle and fought my way to the school.

I was worried for Sara. She needed to be alive for my plan to work. It was all about revenge.

The school was in chaos. The fire department had the tents and was methodically working to remove people from the collapsed building. People were everywhere, some helping, some stumbling around in a shocked haze, others just watching, too lost to help.

I moved into the tent at the end of the line. There was less activity there, and I quickly understood why.

There weren't any emergency people in there, only rows of bodies covered in sheets. It was filled with little lives cut way too short. I knew her kids were in there; I could feel it, and damn if that didn't hurt even more. I wanted to ruin Kyle's life, not hers. I had to leave; seeing all of the kids reminded me too much of burying my own daughter. If she was burying her kids, then hadn't she suffered enough? I stepped out just as she came huffing out of the other tent. I moved to the side. After she took a breath for courage, she made a bee-line for the tent.

"You don't want to go in there," I stated. She completely ignored me. I grabbed her shoulder and tried again. "You really don't want to go in there."

She refused to face me, and I could feel her deflate in my hands. Then she pulled back quickly, rolled my grip off, and said something about her kids before trying to charge into the tent.

I grabbed her arm in a final attempt.

"There are no survivors in there. This is the tent for the dead," I whispered. God, my heart ached for her.

I couldn't let her do this alone. Within seconds, I was following her in. I watched as she searched through the little feet, looking for something familiar. I knew where they were, but I didn't want to be the one to point them out to her. The second she found her kids, she paused for a moment, and my heart shattered with hers. She moved slowly to the shoes that could only belong to her daughter.

She was talking to me but not really. She needed to reassure herself that her little girl knew how much she loved her.

I watched her take care of her daughter, and every ounce of hate I had for her disappeared and was quickly replaced by the love I had missed so much. This was the first woman I had ever loved, and she was breaking. Shattering like I had when Ellen and Samantha died.

When she removed the blanket from her son, the two children were holding hands. You would have had to be made of stone to not feel something at the sight. I needed to reassure her, make her see she'd done everything right with her kids.

"She never let him go, not even for a second," I whispered.

I didn't know if it was true, but she needed to believe it was. I watched her clean the kids up and listened as she spoke. I wanted to wrap her in my arms. I needed to remind her of who I was so I could comfort her, but instead I watched her grieve.

She was struggling to get the kids on her lap. I bent down and said, "Let me help you." I reached for their hands to keep them together as I moved them. She yelled at me with so much venom that I felt its sting. I grabbed her daughter instead and placed her in her lap, hoping their hands held. I watched her kiss them both. In that moment I was glad Ellen died with Samantha because there was no way I could have watched her go through the loss. Observing Sara was killing me.

The outside noise came to a sudden halt, so I ran out of the tent. *Shit.* Another round of storms was coming. In minutes, they would be on top of us. I ran back in to get her moving.

It was a simple request, but she argued with me. I ran back out to get my vehicle moved over to the tent, praying the newest tornadoes would miss us. I didn't feel like dying. Not then, and definitely not like this.

For the first time in years, I wanted to live. I wanted to learn who she was now.

After what seemed like hours, I convinced her to get the kids to safety. She was a bitter woman, but I chalked most of her attitude up to the severity of her loss. We got to her place, and I went through the motions of helping her.

I could tell she was angry with me. She struggled with the

simplest of tasks, and I tried to be supportive, but she had to step up.

After getting a cover over the basement, I went to get Tina out of the back of the vehicle. I needed to get them down there fast before the rain really started falling. Sara looked utterly lost; she was looking around at everything, taking in the sight, but didn't seem to be looking at any one thing. She must have been in her own head. What could she have been thinking?

"Open the door," I urged with Tina in my arms.

She moved like she was in a fog. I could tell she wanted to get Thomas, but I needed her to be safe. I had been watching her from afar and swore she would be the catalyst of what would ultimately be the fulfillment of revenge. However, now all I wanted to do was protect her. "I will get him. Just come down here and show me where you want me to place her," I requested.

She did as instructed, and I moved quickly to get both kids where she wanted them. I tried to make small talk, but every time she spoke, another piece of the shell broke away.

Her whispered offer to stay made my heart beat faster than it should have, but I had to decline. It was all too raw, and so I told the first of the many lies I would tell her.

"Thank you, but I have to try and make my way to my house and see if I can salvage anything. Then I have to try and find Samantha. She wasn't at the school. Her mom called her in sick. I spoke with her teacher before I saw you standing at the doorway leading into the same tent I had just come out of. I knew what was in the tent because I too was looking for my daughter amongst the dead," I interjected.

"I understand, and if I can help in any way, let me know. After all, it is the least I can do," she whispered, and I could tell she meant it.

"Stay safe," I stated, before heading back up the stairs.

I did what I said I was going to do. I went home. Unlike Sara's place, mine was still standing. When Ellen and I built it, we had insisted on extra precautions. There were a few of my neighbors that had weathered the storm. They were outside packing things into their cars, getting ready to head somewhere else. My house was the only one fully standing on the street, but my street fared better than most.

I couldn't stop wondering why I lied to Sara about the girls. It was too late to try and make her pay for what Kyle did. Revenge didn't seem to be as important in that moment. I should have told her they were dead. Would it have made a difference on how she saw me? I couldn't risk my plan. I'd held on to it for too long, and I needed to see it through. I might not hurt Sara anymore, but once I found Kyle, I would be the one who killed him. I decided to go look for my sister-in-law and niece and tell Sara it was my daughter and wife, consequences be damned.

I packed stuff up and took it to my basement—things I didn't want to lose since I knew it would be a while before I could return for them. I grabbed the old box from the closet with the little things I had kept from high school and threw the mausoleum keys in it. It was a low blow, because I knew the minute she saw what I had kept she would be reminded of our kiss in high school. It was selfish, but I needed to know whether I haunted her thoughts like she did mine.

***

Hours passed, and the weather had turned to a heavy sleet and snow mix.

I shouldn't have gone back to her. I should have washed my hands of her and tried to start over somewhere else. My brain and heart were at odds. The heart yelled, *Stay, she needs you,* while the brain screamed, *She is more trouble than you want.* My heart won.

When I got back to her place, the door was wide open, and all I could think was that something horrible had happened. I rushed up to the opening and found her lying in the snow with nothing covering her; she was curled up in a fetal position, protecting her face with her hands. One was covered, but the other was completely exposed.

She was screaming at me before I reached her. "Just kill me! Please, just kill me."

"Sara, what are you doing out here? Are you trying to kill yourself? Hold on," I angrily questioned.

"I hate you, Kyle. I wish you were dead. You should be dead, not the kids. They were perfect and you're a hateful, hateful man. I wish I was strong enough to kill you myself," she slurred.

"Shhh, Sara. It's, Sam, not Kyle," I cooed.

"I loved Sam, but he didn't love me. Kyle told me all the time. Sam hates you, Sara, because you are a worthless excuse of a human who can't do anything right. That's why Sam left me—I couldn't follow directions and he didn't like me anymore," she mumbled.

Her life was so much worse than I expected. She wasn't the happy girl I used to know; she was a worn-down woman with no sense of who she was. He had completely ruined everything that was good and pure within her. That would explain why she lashed out at me so much; she was trying to protect herself. She needed to understand I was not him and I would take care of him, not only for myself, but for her, too.

"I will kill Kyle for you, Sara. Don't you worry. If he survived this, I will kill him for what he has done to you," I promised.

"Thank you, fairy godmother," she giggled while patting my cheek. Moments later, she was passed out.

Great, she's drunk and half-frozen to death. I got her downstairs and quickly stripped her out of her clothes.

"Sorry, kids," I whispered before moving them off the mattress, flipping it over, and placing Sara on it.

I was stripping when the shaking started, so I quickly got into bed with her and held her close. She was an ice cube and obviously thought my touch was killing her because she kept mumbling about burning. Eventually she fell into a deep slumber, and I knew I had to do something about the kids. She would be livid if she found out what I had done. Getting out of bed, I tucked her in and dressed quickly.

I needed coffins, and I knew where to get them.

It didn't take much to get into the funeral home. Obviously, they weren't worried about anyone stealing from them. I went to the office and quickly rifled through the invoices until I found what I was looking for. Lucky for me, they got their caskets locally.

I drove to the warehouse and the main doors were wide open, so I went inside the loading bay and parked. The place was huge. After about twenty minutes I finally figured the system out, which made finding what I needed easier. The white was more of a standard issue, though it had a pearl finish, but the pink one was the exact same one we used for Samantha. For a moment I lost the ability to move as I remembered the day I laid them to rest.

Now was not the time to open that box. I crammed the memory back down and got the caskets loaded.

It was a bitch to get them through the stairs, but I was determined. I didn't want to have the same issues going out after I placed the kids in the caskets, so I moved things around in the basement to make leaving easier.

Sara was moaning in her sleep and sounded like she was in pain. I stripped back down and got onto the bed with her and immediately felt her shaking. I shouted, "Open your eyes, Sara!"

Her eyes flew open and then she started to convulse harder. "Sam," she cried softly.

"Oh, Sara. Hold on—you're going into shock." I pulled her to me as tight as I dared.

She closed her eyes even though I tried to keep her looking at me. Her muscles were loosening, and her convulsions were slowing, but I needed her to stay with me. "You need some electrolytes. Do you have anything in your supplies?" I whispered, trying not to startle her.

"Gatorade, bottom shelf towards the back," she croaked.

With no thought concerning my nude body, I hurried to the shelf and brought back the first flavor I found.

When she reached for the Gatorade she screamed, I should have wrapped her hand as soon as I noticed it. Before she could think further about her appearance, she noticed Thomas' coffin. She lowered her arm and fingers back down and stared.

I put my boxers on and crawled back into the bed with her. She wasn't as cold as before, so I pulled her close to me to keep her warm. With her eyes still fixed on the coffins, I decided to answer the unasked question.

"The other one behind it is a beautiful pearlescent pink," I whispered into her ear.

"How?"

I slipped my hand behind her, urging her to sit up and drink the Gatorade. She parted her lips slightly as I held the bottle to them. She started chugging it, and I was afraid she was going to make herself sick. When I pulled it away, she actually growled at me.

"You need bandages and some antibiotics. Once I get your body temperature back to normal, I will go get you some. If Kyle comes home, he can take my place beside you and I can go sooner," I insisted while positioning us back under the covers even though I hated to think about Kyle laying here with her.

"He wouldn't lay with me to save me. He would tell me to get over it. We haven't held one another for a very long time, and he makes sure I know how disgusted he is by my body. So, don't count on him relieving you," she plainly stated.

That fucking son of a bitch! I was livid at the thought of him not caring enough to save his wife. Didn't he understand how precious she was? I leaned into her, breathed in her scent, and kissed her head.

"What happened to me?" she questioned.

"I found you outside about six hours ago. When I got here, I thought you were dead. I didn't see you at first, but then I found you in the fetal position barely breathing and showing signs of hypothermia. You were covered in a layer of ice, and all of your skin that was exposed has frostbite. You're lucky it was only your hand. I picked you up and brought you down here, stripped us down, and began trying to warm you up," I finished, hoping she wouldn't see through the vague description.

"At this very moment, you are all I have. We need each other to cope with what is happening, and I didn't want to lose you again," I softly admitted.

"I don't understand why you would care so much?"

"Because, Sara, someone has to," I plainly stated.

"If Kyle is so horrible to you, why do you stay with him? I mean, if he is as mean and hateful as you say, then why would you keep yourself in that situation?" It wasn't any of my business, but I needed to know what kind of hold this man had over her.

"I never said he was mean and hateful," she tried to argue.

"You didn't have to say those words for me to hear what you were leaving out," I said.

She sighed. "It wasn't always that way. There was a time when he truly loved me and would have done anything to make me happy."

"What happened? When did things change?" I pushed.

I needed to drop it; it was none of my business. I would kill Kyle and didn't want any additional reasons.

Surprisingly, she answered. "I honestly don't know. It was little things at first, an unkind word, a disgusted look at something I would say. Every time he made comments about me doing something horrible, I tried to change it. Before I knew it, I would change to the way he wanted and even that would be wrong. It got to the point where I felt no matter what I tried

I wasn't good enough for him. Regardless of what I wanted or how hard I wanted to keep him happy, nothing I did sat right with him. It could have been me—maybe I changed him. He was so wonderful when we got married. Attentive, loving, concerned about me all the time. I miss that, I miss who Kyle was. I have fallen into a life of going through the motions. I do what I know he wants because it's easier to keep him content than worry about my happiness. One day he will see everything I do for him. He loves me the only way he knows how, and that has to be good enough for me."

"Why did you marry him?" I spat more forcefully than I intended.

Her answer made me physically sick to my stomach. I listened to the words and heard what she wasn't saying. He had tricked her, lied to her, and misled her into believing he was this great guy while hiding who he was until he had her tied to him. He knew she would never leave him; she was raised to believe once you married you stuck it out. When she finished, I wiped the tears from her face—ones I don't think she realized she was shedding.

My heart ached for her, and here was a chance to be completely open with her about everything. Instead, I lied.

"I understand where you're coming from. I thought Ellen and I would be married forever. Some things are meant to last, but she and I weren't. We never talked, or argued, we never discussed anything. Our marriage was missing a key element, communication. I came home from work one day to find her saying enough was enough and she was leaving. The worst part of it was she never gave me a chance to change or correct what was wrong. She just packed her and Samantha's things and left. The following week I got served with divorce papers citing un-reconcilable differences. I never stood a chance."

I was playing on her sympathy and knew it would work. I didn't want her to see me as a widower—I needed her to see me as heartbroken and lonely just like her.

"You still love her?" she whispered.

Finally, I could give her some truth. "I'm not sure I ever really loved her. She reminded me of someone I had loved for years but couldn't be with. I think I was subconsciously trying to extend my love for the other woman by marrying Ellen. I thought if I loved Ellen, I would stop loving the woman I couldn't be with. I loved Ellen in my own way, but I'm not in love with her."

She had stopped shaking completely, and I had no reason to still be holding her, but I wasn't ready to let her go.

"I think the neighbor had some prescriptions she used to keep in her medicine cabinet. Since I've stopped shaking and convulsing, perhaps you can go check. If you could find something to help ease the pain in my hands, I would appreciate it. There also used to be a drugstore up off of Route Nine. If it is standing, maybe they could help us?" She was still hurting, and I should have thought about that.

"I'm not sure I should leave you yet. I don't want you to have a relapse, or worse. Can you promise me you will not get up or try to move around?" I roughly stated. I wanted her to promise if Kyle showed up she wouldn't let him down here with her, but I knew I couldn't.

"I promise you I will not move from this spot until you return. The truth is, I hurt too bad to want to move, so I don't foresee it being a problem."

I exhaled, and before getting up I looked into those sad, lost eyes of hers and whispered, "I will come back to you. I know you remember me. You have to, because we're all we have."

I leaned in and kissed her forehead but really wanted to kiss those soft, luscious lips. I got up, tucked her in, and dressed quickly. I had things to do.

I ran back over to Mrs. Johnston's and dug through what was left of her medicine cabinet.

The next stop was the pharmacy, but someone had beaten

me to it. I crawled through the broken door and collected the things that I thought would help with infection and pain. I took way more than we needed, but I was unsure of exactly how long the world was going to be upside down.

I stepped out of the pharmacy when a voice in the dark called, "Did you tell her about all the people you've helped kill, or your plans for Kyle and for her?"

No, it can't be.

"Jonathon, how the hell have you been, man?" I asked with as much passion as I could muster.

"Good. You never came to visit me," he joked.

"I couldn't. The day after you got arrested, Detective Mackaby came to me telling me he thought I had something to do with the deaths. It took everything I had to convince him that I wasn't involved. Hey, what about all the bodies they found on your property?" I replied.

"Other than what I did for you, I never murdered anyone in cold blood. I was contracted to take out precise targets, but hey, that's all water under the bridge now. Did I ever tell you I was a twin?" he interjected.

"No, I had no idea."

"Yep, my brother's name is Adam, and I think he and Sara would really hit it off. She is exactly what he needs in his life. Sara is what I want for all the help I gave you before and will continue to give you," he deadpanned.

"No, you said it wasn't about blackmail. You said you didn't want anything from me," I spat hatefully.

"Correction, I told you that one day I would ask you for something and you weren't allowed to say no. At the time of the murders, I didn't want anything from you. Things have changed. You can either let my brother have her, or I'll kill you and he will have her, anyway. Do you really want to break her heart by dying on her? The choice is yours. Oh, I know the officers from your wife's trial were on the bottom of your final kill list, so I will take care of them for you too just to show you I always keep my end of a deal," Jonathon advised before walking away.

This can't be happening. No, you can't do this to me!

PART 3

SARA

Chapter 15

I woke to Sam screaming in his sleep. He was thrashing at the air yelling, "No, you can't have her—I won't let you!"

I rushed over to him and shook him hard. "Sam, it's Sara. Wake up! Sam, WAKE UP!" I yelled.

He bolted up, looking at me with the most intense eyes I had ever seen.

"Are you okay?" I asked, sitting down beside him.

He was breathing heavy and kept clenching and unclenching his fists.

"I want you, Sara. Right now. Kiss me, please," he begged.

How could I refuse? He looked so lost. I leaned in and kissed him. I felt him melt in my arms and I wanted to cry. This was the man I had loved for years.

I wouldn't have denied him even if I could; I leaned and pressed my lips to his again. Everything was there between us—the electricity, the passion—the things I felt with Adam I was feeling with Sam as well. He slid his arm around me and pulled me up onto his lap. He moaned as his tongue moved across mine. I was so lost in the feelings I didn't hear the door open or Adam come in. The bed dipped behind me, and a soft caress glided up my back. I jumped at the sensation and quickly released Sam.

I turned to Adam and quickly apologized. "I'm so sorry, he

looked so crestfallen...I..."

What could I say? I wanted to kiss him, so I did? There was no other reason for it.

"Don't apologize, I know you love him. I can see it when you look at him. I knew it when you thought he was dead. I don't mind sharing if you have enough love for the both of us?" Adam replied with complete sincerity.

Who was this man? How could he be so open about all of this? I looked between the men, not sure exactly what should happen.

"Adam, I want to make love to this woman more than I want to take my next breath. I'm not sure she is as open as we are. I don't think she can be with me while you're here because she loves you too," Sam stated.

Oh god, he was right. I loved Adam too. I looked back and forth between both men. How could I love them both? It was all confusing. I couldn't love them both—it was not proper. People don't have more than one lover. It wasn't natural, was it?

Adam must have noticed my internal debate. With his hand still on my back, he pulled me over and kissed me softly, and I felt myself melt further.

"You can be whoever you want to be now. No one is going to judge you or look down on you. I love you, Sara, and if loving you means I have to share you, then I will." Adam kissed me again and rested his forehead against mine.

These two men meant more to me than anything else. They were all I had. I kissed Adam softly, a brief meeting of the lips, but I poured all of my love into it.

"I'm going to go back to your old place and load up some more stuff. I should be gone a few hours," Adam said as he broke the kiss.

Adam left before anything else could be said. Still sitting in Sam's lap, I turned back to look at him. He was upright too and wrapped his arms around me, burying his face against my chest. He took a deep breath, absorbing me in.

"I have been stupid for so many years, Sara. I've been blinded by hate, and a better man would say he was sorry about it, but I'm not. I've had this fog surrounding me and viewed the world as a hateful place I had to survive. I loved you so much back then. I was dumb to think you would wait for me as I figured it out. None of the girlfriends lasted because they weren't you, but I didn't figure that out until it was too late," he whispered.

His tone told me he wasn't saying it for my benefit, but for his own. It sounded like a confession, or inner thoughts spilling out. He needed confirmation that he was not alone in the way he felt.

"I thought I would wait forever for you, but every new girl broke my heart even more. Then we kissed and everything fell into place for me, but not for you. That night was when I decided I wasn't going to wait for you anymore. You didn't love me as much as I loved you, and I was tired of being pushed aside. You are who I should have married, but you weren't ready. I was so mad at you—I cursed you and cried over you so many times. I married the next person who showed me an ounce of affection, and the rest is history now. I'm not who I used to be, and I won't pretend to be. I'm broken and slowly trying to mend the wounds, but once it's healed, there will always be a scar. If you can love me for who I am now, then we will get along wonderfully, because I love the woman sitting in front of me. I love your strength and your passion," he said.

I tilted his head up and kissed him, sliding my tongue along his lip, seeking entry. He growled and opened up for me. The feel of his tongue dueling mine was different from any other kiss I'd experienced.

I wrapped my hands behind his head and pulled him into me, trying to get him closer. I wanted to be consumed by him. Wrapping his hands under my shirt, he lifted my top up. It flew off easily, and with a few subtle movements our naked bodies entwined with one another.

Sam's body was hard and throbbing against me. I could feel his desire for me; he was fully erect, solid and wanting. I moaned into his mouth while our tongues danced in tune with the growing passion between us. He rolled me over until our bodies were perfectly aligned. The feel of him aroused and nestled against my thighs was driving me crazy. I rotated my hips, sending sensations singing through me. His kiss went deeper, with more desperation. I matched him with all of my fever and kissed him with all of the love I felt.

He broke away to kiss my jaw, working his way down my neck. I loved the feel of his mouth on me, and then he bit into a tender part of my neck below my ear, making me moan louder. I was unconsciously moving my hips trying to work him into me. I wanted to feel him slide inside of me and make me his on a primal level. I was panting, moaning, and completely overwhelmed by him. His scent was permeating around me—driving my need higher.

He finally gave in and slid into me with one slow thrust. I arched, taking him deeper. Our connection felt exactly like I thought it would all those years ago. We were united as one, moving in tandem, both seeking what the other was giving freely. I ran my hands down his back until I was gripping his ass and pulling him deeper into me. I couldn't stop the sounds that followed even if I wanted to. He felt wonderful inside of me, fitting me so well. His thrusts were coming faster, making me chase him every time he pulled out. I was awash in sensation, not thinking about anything but how well he played my body.

"I love you, Sara," he whispered in my ear, sending my orgasm over the edge. I cried out my release and could sense him reaching his peak as well. He pushed farther into me, so when he came inside of me, he was as deep as possible. The sensation of him finding his release felt phenomenal.

He collapsed down onto me as we both worked to catch our breath.

"I love you too, Sam," I whispered while wrapping my arms around his back.

I don't know how long we stayed that way, but Sam eventually moved off of me. He didn't run away from me and instead pulled me closer, and I fell asleep wrapped in his arms.

I slept the rest of the night with Sam. When I woke, I saw Adam had returned and was sound asleep on the other bed. I pulled from Sam's embrace and walked over to the bed. I sat down on it and ran my hand along the side of Adam's face. He opened his eyes and smiled at me. "Good morning, beautiful."

"You should have woken me when you got back," I whispered, trying not to disturb Sam.

Adam grabbed my hand and kissed it, gifting me with another heart-stopping smile. He sat up in bed and wrapped his arms around me.

"Want some coffee?" he inquired.

"They have coffee?" I asked with way too much excitement.

Chuckling, he got up from the bed. I followed him into the small kitchen area and watched him make the coffee. The smell of it reminded me of when I lived with my parents. I liked coffee, but no one else in my house did, so I rarely drank it.

With the coffee finished, Sam came shuffling in with his arms full of folders. "I'll take a cup too, Adam, if you don't mind," he requested.

"Sure thing," Adam replied.

"What is all of that?" I asked as I added a little coffee to my cream and sugar combo.

"The files we found under the cabinet. It looks like Derek had them sorted by who was at the prison and who was at the hospital. I've only glanced at one file, but it seems like these are the people he found the most dangerous," Sam said.

Looking over to Adam, Sam asked, "Adam, can you look at the pictures and see if any of these are ones that you already buried at Cerritus?"

"Sure." Adam sat down beside me and started to thumb through the files. He would open one, look at it, and set it on one of two piles. There had to be more than two dozen folders, but he made fast work of them.

"These people I buried in the lot at the facility. These are the ones I don't remember seeing, but that doesn't necessarily mean they are alive. I would have to go back and check again," he said.

"That's actually a good idea. Adam can go to the facility, and Sam and I can go to the prison and see if any of those people are dead," I said.

"That is a good idea," Adam added.

"Maybe I should just go myself," Sam offered.

I looked at him like he had lost his mind. Why would he think I was going to be okay with that? I huffed at him and grabbed the other stack of files and thumbed through them looking for two in particular. I grabbed Marcus' and pulled it out. I went over them again and looked back at Adam. "Why isn't the file on your brother here with the others?"

"Because he was moved to Cerritus last year. He was having identity issues, and the prison wasn't a safe place for him anymore," Adam answered.

"Oh, makes sense. Well, this guy is definitely dead. I saw his body hanging from a tree," I finished.

I grabbed the files from Adam and looked through them, adding another to his deceased pile. "Chris is dead already," I stated.

We finished our coffee in silence, each thinking about what we needed to do and not wanting to discuss the details.

"Should we try to contact the people on the radio yet?" I asked.

"I think we should wait and see what we find at the properties first," Adam suggested.

"I agree with Adam," Sam advised.

"Then it's settled. Adam, we will see you when you get

back. Be careful," I cautioned, moving over to him and kissing him gently.

"Always." He smiled.

That smile never failed to make me melt. I chuckled as he made his way out.

"Oh, Adam. Would you mind finding stuff for the cats, please? Food, litter, toys—anything you think they might need?" I asked.

He turned to look at me and winked.

Getting up, I grabbed the files and walked back to the bed. I sat down and thumbed through the folders.

"Before you get too involved in what might be a problem, let's go see if any of them are dead in their cells," Sam suggested.

"Sounds good," I said.

The drive to the prison was uneventful. Most of the building was still standing, and my heart sank a little because that meant some inmates had survived.

We drove through a plethora of broken gates and walked into the prison by way of a missing door. We came to an office, and I glanced around to find some kind of a map. There was nothing that told us which way to go. The smell of decomposition permeating the air told me there were dead people throughout the prison.

There was one hallway leading to the part that housed the inmates, so we went towards it without discussing the game plan. There couldn't possibly be anyone left alive. The smell alone would take them.

"Do we need keys?" I asked.

"I brought this." Sam showed me a crowbar.

I shrugged. Hopefully, it would work if we needed it.

The first set of cells we came to were open and, thankfully, empty. Around the corner we could still see every single door completely accessible, but this time there were people inside. It was difficult to see exactly what killed them. It could have been head trauma, gunshot wounds, or they might have been beaten to death. It didn't matter. They were dead and decomposing.

"I don't think this is the correct section," I guessed.

"I agree. I bet we have to get into the other building to find who we're looking for," Sam agreed.

We walked past the next heavy set of doors, and I stood to the side as Sam broke the following door open.

"It's about damn time!" A man came running up at us.

"Back the fuck off," Sam hissed.

The guy stopped, startled. "Wow, man, relax. I've been locked in here for weeks, and I didn't think anyone was coming."

"Who are you?" I countered while covering my nose. He smelled horrible.

"The name is Chadrick Tethers. I'm nineteen and a shoplifter," he said.

"Are you a druggie, Chadrick?" Sam hissed.

"No, I stole because I enjoyed the rush. My parents are loaded, and I could have bought anything I wanted, but stealing was more fun. Then my old man didn't buy my way out, so here I am, stuck in jail rotting away. I wasn't even housed in this unit. I came down to make sure no one was starving to death, and those assholes locked me in."

"Do you think we should believe him?" I whispered.

"Not sure yet," Sam remarked. "Is there anyone in this other unit alive?" Sam prodded.

"There were a dozen people here when I came in, but I never made it out of the chow hall. I have been stuck in here for way too long. Just let me go, and I swear to never try and find you. I need a change of clothes," he begged.

I swung my bag around and dug out the files. "Can you tell me if any of these men were in here when you came in?" I asked.

I placed them on the table and stepped back. I thought I could take the skinny guy, but isolation does funny things to the mind, and I didn't want to test his resolve. He sat down and slowly opened each and every folder. He put two over to one side and then slid the others away from him.

"These two were in here. The rest I don't recognize," he said. He got up and walked away from the table. "Can I leave now?"

"You are going with us down that hall to see if any of these guys are in there," Sam interjected.

"Fine, man, but let's hurry. I need fresh air," he edged.

Sam walked over to the other door in the room and placed the crowbar along the inner edge of the door and pried it free, giving us access to the hall. The smell that followed made me gag, then I fell to my knees and dry heaved. I had to get it under control if I was going to walk down there.

"If you look at the files, it gives you a room number. The numbers are above the cell doors. We can find your people that way," Chadrick said.

I stood up and nodded to Sam. He didn't say anything. His brows were drawn down, causing his forehead to crease. Was he worried about me or what we might find? I grabbed the files from the table, put the two that were confirmed alive back in the bag, and held the others in my arms.

The first five cells were occupied with dead bodies. "I thought they opened the doors?" I demanded.

"They did, but there is a fault in the system. You can shut the door, but unless you have a key, you can't re-open it. When the system opens the doors, you have to move fast or some asshole is going to lock you back in," Chadrick hissed.

"How many did you lock back in?" Sam insinuated.

"None. Starving to death like a trapped animal is no way for anyone to die," he countered.

"Here is the first number on the files." I stopped Sam.

"Yeah, he is dead," Chadrick said.

He was much more than dead. The person was bloated, mostly black in color, and there was a slimy look to their skin. You could see how it was decomposing, and the mattress was absorbing the excreted fluids. It was revolting. We didn't linger and kept moving. The people in the cells all looked about the same, although some were on the bed while others were on the floor near the door, probably to plead for someone to let them out. Three more numbers, all dead.

"This is the next number," I stated.

"Lucky bastard, looks like he made it out." Chadrick chuckled.

We finished as quickly as we could and exited the secure ward. Three of the people in the folders seemed to have made it out as well as ten others, according to Chadrick. They weren't on Derek's list, so I wasn't too concerned with them.

We walked back into the main section. Sam pried open the door to the warden's office.

"Chadrick, let's go find the files on the guys who made it out. Then you can go wherever you want," Sam insisted.

"Deal." Chadrick strutted into the office and went directly to the file cabinet in the far corner.

"How do you know they are in there?" I inquired.

"The receptionist was sweet on me. She and I have been in here a few times for privacy, and she loved to talk about all of the responsibilities the warden put on her," he replied.

"I'm surprised she didn't try to make sure you got out," I surmised.

"She did, and they took her with them. I don't even know if she is still alive, or if she wants to be if she is," he deadpanned.

"Sorry," I whispered.

"All good. Here are the people you guys are looking for." He handed the files to Sam. "I hope you don't run into any of them, but if you do, give them hell for me. I'm heading upstate to my parents' hunting cabin. Fingers crossed it's still there." He grabbed a set of keys off the wall marked "vans."

"Hey," I started.

"Not going to rat me out for taking a vehicle, are you?" he sighed.

"No, there are only like two useable ones out there. I was going to suggest you take all the keys to make sure you have a usable set," I said.

"Oh, thanks. What are your names anyway?" he asked.

"I'm Sara, and this is Sam," I responded.

"Thanks for being my white knights. If I can ever repay the favor, let me know. I do have a ham radio at the cabin. If it works, you can reach out to me." He turned and left without giving us a last thought.

I looked down at the top file he handed me; It was his, and I glanced through it.

"He wasn't lying to us. He really is just a young shoplifter." I chuckled.

"Let's get back and see what Adam has found," Sam suggested.

I nodded.

Outside, Chadrick was nowhere to be found. He sure did move fast. We drove back to the bunker in silence.

***

We were greeted by two angry kittens. I knew they had to be hungry, but I still didn't have anything for them. I gave Sam the folders and went to go look through Derek's house for something to feed them.

The little brats were in luck; he had tuna in the cabinet. I grabbed it and made my way back down and found them waiting at the bottom of the ladder. I opened the tuna and gave them each their own can. I chuckled at the way they wolfed down the food with little regard to their surroundings. You could hear them growling at each other as they scooted the cans closer to one another.

I walked into the room, leaving the door open for the boys to join us when they finished. The first thing I noticed was Adam hadn't returned yet.

Sam had the files out in front of him and sorted.

"These six are in for assault, mostly domestic, but they are repeat offenders. This guy is in for killing his girlfriend in a car accident. These two are child molesting, low-life scumbags.

"This guy is in for medically assisted suicides. The last two were on Derek's original list and were both listed as serial killers. They have multiple convictions for murder. I think the others were just following the scariest of them," Sam finished, placing his head in his hands.

"I take it you got more than you were bargaining for on your search. I know I did," Adam called as he headed in.

I ran over to him. "What the hell happened to you?" I asked, seeing his swollen eye, bloodied nose, and busted lip.

"I can confirm one on the list is still very much alive and living in the part of Cerritus that still stands, along with two women who were former patients. I don't think he will seek to hurt anyone, but he definitely made sure I knew I wasn't welcome. The others were still locked in their rooms dead." Adam sighed. "I should have checked the high security section last time I was there. Perhaps I could have saved some of them," he stated, crestfallen.

"You can't think that way. You did save Naomi, and the other two," I interjected.

"I know." He laid his head on my shoulder and wrapped his arms around me.

"I think it's time to reach out to whoever is on the other side of that radio, Sam," I pleaded.

"I think you are right," he replied before picking up the radio.

I don't think any of us breathed as he turned it on. He depressed a button and said strongly, "Hello, is there anyone out there?"

He released the button, and we listened to the silence extend.

"Hello?" Sam said again.

Silence once more.

I jumped up and took the radio. "We are looking for Derek's friends. Please, if you can hear us, say something."

More silence followed. I handed it to Sam and sat back down on the bed next to Adam. The radio crackled slightly. "How do you know Derek?" a young voice responded.

I wanted to cry; he was still available. Sam motioned me with the radio. "He answered you, not me," he stated.

"I met Derek at the police station before he died. He told me about his bunker. We are here now," I said, needing to be as honest as I could.

"How do I know you're telling the truth?" the boy edged.

"He has a great painting in here of the solar system and enough MREs to feed a small army for years," I answered.

I had no idea how else to convince him who I was or that I was where I claimed to be.

"I painted him that picture," the voice chuckled.

"My name is Sara." I paused and looked at both men before continuing.

"My name is Sara, and I'm here with my family, Sam and Adam. We know there are some bad people loose in the world, and we want to stop them. We want to help re-start the world. I was hoping you knew where to start," I confessed.

"My name is Derek Merrow. Your Derek was my uncle. I am with a group of survivors, military men. What type of people are you?" he questioned.

"I was a housewife, but I'm smart and can figure out almost any problem. Sam was in insurance but has years of construction under his belt. Adam is..." I paused.

I turned to Adam and waited. He grabbed the radio and finished for me. "Adam is someone who knows how to get answers when someone doesn't want to talk. Tell your military guys that, and they will understand."

Adam handed the radio back to me. I knew he was hiding something more from me. Surprisingly enough, it didn't bother me. Not even a little bit.

347

"Give me a minute," Derek directed.

We waited for what seemed like forever before another male voice broke in, "What station?"

Adam once again motioned for the radio, so I gave it over to him. "Delta White, sir."

"Hot damn, son. You've been missing for years. Where have you been?" he asked.

"I took some R and R to help a friend deal with an injustice, and a few other classified items," Adam stated while looking at Sam the entire time.

Some kind of knowledge passed between the guys. I felt lost and wanted to ask them what the hell was going on, but I couldn't bring myself to. I noticed Adam's demeanor changed.

He pulled himself up taller, more confident. His facial expression hardened, his jaw seemed more angular, and the playful hint in his eyes was gone. He ran his fingers through his hair before touching his lip lightly.

"Okay, I will fax over some coordinates. You come to us and bring your family. It'll be damn good to have you back, son," the guy filled in ecstatically.

"Thank you, sir. We will pack up everything from here and make our way to you," Adam finished strongly.

There was a brief pause before the radio crackled to life. "Have you been to the prison?"

I grabbed the walkie from him and answered, "Yes, we have."

"Was there anyone there alive?" he hesitated.

"There was one guy in prison; the rest that survived had escaped. Are you looking for someone in particular?" I hesitated.

"Yes, my son, Chadrick Tethers. It was my idea to make him learn a lesson, and I am worried he didn't make it out," he confessed.

"He said his parents were rich?" I questioned without thought.

He chuckled, "His mom has money. Her family is well off,

and because of this he always thought he could do anything without consequences. With the help of her family, we made sure he would understand he wasn't untouchable."

"He got out, sir. He helped us and told us he was going to the hunting cabin," I relayed. "Thank you," he whispered.

"Wait," I quickly added.

"Sir, there are survivors here in town, waiting for help. Could you send people to collect them or help them?" I anxiously waited for a reply.

"We know the bunker's location. I'll organize a rescue party and send help," young Derek replied.

With that done, I instantly came back to the moment at hand. I stood up quickly, but Adam grabbed my hand. "Don't be afraid of me. I won't hurt you."

"What the fuck, have you been playing us this entire time?" Sam demanded, walking over towards us.

I looked between the men and wanted to cry. I started to shake. "Who are you?"

"I am a weapon trained, molded, and modified by the military," he deadpanned.

"Jonathon?" I begged.

"This body was born, Adam. When I, Jonathon, pulled the gun from Adam, I got shot and died. Or so I thought. Somehow my conscious self-connected with my twin and we have been sharing the same mind for years. When the military found out the Ellis brother who didn't mind torturing was still alive, hidden within his brother, they taught me how to come forward when I was needed. They taught me how to recede when I wasn't. Adam still believes I am alive; I have replaced his memory of the night I died. Since they locked me up, I have let Adam take over. He convinced the court he was suffering from an extensive blackout and couldn't remember doing what they said he had done. I put him to sleep when I work. He doesn't even know I am here. I ask that you two keep this quiet. I don't want him knowing any different. There is no reason for it. Are we clear?" he stated.

"Can you see everything Adam does?" I cautiously asked.

"Not always. I try to give him his privacy, but there are occasions when I need to see what is happening to protect him," he reassured me.

"That day in the loft, when I was sure he was holding back, that was you," I questioned, although I already knew the answer.

He dropped to his knees, grabbed my hand, and pleaded, "Adam's inner monologue was driving me crazy. He kept going on and on about how beautiful you looked beneath him. He was caught up in your passion. I had to see it for myself. I pulled forward and looked at what he was seeing. I'm sorry I took what you were giving him. But he was correct; your passion is intoxicating. I wanted to taste a part of it. I promise to protect you no matter the cost. Don't you understand, Sara? I am yours."

I got down on the floor with him, pulled his hand to my heart, and gave a heartfelt response. "Yes, Adam or Jonathon. I accept both."

I didn't have much of a choice, and I wanted Adam back. As long as Jonathon felt safe, he would let me keep Adam, and I would be a fool to not think that he was who we would need to survive the new world.

"Yeah, we are good," Sam stated.

"Glad we have finally come clean about everything," Jonathon chuckled.

"I'm checking out. I'll be back when you get to the military installation. Tell Adam he closed his eyes for a moment from the pain and that is all," he requested.

I shook my head and sat back down. For the first time, I understood what the voice in the tent meant when it told me one day I would thank him. I missed my kids with every breath I took, but I was glad they didn't have to experience any of what the world was about to show us. Jonathon laid his head on my shoulder and closed his eyes. When they re-opened, I was looking at my Adam. I gave him a kiss before saying, "Let's get you cleaned up. We have a drive ahead of us."

We stood together. "Good news. Help is finally coming for the survivors. I need you to write down the address of where Naomi and any of the others you remember are. There were a few on the main drag in town, too. We need to make sure they are added to the list," I suggested.

As soon as the words left my lips, the fax machine rang, and the page was coming through.

"Welcome to our new lives," Sam chuckled as Adam and I walked into the bathroom.

Acknowledgments

To my family, I love you and appreciate all you do to support me.

To Andrew, because you wanted to see your name in print, lol. Never stop pushing and driving forward. You can accomplish anything you put your mind to. I love you, babe!

Ali, I am proud of the woman you have become; keep believing in yourself and striving for more, and you will have everything you want in life. I love you!

To my Muse, where would I be without you? Still working on the book, probably. Thank you for always diving down the rabbit hole and having those deep discussions with me. Thank you for being supportive and listening to every crazy scenario I threw at you. Thank you for being a fellow artist who understands passion. I am grateful that I met you and have you in my life. You hold a special place in my heart.

Special shout out to my Middle Fork peeps... You guys are a fantastic group! I am lucky to call you all my family.

Thank you, Jen, for continually believing in me even when I disagreed.

Nikki, thank you for being you! Never judging; you just listened and helped when I needed it. Whether it be encouragement or a stern bought of 'get it together.'

To everyone who has offered encouragement, a kind word, or a simple 'you've got this.' There are too many people to mention by name, but you know who you are. I love and respect you all.

About Atmosphere Press

Atmosphere Press is an independent, full-service publisher for excellent books in all genres and for all audiences. Learn more about what we do at atmospherepress.com.

We encourage you to check out some of Atmosphere's latest releases, which are available at Amazon.com and via order from your local bookstore:

Icarus Never Flew 'Round Here, by Matt Edwards

COMFREY, WYOMING: Maiden Voyage, by Daphne Birkmeyer

The Chimera Wolf, by P.A. Power

Umbilical, by Jane Kay

The Two-Blood Lion, by Nick Westfield

Shogun of the Heavens: The Fall of Immortals, by I.D.G. Curry

Hot Air Rising, by Matthew Taylor

30 Summers, by A.S. Randall

Delilah Recovered, by Amelia Estelle Dellos

A Prophecy in Ash, by Julie Zantopoulos

The Killer Half, by JB Blake

Ocean Lessons, by Karen Lethlean

Unrealized Fantasies, by Marilyn Whitehorse

The Mayari Chronicles: Initium, by Karen McClain

Squeeze Plays, by Jeffrey Marshall

JADA: Just Another Dead Animal, by James Morris

Hart Street and Main: Metamorphosis, by Tabitha Sprunger

Karma One, by Colleen Hollis

About the Author

DAISY DEMAY lives in Illinois with her children and husband of 25 years. She loves sitting and watching the storms roll in. She enjoys reading outside in the warmth of the sun. When she's not working, she creates stories to share. She has a fascination with the macabre. She approaches everything in life with a mix of passion and logic.

Made in the USA
Monee, IL
03 July 2023

38626050R00215